The House with No Roof

for Pauline and Douglas.
With love and Best Wishes

Jessie Ritchie

August 2017

About the Author

Jessie Ritchie was born on the East Coast of Scotland, trained as a nurse, midwife and health visitor in Edinburgh during the Swinging Sixties; she has worked in two different continents and travelled the world extensively. Now retired, she resides in Scotland with her family and grandchildren. Prompted by her eldest daughter to write a book, *The House with no Roof* is her first, incorporating many stories told her by her parents and grandparents of the east coast fisherfolk. This romantic fictitious tale was written, dedicated with the greatest respect to all those who challenge the seas to make a living and in particular from her beloved 'Kingdom of Fife'.

The author is now currently working on *The House with No Roof* book 2.

The House with No Roof

by

Jessie Ritchie

DIADEM BOOKS

The House with No Roof
All Rights Reserved. Copyright © 2017 **Jessie Ritchie**

Published by Diadem Books

For information, please contact:

Diadem Books
8 South Green Drive
Airth
Falkirk
FK2 8JP
Scotland UK
www.diadembooks.com

Cover artwork by Alex Bird

ISBN: 978-0-244-32000-3

To my family and in particular Sophie, Laura and Kay – for all their support, encouragement and without whom this book would never have been written.

He who fights and runs away lives to fight another day
But he that is in battle slain, will never rise to fight again.

BOOK ONE

Part One

Introduction

GREAT AUNT JANE died in the early hours of a late summer's morning. She died alone.

Arriving home after a busy night shift at the local Hospital, I was grateful to get into bed and get some sleep. My fiancé Johnny and I were meeting in London and I had to catch the six o'clock flight from Edinburgh to Heathrow to meet up with him. Johnny Geiger was an airline pilot with *TWA*; we met in-flight when I flew to the States for a six months elective, during my University years. We were looking forward to planning our wedding in Scotland, after which we would move to Johnny's home State... Texas.

I heard the phone ring downstairs, my mother answered it.

"Hello, hello?"

From the tone of her voice, even although she had lowered it to avoid disturbing me, I sensed something was wrong. I went back downstairs now fully awake. There was no way I could sleep with such an early morning call – might be the hospital? Please don't tell me I am needed to do an extra nightshift... I would have to cancel my London trip.

My mother looked up and saw me enter the room. No need for her to speak quietly now, but mouthed to me: "It's Cathie."

Realising the phone-call had nothing to do with work I sat down to wait for her to finish, hang up and let me know what was going on before I went back to bed. But mum seemed to be talking forever; I knew... all was not well.

"Yes-yes, I will phone Nan right away; she knows all Aunty's business... will know what's to be done. Thank-you for phoning Cathie… yes… it must have been a shock. You have been with Aunt Jane for a long time now. Make yourself a cup of tea, leave everything as you found it and wait," mum advised her. She continued:

"I will phone Mr Wright the undertaker. I'm sure he will be with you in the next hour… Yes, it is a sudden death, but her G.P. Practice will know her and her Doctor will sign the death certificate." Mum nodded. "No… no need to call the police. What was that you said… did I hear you right?" There followed a long pause as mum listened to Cathie.

"Not in bed?" Mum gasped, looking straight at me.

Obviously something out of the ordinary had happened from what I overheard. I waited for Mum to finish, but she kept on talking, listening, shaking her head, expressing her sympathies and trying to reassure Aunty's live-in housekeeper. I began to think the call would never end.

"Oh dear, how awful for you" – and with a few more "yes… yes's" and "no's" she hung up.

"No need to tell me Mum, I guess we have a funeral to arrange," I said sadly. My great aunt had become one of my best friends.

Mum frowned. "Cathie said she has just found Aunty… but not in her bed where she left her last night. Cathie says she's a light sleeper, she heard nothing untoward."

"So?" I replied a little vague, my thoughts elsewhere.

"Cathie said for some time Aunty has been afraid to come down the stairs by herself, for fear of falling. So in the morning Cathie always goes down to the kitchen first, puts the kettle on then goes back up. When she has helped Aunty wash and dress, they go down to the morning room together. Cathie serves her breakfast, the same routine every day. This morning when Cathie went into Aunty's room and she discovered the bed empty, no sign of her anywhere…" Mum shrugged her shoulders in disbelief.

"Well, that doesn't mean anything. Maybe she did get up by herself for once... you know... the elderly are unpredictable." But I knew as I said it that it sounded a bit lame.

"Just listen!" snapped mum. "Listen, what concerned Cathie most was the mess. Cupboards normally locked standing wide open, contents strewn all over the place. Sheets, blankets in a heap on the bed, quilt on the floor and far more worrying for the woman... it looked like both pillows had been slept on. That's what's weird." Mum shook her head in disbelief.

"Apparently Aunt Jane rarely moves at night, even to go to the toilet. So Cathie couldn't understand how this had happened without her hearing and I have to agree with her. 'A place for everything and everything in its place' is the old woman's motto. Anyway Cathie began to search the rest of the house, afraid Aunty might have fallen or wandered outside; it's a big house..." Mum paused.

"That's ridiculous. Aunt Jane's mind is as clear as a bell; the last thing she would do is wander outside in the middle of the night... Maybe she had a party?"

"Enough. That's not funny!" mum snapped. "Cathie found Aunty in the lounge; she said she would never forget the sight in front of her... It would haunt her till the day she died. From inside the lounge door she could see the curtains had been closed, the fire lit, embers still glowing in the grate... table lamps on."

I thought Cathie's imagining things and I blamed sleep deprivation for my thoughtless remark.

"Going into the room, Cathie said she could see Aunty's back to her... at the side of the fireplace one hip on a low footstool, her body twisted towards the seat of the Parker Knoll. Thinking this odd seeing her in that position, Cathie went closer, thinking Aunty might have fallen and hit her head… she hadn't… she was dead!"

"Dead lying on the chair… not sitting on it – what the hell's going on?"

"Your aunt's arms, it seems, were stretched out in some sort of embrace with a cushion on the seat, her cheek resting on it. And wait for it… she was wearing a beautiful pink, silk, quilted dressing gown. Cathie says she's never seen it before, has no idea how Aunty could have kept it hidden. She's been Aunty's housekeeper for more than twenty years." Mum paused, unsure whether she should continue, thinking this was all beginning to sound farfetched. Privately I thought the whole scenario from Cathie sounded farfetched, but Mum shrugged her shoulders.

"Listen to this." Mum put her hand out to me to emphasise the point she was about to make. "By the position of the old lady it seemed to Cathie… it suggested… that Aunty had been reaching out for something… or to someone? And Aunty was – smiling!"

My mind began to race with this last bit of information. Nothing was funny any longer.

Mum cleared her throat, blinked a few times as if to hold back her tears.

"Well…it looked like the old lady was happy to go – that's a comforting thought. You will be glad of Johnny's support when he hears the news; the old lady was fond of you both… I hear she was looking forward to the wedding, planning a very special gift for you both and a new outfit for herself… it's like the end of an era, the last of that generation in our family to die." Mum sighed. She seemed lost in thought for a moment.

"Cathie decided to phone us with the news right away as she wasn't sure what do. There's no evidence of a break-in…" She halted. "I'll phone Nan…" She'd changed the subject, Mum being practical as always. "Nan lives the closest to Aunty and she's nothing better to do with her time." Mum gave a wry smile remembering her sister's controlling ways.

"We'll let her get on with organising the funeral; miss bossy-boots will relish that... goodness only knows what's to be done with all that stuff of Jane's – she's been hoarding for years. Well we better all meet at the house.... do a clear out. At least go through her personal things before somebody else does." Mum was thinking out loud, distracted and talking more to herself than me. "M-mm – maybe we can get one of those Companies who do house clearances and the Antique Dealers. Oh! I forgot, I hope Nan remembers to phone young Mr Cunningham, Aunty's lawyer. Old Mr Cunningham's been dead for years. I'll remind her when I phone her..."

Mum began folding the clean washing ready for ironing. As she was dropping a sheet into the laundry basket, she looked up, and started to say:

"Oh, by the way, I've just remembered Cathie said she found a parcel... no, a box, on the coffee table addressed to you..." Mum now looked directly at my face and gasped...

"What's the matter? For God's sake lassie... you're as whites as a sheet...you look as if you have seen a ghost!"

I shivered... whispered: "I feel as if someone has just walked over my grave."

I put my head in my hands. Oh my God... now I understand... now I understood everything she had been telling me. In those few short minutes... a moment in time... all had become crystal clear.

Chapter 1

MY EARLIEST MEMORIES as a small child were of driving along the coast road with the women-folk in my family. One Sunday in each month, we did a statutory visit to Great Aunt Jane. A duty visit to my mother's aunty, an elderly maiden lady living alone in one of the fishing villages of Fife. By the age of six I knew the journey off by heart, every bend, twist in the road and landmark. I had no idea at that time where these journeys and visits would eventually lead me to when I grew up. For each visit my family waited to be collected by my Aunt Nan, from their respective homes. There was only one car in the family at that time – my grandfather's Standard 10. With no regular bus service, it was essential for us to travel together. My cousin Margo with her mum my Aunt Jessie collected first, my mum and I last. The two mothers each with their young daughters in the back seat, me on my mother's knee as I was the youngest... no seat belts in those days. In the front my Aunt Nan in the driver's seat and my granny in the passenger seat beside her. Aunt Nan, a spinster, lived with my grandparents... she believed the car was hers. During the week Nan used it for work, but at the weekends felt she had sole rights to it as well.

This bugged Mum; she was proud of her driving skills and rarely had the opportunity to drive. Mum had joined the WAAF during the recent war, admitting she had been motivated by the desire to learn how to drive. Posted to RAF Bomber Command Dyce in Aberdeenshire, she did just that. Mum was a nursery nurse, certainly not a qualification needed to fight a war. Therefore the war office did not consider her suitable for officer status. So instead of gaining her driver's licence by learning to drive the staff cars transporting the officers on the base, she learnt to drive the Commer Lorries – no mean feat at the age of nineteen.

Mum drove the air crews out to the Lancaster bombers warming up on the tarmac ready for take-off. Dad used to tease her about learning to drive an RAF lorry, but in private he bragged and boasted to his friends how proud he was of her. He said she was the only woman he knew who could not only drive a lorry, but could do an oil change as well. Mum only smiled; I think she had some sad memories, the sights she had witnessed at such a young age. She remembered the bombers returning to base, the state of the aircraft and their crews. Those young men who did not return – were they floating in the North Sea, alive, badly injured or dead? I don't think she wanted to think too deeply about it; certainly when I was around she never talked much, except to say the rear gunner always seemed to survive. Now she felt fully justified in wanting to take the wheel of her father's car… she was his daughter as well, wasn't she? She knew she was the better of the two drivers because of her wartime experiences, and that fuelled arguments between the sisters.

Aunt Nan had joined up; she was accepted into the Royal Navy having a professional qualification that the War Office did want, and she was automatically given the rank of Lieutenant. Occasionally, Aunt Nan, trying to be funny, would pull rank on Mum, reminding her that she had to salute her during the recent conflict, so she should take priority. To which my mum calmly reminded her, it was the uniform she was saluting… not her sister. Poor granddad – goodness only knows where he figured in all this, probably glad he didn't have to do the visits with us. After the usual argument about which sister was going to drive, it was usually Aunty Jessie who settled the matter. Although she herself did not drive and in truth she couldn't care less which of them was going to drive, demanding impatiently that the pair of them hurry up, make up their minds, decide and stop arguing. Aunt Jessie wanted to get on with it, so they would have more time to enjoy the visit with their aunt. Which was the purpose of the trip, instead of hanging about on the pavement while her sisters squabbled over who would drive the blasted car.

Once settled with Aunt Nan (having won again) at the wheel we were off. Secretly I preferred her to drive for I did not like sitting on Aunt Nan's knee, and she always complained that the buckles on my shoes ripped her nylons. Otherwise we enjoyed our car journeys; it was rather nice for us to be together once a month. We took the same route every time along the coastal road and that seemed to make the journey go faster. My cousin and I pointed out to each other familiar landmark's on the way. We knew them by heart and tried to see who could spot them first. A short steep hill by a Glen followed by a golf course on the Link's and last of all the woods where we stopped to pick brambles in autumn. It wasn't surprising that after this game my cousin and I started to get restless. Bored and not in the least bit interested in the adults' conversation which always followed the same old pattern: news in general; whether viewed on the BBC or read in the local newspapers: followed by local gossip, births, deaths and marriages.

As Granddad and Grandma were the only family members who had a television, Mum and Aunt Jessie were always keen to hear what was on the T V. Aunt Nan, living with her parents, was only too glad to show off her acquired information regarding the news.

It's odd, but looking back as there was no car radio to entertain us, we made our own entertainment. It was at this point we would start to interrupt the adults' conversations.

Realising they would get no peace unless they turned their attention to us, we all started to sing. Same songs every journey– 'There was a Wee Cooper wha' lived in Fife' and other Scots songs. But my favourite was a poem, 'The Laird o' Cockpen.' By the time I was old enough to have developed sufficient memory skills, about the age of four, I joined in. After a while the adults would drift back to talking amongst themselves. Margo and I, now fed-up, would start to annoy each other. The journey was not that long, but for children confined in a small space it seemed like hours.

On my mother's lap, her arms around my waist, meant my head was higher than my cousin's, a distinct advantage. Margo was squeezed in between her mother and mine; this meant she was unable to move freely. Our quarrels usually began over the bags of sweets that our grandmother had given us for the journey. On one occasion I hit on the idea, if we ate Margo's sweets today, we could eat mine tomorrow… clever? I knew she would be back in her own home next day so it would be highly unlikely she would be around to share mine. Four years older, she was not fooled by my suggestion and hid her sweets so she could eat them all herself. Having informed me in no uncertain terms she wasn't sharing, I'd seized an opportune moment to lunge forward over my mother's arms at Margo's poke of sweets and grab it; tore open the bag and a shower of sweets cascaded up into the air and down onto the floor. That caused an almighty uproar with the adults.

In revenge Margo sometimes managed to nip me on my thigh, my leg being in a vulnerable position right next to her hand. I would yelp in pain and that would lead to yet another outburst from the mothers, each accusing the other of not controlling their child. With such choice phrases as "you will need to control Margo, she's the eldest… should know better" and "look at the mark on the wee one's leg, I bet that turns into a right bruise" my mother would rub the offended red skin.

Naturally I howled, rather enjoying the attention nevertheless. "Don't be ridiculous, she's hardly touched her," Aunty Jessie defended Margo; Aunt Nan would then enter the fray: "I am going to crash this car if you don't behave yourselves. How can I concentrate with that racket going on in the back!" "Then maybe I should be driving!" my mother would chip in...

Grandma, who had a placid nature, never paid any attention. She knew it would all blow over, which it did. Meanwhile we girls had made up and were friends again, long before the adults. Peace restored, each child was encouraged to say sorry to each other. When I look back I am not sure which one of us was the most spoilt. Both our mothers felt justified complaining about the other child's behaviour; the other was at fault, not their darling daughter. They were also well aware that there would be no more children for either of them.

One never knows the exact moment that the memory develops, the moment the brain retains an imprint of what the eye sees. Without being prompted by some external stimulus, you know what will come next, even in a child's memory. So there it was... No one had brought it to my attention, but every time we visited the old lady after a certain bend in the road, I would look out of the car window and there on the road between the villages was 'The House with no Roof'.

I cannot remember when I first became aware of its existence. There were several imposing houses on the journey along the coast road. Why did this particular house hold special fascination for me? I don't know. But this was not just a grand house; this palatial grey sandstone, eighteenth-century mansion of considerable proportions, was what I saw out of the car window. My position on my mother's lap, behind my grandmother gave me a clear view of the mansion and the surrounding estate. At the bottom of a long drive stood high ornamental wrought-iron gates, heavily chained and padlocked. Thick with rust, and sagging to one side, clearly they had been closed for a very long time. On each side were tall stone columns; one was still graced by a carved stone animal while the other had lost its stone guardian. Beyond the gates the long driveway, overgrown with weeds and deep ruts where the weather had eroded the surface, led to the house. Neither coach nor car could travel along it now. Giant ancient trees, waving their heavy branches, leant in support of each other, forming a canopy over the drive as if bereft, mourning the loss of a former life…

The whole scene was one of neglect and decay. Did no one care? It could have been a depressing sight, but not for me – I was intrigued. The high dry stone dyke attached to the columns curved gracefully outwards from the exit leading to and along the main road. Many of the stones were missing, holes embedded with weeds. A fence no longer attached to the wall lay on its side but still gave way to unimpeded views from a road that probably did not exist when the house was built. I felt a special connection… a bewildering fascination for this house.

As teenager I imagined maybe I had lived there in another life. In the depths of my pleasant daydreams I was also vaguely aware of a feeling of sadness; perhaps some unfortunate event had taken place… a dramatic turn of fortune, a quirk of fate causing the roof to be removed. It certainly did not look as if it had caved in or been demolished; the chimneys and walls were still standing proud, but on the return journey shafts of the setting sun were visible slanting through the empty windows.

In later years it would be just my mother and I doing the monthly visits. Mum very happy to be driving our own car, would wake me from my daydreams. 'A penny for your thoughts, what is it you're so deep in thought about? Why my dear girl, you look sad, what's wrong?' I knew I was struggling to understand the feelings going round in my head. But there was no point in trying to explain how I felt, when I could not explain to myself; it did not make sense. I had no ties to a derelict, old house.

"Mum, why does that house have no roof?" I'd ask. "I don't know," she would reply, "it has always been like that as far back as I can remember." But I would not let it rest; each time we passed the house I would demand to know the answer and each time, she would patiently reply, "I don't know." I was irritating, annoying, probably getting on her nerves with my refusal to accept her explanation. "But mum?" The day came when she replied, but not as she had done a hundred times in the past: "I don't know but I know someone who might… your great aunt. Why don't you ask her?" I shrank back in the passenger seat at this suggestion.

Great Aunt Jane always seemed a formidable character to me. Her beautiful, spotlessly clean and well-furnished house was full of stiff unwelcoming leather chairs in one room, not unlike their owner. Exquisite rose coloured brocade suites upholstered by a master upholsterer in another. Solid wooden furniture heavily embellished with gold inlay work, marquetry floors, Persian rugs, priceless antique china. Italian crystal chandeliers hung from the ceilings. Incredible works of art hung on the walls; hardly the place for a young child to visit never mind ask questions. I always felt relieved when we left, glad to be going home, glad I had been able to sit still long enough, not receive a sharp rebuke to 'sit still!' from her. Once when I was very young she had screeched at me: "You're breathing on my windows!" I'd been standing… bored, looking out of the window. I nearly wet myself and promptly burst into tears. I had no intention of asking aunty; memories of the rebukes I had received as a child were still fresh in my mind, of the unapproachable old woman.

In my twenties I was my mother's friend as much as I was her grown-up daughter and for various reasons we were the only members of the family visiting Aunty now. Margo, now married, was living in England; Aunty Jessie, occupied with her bowling, didn't have time to come with us; and Aunt Nan was occupied with her Bridge group on Sundays. I had temporarily forgotten my interest in the house. On this particular journey however my previous obsession returned.

Able to drive, I alone visited my great aunt, my mother having joined her sister's bowling club, Aunt Nan occupied with her bridge group and Great Aunt Jane had mellowed with the passage of time, making it easier for me to ask about Leightham House. I wouldn't put it past her to tell me to mind my own business in the same sharp voice she used to rebuke me as a child. I sensed over the years Aunt Jane had formed a sort of affection for me as I had for her and that gave me confidence to ask. I had nothing to lose.

I will never forget that particular Sunday. It was a beautiful day in late summer, the sun high in the sky, fields of golden corn ripening in in the fields. I knew as I approached the bend in the road I had travelled so often in the past, it would be in front of me and there it was... beckoning, pleading with me not to delay... ask! I got the feeling on that day Aunt Jane would be waiting for me, prepared for my question. With her advancing years perhaps she had a premonition her life was coming to an end. Was she the last person alive who knew the truth? On that first visit we exchanged the usual pleasantries. I gave her messages from the family, enquired after her health and had a cup of tea and one of her ginger biscuits. Sitting in the lounge I decided it was time... now or never.

"Aunty, why does that old mansion on the coast road have no roof?"

It seemed to me the old lady stiffened, inhaled deeply... then sank back into her chair. A wistful look came into her watery old eyes. Sitting upright as if coming to a decision, she looked straight ahead at the wall behind me... still silent.

"Aunty, were you involved? You don't have to tell me if you don't want to." I tried to encourage her to answer me one way or another.

"No!" she snapped as only Aunt Jane could, as she seemed to return to the present. I drew back reprimanded, as if a child again. I'd blown it, maybe Mum's wrong. She doesn't know the answer or doesn't want to divulge… a secret, and now I'll never know.

As if thinking better of her sharp reply, her voice softened.

"No." And after a slight delay she continued: "…but my very good friend Alice was, and I will tell you her story."

So here I was… once more on a journey along other roads and paths, this time not from the wheel of a car, but from the comfort of my great Aunt's sitting room. This is the story she told me. It would take me many more Sunday visits and from the start I was enthralled, hooked, but I would never have guessed, what the long term implications would be…

My great Aunt Jane would be dead before the final chapter came to light!

Chapter 2

A FEW WEEKS LATER I phoned my Aunt Jane to arrange my first visit regarding the house. The phone rang... it was Cathie who answered.

"Hello?"

"Hi Cathie, it's me – can I talk to my aunt please? I hope she's not busy."

"Aye, hello lass, I'd recognise your voice anywhere. No, she's no busy. Hold on, I'll take the phone to her. She's sitting across from me."

Now sitting in the large bay window of her beautiful home on a bright summer Sunday, I felt quite excited. At last I would find out the answer to the burning question I had lived with most of my life. Having enjoyed a cup of tea and a Perkin biscuit, I waited to hear Aunt Jane's story... Why a magnificent palatial mansion from another century stood derelict...

"Are we ready to begin?" she asked me.

"Yes," I nodded.

"Well, I must warn you before I do, you will have to bear with me, trust me. Not all will seem relevant or make much sense at first, but it will eventually. Do you agree to be patient? Or is there no point in my wasting both of our time?"

"I understand... please begin."

Chapter 3

ON THE EAST COAST of Scotland a small fishing village stands, situated at the estuary of a wide river and looks out over the North Sea. It seems as if it has been there forever. A small, insular community where everybody knows everybody else and everybody else's business. That's not a surprise as the residents are all married to each other, though it is rare for a couple with the same surname to marry. The village of Pittendreal has a wide cobbled High-Street, a place for shawl-draped women to meet, shop and exchange the latest gossip. The Parrish Church, Manse and graveyard stand at one end. A new Library and a school, named The Academy which doubles as a community hall at the other. Local philanthropists, the Phimister sisters, donated the buildings; spinsters from a well-to-do background, they also teach the children. The High Road connects Pittendreal to other villages in the area, and a recent welcome addition... the new railroad. Newspapers, mail and parcels now arrive on a regular basis. Off the High Street are several other smaller streets, where the villagers live.

But the hub of fishing village life is the Harbour. The Mid-Shore is reached by the steep Kirk Wynd below the church, the Lang Brae, a gentler slope, from the other end of the High Street. A newly constructed harbour and sea walls protect the fishing boats, so they no longer have to be pulled onto the beach. The open fish-market on the days when the herring catch is landed is normally busy, but on this particular scorching July day in the late afternoon of the mid-1890's, the Mid-Shore was deserted, except for one local character. Auld

Jock Bowman entered The Pirates Inn. He was in sore need of a drink.

Davie Muir looked up from behind the bar as he heard the swing-doors of his Pub open and saw one of his regulars enter, auld Jock wearing his ex-Army great-coat as usual.

"Aye, I'll hae a wee dram o' Himsel," announced Jock in response to Davie's greeting.

"What' ill ye have Jock?" and without waiting for the reply, Davie, knowing what Jock's response would be, threw the dishtowel that he had been drying last night's glasses with over his shoulder. Taking a dry glass, he filled it with a dram of Haig and handed it to Jock. "You're in here earlier than usual man, am no open yet."

"A' weel, I'v come tae wet the bairn's heid."

"Eh!" Davie responded, surprised. 'Yer a bit early for that are yae no, Jock? The bairns no born yet."

"Aye a' ken it's no, but ye never can start too early with a wee dram." Jock credited whisky with human qualities, if not religious ones, and this drink he felt was more than justified under the circumstances.

Davie took the dishtowel from his shoulder and continued with the task, drying last night's glasses. Davie shook his head, smiled with affection at his old customer and friend. What a character, the whole village knew him; especially when he was fou'o the demon drink or the craitur' as Jock called it. Harmless, well liked in the village, especially by the schoolchildren, when Jock he passed by the Academy at playtime, he always had a poke of Pandrops with him. The children knew this and those standing closest to the school's railings, would be rewarded with a sweetie.

"I can niver understand why you wear that auld Army coat of yours? Especially in this heat, nae wonder they call you 'Sodger Booman' – dae ye' never take it aff?" Davie leant closer. "What are ye hiding in thay pockets, a wee flask o' somethin'? I'll bet ye sleep in that coat… it'll be the death of you Jock."

"You mind yer ain business, Davie Muir; this coat has done me prood over the years. Many a cauld winter's nicht it's kept me grand an' warm on my wye hame. When the groonds thick wi snaw, blaw'n a gale o' wind, or you've *thrown* me oot…" – Jock emphasised the word 'thrown' – "This coat… got me through the Crimea!"

Privately, Davie doubted Jock had actually been in the Crimea, but he was certainly attached to that coat.

Dismissing the subject of the coat Jock pressed on. "Fine, well I ken the bairns no here yet, but three days Davie a'm that worried, she's never taen that long afore." Concern was etched on the old man's face.

The two men stood together, only the bar separating them. Jock indicated with a finger for Davie to draw closer, and Davie drew in.

"Aye, twa bits o' bairns already up the Cemetery Davie, neither o' them reached their third birthday." A tear had started to form in the old man's eyes – eyes sunk in the weather-beaten, wrinkled old face of a fisherman.

"Now, now Jock," Davie tried to reassure the man. "Drink up. When Junet gets here, she'll sort it all out and the bairn'll be born afore ye' ken it."

Jock lowered his voice to a whisper.

"Well, a ken that man, but three days since Aggie… ye ken." He nodded encouragement to Davie to understand what he was talking about. Men did not discuss such female matters in the village. That was 'wuman's' business.

"Maggie sent word about an oor ago with Wullie tae find Junet the Howdie; Maggie ken't things weren't going well early this mornin'. Ye ken ma son-in-law Wullie? He's been staying with me for the last twa nichts out of the road. A woman havin' a bairn is no place for a man," Jock whispered.

Davie knew full well that Wullie was Jock's son-in-law but said nothing to that effect. Instead he nodded in agreement.

"Aye, you're richt aboot that, Jock," Davie agreed with him. "Best let the women folk just get on wi it. Let's face it they dinna want us aboot when they are deliverin'." Reflecting on the subject for a moment he remembered his wife's opinion. "Even the new Doctur.... he's too young my wife says," Davie quoted her. "She says the Doctor should only be called oot in an emergency and I am very grateful I'v niver been involved in such matters."

The last thing Jock wanted was to have to call the Doctor. Oh, dear Lord no. Jock vividly remembered the last time the Doctor had to be called for another poor lassie in labour. Young Dr Forman had arrived in the village the day before, when he hardly had time to hang up his coat before being summoned. Arriving at the house the Doctor quickly realised there was little he could do. In the man's defence the local population only made a request for house calls in cases of dire emergency, or death. In this case, it turned out to be both. The new Doctor in desperation contacted an obstetrician from the City and spent the next two hours waiting for the man to arrive, doing his best to alleviate the woman's suffering.

When the Consultant finally arrived, the two Doctors stood at the end of May Smith's bed and the consultant shook his head. "After five days? Nothing to be done here; maybe if I had been called earlier... no, it probably wouldn't have made any difference... too late."

May Smith, semi-conscious and having finally given birth to twins, slowly bled to death. A grim business no one would ever forget, it left the whole village reeling with shock. The Consultant stood on the doorstep and said 'Very sorry for your loss Mr Smith... You'll receive my bill in due course' to the infants' father and with little more than a grim smile and a perfunctory shake of the hand, departed leaving Harry speechless.

Turning without a backward glance, the man got into the carriage waiting to take him to the station, ignoring the huddle of anxious women waiting on the pavement for news. Right enough, the bill arrived a few days later – a demand for five guineas. That left Harry Smith reeling and no longer speechless.

"Wake up Jock! Your awa' in a dwam man, I dinna like the look on your face! Can I dae onythin' tae help?"

'No, it's a' richt, I was thinkin' thoughts I really dinna' want tae. I ken you mean it kindly, but Davie, listen, I have somethin' else on my mind… somethin'… strange." Shrugging his shoulders, mystified and rubbing his unshaven chin with his hand, he continued:

"Junet normally just materialises, like the sound of the fog horn out o' the mist. It's like second sight with her, she just appears from nowhere when ony o' the lassies are having their bairns, but the day nae sign o' her… Tam was deliverin' coal in the next street, he says he's no seen her either this morning."

"Aye yer richt there Jock, she does seem to sense what's going on in the village. Ah de ken whit we would do withoot her and she's that young and if onybody knew her whereabouts it would be auld Tam."

What Jock was saying was not that far from the truth. Janet rarely had to be sent for. Having previously conducted the conversation in low tones, Jock now wanted to shout for someone to come… help his daughter. Raising his glass to his mouth he downed the last of his whisky, and was about to order another thinking the situation more than justified it. Before he could do so the door of The Pirate's burst open. Both men turned to see who it was. There stood Wullie Gardner, Jock's son-in-law panting like a war horse.

"She's here Dad, Junet's arrived!" The man's relief was obvious. "But no the bairn... yet."

"Well that's grand... what about anither wee dram Davie?"

"Just a minute Jock, I want tae hear what happened." Davie put his hand up to stop any further discussion. "We'll have no more talk aboot another drink. Go on Wullie – where did you find her?"

"Ah couldn'a find her in Pittendreal so I decided to run a' the way to St Creils; the full six miles I dinna' mind telling you." Wullie paused for breath. "But there was neither sight nor sound of the wuman. I asked some of the local lassies that were gutten the fish, had anyone seen Junet? They all shook their heads." Wullie stopped.

"Gie me a glass o' water Davie, my throats that dry I kin hardly speak."

Davie filled a glass from the tap and handed it to Wullie. Not taking his eyes off him, Wullie gratefully took a few gulps, got his breath back.

"Ye ken what it's like about here, the jungle telegraph; a body kens a body's business. If a bairn's on the way we soon a' ken about it and Junet just appears like magic."

"Weel a ken that... hurry up, get on wi it." Jock wondered how much longer he would have to wait for Wullie to finish his story.

"I'm trying to tell yae." Wullie took another gulp of water, this time emptying the glass. "When I got back tae the hoose, I didna' ken what I was going to tell my mother-in-law."

"Aye, ye dinna have tae tell me," Jock butted in. 'She's got a voice like a Kirk bell that wuman."

Wullie ignored his father-in-law. "My worst fears came when I thocht I would hae tae send for the Doctor. A mean three days... When I turned into Rodger Street I could see the wuman on the pavement outside our hoose. They were a' huddled the gither; my heart sank and by the look on their faces I thocht the worst."

Wullie closed his eyes for a moment remembering the relief he felt when Rena McKay broke free from the group of women and shouted:

"Calm yersel Wullie… Junet's here, she arrived half an hour ago. Then she shooed me awa' telling me she saw you heading towards the Mid-Shore. Adding it wouldn't tak a genius to work oot where you'd gone. Awa yea go, auld Jock will want to ken what's happening… maybe… that's if he's still sober!" she added.

"So I ran here to tell yea."

"Humph, whit a cheek," Jock protested at Rena's comments.

The relief Wullie felt knowing Janet was now with his wife was tangible. But by the look of disapproval on Rena's face Wullie knew exactly what she had been thinking. That look said it all: *there's nothing more for you to do here, the damage was done nine months ago.* Wullie cringed with embarrassment. Rena might have been surprised to hear he fully agreed with her. Aggie and he were getting too old for this.

Wullie had been glad to leave Rodger Street. A high pitched moan like that of an animal in agony came from inside the house, a sound he would never forget. If Agnes and the bairn survive there would be no more, he'd make sure of that. He then made his way to the Harbour where he knew he would find his father-in-law.

"So am here, I knew you'd be worried. Thank heavens we have Junet – we're that lucky to have her. Wi a bit o' luck yer grandchild should'na be much longer… I hope." He had dropped his voice for the last two words. Wullie was well aware of the imminent danger his wife and unborn child were in and it might be a while yet before the child was delivered.

But he gasped in disbelieve at his father-in-law's next words. He couldn't believe his ears...

"Ah, well, that's a relief, Junet's wae Aggie." All previous concerns about his daughter were forgotten. It was as if Jock had heard nothing. He was now pre-occupied with his own needs, offering no words of gratitude or comfort to his son-i-law. Instead he demanded...

"Anither wee dram o' Himsel, Davie."

Chapter 4

"**L**IKE A SEED** blown in on the…"

Without hesitation, Aunty proceeded with her story, while I was struggling to understand why she was telling it in such a manner, as if she was reading from a book. Why? I had to stop her… ask where was this leading and what did these people have to do with Leightham house?

"Wait! Hold on a minute Aunty! I am sorry to interrupt you, but I'm confused."

"What? What do you mean, confused?" the eyes narrowed.

I shook my head, mystified. "I don't understand," I said. "What you have just told me is delightful. I feel I know the people; you describe them so well… but how would you know all those details? How do you know who said what to whom? You were not party to their conversations. You weren't even born then… and…"

"And what have they got to do with Leightham House? If you would exercise a little patience my dear… you will find out," she pre-empted what I had been about to say.

Stiff, still upright in her chair, the steely pale blue eyes looked straight at me. I withered under her gaze.

"No more questions," she said, sternly. "You will understand… all in good time… all will be revealed. Remember what I said before we started. So… shall we continue?"

Who would dare argue with that?

I nodded. I had returned to my childhood and had been rebuked for interrupting my elders. If I wanted to hear what happened to the house, I would have to be patient. I realised this was going to take a lot longer than I had anticipated, so if I wanted to hear more I should just sit quiet and listen.

I was glad we had chosen Sundays. I had no other commitments and I had to admit Aunty's story had begun to interest me. Whatever way she decided to tell her story, it certainly wasn't boring.

Without further ado she continued. I sat silent and listened.

Chapter 5

LIKE A SEED BLOWN in on the wind from another land… taken root and flourished, Janet settled into village life as if she had been born there. No, Janet had not been born in the village; she would be the first to admit she had no idea where she had been born, had very little recollection how she came to Pittendreal. The nightmares Janet woke up from, sweating and gasping, might well have been the reason that in her waking hours she did not want to remember. However, the dreams were becoming less frightening since her arrival and for that she was grateful. A young woman just past girlhood, she was an imposing figure, once seen, never forgotten. Tall, slim, head held high, a mane of dark brown hair twisted into a bun, tied in place with a colourful scarf. Her lightly tanned skin suggested many years on the road, along with her aquiline nose and high aristocratic cheekbones that betrayed possible foreign origins. But it was the eyes, eyes that brooked no arguments that held people spellbound; deep blue, heavily fringed with long black eyelashes. Silent, still, betraying no emotion, they conveyed a coldness that many drew back from. Eyes that invited no conversation or enquiry; instead, they seemed to add to the shield of anonymity that surrounded her… an invisible veil of privacy. Janet may have forgotten her past, but she remembered vividly the night she arrived.

Where had Janet come from? She did not want to know. Apart from an old sealed box she brought with her, her possessions were few. She had little more than a change of clothes and they had seen better days. Janet could have been left behind by the travelling people that visited the Scottish countryside, Rumanian or Gypsy, left by mistake or intent. For some time now transient foreigners had been arriving, passing through the village, trying to make a living. Others stayed speaking of terrible unrest in their own lands, wishing only to live in peace, earn enough to feed their families. They came, Polish, Russian, Austrian and Italian, some smiled, others never did. Sad faced adults with their sickly-looking children. Others came and went, selling their wares and services for a little money. Some stayed, others were seen once, and never again. At times it seemed to the villagers as if the whole world was on the move.

These strangers spoke of places the locals had never heard of and at times in languages none could understand. The kindly fisher folk did their best to purchase the goods on offer with whatever spare cash they had. They gave the refugees something to eat and shelter for the night. The regulars sold onions or clothes pegs and no wedding was complete without Paulo and his squeeze box. He played his accordion so young couples could celebrate their marriage with a dance; his playing on the Mid-Shore on fine summer evenings was always welcome. The villagers out strolling on a Saturday night paused for a dance; no one on the planet could match the ice-cream Marcello made in his new shop on the Mid-Shore. His sliders and cones were the best in Scotland. It seemed as if the word 'Prejudice' was unknown or belonged to another world. The villagers welcomed all newcomers irrespective of colour or creed.

In such a small community, everybody's nose was in everybody else's business. So it was unknown for a girl to arrive alone and stay, with her only connection to Pittendreal… auld Tam. Tam had been the dunce of his class at school; he had never been able to sit still long enough to learn anything. Taunted by the other children because of his dirty, torn clothes and muddy boots, he was often set upon, unable to defend himself, kicked in the playground and on the way home by the other boys. Eventually he'd had enough. After a lashing he received from the teacher Miss Smith, with the tawse for not being able to spell, Tam was finished with school. He'd had enough of the injustice, the humiliation, not able to understand what was behind the woman's contempt for him; and so he left for good. When the bell rang for playtime, he left the playground, his hand still stinging, swore it would be the last time he would be belted by her. Never again would he be subjected to such physical abuse.

Tam, an only child, lived in isolation up the Comentry Road, a mile or so from the village. With forest and bog-land around the cottage, no one, least of all the village children, visited him, in case the bogie-man got them... such was the power of suggestion told by their parents. Over the years Tam was forgotten by the community to a certain extent. He was a nobody, of little consequence, certainly not in the academic scheme of things.

Miss Smith did not even bother reporting him missing to the authorities. She also did not miss the smell of his unwashed body and dirty clothes in her classroom.

Tam was used to looking after himself. His mother was deaf; a dose of measles in her childhood had robbed her of her hearing. Unable to cope with the silent world around her, Jenny withdrew from village life into her own world, relying more and more on her son. Tam did such shopping as was necessary and tended the vegetable garden. Tam's father quite frankly did not exist. According to his mother he had left to find work in the City and had never returned. The poor man suffered from seasickness, so earning a living in the fishing industry was out of the question. At least that was his excuse for abandoning his wife and child.

As the years went by everything changed. Jenny passed away, leaving Tam to fend for himself. Having had little attachment to his mother and being self-sufficient, he thrived. Now possessing a horse and cart, no job was too big or too small, he happily picked up odd jobs here and there in the village. Local farmers and the manager of the Leightham Estate gave him work. Everyone employed Auld Tam regardless of the fact he was not that old. As long as the job paid in cash or in kind and as long as the cart did not smell too strongly of manure, he got work. A house flit'n one day, sacks of potatoes to be shifted from Leightham home farm to the railway station the next, then a load of manure, all in a day's work for Tam. Tam held no grudges against those who were the torturers of his schooldays. In adulthood they became his friends. The men kept a kindly eye on him, and after a while they stopped calling him 'ye stupit eejit' when he got it wrong; instead they ran to help. If his horse reared up in the High Street and dumped a load of dung on the pavement, they shovelled it back onto the cart and helped themselves to a bucketful here and there behind his back for their vegetable gardens. Tam knew fine what they were doing; he didn't care – it wasn't his manure, it was the Estates or the farmers. Tam was no gowk; he knew what the payment would be for him to turn a blind eye… a dram or two in The Pirates later that night.

He enjoyed the company of his friends and they welcomed him. Sometimes they wondered why he didn't feel lonely up the Comentry Road. Many a night he enjoyed a wee dram and the company of the fishermen in The Pirates. Tam's special friend was Jock Booman; being much the same age the pair had struck up a fine friendship. Jock didn't seem to mind the smell of manure; so the pair spent many a happy night together in The Pirates. At least till Davie flung the pair of them 'oot'. It was on one of those nights when Tam 'four sheets to the wind' had been flung oot by Davie. Climbing up on Nellie's back, he give a fair rendition of 'I'm no awa tae bide awa' till he fell asleep. Swaying back and forth on her saddleless back, clinging onto her mane to prevent him falling off, the two of them set off together up the Comentry Road.

Nellie was a seasoned campaigner and tonight was no different from any other. Her job in life on these occasions was to get Tam home and herself into her stable. Easy, she had done it a hundred times before. As they drew closer to the cottage, Tam, sprawled full length along the animal's spine apart from his arms and legs which were dangling on either side of her rump. Nellie suddenly reared up, almost throwing Tam back over her hind quarters. Tam rudely awakened, grabbed at her mane and gave the beast a few encouraging dunts on her sides with his heels to get her going. No luck, she refused to move and wouldn't budge. Something was wrong and the animal sensed it. Normally when Tam fell off her back he slept soundly where he fell, oblivious to all. Left, Nellie could look after herself… until the human was sober enough to look after Nellie.

But on this particular night Tam was forced to get down, take a hold of Nellie's reigns and try to pull her towards the stable… but it was no use. The animal still refused to budge. Neighing and shaking her head, Nellie started to irritate Tam.

'Whit's wrang wi ye noo ye daft auld bugger? Move!' he shouted.

Then he went round to her head, aiming to drag the beast in by force if he had to. Tam burst out laughing when he discovered the cause of Nellie's refusal to move. In his cups, Tam had been trying to force the hapless beast to enter through the hedge. The wise old animal had not only balked at being forced to plough through an impenetrable object; she had become aware of an unknown presence in the shadows…Tam had not. Horse sense… horses are no daft. Tam still unaware of what had frightened Nellie, now took the poor beast round the right way to her stable. Having sobered up somewhat, he led her into the stable and gave her a bale of hay to eat as some sort of apology. Nellie neighed her thanks and tucked into the unexpected treat.

Closing the stable for the night, Tam made his way round to the front door. No need to fumble for keys, no need to lock the door in the first place and in some of the states Tam arrived back in; he would have had a hard time finding his key or the lock.

"Oh!" Tam drew back in fear. There, huddled on the doorstep, a figure… a figure unknown to Tam.

"Who is it, who are ye?" Tam ventured.

In the gloaming of the darkening sky, he could just make out it was a woman, because of her long skirt. As he spoke she rose up and came towards him. Tam started to back away.

"What dae ye want? I hiv'nae ony money." He tried to sound brave.

He had no idea what to do or how to cope; worse still, the old gnawing sensations in his stomach returned. The same he felt as a young child about to be attacked by the boys in school. But something made him stand still; he began to realise the apparition in front of him meant him no harm. As the presence floated towards him he began to feel… calm. But panic once more surfaced. His hands trembled.

"Ye canna' bide here," Tam ventured, drawing back. On peering closer he realised, to his astonishment, the 'person' was little more than a young girl.

"But I have nowhere else to go," a well-spoken soft voice drifted from out of the gloom.

"Oh dear, oh dear!" Panic began to rise in Tam's befuddled brain.

He began to wring his hands. The figure seemed to hypnotise him. He stood fixed to the ground unable to move. The young woman drew close, reached out and took hold of his hands. For the first time he became aware of a scent – of lavender. Inhaling deeply, his heart stopped thumping in his chest. Life had taught Tam to trust no one, be wary of everything, but at that moment he sensed she was no threat to him. Quite the opposite, he had nothing to fear.

Till the day he died he would never understand what happened that night. What he didn't know was his life was about to change forever as was the girl's. Tam was filled with a feeling previously unknown to him: the desire to protect. Protect this stray who had arrived on his doorstep from nowhere pleading for his help. This girl had come into his life unasked, uninvited and over the years the relationship would develop as if she were Tam's own daughter. She made up for all he had suffered in his youth and for the first time in his life he felt… needed. The truth… it was the girl who needed him, but she never let Tam know. She would never leave him. He took her in… a total stranger, and let her stay. It was like a miracle. At last she had a place to call home. Her gratitude was endless.

Tam found himself in a world previously unknown to him. He had someone to depend on, someone he had feelings for. In the fading light of that special night Tam found himself saying:

"Yer' welcome tae bide, what's yer name lassie?"

"I don't know," the soft voice replied.

"Then I'll gie ye a name, gie me a minute to think… Junet, aye that's it... Junet!"

Chapter 6

"**WHERE ON AWE** the earth have yae been?" Maggie accused Janet. "I'm frantic, a' dinna ken what to dae... a' think she's' dying... are we gonna' lose her, Junet?" Maggie, wringing her hands, was pacing up and down the kitchen floor. Lifting her apron to her face, she wiped away the tears running down her cheeks. Agnes was Maggie and Jock Bowman's only child. There had been other children; Aggie was the only one to survive childhood.

"Help her Junet! Dae somethin'. You always said niver let the sun set twice on a woman in labour; well, in a few hours the sun will have set three times!" accused Maggie. "Aggie started with the pains twa days ago, not that bad at first, but yesterday and through the nicht." Maggie raised her eyes to the Heavens. "Ah expected you at the door at any minute."

A low weary moan came from within the recess of the box bed. Aggie Gardner was past caring whether she lived or died. She was exhausted; the pain seemed to start at the base of her spine, reaching a crescendo of agony in her ears and heels. Maggie had approached the bed every time she saw the bedclothes move and her daughter's figure wrestle. Holding her daughter's hand, she wiped the sweat from her forehead with a wet cloth. At first Aggie had welcomed her mother's attention, but now Aggie brushed her mother's hand aside.

"Dinna' touch me!" the labouring woman hissed.

"Now a' dare na go near her, with every contraction she pushes me away; she's nearly lost her voice with crying out in pain that often." Maggie stopped for a moment looking at the

36

figure in the bed and turned to Janet holding her hands out, pleaded for help.

"She keeps telling me… keep away… she says I'm starting the pain."

"Maggie I am here now." Janet spoke in her usual soft but commanding voice, walking from the door to the bed. It surprised the villagers when Janet spoke; no one could detect an accent, but they understood her perfectly.

"Has Agnes' water broken? No – you don't know?" She answered in response to Maggie shaking her head. "Have you looked?"

"A didna' look because as I'v tried to tell yae, every time ah touched her she yells at me to stop. To leave her alone. I'm terrified to go near her!" Maggie defended herself. "She's never complained about the bed being weet or onythin' or that she wanted to push. So I just decided it couldna' be time yet and left well alone… expecting you to arrive at any minute." She tailed off feeling she was being blamed for the state her daughter was in. She looked ready to collapse.

"Well I am here now and I need your help; put the kettle on and keep the water boiling. Perhaps we could start with you making us a cup of tea?" Janet had a lot of experience handling those depending on her in a crisis. It was important to distract Maggie, to give her something constructive to do, to occupy her mind. "But first get me a basin so I can wash my hands, and then bring me the clean towels I asked you to boil last time we met."

Janet took a bottle of clear looking liquid out of her holdall. She poured some solution into the basin Maggie had brought, thoroughly washing her hands, wincing as the salty solution nipped the odd bits of broken skin. Drying her hands, she turned her attention to Aggie.

"Let me see what stage she is at and then I will decide what is to be done." She turned towards Maggie. "It may come as a complete surprise, but I don't have the second sight. I certainly am no psychic and I do get it wrong, I am not infallible," Janet informed Maggie with a wry smile. Maggie was too distracted to understand and had no idea what the word infallible meant.

"But you are right, I do keep an eye on the women in the village who are pregnant," Janet went on. "And generally speaking I do have a reasonable idea when they are due to deliver their babies. I watch their expressions, physical movements, when they are nearing their time." She nodded wisely. "But my observations with your daughter were wrong and I assure you I get no pleasure admitting that."

Janet had been observing Agnes for several weeks from a discreet distance. She had come to the conclusion; that Agnes Gardner was carrying her baby high, close to her ribs; either her dates were wrong, or the woman was having twins. Roll on the day when women would overcome their embarrassment about the fact they were pregnant, admit to it and not hide it. With no real examination, guessing the likely due date was impossible. You would think these women had committed some shameful sin becoming pregnant and had to hide the evidence.

"I have made an error of judgement, let me see what's to be done to put it right and try to alleviate her suffering."

Another moan came from the bed recess. Gently Janet pulled back the bedclothes until a huddled figure in a sweat soaked nightdress was exposed.

"Agnes, it's me, Janet." There was some movement from the bed as Aggie recognised the voice. Turning slowly and with great effort Aggie managed to turn toward Janet.

"Help me," the stricken woman pleaded.

Janet with all her experience was shocked at the sight. Aggie's ashen face made her look as if she had aged ten years in two days. It took all of Janet's strength and self-control not to gasp. The woman was unrecognisable. Aggie's eyes were sunk into the back of her head, black circles under them. Aggie Gardner was in trouble...

"Listen to me Agnes, I need your help get this little one into the world; we need to do this together and as quickly as possible." Janet spoke slowly and deliberately, trying her best to sound as reassuring as she could under the circumstances. Never once did she raise her voice or betray her anxiety.

Turning back to Maggie: "There is a bottle of brown liquid in my bag. Pour a small amount about an eggcup full and hand it to me... *now*." She emphasised the word now. "Then I want you to fill a jug full of cool water and add some sugar to it along with a small amount of salt. Say three tablespoon of sugar to a level one of the salt. Stir the water till everything has dissolved, then bring a glass full and be quick about it." There was no time for niceties.

After another one of Aggie's contractions Janet managed to get a second pillow under the woman's head. Using her free arm she was able to get Aggie sufficiently upright to get the eggcup to her lips, to enable her to swallow the thick brown liquid, followed by the sweeter tasting fluid that Janet wanted Aggie to drink as much of as possible. Aggie gratefully obliged, to get rid of the vile tasting first lot and to wet her parched mouth. Putting the glass down on the table, Janet gently raised the nightgown to look at Aggie. There was no need to distress Aggie further than she had to, no need to examine her; all Janet needed to know was self-evident.

No point in worrying Aggie's already agitated mother. "Listen to me, I need your help, we have to move your daughter."

"Move her in this state?" Maggie gasped dumbfounded. "Where to?"

"Are you going to help me or not? Don't talk... just listen." Janet's tone never wavered.

"We are going to remove all these crochet frills from the bed. Then we are going to turn Aggie round until her feet are on the edge of the mattress, so I can see what I am doing." These frills are probably full of dust, Janet thought, shaking her head at the senseless decoration.

"Wait! I will get on with this; get one of the women on the doorstep. See if Rena McKay is still there – ask her to come; we can't manage by ourselves." Janet knew Rena was one of the best, a stable sensible woman and she kept herself to herself.

Maggie left to find Rena while Janet started to strip the trimmings off the wooden box bed frame. Unknown to Maggie Janet had made an alarming discovery when she had pulled back the sheet and lifted Aggie's twisted nightdress. Lord! A footling breech; the baby's foot was still pink and reasonably warm to the touch, but for how much longer, Janet asked herself? Mercifully the cord had not prolapsed, so there was still a chance, a faint hope of delivering the baby… alive.

"What's happened, Junet?" Rena asked, arriving in the kitchen "How can I help? Maggie could hardly speak or tell me onythin', so a' dinna' ken what's gawn on. I guessed somethin's no richt; just tell me what you want."

"I am glad you were still there Rena; yes, we have a problem, but there is something we need to do first. I want you to help me turn Agnes to the edge of the bed facing into the kitchen. Then you will see what I mean by a problem. To be honest I am rapidly coming to the conclusion we need medical help and will have to call Dr Forman in."

"Oh my God, is it that bad?" Maggie gasped when she overheard what Janet said to Rena.

"Never mind God, we will appeal to Him later if we have to. In this situation, we have no choice, the Doctor or God, depending on who gets here first."

Janet kicked the pile of crotched lace out of the way. "Where are the rest of the clean towels I asked you for Maggie?" Maggie pointed to the pile on the chair. "Bring two, put one on the floor and be ready with the other. I want you to stick it under Agnes' bottom when I tell you... do you understand?"

Maggie mutely nodded.

Janet tried to rouse Aggie and failing for a moment, began to stroke her cheek. "Look at me Agnes, look at me," she repeated. The brown elixir was beginning to take effect.

"No more, no more," Aggie pleaded.

"I am sorry my dear, but I have to disturb you for the sake of your unborn child. Please, you must follow my instructions. I want you to look at my face and when I tell you, I want you to start taking in deep breaths. Listen to me... in through your nose and out through your mouth. Do you hear? Do you understand?" Aggie nodded. "We will practice with the next contraction. I am sure you will find it helpful and it will distract you from the pain."

Janet called Rena over beside her and explained to the woman what she wanted her to do. "You will get one of Agnes' arms and I will get the other." Rena nodded. "On the count of three we will twist her round until she is at the edge of the bed with her knees up, feet on the edge." Janet decided that Rena should climbe onto the back of the box bed. Rena, shoes off, with her sleeves rolled up, made her way to the back and awaited further instructions. Rena took a good grip of Aggie's arm with one hand and shoved her other one behind the pillows as instructed.

"A'm ready Junet."

"Right, we will wait for the next contraction. It won't be long as I have just given her more of my elixir. Maggie, stand beside me. When Rena and I move her into position, lift your daughter's feet, bring them round, keep her knees bent, place them on the edge of the bed when I tell you. Then Rena and I, we will raise her buttocks; you can place the towel beneath them. Have the towel ready. Do you think you can manage that?"

Maggie nodded.

"Agnes," Janet commanded, "I need you to look at me! Remember, breathe in through the nose and out through the mouth." Aggie nodded, grateful to have something to distract her… to cling to… instead of the awful pain. At the next contraction Janet took control.

"Ready?" she asked the group. "Agnes. Take in a deep breath – one-two-three – go!" With the three of them working together they managed to get the labouring lassie round into the position Janet wanted. Having distracted Agnes with the breathing exercises, the move did not seem as bad as Janet feared it might.

"Now we have to wait … hands off, there's not much more I can do until nature takes its course. So we wait." Janet beckoned for Rena to follow her into the corridor out of Maggie's hearing.

"Rena," Janet instructed, "I want you to run for all you're worth, find Dr Forman, explain what is happening here. Tell him there is an emergency in the Gardner house." She lowered her voice still lower, and whispered in Rena's ear: "Tell him he might need his forceps. This baby is not coming the way nature intended. The twists and turns that a baby's head make during a normal delivery are not going to happen here. The diameters are all wrong." Janet drew in a breath, wiped the sweat from her brow, brushed a stray wisp of hair back into its net and with those few gestures in front of Rena, showed how serious her concerns were.

Rena did not have to be told twice. She had seen the baby's foot hanging from its mother and was more than aware of the danger. Even although she did not fully understand what 'diameters' meant, Rena knew to find the Doctor and be quick about it.

"Now go!" Janet had raised her voice and that meant trouble. Rena, ignoring the shouts of the other women standing on the pavement waiting for news, ran full pelt down Rodger Street without as much as a backward glance.

Chapter 7

JANET was always the same, calm, reliable, never fazed in a crisis. This last confinement had given the young woman cause for concern and a few heart-stopping moments. Some of the locals said she had no feelings, but that was not true. Unknown to the villagers, Janet kept a tight grip on how she felt, refused to become emotionally involved. No one knew her surname and no one asked. No one risked enquiring in case she took exception and left as suddenly as she had arrived.

Janet despite her youth knew she had to remain impartial. Emotion was all very well, but not much use when comforting others, or giving bad news. Empathise, never sympathise, was her motto. This was the strict code of conduct Janet imposed on herself. Listen, never judge nor volunteer an opinion. The less her clients knew about her, the better she liked it. At times Janet felt alone, but this did not bother her. Deliberately she kept apart, living less than a mile from the village; she had good reasons… she wanted to keep a discreet and respectful distance from those she cared for.

No one knew where she came from and they would be hard pressed to name the day or the month she had appeared in their midst. She had been in the village little longer than the new Doctor; tirelessly appearing for the deliveries of the women in labour without being called. As old Jock had observed… it was as if she had the second sight. None of the local lassies would dream of going into hospital to have their babies… waste their hard earned money, ah no. Janet was better that any hospital. The villagers were grateful to have her.

Janet smiled when she discovered she had a title – 'The Howdie'. What on earth was that? She discovered it was a title of great respect given to untrained women, women wise in the ways of healing and midwifery; the one who treated the sick, the one who cared; Janet's herbal teas, salves and lotions brought relief and comfort to those in need. She was their Howdie. In a time where Doctors were few and far between and cost money, the Howdie could be paid in kind. Janet was not too sure about the title, fearing the fisher folk might think her a witch. Gradually, as the village accepted Janet, she accepted the title… Janet became part of village life.

Young Dr Forman appeared at the door out of breath, Rena hard on his heels. Aggie was now safely tucked up in bed the right way round and the bairn tightly swaddled in an old Shetland shawl, its faded colour and slightly matted feel indicating it had been used for several generations of Gardner babies. The wee bundle was lying mewing quietly in the old fishermen's cradle, brought down from the loft and restored with a lick of varnish for the family's newest member.

Aggie was trying to sleep after her ordeal, barely aware of what was going on around her, too many people in the room… too much noise. Her mother's tongue echoed down the hall as she called out to the neighbours to tell them all was well. Exhausted, she wanted to be left alone. And now the Doctor… what next? Aggie was weary, she had had enough. Couldn't they all just go away, leave her in peace?

Dr Forman had run along Rodger Street and was anxious to be present at least at one delivery. He wanted to gain the confidence of the local population and in particular the women, anxious to redeem his reputation after the catastrophe at the Smith house. At present he seemed to see only men and children and they were few and far between. Doctor Alasdair Forman having recently opened his Surgery in Pittendreal, was anxious to show how well qualified he was and make a good impression.

"Ah, Mistress Bowman, I am Dr Forman. Mrs McKay tells me your daughter's in labour. I believe there might be a problem?" he managed to pant out when he saw Maggie at the front door waiting for him.

"Aye, that's me Doctur, Maggie Strachan, Jock Booman's wife. There's no need for ye' tae hurry noo; am awfie sorry you've been troubled; it's a' ower thanks to Junet. A fine wee duggie-mel… aye, what a braw bairn, but yer welcome to come in the hoose Doctur now you're here; come awa ben, would yae like a cup o' tea?"

"Err no thank-you, perhaps another time," Alasdair replied, courteously removing his hat, not wanting to offend the woman. He silently cursed the fact he had missed a golden opportunity to show off his obstetric skills. Walking ahead of Maggie as she had bidden, he opened the door on his right and went into the room.

"Oh! No Doctur, no in there, that's the guid room we keep for company."

Alasdair turned back to follow Maggie down the long corridor to the kitchen, to where the box bed usually was. Thank goodness, Alasdair thought, I don't have to stay in the 'guid room' – I wouldn't like to sit for any length of time on that sofa or the chairs. It's a miracle how the upholsterer managed to get that amount of horse hair stuffed into one leather chair! It must be as hard as bricks and heaven help me if I'd swung my bag out. I would have knocked down and smashed a mass of china and glass ornaments. I would never have been let back in; they were everywhere, including metal ones in the fireplace. What was that written on those cups and saucers – a 'Gift from Great Yarmouth'? But he also noted that along with the mementos were some seriously beautiful artefacts.

On the sideboard and the shelves of a 'What-not' was a fine collection of Crown Darby and Serve porcelain. As Alasdair turned to leave the room he glanced toward the window… darn near stopped in his tracts, astounded. On a polished mahogany drop-side table, placed on a lace crotchet doyly… one of the finest pieces of Meissen he'd ever laid eyes on. He had to blink twice to make sure his eyes were not playing tricks on him. All of eighteen inches high, a soft ceramic, colourful representation, of rural life captured in fine china. Shepherds, shepherdesses, animals, trees, flowers standing in relief, at every angle, a confection of the artist's skill, a true work of art. There, hanging above the fireplace, a fine oil painting of an old sailing ship in full sail painted by a Dutch Master; waves breaking over its bows, a glorious blue sky and billowing clouds on the horizon, a masterpiece. With his privileged upbringing Alasdair had seen plenty antiques, paintings and fine china ornaments in his own home, but he never expected to see such a thing in the home of a fisherman. Where had all this come from? He smiled, shook his head in disbelief, as he followed Maggie out of the 'guid room'.

In the few short months he had been practising, Alasdair had developed a great respect for the fisher folk. The sheer volume of back-breaking work would have put many off that lifestyle, but born into the fishing community, they had no other choice. Despite the hard daily grind… they still smiled, as Maggie Bowman was doing now. The conditions their men endured at sea were just seen as part of life. He took his hat off to them. His train of thought went back to the collection of ornaments he had just seen. Well, why not? These folk deserve to have beautiful things in their homes. Were these not the fruits, the rewards of their hard labour? But how had so much stuff been accumulated?

"Ouch!" Alasdair yelped. Not paying attention, his mind on other things, he had stubbed his big toe on a fierce looking iron metal doorstop.

"Aye Doctur, watch yer feet, I'v been meanin' tae move that," Maggie announced unsympathetically, now marching ahead of Alasdair.

"Good grief," he muttered under his breath, "how am I supposed to see where I am going, the damn hallway's so badly lit."

A dark oilskin engraved wall-covering was glued to the bottom half and a coat of mustard coloured distemper on the upper half of the walls. They should have a lamp burning day and night to see where you're going, he thought, his big toe now throbbing in pain. What next? The pictures hanging in the hall in thick gold frames made Alasdair suppress a smile, in spite of his pain. He recognised the same prints he had seen in other houses of the fisher folk. A set of boring, depressing scenes of 'Highland Coos', perhaps the Monarch of the Glen was slightly better depending on your taste. Alasdair also felt he wouldn't like to argue with the ferocious looking stuffed stag's head hanging between the pictures. At nearly six feet he had to duck to avoid hitting his head as he passed.

"You have some beautiful possessions, Mrs Bowman," Alasdair announced, trying to strike up a little conversation and distract his attention from his toe.

"Aye, my great grandfather sailed in the Tea-Clippers more or less round the world, but mainly he was in the Far East and Europe. He brocht a' sorts o' stuff back, but the stags head… that came from Peterheid. But according to ma granny, ma' dye, always said the best crystal came from Italy… the best china from the French and German factories."

"Oh your dye, that means grandfather… yes?"

"Aye that's richt Doctur, ma grandfather."

"Well he had a good eye. The objects are very beautiful to look at and they could be quite valuable."

"Och, I dinna bother wae such thing, Doctur; am no that house prood, they're just a hair for dirt, aye needing tae be dusted…" Maggie prattled on happily. "This is not ma house, Doctur, its ma' daughter's, Aggie Booman… her man's Wullie Gairdner… we live three doors up… we're grand and close."

"Janet isn't it?" Alasdair asked when he finally reached the back kitchen. "Looks like you have managed without me."

Janet detected a slight edge of sarcasm in Alasdair's voice. Alasdair noted the pleasant smell of lavender coming from the woman. When people had little or no access to frequent bathing this made a pleasant change for the young man.

"Yes, but I am very grateful that you are here now, Doctor. I know you will check all is well with Agnes and the baby. I hope they have suffered no ill effects." Janet was always diplomatic and mindful of the role she played as unqualified midwife.

"Tell me what happened?"

"When I arrived, Agnes had been in labour for two days and according to her mother she had made no progress. On examination I discovered the baby was presenting in the breach position. I don't have to tell you this is quite rare and is dangerous for both." Janet paused to gather her thoughts and to make sure she had not missed anything regarding the sequence of the events, or had said too much. Alasdair just stood and listened… a slight smile on his face.

Janet continued with her report. "I decided to call you at once. Then after Rena left, most of the baby's body delivered. We had previously moved the position of the mother to the edge of the bed; I left well alone and let the baby hang for nature to take its course. With the next contraction I slipped my forearm along the baby's body leaving the legs straddling either side. As labour progressed I put two fingers on either side of the cheeks. I was helped by the fact that this was Agnes' third delivery; with a little manipulation, the head delivered. So there was no time to wait for you."

"Err, no Janet, it is more likely the baby came not because of the mother's previous obstetric history, but more likely with a little help from your special pills and potions." But he had to acknowledge that very likely Janet had saved the woman and baby's lives. Alasdair was a tall young man and looking down at such close quarters he discovered a startling fact… Janet was much younger than he had previously realised.

Looking down into Janet's deep blue eyes, he felt a sensation previously unknown to him regarding young women. An unexplained feeling, he had become aware of the opposite sex as if for the first time in his life. Was this what the poets and novelists wrote about? Dear God, what is wrong with me, he thought, cursing his shyness, why don't I have the nerve to get to know her better? Mother has a lot to answer to. I have allowed that woman to control me most of my life. Get to know Janet better, that's a joke… how? The very thought of it turns me into a drivelling idiot. Am I afraid to speak to her on any matter except professional ones?

Alasdair turned away, praying she had not seen the reddening of his cheeks. Don't think about her, put her out of your mind; he cringed at his response to a beautiful young girl. To hide his embarrassment, take his mind off Janet, he turned his attention to Agnes and gave her a thorough and very professional examination in the hope of impressing the family; he also took a good look at the baby, but could find no immediate ill effects.

"Well done Janet, I doubt I could have done better; all is well as far as I can make out," he announced over his shoulder, not daring to look at her. Then he changed his mind… he turned and looked straight at Janet. This time he discovered she would not look at him. Why, she feels the same way! Alasdair was pleased with his discovery. So, the chemistry is mutual?

"Now ladies," Alasdair said, recovering. He cleared his throat and continued. "As far as I can ascertain from a medical point of view, I believe all is well, but who is going to break the news to Mr Gardner?"

"What, news… Doctur?" Maggie asked hesitant, fearful.

"Yes, Mrs Bowman, the news… not only does Mr Gardner have a daughter, and I must confess one of the most beautiful infants I have in my experience ever seen, but who's going to tell her father… she has red hair" The Doctor smiled at the assembled company.

The superstitions Alasdair had encountered in the short time he had worked in Pittendreal never failed to astonish him. It was beyond his comprehension, the beliefs… unimaginable catastrophes, the fear of bad luck seemed to dominate their everyday lives. Never cut hair or horn on the Sabbath – such acts carried dire warnings of gloom and doom; a pinch of salt had to be thrown over the shoulder, if spilt. Sailors never swung their compasses against the sun. Every day he heard some new prophesy of doom. Alasdair knew that although Wullie would welcome his baby girl, he would hide his disappointment that she wasn't the longed for son; but no way would the proud father allow a red-haired female on his fishing boat and that was that, daughter or no daughter.

After the trauma of Aggie Gardner's delivery and an uneventful lying-in, things went back to normal. Village life returned to the daily back-breaking grind just to exist.

Chapter 8

I SAT AS I HAD BEEN TOLD... ordered like a small child to be a good girl, and so more than two hours had passed before I dared interrupt my aunt. It was now my turn to prove I was no longer that child. I would have my say, assert myself or it would be all over as far as I was concerned before it began. She wasn't making any sense and I didn't have time to waste – however curious I had been.

"Aunty, wait!... wait a minute. I know what you said a couple of hours ago, but I never expected anything like this... I thought what you had to tell me would take half an hour at most. We might have a cup of tea then I'd leave. Never dreamt the answer to my question would begin in the 1890's. I'm puzzled by that. As I said, how do you know all the detail of Aggie's delivery?" I dared to challenge her. "You weren't born then and a small child would not remember such intimate details, or you must have an incredible memory for your age, never mind your ability to speak in the local dialect!" I twisted my head to the side, sceptical. "Are you sure you are not making it up, maybe to keep me visiting you?" The thought had crossed her mind how old people enjoyed company and apart from Cathie, who else did her aunt see on an average week? "There's no need to feel isolated from the family, you know," she said reassuringly, "I like driving along the coast."

My aunt stared at me.

"I'd visit either way..." I tried to continue but was interrupted... with a sharp reprimand. She had been ignoring what I had just said... as if she had not heard a word.

"Of course I'm making some of it up! And I'm not suffering from the lack of company. Call it an old lady's prerogative to embellish the truth! If I had said the roof of Leightham House had blown off in a storm and the family did not replace it... well? You would have had little reason to visit me one way or another... Am I right?" She said this in a matter of fact, flat tone, to emphasise how bored or perhaps disappointed I would be. I knew from the start there had to be more. My suspicions grew.

"And that's *not* what happened to it, missy; the roof did not blow off in a storm. Yes, I enjoy your company, look forward to your visits. Sometimes to be honest I do feel alone... not lonely... and I have an ulterior motive... the reason I agreed to tell you what happened in the first place," she added mysteriously.

"You're right," she conceded. "No way could I have been at Aggie's Gardner's confinement. So... you want the truth? Over the years I have wanted to write a book about the house and Alice..." She shrugged her shoulders as if apologising for tricking me. "I started to write a few chapters but never got round to finishing it. That's why it sounds as if I am reading from a novel. Technically speaking, I am. It's all in my head. It's important to fill you in on the background, the details, the people involved, make them known to you, before we get to the reasons for your intrigue with Leightham House. Now it's too late for me to finish my book, but not for you – you can complete the story for me. I'll give you the information and you will write everything down... tell all someday."

Once more she had defeated me. What she was saying was perfectly logical.

"You have already had a flavour of the narrative and I promise you as we continue on our journey you will not be disappointed. I'll give you an in-depth account of the people I once knew. Their loves, happiness, betrayals, that part will be the absolute truth... I will take you through the seasons of their lives… the emotional pain, births, marriages, deaths and at the end, the secret I have kept will be revealed."

Should I feel privileged? Had she many secrets to reveal? If my suspicions were right… had she an ulterior motive, along with the narrative?

"I remember the stories, the village gossip… my mother, grandmother told me and I will include my own experiences… a handing down from one generation to the next and the next." I began to feel hungry for more.

"It will be your job to distinguish between fact and fiction, decide what you want to write, but leave nothing out." She stopped to let me digest this. "Listen to what I tell you as if you were there. A witness to a past age… to past lives. Believe me, you will feel you were, but…"

Here it comes, I thought.

"But I have a condition… if you agree to undertake this work; under no circumstances will this information be revealed or published, while I am still alive. Do you understand me?"

My brain buzzed, astonished at this demand. I couldn't answer. She took my silence to mean I agreed.

"We have only just begun; I hope you have the patience to listen to the end. I give you fair warning, you are going to have a long wait before you find out why the roof was removed from Leightham house. If at times you think my memory is failing, ask Cathie to confirm the facts. She knows a little and has lived here all her life. Better still, go visit her grandmother. The lady is older than I am, but her memory is as sharp as a tack and she might know something of local folklore. But that's what it will be. Folklore… but I know the truth." Aunty seemed to hesitate, unsure whether to continue.

"There is another reason I have agreed to speak of certain times in the life of my friend Alice. I have never broken her confidences in over seventy years… but I must tell you everything before I die."

53

I was right; it had something to do with her age… I *knew* she had an ulterior motive… something she had to get off her chest before she died. As for proof, why would I doubt her… and surely Cathie's grandmother must be due her telegram from the Queen.

Very softly Aunty continued. I almost didn't catch what she said.

"Then you will understand… it will become clear to you what really happened. How you are… involved."

"What! What did you say?" I exclaimed, jumping halfway out of the chair. "How can I be involved? That doesn't make sense, I know nothing…"

"Oh shush, sit still and listen, you're not involved… directly; you and I are the picture frame of Alice's life story. What I tell you is the description of the painting itself, the people, landscapes, the colours. So make your mind up. Well… shall I continue? What's it to be?"

"Give me a moment to think, I'm overwhelmed…" We sat silent for a minute… or was it an hour? It seemed like that. I did not answer till I made sense of her proposition in my mind…while I tried to work out whether or not I wanted to be burdened, make a commitment to recording the life of Alice. I had little enough free time as it was.

"Run this by me again," I said, "I need clarification. Have I got it right? You want me to write down all you tell me about Alice, her family and friends and her connection to Leightham House?"

She nodded.

I came to a decision. Made a commitment, a no brainer really… no one would or could refuse such an offer.

"Okay then," I said, "here's the deal. Real life… fact or fiction… go for it. From what you have already told me it will be almost impossible to separate the two. Let's get started. I will write from memory today, but from now on I take notes. One last question… Even I can be forgetful at times, but you… how at your age can you remember? Do you still have notes from your book... manuscripts, etc., that I can look at?"

"That's a very intelligent question under the circumstances," she conceded. "No, I have my ways of remembering, I have my secrets stored in a box of relics from the past. Documents, newspaper cuttings, letters, a scrapbook full of information and even some old photographs to refresh my ageing memory... as you've just point out to me."

"Can I see them?"

"No! That's not necessary. I will be fully prepared and will have done my homework for each of your visits. I have to decide exactly what you should hear. Much of what I have to tell you is private... no-one has seen or heard... or knows." She fell silent. I thought I detected a look of sadness on her face. "When the time is right I will allow you to read some of the correspondence I have between me and my friend, but at present it is not relevant."

Good, bad or indifferent, it looked like we had reached an agreement. No going back, we understood each other. We had set up the goal posts. The contract signed, the tension eased... Alice's story... my silence... nothing to be revealed or divulged till after her death. Why had she kept this secret all these years? What had Alice done... murder?

Thankful I heard the sound of Cathie bringing the tea trolley down the hall.

"Just got back from ma sister's, thought you would like a cuppa," she said as she entered.

Driving down the long tree-lined drive from my aunt's house, I looked back, reflecting on today's visit. With a sense of peace, calm, belonging... but my aunt had intimated I was somehow involved and then had quickly retracted the statement. Until my next visit I would have to wait and see what she meant. But that sense of peace and calm changed, left me feeling emotionally wrung out... exhausted.

Chapter 9

A MONTH had passed from my last visit and I was on my way back to Aunt Jane's. Refreshed and restored, I was looking forward to today's visit.

"Is that you away?" Mum asked as I left. "I feel a bit guilty not going with you. Give Aunt Jane my love and tell her I'm asking for her, but I have choir practise – I can't miss it."

"Yes I'm off. Aunty won't think any the worse of you for not coming. Anyway, it's only me she wants to see. You know Mum, since I've been one-to-one with Aunty I've noticed she doesn't speak with a local dialect. Any idea why?"

"Now that you mention it, no… you're right, I've never thought about it. I've no idea why. Ask her. It's only you she wants a visit from these days. Be careful, that's a bad road; the subsidence from the coalmines…"

"Mum I'm more likely to be killed by a drunk driver. It's about time they enforced the new drink-driving laws… Ah, a nod to my working life, if you could see some of the sights I see in A and E; driving should be banned altogether if you have been drinking."

"Why is it only you she wants to see? You're up to something the pair of you, thick as thieves! What is it you're doing?"

"Believe me Mum, after my last visit, I wasn't sure I want to go back. She makes me feel as if I am facing old Miss Richardson, my English teacher. But I have been doing some sort of research for her, it's of no real interest." I shrugged my shoulders. Mum seemed to have lost interest, which was a relief as I had no desire to lie to her or refuse to answer her questions.

"What's that you're taking with you?"

"A packet of Kit-Kats. I don't think I can face another Perkin biscuit. I thought I should take her flowers, but there's no point. The house is full of professional flower arrangements, I believe brought in weekly from the local florist. Cathie says she has a standing order with them. She must be wealthy; I wonder where all her possessions came from... and the mansion?"

"I don't know. I do know she came back to the village before you were born, but you don't question Aunty, you have to wait till she's ready to tell you. Play your cards right though and she might leave you something in her 'Will'!"

"Mum! You know I have a genuine affection for the old dear. Sometimes I can sense what she's thinking... it's spooky."

She laughed. "You're imagining things; nobody knows what Aunt Jane's thinking and I've known her a lot longer than you. Remember, dinner tonight six o'clock... don't be late... don't have me worrying."

On my way along the coast road I noticed the corn in the fields on either side of the road ripen. Soon it would be harvest gathering. Which brought me back to today's visit with a mixture of anticipation and trepidation after our last encounter. I mulled over what the best approach would be... a post-mortem on the last visit? I felt it would be better to start with a light-hearted discussion, ask her opinion on what I had written. Confirm that it was what she wanted?

"Come awa in ma lass, your aunty's waiting for you in the sitting room."

"Thank you, Cathie. Here's a packet of Kit-Kats, do you think you could sneak them onto the tea-trolley?" Cathie smiled; perhaps she was fed up with ginger biscuits as well.

"Hi Aunty," I called out as I entered the room and sat down in the big Parker Knoll chair opposite her. "I finished from memory what was said last time. I hope it's correct; in fact here's a copy in case you want to check it."

"That's not necessary, I trust you to remember the details and record them. I don't have time to go over everything again. You're a Doctor, your memory is your ally… you don't forget."

"Thank you. However I would like to reiterate some of the details before we begin, add my own thoughts."

"As you wish. What did you want to discuss?"

"I agree with you for the sake of history all should be recorded for posterity. You made me think back over the stories my granny told me and if I don't record them somewhere, they will be lost in the annals of time. I think… if I am not mistaken the Smith twins Elspeth and Lindsay were distant relatives of a cousin of granny's. I think she said she went to school with them and if I remember rightly granny said the twins' older sister Lieb had to leave school at a young age to care for the family. She probably was only fourteen." Aunty nodded in agreement. "To get back to today… to clarify what you want me to record, the history of the people, the area… is that right? Well, I'm with you a hundred per cent on that score."

The more I had thought about it over the past few weeks, the more I realised I was being handed a gift from her. Better than some cheap china ornament left in a 'Will' my mother talked of. Local historical facts, no real interest to anyone, but I would have something more precious at the end of the day. A history and how it affected me and my family… indirectly. At least that's what I thought she meant.

"Next time I come let's go out, I'm sure you would like that. I can drive down to the Mid-Shore and we can get an ice cream from Marcello's – how does that sound to you?"

Aunty seemed to be nodding consent.

"Marcello's been dead a long time, so are all my friends. His grandson young Marcello runs the business. It's a long time...." The old lady's mind had wandered. I pressed on conscious of the time and we hadn't even begun.

"I can't believe Aggie Gardner had a home delivery? No one in their right mind would stay at home in labour for one day, never mind three. Delivered by an untrained woman acting as midwife... unheard of... incredible. Occasionally you hear of a woman delivering in an ambulance... not making it to hospital, but the ambulance men have been trained to deliver babies and you only hear about it because it hits the local press.

"Aunty, nearly all breech babies are delivered in the maternity hospital now. I have known the obstetrician order an X-ray to confirm the baby's position... a breech delivery is no joke. It's dangerous for both mother and the baby. Some of the obstetricians are rapidly coming to the conclusion, that all breech presentations should be planned C-sections – the lesser of the two evils." Aunty seemed to be listening.

"So getting back to what you were saying at my last visit, the baby and the mother survived, yes?" I tried to jog her memory. There was no response so I chattered on.

"You know I have read about the Howdie's – do you know it's a Scottish word? M-mm, seems women practised the art of healing and midwifery in every country in Europe over the centuries. In France these women conducted the deliveries in 'la Chambre-des Sages- Femmes'... yes, the chambers of the wise women.

"They were the mainstay of their communities from a healing point of view; I doubt they did much harm with their herbal medicines. Medicine was in its infancy; probably the Doctors did more harm. Think about it – they bled the patients almost to death. Did you know it was Doctors who accused the female healers of being witches? Guess what the villagers did to these poor souls!"

Maybe I had chosen a bad day to visit; I seemed to be getting little response. Suddenly... she looked back, stopped gazing out of the window.

"I know what they did, hanged them or worse," Aunty interrupted as if she had just woken up. "They also burnt their cats, poor things. See, you're not the only one with a bit of knowledge." She had been listening after all.

"Well, I'm very glad they did not burn Janet!"

"Why would they? I remember my mother telling me, the young Doctor had not long arrived in the village. Before that they had to travel into Leightham to see Dr Henderson. But you are not the only one with some knowledge of witches. Did you know that this area has a history of witches living in the caves not far from here? I am not absolutely certain, but I think they burnt or hanged the last witch in Scotland just along the coast."

"Witches here? Interesting – maybe I'm descended from one! No, that's wrong, its nurses that are descended from witches. But I have the witch's thumbs." I held my hands up, spreading my fingers at the same time.

"What on earth are you talking about?"

"It's true, look, look how short my thumbs are. They barely come beyond the palm of my hand. They call them witch's thumbs. Anyway that's not important..." I dismissed the subject. "Tell me about Janet; I have a lot of respect for that woman... no, girl. I think she was much younger than the villagers realised, maybe in her late teens, what do you think, Aunty?"

"I don't need to think," was the tart reply. "Are we ready to begin? I don't have all day, to be blethering about witches..."

Knuckles rapped, I got my notebook and pencil out of my bag ready to record details of today's visit.

The woman's right, we seem to skirt round useless subjects... When is she going to get on and answer my questions and when are we going to start hearing about Alice and Leightham House?

Chapter 10

ALASDAIR FORMAN had a grudging respect for Janet, formed on the few occasions their paths crossed, even if she did lose him some of his income. His newfound feelings for her made him magnanimous. He felt she was worth the financial loss. He was a bachelor with only himself to feed, he wouldn't starve. He looked forward to other encounters with Janet; perhaps he could get to know her better. Maybe she would impart some knowledge of the natural remedies she used. It was not the first time he had resorted to Foxglove Tea – for older patients with heart problems who were resistant to the more conventional treatments. What was it Janet gave Aggie stimulate her contractions?

Alasdair survived his first few months without earning a bean; he found out he didn't need money to survive. 'Look at the amount of fish the villagers bring in payment,' he told himself. 'Alasdair, if fish gives you brains, you will be a genius by the time you're thirty.' He laughed, smiling at the local generosity. 'Maybe I've gone back in time, a return to the dark ages, the barter system? It's your own fault you don't get paid. They know a real softy; you find it hard to bill them... well. How can I when they have given me such a warm welcome and they are determined I won't starve!' If it was not fish the villagers brought, it was pots of home-made soup, eggs from their hens, shortbread and the like.

Alasdair loved the area from the first day he arrived and the fisher folk; he would not change his new life for a fortune. Sitting at his desk in the surgery, his thoughts momentarily strayed to the sounds of the sea and the waves on the beach. He loved watching the sea spray rising in the air, ever higher in stormy weather, crashing over the harbour wall. Standing under the sea wall, risking a soaking, to watch the fishing boats, berthed, tied up at the pier, rock back and forth with the swell, buffeted by their fenders from the sea wall and each other, their chains clanking in chorus. Bracing winds in his face, the invigorating smell of the salty air. Walks along the sea shore barefoot, with his shoes tied together by the laces slung round his neck. The sand under his feet, he ducked back and forward to avoid the white horses as they pounded the shore in front of him. Thinking he might get a dog, something he'd always wanted, but as a city dweller denied to him as he grew up.

He respected the fisher folk, particularly the women's fortitude in adversity. Frugal with money, never knowing whether the men would bring back a good catch or poor one; never knowing whether they would return from the greedy jealous sea. God, what a life, he thought as he watched them huddled together on the pier, shawl clad in all weathers watching their men folk sailing out into the Forth. Silently praying for their safe return, the same women, backs broken from carrying heavy creels full of fish, hands gnarled, skin toughened with the salt from gutting the fish. Hours spent up the garret mending the nets, rocking the latest addition to the family in the cradle with their feet, the same time as their hands did the work. No time to stop when their entire existence depended on nets for their men at the fishing. These women just got on with it, smiled, never complained. Alasdair shook his head... How? He loved every new experience and was developing an 'ear' for the local dialect; every day brought a new experience. He had been brought up in the smog and smell-infested city... There no one smiled, kept themselves to themselves, as grey as the weather. He was glad he had made the decision to get away... escape.

Alasdair's new love... the sea. He vowed that when he got to know some of the fishermen better, he would persuade them to take him out on their boats. A short journey from one village harbour to the next would do nicely when they delivered the boxes of fish to other fish markets along the coast. To hang with superstition, all right, he had red sideburns, but he was male, the right sex. Who could argue with these facts? Surely they wouldn't hold that against him, for a few short trips?

The area first interested him when travelling along the coast with his father on their way to play golf. Not long after Alasdair qualified, he rapidly came to the conclusion hospital life was not for him. Feeling more and more disillusioned with what he saw. Powerless to do anything he felt he had to get out. The discrepancies between rich and poor determined the treatment. Levels of disease in the poorer areas of the population got to him. He decided to look towards the less privileged in society where he might do the most good. Turning a deaf ear to his mother's pleas not to go... she pleaded with him, pointed out that he could have a brilliant professional hospital career; reap the financial rewards, private medicine, and the recognition. All pleas fell on deaf ears, his mind was made up. When his old mentor Professor Sir David Scott, a fine surgeon, heard of his decision to leave he simply shook his head in disbelief. Alasdair had developed an interest in Paediatrics; the death rate among the very young was appalling, leaving him feeling helpless. Maybe he could try some of his own theories as a G.P... put them into practice. Where did these epidemics come from, what was the cause? Moving to a smaller area could give him more time to do research, write up his findings for the new medical journals beginning to appear.

The opportunity to escape came from an unexpected source... his Godfather Dr Harry Henderson. A distant relative and golfing buddy of his father, when he visited the family in

Edinburgh and hearing of Alasdair's decision regarding his future, he informed the young man he had the solution. He wanted to open another surgery, further along the coast from his practice. He assured Alasdair there was the need. Dr Harry Henderson would take all the official matters into his own hands, prepare the way. He would inform the local authority and register the boy as the new G.P… he was only too glad to keep an eye on him. Pay for a locum to work in his own practice for a couple of weeks, help him settle in. So what did Alasdair think?

The work was getting to be too much for Harry, who had practised in Leightham for all of thirty years. His workload had increased dramatically with the expansion of the docks and new families arriving all the time. There had been many changes, but the biggest change of all – the town's expansion and his rheumatics! The older man laughed at his own joke. Alasdair and his father didn't think he was joking and both agreed it was a plea for help. With the need for extra Surgeries… house-calls in Leightham; Harry said the visits to the outlying villages were becoming too time-consuming. It left him little time for himself or his family. Worse still his golf was suffering, no time for a round of nine holes on the local golf course. The area really needed another Doctor to practice and Pittendreal was the very place, but if Alasdair was not interested then he would advertise.

"Alasdair," he said, "this job is made for you! Develop the work, expand as you wish, you have my full support. There is a vacant, pleasant house in Pittendreal up for sale, on the High Road as you come into the village. Would do you fine to start with. The two front rooms can be adapted as a surgery and waiting room. Easy for patients to reach, even with children, but far enough from the village to give you privacy when you are off duty, if you ever are." Harry let this information sink in.

"The back of the house has a fine view of the river and a grand wee garden to sit in when the weather is fine, away from the main drag."

As a further incentive he offered to throw in his old horse and buggy to clinch the deal.

"Like me, the horse is getting on, but we have a few years left in us yet." The older Doctor laughed. "I'm going to employ a locum anyway, you see, once you're settled. I want to travel around the Continent. Maybe even get to America... always wanted to visit the States... see what new forms of transport are available. I hear some of the engines are petrol driven, oops, made a mistake, the Americans call it... gasoline." Again he laughed at his own joke. "Cars they call them, or was it automobiles?"

After that meeting with Harry, till Alasdair left his parents' home, everything just fell into place. The house on the High Road was purchased from the money he'd inherited from his grandfather. The remainder would give him the financial backing he needed to start him off, or at least until he started earning enough to support himself. After a few months Alasdair felt he had been there forever. Life could not get any better; he was content and he could not imagine tiring of the village, or of its people.

Having asserted himself for once against his mother's wishes, he'd refused to allow her to buy him new clothes. "Buy them if you insist but I won't wear them," he insisted! The last thing he wanted was for anyone to discover he was only twenty-four and how inexperienced he was outside the comparative safety of hospital life. New clothes certainly would not lend themselves to that illusion. His mother accepting defeat, gave in, and off he went to Pittendreal wearing his grandfather's old tweed waistcoat, the old man's Half- Hunter gold pocket watch in his pocket, gold chain draped across his midriff. Thus he set forth to conquer the fishing villages, but not before he cultivated a fine moustache in an attempt to look older. He also tried in vain to slick down the bane of his life – his unruly forelocks. It made no difference how much Pomade he plastered on his hair, in a few minutes his hair stood up in a 'Cow's lick' as his mother fondly called it. She had constantly stroked his hair when he was at home. "Mother!" he'd snapped at her, brushing her hand away. Didn't she realise how annoying it was? He was a grown man, not her little boy any longer.

Thus kitted out, attired in his oldest clothes, Alasdair went forth to work. Full of ambition, enthusiasm, determined to be a success, ending up a few months later, in bed with an infected left hand… What a start to a new job.

Chapter 11

JANET watched Alasdair Forman leaving a patient's house a few weeks after Agnes Gardner's delivery. Nothing unusual in that, they often passed in the street. Alasdair doing his house-calls and Janet going about her business; after all it was a small village, not a large town. The Doctor would nod; tip his hat in recognition when he saw her, Janet would bob a very slight curtsy and move on. But today no response. That's odd, she thought. Normally the young man strode purposefully along, whistling at the same time. So it dawned on Janet that something was wrong: anyone looking at him would realise this. His unsteady gait like a drunk's had nothing to do with alcohol; it was well known the Doctor didn't drink.

It so happened a few days earlier in the surgery, Alasdair performed some minor surgery on a patient with an abscess. Cupping his left hand over a carbuncle on the patient's backside, he had proceeded to lance it. The patient jerked upward with the pain, knocked the scalpel now covered in puss into the palm of Alasdair's left hand. The infection transferred from patient to Alasdair and was rapidly forming an angry looking abscess. The inflammation was now creeping in the direction of his fingers and wrist. His fingers were swollen to the point where he could hardly bend them.

Alasdair did not have to be reminded of the danger from sepsis; he knew what the complications were. He knew the angry swelling creeping up his arm could lead to gangrene and the only cure... amputation. If the infection did not respond to treatment and septicaemia set in... he was a dead man. The pain was almost unbearable; he didn't know what was worse… loss of his arm or his life. That was if he could concentrate on anything at all.

Janet had observed him going into the house, no doubt doing a house call. If her instincts were correct and they usually were, she was looking at a very sick young man. Alasdair was fighting the desire to be actively sick, he was sweating profusely, had a thumping headache and was dizzy to boot. He longed to lie down and die; or at least get into his own bed and die there. Making a determined effort to clear his mind, he concentrated on steadying his trembling left hand with his useable right one. He bit his lips in an effort not to yelp out in pain every time he had to use them together. The left one was now almost useless; and every movement of the fingers agony. Praying the patient would not notice he paused at the man's bedside, blinked and wiped the beads of sweat from his forehead with the back of his good hand. He tried to clear his head so he could think straight. The patient started to give him funny looks. "Is there onythin wrang Doctur?" he thought he heard the man say.

"No, I'm fine thank you," he heard a voice answer, presumably his own coming out of his mouth in response to the question. Leaving the patient's house he realised he just could not go on working; or dosing himself with laudanum. It was making him lose his balance, stagger as if he were drunk. He reached a low stone dyke and sat down. He did not realise he was moving his lips; he was talking out loud to himself. "Have to do something," he muttered. "I'm becoming delirious." He gave a funny sort of chuckle. "I'm raving – anymore of this drug – I will be dancing in the street, maybe like one of the monkeys I saw at the end of my bed last night!" He laughed mirthlessly. He closed his eyes, placed his good arm over them, then removing his arm tried to open his eyes sufficiently to see where he was. A stupid look came over his face – there was someone in front of him.

Janet had waited for the doctor to come out of the patient's house before approaching Alasdair, who was now sitting on the wall. "What is wrong Doctor? I don't like the look of you, something is not right."

Alistair blinked a few times, peered at the figure until it dawned on him who it was. "I am ill Janet… I'm not well," he said indicating his bandaged left hand.

"Go home Doctor Forman, get into bed and I will meet you at your house in about an hour. Perhaps I can help, but first let me look to see what the problem is, so I can decide what treatment is required and if there is anything in particular I need to bring." Who would argue with that? Certainly not Alasdair, the way he was feeling. It was the best offer he had had that day.

With a deepening sense of relief, Alistair took his arm out of the sleeve of his jacket and undid his shirt cufflink with Janet's help. Together they pulled up his shirt sleeve to just below his elbow. He gasped in pain at having to move his arm. Completing a minor examination of his hand and lower forearm and gently disturbing the bandage that Alistair had crudely managed to apply to himself with the help of his teeth, Janet saw what looked like a nasty abscess on the palm. Not wishing to alarm the man with her fears she replaced the bandage, shirt sleeve and helped him on with his coat.

"Hmmm, I might be able to help. See if you can get into bed by yourself, I will send for Tam to help when I get back, if you haven't managed."

Alistair would have agreed to meet the Devil himself if he thought he could help. Later he had no recollection of how he made it home or got upstairs; all he remembered was throwing off his outdoor clothes on the floor where he stood and falling onto the bed. And that's how Janet found him an hour later.

Janet returned with a bag filled with all sorts of unusual looking lotions and weeds. She was a firm believer in working with nature, not against it, but at times she acknowledged even nature needed a helping hand.

Alistair had heard the back door open then quietly close. A wry smile crossed his face. He knew it was Janet who being well aware of the narrow minded villagers, had arrived, quietly and unobtrusively. He was an unmarried man and living on his own. To be seen visited by a single woman would have prompted much speculation and gossiping. How tongues would clack! The newspapers only arrived once a week from the city, so any news from the outside world took days to arrive. Was it any wonder they gossiped? In the insular news-starved village, the more sensational the gossip the better they liked it. Flouting the conventions – a woman alone with a man – in his house: Oh, scandalous! "Did ye hear aboot her...?"

Janet couldn't care less about the convention of the times, or giving the locals cause to gossip – in fact she quite enjoyed the thought, but she did care about Doctor Forman's reputation. Nearly all Janet's work was with the women and children; normally she would have had a quiet smile about being alone with a man in his home. But not today. Today there was nothing to smile about when a life was at stake. The kitchen was at the back of Alasdair's house and it was rare for any of the doors in the village to be locked. Janet had come in by the back entrance, to reach the kitchen quickly and to put her bags down, so reducing the noise of her arrival. If Alasdair had managed to fall asleep she did not want to waken him.

She gasped as she looked around the kitchen; then she remembered he was a bachelor living alone. The kitchen wasn't dirty, but it would certainly benefit from a little female attention. Plates, cups, cooking utensils, pots and pans, clean and dirty, were strewn over the table; dumped in a heap in the sink and on the cooker. Janet argued in his defence, as he begun to feel rotten; no doubt he left the mess intending to clean it up later. She sighed. 'What this young man needs is a wife or at least a housekeeper until he gets one. – Ah! Rena McKay, the very person! I'll have a word with her after I have spoken to the Doctor about it.'

Janet remembered Rena's husband had been drowned in the harbour when two of the fishing boats moored together had collided. Thrown into the water, his heavy boots had dragged him under. The water was deep and there had been quite a swell that day. Sad to say no one saw him fall, the rest of the crews' attention being taken up on the starboard side of the boat, intent on unloading crates of fish onto the pier. Rena, now a widow, was dependent on what work she could get from gutting the fish. With two small children she couldn't follow the fishing fleet as the single lassies did and was dependent on her mother. 'Yes, that's the solution! I will have a talk with him about employing Rena. For a few shillings a week Rena will be only too glad to work for the Doctor, she'll do a good job.'

Rolling up her sleeves, Janet set to work lighting the gas cooker. Filling two large saucepans and the kettle with water from the sink, she put them onto boil. 'Lucky man, a gas cooker with four burners! I can get everything ready at once and not have to wait.' Digging in her ample bag Janet produced two stone jars, one containing a quantity of rough sea salt she had procured from one of the fishing boats in the harbour and the other containing homemade soup. From the same source as the salt, Janet had filled a large oil skin bag with as much ice from the hold as she could carry. 'I need somewhere to store this, somewhere cold,' she thought to herself, 'but where?' She rummaged about, thinking whoever had organised this house for Dr Forman had thought of everything and it appeared that money was no object. 'Would you look at that!' During her search for somewhere to store the ice, to Janet's amazement, there in the pantry stood an ice-box! This kitchen couldn't get any better or any more modern, it was superb! 'I can keep the soup fresh, better still the ice frozen. I doubt he's eaten in the last day or two; I'll try to get him to take some of the soup later. Lord! I hope you know what you're doing, Janet.'

Placing a small sharp knife in one of the pots, she added a quantity of Boracic Powder and left it to boil. Searching around in the kitchen cupboards and drawers Janet was delighted to find out how well equipped they were. Without doubt this kitchen had benefitted from a woman's touch. Some of the utensils had a worn look about them, but still had plenty use. These utensils and pans must have belonged to the Doctor's family. 'I will probably never know,' she thought. 'But one thing is for sure... this man is well loved, for someone to go to such lengths for his comfort.' Janet rarely allowed herself the luxury of looking back, where she might have come from... who her parents were. What they might have done for her. She frowned, shrugged her shoulders, wondered if... 'Do I miss... this is not the time or place,' and she dismissed the thought.

In the kitchen press Janet found two large bowls and filled one with ice. Into the other she poured the relatively hot water from the kettle and a few shavings of Lyle soap. 'Cleanliness is next to Godliness. If that is true, my methods can't do any harm.'

Janet had decided the abscess she had discovered on the palm of Alasdair's hand would definitely need to be lanced. Both hands full and a clean towel found in the table drawer over her shoulder, she went upstairs like a soldier going into battle. Dr Forman was her patient and she would use every shred of knowledge she had, to help him and hopefully save his hand. It never occurred to her... it might be his life?

A feverish young man looked up from his bed which was opposite the bedroom door. He could see Janet entering the room. In a hoarse voice, because of his dry throat, Alasdair asked her:

"What about my patients?" Even in pain his only concerns, to his credit, were for his patients.

"Now – now Dr Forman," Janet replied patiently, sounding like a mother consoling a fractious child. "Stop worrying, try to rest, I have thought of that. Tam is on his way to Leightham to inform Dr Henderson. If the Doctor is not in his Surgery, Tam will leave the message with his wife. I am certain Dr Henderson will be willing to cover the practice for you." She hesitated, not wanting to admit she had no idea how long it would be before Dr Forman would be fit for work. She tried to reassure Alasdair by chattering in a lighter tone. "I know Dr Henderson is getting on in years, I hear he is kindly – has great respect for you; I am sure he will be more than willing to help out... should there be any real emergencies." She continued:

"When Tam gets back he's to go directly to The Pirates, ask the men to spread the word... to find Dr Henderson for emergencies over the next few days. You have a bad cold... might even turn in to flu... Until you know for sure, you don't want to infect anyone, so they are to keep away from the surgery. Tam will also call at the Manse and tell the Rev Mc Dougall, he's to make an announcement at the service on Sunday so everyone has heard you're indisposed." Secretly Janet was not too sure about this last instruction she had given Tam, whether to inform the villagers or not. It was not the amount of praying that would be done in the church for the Doctor's recovery that bothered Janet, but that by Monday morning they could be floating in home-made soup for the Doctor!

Janet worked away at the Doctor's bedside, placing the towel she had brought from the kitchen under the affected limb. Well aware of the responsibility, she felt it necessary to voice her fears. "Dr Forman, I must tell you," she began.

"Janet," he interrupted, looking straight at her. She stopped trying to unravel the tattered remains of the bandage on his hand, took pleasure in having an excuse to look directly at Alasdair's handsome face. "I think for the present and under the circumstances it is you who are the Doctor now. I am the patient so I would be grateful if you would call me Alasdair, not Doctor. Once I am well we can revert to you calling me Dr Forman. You understand?"

Janet nodded her head; familiarity would end with his recovery. She knew what he was asking of her and was quietly pleased… but she also knew her place.

"Yes Doct – Alasdair," she continued. "I am no Doctor and I do not work with medicines, I work with nature. For the present we will exchange roles, Doct… I mean Alasdair – how nice that sounds!" Janet stopped what she was doing, smiled, then cleared her throat to cover her embarrassment; she hoped her cheeks were not turning pink.

"As I was saying," she continued, "my only concern is Dr Henderson. I feel certain he will try to visit you if he is called out. He may decide on a different course of treatment." Interfere and change her treatment before it gets a chance to work was what she really meant. "Naturally I must leave all decisions up to you regarding your health. If you are no better…" She frowned, to work out what was the best course of action in her mind. "Shall we say in two days, I will hand you over to Dr Henderson? For now all I ask is that you trust me, trust in my judgement." She waited for a response from Alasdair. She could see how tired he was becoming and might not be able to think clearly, or be able to decide what he wanted.

"Alasdair, if at any time in the next two days I feel there is no improvement – we have to be realistic if you take a turn for the worst – Tam and I will take you to the cottage hospital. Trust me, if I decide on this course of action there would be no point in calling Dr Henderson; he'd come to the same conclusion and it would waste time. By the time he got here from Leightham, we would be on the road... probably pass him on the way."

Janet was aware that she was untrained. But she trusted her own instincts and experiences regarding the care of the sick – although she had no idea how she had acquired them. As things stood now the worst case scenario would naturally be hospitalisation for Alasdair. She had little faith in hospitals and even less in Doctors. It appeared Alasdair felt the same.

"You seem very confident, that I do have a chance of recovering."

"Enough of that talk, negative attitudes help no one." Janet had returned to her usual soft voice and recognising the quiet voice of authority, Alasdair knew not to argue. Overcome by another wave of excruciating pain, he clenched his teeth and bit into his lips to avoid crying out. The throbbing in his left hand seemed to reach a new level of hellish agony.

"I am sorry my dear Alasdair, this is going to hurt." Janet had unconsciously used a few words of endearment. In those few short seconds, unknown to them both, their relationship changed forever. "I must get this bandage off. Wait, I'll try something else."

"I don't care what you do, get on with it! Get the bloody thing off. I don't know how much more I can take."

"I was going to have you grasp a fist full of ice. I know that might have reduced the pain a little, but not sufficiently; so let's put everything – hand and bandage – into the basin of salt water. The salt will stop the stinging and I have to warn you the hot water will increase the throbbing, but this is our best, really the only option left. The bandage has adhered to the palm of your hand... it's stuck fast. How did this happen anyway?"

Weary, Alasdair gave a short account of events leading up to him injuring himself. Janet realised Alasdair was becoming despondent, so resorted to the local dialect to cheer him up.

"Well, I am going to 'plot' your hand, steep it in hot water."

Alasdair gave a wan smile at her attempted joke

"Sorry, I am not much good at telling jokes; sometimes I find there is very little to joke about."

'God,' she thought, 'I'm trying to cheer him up. I sound as low in spirits as he is. Negative attitudes…?'

Janet left the bedroom, calling back to Alasdair that she needed to collect the rest of the things she had brought. "So to be brave," she said, speaking louder, "try to endure the pain a little longer and please don't spill any of the water out of the bowl onto the bed sheets; just hold your hand still till I'm back."

Hold his hand still! Was this another joke? He had no desire to move his hand… not a single inch. Every involuntary twitch of a finger was agony. Concentrating on keeping still, Alasdair let his thoughts wander. He'd realised at Aggie Gardener's delivery, that Janet was much younger than he first thought. He was confused by her. Where had she acquired her non-existent accent? Where had she learnt such phrases as 'negative attitudes', speak in an educated voice? One thing for sure, Janet was no local; it was highly unlikely she was even Scottish. When he recovered he would ask her; at present he was in no position to ask anyone anything.

"Aaaah!" he yelped as he must have involuntarily moved his hand. The pain reminded him to keep still as Janet had ordered. 'Hurry Janet, hurry, even the smell of lavender that wafts from you, helps to take my mind off the pain. Come back upstairs please, stay with me. Oh be quiet, just listen to yourself, you're like a whimpering child wanting its mother! Thank God my mother's not here fussing, annoying me, I couldn't take her on top of everything else…" With that thought of his mother in his mind, Alasdair gradually drifted off into an uneasy sleep.

Chapter 12

JANET WAS RIGHT. Dr Forman's house had been furnished by a professional.... his mother... and a good job she had made of it. Audrey was not enamoured with the idea of her darling boy, her only child leaving home. She harboured secret thoughts of Alasdair making a brilliant match with some heiress and staging an equally glamorous society wedding, to impress the neighbours. She secretly hugged herself with pleasure at the thought. Some wealthy and very acceptable young socialite from an upper class Edinburgh family would do. At the same time she was equally horrified at the thought of him giving up... no, throwing away a glowing career in the Medical Profession. As far as Audrey was concerned it was one thing to abandon a promising career, but to move so far away was another.

"Oh, Alasdair, what are you thinking about?" she had railed at her son, acutely distressed. "Why move so far? Do you have to take up Harry's offer? You have the promise of several excellent jobs in the city." The very thought of her darling son leaving gave Audrey reason to take to her bed with her 'nerves'.

Audrey Forman was not used to having her will thwarted. For the first time in her life she realised she no longer had control over her son. He was determined to go and nothing she could do or say would stop him. To give the woman her due, once she realised all reasoning with Alasdair was futile, she began to relish the challenge of 'sorting out' her son's needs. It made her feel needed, that she still had some control over her son. It also crossed her mind to be thankful he wasn't getting married as his wife would take over and she'd be out for good.

On the subject of the move, her hand on her forehead, she sobbed: "How would Alasdair get on without me?" In a moment of truth she realised it was the reverse: how would she get on without him? Her whole life since his birth had been devoted to her boy. What would she do with her time once he'd left? Angus, a Naval Commander-in-Chief based in the Dockyard, had been frequently away at sea or abroad. After the birth of Alasdair, Audrey stubbornly refused to join her husband on his tours of duty. Quoting infectious diseases that might affect her son... not *their* son. It would interfere with Alasdair's schooling, she said. As if there were no schools abroad, or boarding schools in Scotland. Secretly, Angus saw this as a blessing, not a curse. It let him get away from both his neurotic, controlling wife and her mother who lived with them. Two women of the same ilk was enough to send any man to sea. Sadly, the end result was little communication or companionship between Audrey and Angus.

Alasdair finally exploding, reminded his mother once and for all it was the East Coast he was moving to, not the bloody Far East! On one particularly trying occasion, Alasdair, totally out of character, actually raised his voice and non-too politely shouted at Audrey, advising her:

"Get to know Dad better? Start socialising with him!" Giving in gracefully, Audrey had to admit he had a point; she had lost and it would be far better for her to acknowledge the fact. Realising that if she didn't and kept going on in this vein, she might end up losing both the men in her life, if she hadn't already lost Angus. Recovering somewhat from the disappointment, Audrey decided to take up the challenge and do what Audrey did best... take control of Alasdair's move to Pittendreal; arrange a visit to the village; see what kind of property her son had bought without her blessing. Have a good nosey around, see what was needed, investigate the neighbours, and find out if they were good enough for her son – although she recognised there wouldn't be much she could do about that.

Recovering, Audrey reached a decision. "I'll go next week to Pittendreal," she muttered to herself. "I have nothing to do on Thursday. I'll take the inch tape with me to measure for carpets and curtains, decide which rooms need what. Now let me think, what have I got that could be used? What's up the loft and in the garage? There is bound to be stuff no longer needed but still useable." Casting her mind back she remembered her father-in-law's belongings, put into storage after his death. He would be delighted to know his old Practice furniture was getting a new lease of life, for Alasdair's surgery in Pittendreal: his desk, swivel chair, examination couch and filing cabinets which he had used himself as a G.P. Old Philip's heart would have filled with pride at thoughts of his grandson and a new generation of Forman Doctors going into general practice. Oh, and a trip to Fordyce's Emporium, the general department store in Princes' Street, would be necessary.

Audrey knew the house had only two bedrooms. "I will furnish one of them and the other can be used for storage. I have no intention of becoming a golf widow. Alasdair needs only one useable bedroom, so that puts paid to any idea of week-end trips Angus might have in mind. Prevent him from escaping, play endless rounds of golf, spend time on the nineteenth hole with his son and Harry Henderson. No way." Short sighted, it had not crossed her mind that her plan would also prevent her from staying with Alasdair as well.

Audrey thought of taking the ferry across the river, but decided to take the train over the bridge instead. The local timetable showed she would be slightly quicker by rail to Pittendreal. The train was not much faster, stopped at every village and town on the way, but at least it would take her right into the village. Alasdair arranged the visit for his mother and told her when she arrived she was to wait in the waiting room. A Mr Tam would collect her and he would escort her to the house. Mr Tam would assist Audrey in every way he could. He had the house keys and knew exactly where it was. He also knew the village, so if she wanted to go anywhere else he would take her.

"Is he a local?" Audrey asked innocently.

"No, not really, but he lives close by," Alasdair answered. The look of guile on his face would have done credit to the angels.

On the following Thursday Audrey, alighting from the train, was expecting the local housing agent to collect her with his horse and buggy. She sat down in the waiting room of Pittendreal station. After adjusting her hat, she proceeded to straighten her coat which had opened on either side of her ample thighs; twitching the edges together, she began rearranging the buttons, till she was satisfied with her appearance. To pass the time she dug into the portmanteau she had brought, filled with inch tapes, pencils and writing paper, retrieving a copy of *The Lady* purchased at the newsagents in Waverly Station and started to read. Preoccupied with an article that had appealed to her while travelling on the train, she had not heard the waiting room door open. Gradually she became aware of an unpleasant odour emanating from that direction, which was getting stronger by the second. Looking smartly up to see what the source of the smell was, she stared in disbelief at the vision in front of her. Blinking several times to confirm that the apparition was human, she could scarce stop herself from gasping out aloud. Horrified, she drew back in the chair, fought a strong desire to leave... run to the platform and wait for the next train to take her back. Then it dawned on her... Alasdair had played a trick on her and sent auld Tam.

"You Mistress Forman? Am auld Tam sent tae help ye," the source of the smell spoke. The smell was now standing almost in front of Audrey, grinning from ear to ear, twisting its bunnet in its hands. Its hair obviously slicked down with some sort of grease… no doubt to impress Mrs Forman.

'You rascal, play a trick on me eh?' Audrey whispered through her clenched teeth, when she realised what Alasdair had done. 'Well let's see who gets the last laugh! I will sort you out, boy, when I get back! A joke, eh?'

In real terms Alasdair's choice of guide was a good one. No one knew the village, the area, removals or 'flittens' as he called them better than auld Tam. Pleased with her decision not to run but get her own back, Audrey decided she would pretend nothing untoward had happened… 'Ah-ha! But let's get on with job – before I throw up!'

There Tam stood still twisting his bunnet, reeking of manure – the cargo he had shifted yesterday. He didn't think he smelt too bad, but then he had very little sense of smell. It was only when folks held their noses and backed away that he realised something was up. Now this was an important job he had been given to do. He wanted to please the new Doctor and he had done his best, had scrubbed his cart, but perhaps some of the dung was still on the soles of his tacketty boots; he hadn't thought to scrub them. However the odour was still pretty strong, even if he couldn't smell it.

"Come awa," Tam indicated the door of the waiting room, sweeping the floor with his bunnet as if Audrey were some visiting dignitary.

Audrey swallowed hard, but she had made her mind up and had decided she would go with Mr Tam. Standing, she smoothed out her coat, folded her magazine, put it away and retrieving a small bottle of lavender water out of her bag, poured a considerable amount of the perfume onto her handkerchief, feigning a cold. She followed the man out of the station with her hankie next to her nose to the awaiting transport…. Auld Tams Kirt!

"I bloody well will kill him when I get home!" she hissed under her breath – furious with Alasdair.

Chin up, she graciously held out a fine leather gloved hand for Tam to help her, realising she was expected to hop up onto the cart for transportation instead of the horse and buggy. Unless she wanted to walk? "Ugh," she exclaimed, her handkerchief held close to her nose. Raising her head proudly, legs dangling over the side of the cart, Audrey indicated to Tam they should proceed.

As it turned out, Tam was invaluable, held the inch tape, and measured all the rooms and windows to Audrey's satisfaction till they were finished. Audrey estimated the yardage of fabric that would be needed and decided on the size of the carpets and what would go where, furniture wise. She might have imagined it, but after a short while… it seemed the smell was definitely lessening.

"Nah misses dinna' use thon dear companies from the big town tae bring the Doctur's stuff oor," Tam advised. "I'll sort that oot, I ken some fine lads with twa Kirts' livin' Leightham. They've got family in Portobello that they can stay the nicht wae. First thing in the mornin they'll come tae yer hoose and collect whatever it is yer wantin shifted. Mind you ye'll need tae give them the ferry fares. A canna' tell ye mistress how pleased we are tae be getting the young Doctur yer son…" Drawing in closer so no one could hear, Audrey held her handkerchief up to her nose and inhaled deeply. Tam whispered, "Auld Dr Henderson… he's getting passed it, yae ken whit a mean?" Tam tapped his balding skull and talked all the way back to the railway station. Mission accomplished, he was pleased with himself and how the day had gone.

'That's choice coming from an old codger like you, Tam,' Audrey thought, finally tuning her ear to the local dialect, until at last she could understand what the man was saying.

"Ah well, he's getting a bit donnert in his top story, its time he went, retired?"

'What does *donnert* mean… drunk?' Audrey shrugged her shoulders.

'Wait till I tell *auld* Dr Henderson what Tam said, Harry will know what *donnert* means. Hope it's not too humiliating.' She had a good idea what it meant and knew Harry would find the description funny or might even agree with Tam.

Audrey took her farewell from Mr Tam, thanked him very sincerely for his help and gave him a tip – a shilling. He was delighted with so much money. He mentally worked out how many wee drams this amount would buy him in The Pirates. She assured Tam she would be fine and that he did not need to wait at the railway station with her. Tam bade farewell… turning on his heels and almost skipping away from the station taking the awful smell with him. Audrey called out to him she would not forget to give the men the ferry fare – mentally noting she would give them a tip as well.

A few weeks later, true to Tam's word, very early in the morning there stood the 'twa kirt's' as promised. Fred Macdonald and Henry Cummings stood caps in hand, fags hanging from the sides of their mouths, both unlit, smiling from ear to ear ready for the move. Anxious to get them off her doorstep, away from her posh Morningside address as soon as possible and preferably before the neighbours woke up, she personally supervised the loading of the 'Kirts'. Her domestic staff had spent the last week enveloping every bit of furniture in heavy draw sheets and binding them with twine, Audrey having threatened them with dismissal if they said a word about Alasdair leaving for Pittendreal to the neighbours. With everything on its way, she sank back into the easy chair, a large cup of tea in her hand to calm her nerves.

Reflecting on the past two or three weeks, she had to admit she secretly had enjoyed supervising the move. But now alone in the lounge Audrey, a tear stinging her eyes, suddenly felt lonely. It had become a reality her precious son was leaving. 'What am I going to do? Alasdair has no use for me anymore.' She was left feeling very sorry for herself.

"I'll phone Marjory," she said to herself, recovering somewhat. She lifted the receiver of the new telephone and asked the operator to put her through to Morningside 161, her best friend.

"Well, what's the use in having a telephone if you don't use it? I'll surprise her and she's not the only one with a telephone!"

The spirit of Morningside snobbery had returned.

Chapter 13

"THERE'S A PHONE CALL for you, Mrs Bateman," Sally the housemaid interrupted her employer with a tap on the morning room door.

"Enter!" Marjory Bateman was enjoying her morning coffee and reading her newspaper after breakfast. "Who is it Sally?" Marjory demanded to know. "You know eh don't like to be disturbed when eh am having my coffee, why did you not take a message?"

"I-I don't know Madam, I don't know who it is, I'm not used to the telephone. The thing… frightens me," wishing her employer would just say *I* when she spoke instead of *eh* which sounded like a hiccough. Who did these Morningside women think they were anyway, Queen Victoria?

"Well you better get used to it!" Marjory snapped at the hapless girl. "Eh get the feeling 'the thing' is going to be around for a long time." She added in a matter of fact voice: "Well, I'd better go answer it." Putting her cup down on its saucer and folding up her newspaper which she placed beside the cup on the side table, she made her way to the Hall.

Picking up the receiver from the hall table with one hand, she placed it next to her ear. With her free hand she wrestled with the long tube like part of the new contraption. Untangling her forearm from the long twisted cord that connected the instrument to the wall and once the crackling ceased in her ear, she announced:

"Mrs Bateman here!" in her best Morningside accent.

"It's Audrey!"

"What's wrong Audrey? You are calling awfully early, are you not?"

"Oh, Marjory, I just had to phone you! Who would eh turn to in my hour of need?" Audrey, her voice trembling, proceeded to give a performance worthy of an actress. "He's left me... he's leaving me... eh am devastated... eh will be all alone, what will eh do with myself?" she stuttered down the mouthpiece, catching her breath and pausing between each statement for maximum effect.

"Who's left you?"

A short silence followed. Marjory gathered her thoughts. Who on earth, she wondered, is the woman talking about? "Angus?" she volunteered.

"No, not Angus!" Audrey retorted sharply, Morningside accent temporarily forgotten, and then she recovered remembering it was sympathy she was looking for. How could Marjory be so stupid; how could she not know what Audrey thought? "We've known each other practically all our lives. Would I be that upset if Angus had left me?" Returning to her performance of the abandoned mother, Audrey continued her lament:

"It's Alasdair, my boy, my baby!" she wailed. "He's leaving his job as Registrar at the Infirmary, found another position and so-o far away. What am eh going to do without him? What am eh going to do with myself?"

"Alasdair!" Marjory exclaimed, utterly astonished as it dawned on her who Audrey was talking about. Now the amateur dramatics started to make sense.

"Your Alasdair, your son Alasdair?" Marjory gasped, utterly confounded.

"Yes, how many Alasdairs do you know Marjory?"

"Well, it's about bloody time. Good for him, I am on his side!"

"Oh!" Audrey drew in a sharp breath, stunned. This was the last response she expected.

"You don't understand, you don't have children or you would know how I feel. Hurt... wounded to the core. I have devoted my life to that boy."

"No children! No children!" Marjory's voice started to rise. "What a cheek... that hurt, Audrey Forman. Yes, I have no children, but it was not for the want of trying. It just did not happen, however hard Callum and I tried." Let her mull over that bit of information instead of feeling so sorry for herself.

Marjory caught sight of herself in the Hall mirror, thinking back... smiled. The memories, the fun she and Callum had had in the hope of starting a family. The mornings spent in bed together, glowing, feeling sure this would be the time it would happen for them. Their trip to San Moritz, Callum making her laugh as he staggered across the hotel bedroom floor pretending exhaustion from their lovemaking. Seemed like all their birthdays and Christmases had come at once. But no, it was not to be. There was some cold comfort for Marjory. One of the infertility Consultants suggested it might not be her fault, but Callum's. To go home... discuss whether or not to have him tested, find out what the problem might be. But Marjory and Callum talked it over, decided to leave well alone, better they didn't know. Now with the passage of time they knew it would never happen. But looking back, remembered, they'd recovered from their disappointment and both decided it had been one of the happiest times in their married life, and they had no regrets.

"Now you just listen to me, Audrey Forman! Stop thinking about yourself! Don't you want Alasdair to become independent? He might find a nice girl, marry, have children? Well, it's not going to happen as long as he is tied to his mummy's 'apron strings' living here with you." Marjory hurried on, giving Audrey no time to protest. "He's just a big

Jessie; you have sapped all the gumption out of the boy… no, man… he's a man, Audrey!" Marjory was on a roll.

"Instead of encouraging him to go out into the world and stand on his own two feet, you have turned him into a shy introverted tongue-tied Nancy-boy! Well, good for him, my Godchild has asserted himself at last. I want to dance at his wedding, don't you? I want to be some sort of aunt to his children. Well, it's not going to happen if he continues to let you control his life… stop being so selfish." Marjory realised what she'd said… maybe gone too far? Better change the subject.

Audrey knew what Marjory had said was true, but refrained from making further comment in case she got another tongue lashing from her friend.

"Where is he going to anyway… The Moon?" Marjory tried not to sound too sarcastic.

"No, Pittendreal, he's going to Pittendreal."

"God Almighty Audrey, that's just over the water a three-hour ferry or train journey! What the Hell are you going on about?" Marjory shouted down the receiver, her posh voice momentarily forgotten. "As to what you are going to do, eh can think of half a dozen things Audrey Forman. How about more charity work for starters, take up knitting, learn to play golf? How about giving Angus a bit more attention, poor soul? Continue the way you have over the years, he might be the next man to leave you. Now is there anything else, dahling? My coffee is getting cold."

"Forgive me Marjory… I don't know what I have been saying," posh voice once again forgotten. "Do you think you could meet me in town? I have visited 'that' house in Pittendreal, the house Alasdair has bought wasting the inheritance his Grandfather left him… Marjory, it needs everything. Thank goodness there's nothing in it. It's empty, just as well, I would have taken it all out and burnt it. The place stinks of damp and old fish. Eh don't know how my boy will survive – his chest…"

"There's nothing wrong with his chest!" Marjory interrupted unsympathetically. "How that boy has not turned into a chronic hypochondriac like you, eh will never know." Getting bored with listening, Marjory shook her head and spoke before Audrey could interrupt.

"Audrey! Alasdair has the right to do whatever he wants with his inheritance, spend his money whatever way he likes. I remember his grandfather and I can categorically assure you he would have approved. Maybe that was why he left his money to Alasdair, not you and Angus. The old man adored Alasdair, he was so proud of him and going into general medicine… another G.P. in the family… what more can I say?"

Audrey continued to ignore Marjory's placatory remarks.

"A Mr Tam, the man who met me last week in Pittendreal, took me to the house. He has assured me he will get the house properly aired. I have arranged for him to put a fresh coat of distemper on every wall. Marjory, I need your help and support in this," she pleaded with her friend. "There is so much to be done – so much to be bought. I can't do it by myself. To start with… curtain fabric. I have the measurements, but need to work out how many yards. Carpets, small chairs for the surgery and waiting room, towels, pillows, oh Lord, just everything."

Abandoning the grieving mother act, Audrey was genuinely in need of help. She knew she could count on her friend. Marjory would rise to the occasion and do just that… take over.

"Audrey!" Marjory barked, "That's enough. Take a rest, you are working yourself into a right state, your nerves are getting the better of you."

'What would Audrey do without her nerves?' Marjory thought. 'I feel sorry for the Doctor who has to listen to all this twaddle. I doubt he cares; bet he just dishes out the pills and sends the bill naturally.'

"Naturally eh will help you dahling, that is what friends are for," she drawled in her most sympathetic voice. "Listen… this is what we will do, meet at Miss Margaret's Tearoom in Princes Street about three o'clock… enjoy our afternoon tea and that will put you in a better frame of mind. We can then discuss furnishing the house. What a terrible experience for you, your one and only precious son leaving home! Eh cannot bear to think of what you're going through." Marjory did her best to sound sincere. "We will make a list and after tea, proceed to Fordyce's Emporium. How about that for a plan?"

Since the girls left school they had been inseparable. Hardly a week went by without them meeting for some reason or other. The two women used each other shamelessly as and when it suited them and this was one of those occasions.

"Oh do stop worrying Audrey. Eh will telephone Monsieur Gregori and make sure he reserves our table by the window." This new-fangled instrument has its uses after all, Marjory thought. "Remember three o' clock sharp, that will give us time to enjoy our afternoon tea. Remember Alasdair cannot make this move without your help; see how he needs you?" Marjory dripped sympathy, knowing how patronising she sounded, but it seemed to work. Frankly speaking, she had had just about enough of this conversation. Maybe she should be grateful she never had any children, she thought.

Chapter 14

AUDREY FORMAN descended from a horse drawn tram in Princes Street. A sharp wind was blowing in from the west, making her shiver. Catching her hat by the crown, which was threatening to blow away with the next gust of wind, Audrey pulled out the hat-pin and re-stuck it into her head, in an effort to prevent the hat blowing away altogether. She gathered her Paisley shawl tight about her shoulders for warmth and rearranged her handbag which had become stuck under her armpit from her exertions to secure the hat. Bag in the right place, the handle now over her forearm, she marched along Princes Street towards Miss Margaret's Tea-rooms determined to arrive before Marjory.

Audrey felt this has got to be the coldest, dustiest Capital City in the world. Thank God the winter's almost over; at least I can see where I'm going. Between a mixture of fog and smoke belching out of the cities chimneys' 'Auld Reekie' was well named. Audrey's mood, sullen and sombre, matched the dark rain clouds gathering over the Castle. 'Damn, I have forgotten to bring my umbrella; well I will just have to call one of those horse-drawn cabs to take me home when we've finished shopping. I can't hang around here all day waiting for a tram. How could Angus be so selfish, take our carriage today of all days, my need is greater than his. I'll have to talk to him… tell him to check with me first before he helps himself.'

The weather certainly seemed to match Audrey's mood, which got worse when she realised Marjory had beaten her and was already at the Tearoom's main door waiting for her to arrive. The pair embraced with pretend kissing and hugging, enquiring how the other was as if they had not laid eyes on or had spoken to each other for months.

"Madam Forman, Madam Bateman!" a familiar voice rang out as the ladies arrived. Monsieur Gregori, the manager, welcomed them in his strongest, guttural, pseudo-French. He knew the stronger the accent and the more exaggerated his attentions to the ladies, the bigger the tip. Monsieur Gregori was no fool. Taking each of the ladies' hands in turn, he raised them to his lips, gave each a perfunctory kiss above their fine Dents gloves, in case he marked the leather. Normally Audrey would duck her head, giggle like a silly schoolgirl. Today no response. 'Oh-dear, something is not quite right here. But they have only just arrived, had no time to quarrel or disagree. Ignore it, pretend not to notice, Gregori, just play along as usual.' It was none of his business anyway.

"A pleasure as always. Come this way ladies, your table is ready waiting for you just the way you like it. Fredreche!" He snapped his fingers at the young waiter who was hovering in the background. "Take the Madams' coats and be quick about it!"

Fred did as he was bid; fortunately neither the ladies nor Gregori caught the slight scowl that crossed his face. But a cheesy grin quickly replaced the scowl when the women looked straight at him; but then again no-one ever looked at Fred when Monsieur was around. Today both men looked at each other, gave a slight nod. 'M-m something is definitely not right,' that look said. 'We better be extra careful.' Fred whisked the coats away to the cloakroom while Gregori escorted the ladies to their table with much bowing and scraping; the wily old fox knew Mrs Forman would fall for his exaggerated acts of homage. But he doubted it ever fooled Mrs Bateman. "This way," he indicated with an exaggerated sweep of his hand.

Miss Margaret's Tearooms in the middle of Princes Street had recently re-opened its door to the public. Closed for renovation, the restaurant proudly reflected the latest in modern architectural design... Art Nouveau... no expense spared. Marjory and Audrey stopped, stared in awe at the strange apparition in front of them.

If Gregori had had some misgivings regarding the redecoration he kept it to himself, certainly said nothing on the subject to his boss, but he had his doubts... as had this pair of regular customers.

A sea of tall, angular, ladder-backed ebony wooden seats were arranged in groups of four around much smaller tables. The tables were dressed in snow-white damask cloths with matching napkins. Simple white Limoges porcelain and stark silver cutlery graced the tables. A centrepiece on each table emphasised the artist's desire for stark simplicity: tall unembellished shards of clear crystal glass, posing as flower vases, each supporting a long stemmed pale pink lily.

An entire wall of windows looked over Princes Street had been radically changed. Elongated panes of glass from floor to ceiling, in truth each a work of art, were divided and supported by thin strips of black ebony painted wood between plastered columns. Each individual window was then divided into smaller sections by fine narrow strips of moulded lead. Upper sections of each window scrolls and curlicues outlined, a fine pink long-stemmed pink lily in stained glass reflecting the lilies on the tables. Not unlike a row of matching Alphonse Mucha paintings, but with a flower in the centre instead of the girls' heads he used in champagne adverts. Along the other three walls oblong black ebony enamel painted wooden panels separated panels of pale beige distemper; in one upper corner a long stemmed pink lily had been stencilled. High skirting and a lowered upper empty plate rack completed the new décor. Black and white tiles resembling a chess board replaced the carpet. Impressive indeed for the approaching twentieth century.

"Where's my Lloyd-Loom... are we expected to sit on these...?" Audrey grumbled, indicating the odd looking seating.

The chairs did look uncomfortable, unyielding and not particularly inviting for long stays or ladies wearing metal stays. But was that not the whole idea? Miss Margaret was no fool when it came to business; she was tired of table blockers. Bored middle-class Edinburgh ladies seemed to sit for hours gossiping in groups of half a dozen or more, while her other clients waited to be seated. Her master plan... less comfort... more business.

As they moved into the tearoom the ladies were sufficiently magnanimous to admit... at least it was brighter than the previous brown and dark beige paint. Marjory privately thought it resembled a chess board at best, Harlequin playing a joke at worst. Arriving at the table Audrey, negative as usual, announced: "Thank goodness eh don't suffer from vertigo... those windows give one the impression there's nothing between me and Princes Street."

The ladies now seated at the table, Gregori lifted each intricate and skilfully folded immaculate white damask napkin. Elegantly flapping it out, each behind each lady's back in an over dramatized action, he then carefully placed each napkin over each lady's lap... in case they spilt something on their serge skirts or tussar silk blouses. In unison Marjory and Audrey raised their arms to their heads to re-arrange their hats; extra-large hat pins pulled out of their hair and dug back in through each hat's crown to secure them back in place, to correct the angle they had been blown to. Gregori, enthusiastically flapping the napkins, might have had something to do with the fact their hats had moved sideways almost over an ear with the draught he caused. The ladies had their own private opinions about the changes to their favourite tearoom and, in particular, wondered how comfortable these chairs were. Especially Audrey, whose rear-end considerably larger than Marjory's, was lapping over the edge of hers. But they kept their thoughts on the subject to themselves, just in case they were seen to be out of fashion with the times.

Gregori Aksakov, the Manager at Miss Margaret's, had quite a history before eventually settling in Edinburgh. He had escaped from Russia with his family, few possessions and the gold fillings in his teeth. Escaping the recent uprising of anti-Semitism made him realise the situation for his community was bad and rapidly getting worse. Leaving in the middle of the night they finally arrived in France by ship from Estonia; Gregori was convinced they would be safer there. He soon discovered that although it was safer, even although he procured a job in one of the Parisian cafés, life was not much better. Long hours and poor pay made him decide to move on. But not before he cultivated a fine French accent which he used when speaking English. His only desire had been to get as far away as possible from all the previous misery he and his family had suffered. Landing in Dover, onward and onward, the family trekked, till they refused to go any further. "Enough Gregori!" his wife had shouted in Yiddish, and issued an ultimatum: "The next town we come to I will sit down in the middle of the road and refuse to go any further..." The next town just happened to be Edinburgh.

Gregori was not ashamed of being Russian by birth or Jewish, but he had to work to support his ever increasing family. The day he arrived for his interview with Miss Margaret, he turned on his French Gaelic charms. Dressed in his best and only black suit, spotless stiff white high collared shirt, cravat, spats and a pair of the shiniest black patent shoes you could see your face in... his only new purchase in years, he was ready. Miss Margaret, now a middle-aged spinster, was not fooled by his performance, his outfit or curling moustache, but she was couthie enough to know her clientele would be. They would also love the attention this man would give them. He was desperate, needy and if she gave him the job, that would make him dependent – dependent on her and the salary she was offering, for he had known hardship, and she knew he was unlikely to cheat her. To begin, so he didn't get above himself, she gave him the title of Head Waiter for a trial period. After a few months Miss Margaret began to rely on Monsieur Gregori as he proved to be more than his financial worth, so she promoted him to Manager.

Miss Margaret set a few conditions before Gregori began to work. He must use his first name and never use the surname Aksakov as no one could pronounce it. Never grow a beard – she always maintained that a beard was scruffy, unclean and her customers preferred to see the faces of her staff. However he could keep his fine curling moustache and sideburns which he took great pride in, twirling the moustache with his forefinger to emphasis a point. Whether the customers noticed Gregori's moustache or the sideburns was another matter. What was important to Gregori were his customers. Keeping them coming was vital to his future and his existence.

As far as Gregori was concerned Miss Margaret could call him the Tsar of Russia if she wanted, he'd gladly shave his head; learn to play the bagpipes, just as long as she gave him the job. He'd made a vow never to let her down. What! Lose his job in such a beautiful recently refurbished establishment? He was not daft. Wealthy clients and good tips, which Miss Margaret said he could keep... Gregori Aksakov was a happy man. Standing at the heavy black lacquered doors... chest out... a fistful of menus under his arm at the ready, Gregori waited to greet his customers.

Today, standing at the side of Audrey and Marjorie's table, he asked, "Madams, what is your pleasure this fine afternoon?"

"Eh want a pot of Darjeeling, and what cakes do you recommend Monsieur Gregori? Are the scones..." Audrey and Marjory reverted to posh, Morningside accents in front of Monsieur Gregori.

Marjory interrupted. "No Audrey, Eh want a pot of Earl Grey with a slice of lemon!"

Monsieur Gregori stepped back from the table, out of the firing line. 'Withdraw to a safe distance, pretend not to hear, allow the Forman, Bateman battle to continue.' However Marjory had seen her friend's face drop. Realising there had been enough squabbling for one day she recognised Audrey was genuinely distressed and gave in gracefully, beckoned with her finger for Gregori to come in closer and take their order.

"Ah yes, we will have a pot of Darjeeling tea your fresh baked scones with cream and jams, but no biscuits, only cakes, you know Swiss roll, Battenberg, Victoria sponge, that will do nicely, thank-you."

"Perfect choice, madam, our scones are just out of the oven and we have a selection of our own comfitures made by our own cooks in our own kitchens." His praise was lavish. "Raspberries, strawberries sent to us from Perth," Gregori bragged, boasting about the best produce in Scotland served in his tearoom. All spoken in the most exaggerated, guttural French accent imaginable.

"Fredreche will be with you directly to take your order, but I will serve your tea myself. In the meantime enjoy the view, the finest in the city. If there is anything else you wish, please call me, do not hesitate, I am here to grant your every wish." Gregori felt he had scraped and bowed enough and returned to the Lectern at the front of the restaurant to greet his other guests. He had had enough of that pair, but... 'Keep, keep smiling, Gregori, remember... the tip.'

The tea trolley arrived bearing a mouth-watering selection of tea breads and cakes. A pot of Darjeeling tea was brought in by Veronica the young and very pretty waitress, smart in her new tearoom plain black dress and white collar. Starched white apron and a cap carefully concealing most of her hair completed the outfit. This was the new order of things in Miss Margaret's – no frills.

"How are you today Veronica?" Totally disinterested, Marjory made a polite enquiry.

"I am very well thank you madam," Veronica replied, equally disinterested. She bobbed a slight curtsy and gave a weak smile. Conversations between staff and clients were not encouraged so Veronica busied herself moving the glass vase to the side of the table and put the three-tiered cake in easy reach of the two women.

Monsieur Gregori, all five-foot nothing of him in his stocking soles, damn near knocked Veronica off her feet as, appearing from nowhere, took over serving the tea as promised. The Master of the tearoom was in his element; with great aplomb he poured the milk into the cups, then the tea from a solid silver teapot. Placing the teapot back on its stand, he refilled the pot with hot water from the hot-water jug. Last of all he made sure the sugar bowl was well within the ladies' reach. With a few minor adjustments and satisfied all was as it should be, Gregori gave a bow and with a twirl of his moustache and a sigh of relief, announced:

"Madams, enjoy!" and took his leave.

The ladies, as bid by Monsieur Gregori, raised their teacups to their lips, pinkies in the air, and sipped their tea. Normally their heads would be together exchanging the latest gossip surrounding their boring daily lives, contradicting each other with a vengeance, convinced their points of view were the right ones, but today nothing but silence. Gregori returned to the table a little later… Did they wish to have their cup refilled? He had observed from his station at the entrance of the tearoom there had been little communication between Marjory and

Audrey. So except for a few comments on how delicious everything had tasted, he again left them alone to get on with it. At least there had been no complaints so the problem had nothing to do with the restaurant, thank goodness.

Their tea plates empty but for a few crumbs, it was time to start planning Alasdair's move. Marjory was getting fed up with the semi-silent treatment... 'I'm not waiting any longer for Audrey to get over whatever is bothering her. There's plenty I could be getting on with at home,' she thought.

"We need to start, Audrey, neither of us has all day and time is marching on."

Audrey silently dipped into her small afternoon handbag and produced a lady-like notebook, the pencil attached to it by a silver chain. Taking this action to mean Audrey had agreed to make a start, Marjory delved into her almost portmanteau-sized bag and brought out a large school jotter and pencil. Thus the table-blockers continued to sit for another half hour, to work out what was needed to refurbish the Pittendreal house.

Business-like as always, Marjory began, "What do we need to for this son of yours? Let's make a list. Put away that silly looking notebook of yours, it's useless!" ('Just like you, Audrey,' she muttered under her breath.) "Oh! And before I forget, I have some household furnishings that are no longer needed. Rag-rugs up the loft; they will do fine for his surgery and waiting room. Some old curtains, a bit faded but plenty of use left in them, but ideal for a young man starting out on his own; no need to buy new. That would be a waste of money."

"Thank-you." Audrey's gratitude was genuine. "Some new curtains are needed... brass rings, wooden or brass poles to hang them on. There is nothing in the house. Maybe we should get a few prints to hang on the walls. I refuse to part with Alasdair's own bedding. I know he'll return every weekend to get his washing done for him, and have a decent meal." Audrey, bird-brained, jumped from one suggestion to another.

"You mean you hope he will return for good?" Marjory snapped.

"Please Marjory; let's not argue and just get on with the job."

The completed shopping list in Marjory's jotter now complete, it was time to leave. Audrey had ignored Marjory's remarks regarding the use of her notebook and put the useless object back in her bag. Rising from the table, Audrey had to suppress the desire to rub her bottom, numb from sitting on the hard chair. They made their way to the front foyer where Monsieur Gregori was standing at his lectern.

He minced his way towards the two and stated, "I hope everything was to your satisfaction, Madams?"

"The bill!" Audrey snapped, ignoring the man's pleasantries. It was handed to her by the now speechless Gregori who felt as if he had been reprimanded for something he hadn't done. Lips pouting, he looked like a child about to burst into tears. Head in the air Audrey marched over to the desk, paid the bill, took the receipt and tried unsuccessfully to shove the receipt into her functionless handbag.

At the behest of Monsieur, Fred arrived promptly with the ladies' coats and was now hovering over the two ladies. Forget about a tip, Gregori had had enough of them for one day. Marjory allowed Fred to help her on with her coat, quietly slipping him a shilling in the process, but Audrey grabbed hers from Fred and insisted on putting it on herself. Such was her desire to show her discontent to anyone who was interested, but then was Audrey ever content?

Well aware her friend was behaving like a spoilt brat, Marjory decided to ignore her. If Audrey wanted to behave like a child then Marjory was going to treat her like one. Coat on, Audrey swept out of the tearoom, almost tripping down the stairs as she concentrated on fiddling with the buttons, which today were refusing to go into their buttonholes. But as she reached the street another minor catastrophe was about to take Audrey's mind off her coat buttons.

"Oh no, any minute now I'm going to give a very unladylike belch, my stays are too tight!"

"Well, you can only blame yourself, it's your own fault… behaving the way you did. Why didn't you go to the Ladies' powder room before you left Miss Margaret's? You could have undone the top hook in the toilet."

"Maybe I ate too much cake." Hoping no one would notice Audrey tucked her elbows into the sides of the offending stays; twisting her arms from side to side in the hope of shifting the garment so the wind could travel down and not up.

"Any minute now I am going to choke, steel bones from armpits to hips, only a man could have invented such an instrument of torture!" She thought: 'It's just not fair, look at Marjory, not a pick on her, I bet she doesn't even were corsets; but I don't envy her, I have my Alasdair… at least I think I still have him.'

Marjory caught up with Audrey and they made their way along Princes Street to Fordyce's Emporium – a rather grand shop catering to the needs of Edinburgh's elite, the modern woman's shopping paradise; it stocked everything you could wish for, if you could afford it. Ladies fashions, the latest style from London and Paris. Worth perfume, new cosmetic powders and lipsticks, hats individually created by their own milliners. Gents' clothing and toiletries. Furnishing for house and garden, lounge, bedroom, kitchen and bathrooms on each of the shop's multi-storied floors. Fordyce's also provided an excellent after-sales service and fleet of horse-drawn covered wagons, guaranteeing delivery within a few days, ideal for Alasdair's move at the end of the month. Audrey decided to arrange a mid-morning delivery time to make sure the neighbours would see the Fordyce's logo on the sides of the wagons; happy this time to have the curtains twitch, fervently hoping it would obliterate the memory of the 'twa kirts' standing outside her house last time.

The ladies were greeted by the Concierge in a Top Hat standing at the revolving door of the main entrance to Fordyce's. He bowed to the ladies and bade them enter.

"Right dahling, let's make a start. Curtain fabric on the third floor, we will start there and can work our way down to the various departments. Take the lift. Quick, look! The girl is opening the gates. Get in before she shuts them. Third floor!" Marjory barked at the woman. "What do you have in mind, what does Alasdair want... has he made any requests? It's his house."

"To be honest eh did not ask him. What would he know about furnishing a house? He's a man, he's clueless in these matters, but he did ask for cotton sheets, not linen; he says they are too hard and itch. Two wool blankets and a feather quilt, he says he gets too hot. Oh! Feather pillows, not flock. Eh have decided net curtains are sufficient for the surgery and waiting room at the front of the house. That should provide him and the patients with enough privacy."

'Ah, at last an admission!' Marjory thought. 'Her beloved has grown up and made some demands of his own, at least in some departments.' Marjory raised her eyes to the heavens.

"What about heavier curtains for the back of the house, Alasdair's own sitting room? They need to keep the draughts out; remember its damn cold over the water." Marjory pretended to shiver.

"Eh thought Chenille, certainly not Brocade, much too rich, they might get stolen."

'Saints preserve me!' Marjorie thought. 'How much longer do I have to put up with this?' As far as eh'm aware no one bothers to lock their doors in the fishing villages, but let's get on with it, my feet are killing me." If Audrey thought metal boned stays had been invented by a man, Marjory was sure a man had invented pointed toe shoes to torture her feet.

Curtain fabrics chosen, the floor manager took the measurements from Audrey, recommended the correct brass rods, hooks, screws. "Leave everything to me," he reassured her. All would be delivered in time for the move.

The ladies made their way to the basement, which stocked kitchen utensils, via bedding on the second floor, to confirm it was cotton, not linen they'd ordered. After many disagreements and discussions about what was needed, they were finished at last. Together they stood at the last counter in the basement.

Audrey nurtured the hope that Alasdair would return home once he got this madness out of his system. She hoped in a few months to return to Pittendreal to supervise packing up Alasdair's house. But a collection of kitchen tools, china for everyday use, lying in front of her on the shop counter was the proverbial straw that broke the camel's back.

Suddenly it became all too real: Alasdair was leaving and nothing she could do or say would stop him. The control she had once exerted over her beloved child was over. Tears welled up in Audrey's sad brown eyes. Reaching for a handkerchief in her bag, she started to dab at her eyes. The hopelessly inadequate fabric was soaked in seconds.

"Here, take this." Marjory dug into her bag and unceremoniously shoved a man's sized handkerchief into Audrey's hand. "In all the years I have known you, Audrey Forman, you are never prepared. What's wrong now?"

"Who's going to cook for him? He can't cook, he'll starve. Who will care for him the way I have done, how is he going to manage, all by...?"

"He can bloody-well learn to cook!" Marjory interrupted in front of the astonished assistant behind the counter. "Eh have had it... taken enough from you for one day, Audrey Forman. No man in Scotland living on his own has starved to death yet as far as eh am aware. Probably some local woman for a shilling or two a week will be more than willing to 'do' for your son." Marjory was past caring who heard her.

Another woman in her son's life – was the last straw! Tears rolled down Audrey's cheeks.

Could it be any more embarrassing, Marjory thought! "Eh am going home, Audrey Forman. Goodbye." And without looking back, Marjory marched out of the shop, deserting Audrey, leaving her standing there by herself.

'Lord, I hope she remembers... next week... we are taking the train to Pittendreal... to sort this blasted house out once and for all.' Marjory made a mental note to phone Audrey later and make amends. 'Thank goodness her moods don't last long... I need a drink... preferably a large whisky.'

Chapter 15

"**YOU SHOULD HAVE BEEN** an actress, Aunty!" I laughed at her impersonations of the two Morningside ladies. Aunty Jane dipped her head, coy but pleased. I cashed in on the compliment I had paid her. "I will never understand why you did not continue to write your book yourself. I bet you're the better writer than I'll ever be. Your knowledge of the English language, descriptions of people, their lives, conversations, it's phenomenal, especially the funny parts. All I do is fill up forms, write case notes and letters to G.Ps. I hope I can do this story justice." She stopped me right there and then.

"Remember our agreement…"

"Nothing to be told or published till…" I could not bring myself to say the word death.

I sat for a moment, glad to reflect on the vivid descriptions of Alasdair's mother and her friend and not become morbid… hats on their heads, the metal rods of their stays sticking into their ribs, sitting stiff, upright in the tearoom. I could just imagine them and I'll bet my aunt wore the same corsets once. She probably still does, but with whalebone now.

"You know Aunty, when I was a student, Mum would meet me in town and treat me to afternoon tea. I would be there in the same tearooms wearing a pair of jeans, T-shirt and flat shoes… how things have changed!"

"Would you believe I have met another or rather the next generation of those very ladies? Admitted them to hospital and you can tell which part of the city they come from the minute they open their mouths! But their accents are changed. Modified like the beautiful old mansions they once lived in that have been turned into flats. No-one could afford the expense of maintaining those buildings, never mind the gardens."

Aunty nodded in agreement with me and added:

"The women I was talking about, irrespective of their education, once they married, never worked. They were responsible for every aspect of household life. She was manager, but not boss. She depended on her husband for everything unless she had private means and even then he controlled that. The law allowed it and the husband could take advantage of it."

"I guess you are right. I never thought about that; weren't they bored…?" I questioned.

"Oh yes, they were bored, same routine day after day. What the outside world saw, frequently was very different behind closed doors. Remember the men could do what they wanted… go anywhere… no questions asked, no permission needed. The wives were expected to stay home, have children and manage the house. See to their husbands' every whim."

"Aunty, when you were telling me about Alasdair's mother… I couldn't help remembering house-calls I did in those mansions. The elderly couples would be sitting alone together amidst their collections of fabulous paintings, ceramics, furnishings, Persian carpets… you know what I mean?" Not unlike your own, I thought privately.

"There in a prominent position on large ornate wooden sideboards, would be in solid silver frames a photograph of a young man in his twenties or thirties Dressed in Officer's uniform, stripes on sleeves… epaulettes, caps neatly tucked under their arms Royal Air Force, Navy, Army, take your pick. Handsome young men standing upright proud in their uniforms ready to serve their country, posing for their… last photograph? Occasionally the old lady or gentleman would pick the picture up as I was leaving to show it to me... then tell me he was their only child and killed in the war. What did they have to live for now? And yet they were so proud. It's only twenty or so years since the war, how quickly we forget..."

"Man's inhumanity to man. Have you noticed my dear its men who get us into wars? We need more women in power."

"Give us time Aunty, we're getting there. Do you know I can get a mortgage in my own name now... buy my own house... that's progress. Our house is in Dad's name, which reminds me, I need to talk to him about that... put Mum's name on the deeds. Joint ownership."

The grandfather clock in the hall began to chime. "Look at the time!" I burst out. "Five o'clock. Where has the afternoon gone? Mum said to be home by six for dinner. I love having Sunday dinner with Mum and Dad; they look forward to catching up, sometimes, it's the only day in the week we get together. Oh, the pressure of being an only child! Must be great to have siblings." I got up and made ready to leave.

"No, don't go," Aunty protested. "I want to tell you more about... No, go! I forgot its Sunday... away, shoo! Television's good tonight – Songs of Praise, Sunday night at the Palladium..."

I smiled; I'd been given my marching orders. Drat, I had forgotten again to ask if the baby Janet had delivered was Alice. No more time, it would have to wait till my next visit.

"By the way, I'll be able to get today's visit typed up before I come back. Do you want me to bring you a copy? I bought fresh carbon paper."

"No!" That was positive enough. "Some thing's I want to remember, others I don't. You keep it safe, somewhere, and remember that not all my story is funny, far from it."

"Okay. You don't need to see me out, I know my way." Lifting my handbag from the side of the chair, I fumbled for my car keys. "I swear I will return in my next incarnation as a man with a hip pocket. You never see a man searching for keys or lipsticks, do you?" I leant over to that old lady sitting proud, almost stiff in her chair and on impulse placed a kiss on her cheek.

I thought I heard her call out as I left…"Drive carefully and wear a longer skirt, you'll catch your death of cold in that… miniskirt!" She was human after all.

"I'm wearing thick tights!" I called back as I walked to the front door.

Driving down the tree-lined drive, I experienced a sense of accomplishment, a real connection with the past… But how could I be involved, what had she meant? But until my next visit, I would have to wait to find out.

Chapter 16

IT SEEMED LIKE only a few moments in time and here I was back, sitting in the bay window of Aunty's home, pen and notebook at the ready to hear and record the next chapter of great Aunt Jane's story. I could hardly wait to find out what happened next. Was I in for an unexpected turn of events?

Chapter 17

BACK IN THE KITCHEN, Janet poured fresh cold water into a bowl and added the ice from Wullie Gardener's boat.

"Help yersel'!" Wullie had shouted from the hold when she had asked for the ice. "Here, tak it, onythin' yer wantin' tak it… yae dinna hae tae ask, ony thing else? We're that grateful tae ye Junet."

Going upstairs, she spied two cupboard doors on the landing. Having been somewhat preoccupied, she had not noticed them the first time. Now, she could not resist taking a look inside. "My goodness, one of the cupboards is crammed with household goods," she muttered. "Full… they are stuffed to bursting." Extra bedding on the top shelves sheets, pillows, towels, quilts and on the lower shelf she saw a plentiful supply of Izal toilet paper, yellow soap, bleach; in fact, every conceivable cleaner on the market. She could not remember seeing anything like it in her life.

'His house could do with a right good clean and there's plenty cleaning material to do just that, but I'll deal with that later,' she thought. 'Right now I need to attend to Alasdair, but whoever organised this home did a very good job.'

"What about my patients? When can I get back to work?" Alasdair asked, knowing damn well what the answer would be.

"Alasdair trust me and as I have already explained to you, Tam is on his way as we speak to Leightham. He has taken a message to Doctor Henderson, asking him to cover for you. I know he will care for your patients temporarily. He knows

110

them; until recently he was their Doctor. I have asked Tam to tell Doctor Henderson you have the flu and it would be better if he doesn't visit you, in case he contracts the illness." Janet spoke slowly, carefully emphasising every word. But for a moment she was tempted to tell the fractious young man if he would stop complaining, just concentrate on recovering; it would be better for him in the long run.

"Alasdair I have no psychic powers, I am not a witch; I cast no spells and make no incantations. Believe it or not I don't even have a black cat or a broomstick." Changing the tone of her voice, she tried to lighten the atmosphere.

"I cannot tell you how long it will be before you can return to work – maybe in a few days," she lied, averting her eyes, pretending to busy herself. She had no desire to cause him further distress by admitting she did not have the answer. He was asking the impossible and he knew fine well what the answer was to his questions, better than she. Janet tried to placate him; she wanted Alasdair as calm and relaxed as possible. What she was about to do would wake him up soon enough.

"Try to rest; keep soaking your hand. It shouldn't be much longer. That's someone at the back door. Let me go answer it. I hope it's Tam – I have another job for him." Janet retraced her step back to the kitchen and right enough, there stood Tam with a big grin on his face.

"I just thocht ah would come and check on you, see if you're a' richt, do ye need onythin' lassie?"

Thankfully after a short time in the village, Janet no longer needed an interpreter; she understood the local dialect perfectly... well, almost.

"Actually I do Tam; I'm glad to see you, save time now; I don't have to come and look for you. Although The Pirates would have been the first place I would have looked. Have you completed the other chores I gave you?"

"Aye a' have that, chores, oh yae mean jobs and a' didna stop in The Pirates, never swallowed a drap." Tam grinned with pride. "Davie Muir will let the men ken when they come for a drink the nicht, no to disturb the Doctur and mind tell their womenfolk the same. Mr McDougall the minister says he will tell awe body at the Kirk on Sunday. He says he'll come round in a couple o' days' to visit the Doctur, but if he wants onythin' or you need him, yer just to let him ken day or nicht." Tam took in a deep breath and puffed out his chest; he'd remembered everything Janet had asked of him.

"Do ye ken the minister's wife has just had a bairn? A wee lassie?"

"Yes – yes. I had heard, you did well Tam, thank you," Janet interrupted, knowing he would go into every last detail of the chores she had given him; including the news about the minister's new baby at the Manse.

"Now listen carefully. I want you to load that clothes pole, yes that one over there on the back green."

Tam, bewildered, turned and looked to see what Janet was talking about.

"Yes, that one." She pointing at it. "Take it down from the clothes line and load it onto the cart. Go take it to George Wilson the blacksmith; ask him to set it into a block of heavy wood and get him to screw a large hook into the pole about twelve inches from the top? M-m…" Janet thought for a moment. "Yes, twelve inches, that should be about right… now. There's no point in you going all the way back to Leightham to find a joiner. I need this, it's urgent… do you understand me Tam? George will do every bit as good a job as any joiner and he won't charge me. He owes me a favour."

Tam stood transfixed, his jaw hanging open. The man was not particularly bright as everybody knew, but now he looked positively donnert… a stupid expression on his face from ear to ear. Was he hearing right? If Janet had asked him to remove his bunnet, shave his head, he could not have been more dumbfounded. He was almost speechless. Recovering, he shook his head, eyes closed to concentrate, trying to remember the instructions.

"Did ah hear ye richt? I've tae tak that claes pole to George Wilson… he's to set it intae a chunk o' widd, then hammer a screw at the tap, is that whit yer wantin'?"

"That's correct, but a hook Tam, a hook! And it does not matter how he attaches it. Just get it attached." Janet responded with all the patience she could muster. Living with Tam at times could be trying. "Now hurry, quick as you can. I need this this piece of equipment." Janet frowned. "I suppose you could call it that, anyway whatever, I need it for the Doctor. And I don't have to tell you, do not tell George or indeed anyone else who might ask, why you are going to the blacksmith's or why you have a clothes pole on your cart."

"Aye Janet ah ken when tae keep ma mooth shut," Tam reassured her.

That would be a first. "Well… just play dumb. That should not be too difficult for you." She realised immediately she had hurt the old man and in her present state of anxiety she had been too sharp with him. But there was no time for niceties or the patience she usually exercised when dealing with him. Anyway he would soon forget.

"George rarely speaks so it is unlikely he will bother to question you, and just get on with the job. Do remember to thank him on my behalf."

Tam frowned not understanding the word 'behalf'.

"Just thank him for me Tam," Janet repeated patiently before he could ask the meaning. "Tell him I would be grateful if he could do the job right away. Now!"

"Did I hear ye richt, ye want a…" Tam started to repeat Janet's instructions, having forgotten the insulting remarks she made regarding his intelligence.

"Tam!"

"Ah well a' hope I can mind awe this…" With a questioning frown on his forehead Tam scuttled off down the garden path to pick up the clothes pole, but was halted in his tracks by Janet calling out…

"Wait!"

"Ah ken't it wouldna' last, she's aye got somethin' mair for me tae dae," he muttered. "Whit noo?" Tam said under his breath so Janet could not hear him. He turned to face her.

"Oh, one more thing Tam, if you see Rena McKay, ask her if her mother can look after the children this evening, and say you will collect her about six o' clock. Tell her I will explain when she gets here."

Tam stood waiting to see if there were any more instructions… none came. Among Janet's other bizarre requests, he was now to collect Rena McKay and bring her to the Doctor's house this evening. 'Auch I'll just go and collect the woman, her mother lives next door, what else would they be doing at that time of night.' Still somewhat bemused, Tam duly loaded the clothes pole onto his cart, hoping he would not meet anyone who might ask what he was up to 'wi a claes pole'. He jumped up onto the driving seat, picked up the reins and gave them a tug, clucked his tongue at Nellie and with a light tap on her rump, the two of them set off towards the Comentry road where George had his workshop. Turning to look back at Janet he shouted:

"I'll be back in an oor. Junet." He had lowered his voice, but well aware that Janet could still hear him he continued, "Whit kind o' bliddy contraption is she wantin' noo? Ye'd think I was a skivvy – gawn here, gawn there, an' just take a look at ma hoose. Pans billin' awe oor the stove, stinking the place out. Sometimes a think it's the rubbish she's cookin,' a' they foul smelling weeds hingin' frae the ceiling, seaweed, muck frae the ditches. Rows o' jars an' bottles awe ower the

114

place. A' dinna ken what am gonna step in next and the smell –
sometimes I think she has turned the hoose into a byre... It's a
guid job av nae much sense smell. Whit does she think ma'
hoose is... a' need a dram." Tam moaned, halted, when a voice
reached his ears...

"I heard that, don't you dare go near The Pirates!"

Oh that lassie, he loved her. What would his life have been,
if she hadn't turned up on his doorstep that night? He was glad
he would never know now. His world had turned around. He
shuddered at the thought of his previous miserable existence;
he did not want to look back. Janet gave him reason to get up
in the morning, his porridge hot; his boots scrubbed, dungarees
clean. All ready for whatever job he had that day. At night
when he got back tired after a long day, his new slippers would
be warming by the fire. A plate of soup, bread fresh out the
oven, sometimes stovies, he couldn't wait to get home. She
gave him reason to live; no longer did he feel isolated, he
belonged, he had family. Sometimes he realised that Janet was
not there, when he got back – waiting to hear his news, where
he had been, what he had been up to. The cottage cold and dark
meant only one thing, Janet was out, a new life was coming
into the world or an older one leaving it. On these occasions
Tam knew it would be a cold dinner; it made him feel lonely,
but not for long, for he knew she would be back.

"A better awa, get what it is she wantin' afore a' forget.
Whit was it she said was wrong with the Doctur, a bealin
haun?" (Septic hand.)

"Thank-you Tam." Janet had heard most of what he'd said
and she could read his mind. If Tam thought he could not live
without her, in reality it was the other way around... Janet
shuddered to think what might have happened to her if Tam
had not taken her in that night.

Chapter 18

ALASDAIR was awake when Janet came back upstairs, having dealt with Tam.

"The pain is unbearable, Janet please," he pleaded, Janet had to admit his face was grey with pain. "I must have more… the laudanum… in the dressing table drawer… get it for me!" he demanded.

"Listen to yourself; could I remind you, you're in no position to make demands," Janet said narrowing her eyes slightly as if preparing for a fight. "If you are determined to become addicted, that's fine, but not while I am in charge and believe me I can make it to the dresser drawer long before you could even get out of that bed. Want to try?" she challenged.

"I will get there first and down the drain it goes… I mean it!" Janet was not joking. Drugs led to addiction and Alasdair was exhibiting the first sign… personality change.

"Even if I have to sit here all night, it will be my way, we have an agreement remember? So you might have a chance of getting out of this with your hand still attached to your wrist." She refrained from adding, "And hopefully your arm."

"You of all people should know the danger of long term drug use. Laudanum, that's an opiate, a narcotic, is it not? It comes from the Far East? People addicted to it see and do strange things under its influence."

He couldn't argue with that after his episode with the monkeys on his bed. "Well get on with it since you know so much." He turned his head away to avoid looking at Janet. This was a side to the man she had not seen before, but she could deal with it and him.

Getting on with it as ordered, lifting his hand out of the bowl, she placed it on the towel... the bowl onto the bedside cabinet. Going over to the washstand Janet poured the lye soap mixture into the basin and proceeded to scrub her hands then dry them. Now ready at the bedside she began to work on the affected limb.

"Listen to me Alasdair Forman, I could shout, but I prefer not to raise my voice. I can be just as easily heard by keeping my voice down, as raising it, which is more effective I assure you. While I work on your left hand, take the cup of tea I have brought you in the other and drink it. It's on the bedside cabinet," Janet ordered quietly.

"Tea," Alasdair hissed still almost past caring, "what good is that going to do?"

"I have already explained to you, I work with nature, not drugs," Janet continued like a mother coaxing a child. "My tea is a herbal infusion made from the bark of the willow tree; it has soothing and relaxing properties. In a short time you will feel a little better if you give it a chance. But I promise before I leave I will allow you to have a half dose of Laudanum. I am well aware of the pain you are in... bear with me. You cannot go on taking as much of the drug as you have been; it is worrying me, Alasdair, and it should worry you." She stopped.

"Or perhaps you would prefer to be admitted to hospital; they will fill your rear with as much dope as you want, so what's it to be? My way or...?" she threatened.

Alasdair scowled at Janet... she'd won; he reached for the cup and started to gulp down the tea. The threat of sending him to hospital had worked. Janet thought that's not fair, but all's fair in love and war and... illness. She had put a fair amount of sugar and a large pinch of salt into the tea. He screwed his face, growled in disgust at the taste. However, to please her he persevered and the silence answered her question. No hospital!

Janet picked up a pail from under the sink in the kitchen, one she had brought down on one of her trips upstairs. It was now on the floor at the side of the bed... awaiting the soiled bandage. She worked away trying to remove the foul smelling mess from Alasdair's hand, using the scissors, inch by inch till she finally managed to release it. Even after being soaked for over an hour the bandage had stuck to the skin like glue. Nearly fainting, Alasdair cried out in agony several times.

"You have to stop Janet; I am beginning to think death is preferable!"

"Nonsense, I'm sorry, but there's no other way. Look, I have finished, it's all over, lie back, take a few deep breaths."

Alasdair gave a long sigh. "Wow, thank God that's over. Now get that stinking mess away from me," he ordered.

"Keep drinking the tea."

"Janet, the tea is not so bad... when you get used to it. I wonder if it tastes better than whisky." His eyes focussed on her face, ashamed of the way he had behaved and trying not to be sick at the same time. "Janet, you are right. Maybe it's psychological, but I do feel a little more relaxed. Sorry... you know... the way I have been treating you, forgive me. I apologise for snapping at you, don't hold it against me." He shook his head. "I am not myself... I don't know who I am... my hand... pain, I think I am going crazy..." He stumbled on his words... hesitant at times.

"Apology accepted, why don't we just forget? I don't hold grudges against sick people. Trust me, when I have finished you will feel better... I promise."

"I know what you are going to do Janet, and I am not looking forward to it."

"Keep drinking the tea... think happy thoughts."

'Like being here with you?' he thought.

"You know why I keep asking you to drink the tea. Dehydration – and I can't rehydrate you any other way. I know you have been ill for days, unable to look after yourself; it's unlikely you have eaten or drunk anything very much. I'll bet you were only too glad to see the last of your patients, fall into bed without thinking of food and drink. Am I right?" Janet took his silence to mean he agreed with all she said.

Alasdair drew in a sharp breath as Janet turned the palm of his infected hand upwards. She knew it would be bad, but she had no idea how bad. When she saw the abscess she was horrified, bit her lips so as not to show any reaction, either facially or verbally. How the man had been able to function with his hand in this state she would never know. It said a lot for the man's determination; continue working for the sake of his patients. Janet looked at his face and for the first time felt a rush of sympathy for him. A large indurated mass of puss had collected under the skin; a blister covered most of the palm, encircled by red swollen flesh.

"Put your hand into bowl of iced water; try to hold the ice close as possible… close as you can bear. If it is too painful I can put a pack of ice directly into your hand and bandage it on. The ice will dull the pain, it's the best I can do under the circumstances."

"No I will be fine, go ahead," Alasdair agreed as she gently turned his arm and placed the hand into the iced water for him, pressed the ice into the palm.

"S-s-s, ah-h."

"I know… I know," she soothed, "that must have been painful; leave your hand in the ice water to numb it. Your home is very well equipped Alasdair, did you do this by yourself?" Janet struck up a little harmless conversation in an effort to take his mind off what she was about to do on him.

"No, my mother and a Godmother who poses as an aunt, organised the move. I have no other relatives; we are a very small family. Someday I hope to have several children; I would not wish being an only child on anyone… at least not with a mother like…" He was about to say 'like the controlling woman mine was,' but stopped in time, not wishing to appear disloyal to Audrey in front of a stranger…

"Well, Alasdair, she did a very good job and obviously she loves you." While Janet spoke these last words, she raised his hand out of the water. Supporting his palm on her left one she gently opened the fingers.

"Look Alasdair! Look, a seagull on the window ledge!" she called out and secretly reached for the knife she had previously concealed in a towel.

Alasdair turned to look – no gull – he realised he had been tricked.

The abscess lanced, a spurt of green, purulent, offensive, smelling puss poured out, but the overwhelming look of relief on Alasdair's face was joy for Janet to behold. She swabbed the newly opened wound with a thick solution of brown liquid smelling ominously of rotten seaweed and dead fish. She applied a thick poultice of dried sphagnum moss to the clean wound and bandaged it tightly into place.

"What is that you are using?" Alasdair asked, wrinkling his nose.

"I have made friends with Mr McDade the chemist in Leightham. Sometimes, if I make a reasonable request he will allow me to buy the odd ingredient I need to make my tinctures and ointments. I cannot complete the mixtures, because I have no access to what I need unless he sells them to me. He knows I would never use any kind of harmful substance. I think he is more than a little intrigued, interested in what I do. I have great respect for the man and secretly I think he likes me… enjoys our conversations. This particular mixture is boiled seaweed and magnesium powder, that's why it smells so awful. I have read about bacteria that cause infection – this solution inhibits

its growth; it was in one of the books Mr McDade lent me to read. The moss draws the fluid and puss out of the incision and absorbs it. It also has sterilising or antiseptic properties, Mr Mc Dade told me that himself."

Alasdair listened intently to what Janet had been saying. Concentrating so as to take his mind off his hand, he responded, "It's easy to believe Mr McDade has made friends with you Janet, you are unique and unassuming. You would be easy to become friends with..." He stopped, changed the subject and in a matter of fact voice said, "I don't know what the end result will be, but one thing I do know, the relief I am experiencing now... you would not believe... it's like a miracle."

After a moment's silence, he continued, "Oh by the way, there is a room full of medical books on the shelves in the surgery; if you ever feel the need to read more, come help yourself." He smiled at Janet's explanation regarding the lotion she had just used. She was making homemade iodine. He almost informed her there was a bottle of iodine ready-made in the surgery, but he let her have her moment. Who knows, there is no guarantee either will work, Janet's solution... or the chemist's? Maybe her's is better.

"Thank you, Alasdair, but I don't work with miracles. They can be unpredictable. I try to work with nature, she's more reliable. That sounds like Tam at the door and right in time! I hope he was able to get what I wanted. Lie quiet, I need to go help him up the stairs. I won't be long."

Help Tam up the stairs? What is she talking about now...? Alasdair closed his eyes.

Chapter 19

JANET went to answer the back door and there stood Tam, a huge grin across his almost toothless mouth, the 'pole' set in the block of wood, hook at the top just as Janet had ordered.

"Come upstairs Tam and bring the pole with you, you are right on time."

"Upstairs, now whit?" Tam grumbled. Janet ignored the remark. "Whit about ma sair back, this pole's heavy."

"Funny how your back is not 'sair' when you're going to The Pirates after working all day!" Janet responded. "Get on with it, I'll guide from the front, you hold the back." The two of them lifted the clothes pole and staggered through the hall to the bottom of the staircase.

"Lord Junet, this is an awfie braw hoose, I hope we dinna scratch the widd-work or brek the banister," Tam uttered, slightly breathless.

"Then we will just have to be careful, won't we? What a weight in this pole Tam, has George set it in concrete?"

At the bottom of the stair with the pole in position, Janet grabbed the upper part nearest the hook; turning sideways she tipped it towards her, settling it under her armpit. Tam gave up complaining, lifted the base as instructed and between them they made their way up to the top of the stairs at the first landing before having to negotiate the bend to the next flight. Janet gave credit to Tam's concerns – negotiating the bend was no joke. With very little space and the low ceiling, they just managed to miss the gas light on the wall. After a short break they made it to the upper floor without scratching the woodwork. Red in the face from their exertions, Tam sweating like a pig, they stopped just short of the bedroom to get their breath back.

Anxious to complete the job, the unfortunate pair took off at the same time, collided, and got stuck in the bedroom door... pole wedged between them.

"Ah, the circus has come to town." Alasdair, temporarily distracted from his misery, could not resist making the remark; he started to laugh at the hapless pair, now trying to untangle themselves from the pole and each other.

Janet was not amused.

"This is Tam, Doctor Forman; I don't think you have met him. Tam, take your cap off in front of the Doctor."

"Well no, not officially, we have not met," Alasdair responded. "Can't shake your hand old man, laid up, you see. Probably Janet gives you such good care it's unlikely you'd need a Doctor."

"Thank you," Janet responded. "Tam, put the pole at the side of the Doctor's bed. No, not the right side, the left next to his bandaged hand. That side. Oh here, let me do it!" Alasdair is right, she thought, this is becoming a circus.

"Tak care Junet, there's some wecht in it," Tam cautioned, going forward to help her.

Together they lifted and placed the pole on the left side of the bed.

"What's she going to do with that Tam?" Alasdair demanded to know.

"Dinna' ask me Doctur, ah dae ken what she gonna do with it, but dinna worry, Junet knows what she's dain', you have to trust her, yer in good hands." Tam nodded his head wisely and winked at Alasdair, most un-Tam like. He was normally shy with strangers.

Janet smiled at the camaraderie developing between the two men. Tying a long thin strip of torn sheeting to Alasdair's wrist, making sure it was not too tight, she tied a knot at the loose ends, slung it round the mysterious 'hook' and pulled it up, elevating Alasdair's arm above his head.

"This will help drain the fluid, help get the swelling down and with a bit of luck reduce the throbbing pain. Now you can persuade me to give you a small dose of Laudanum. Can we settle for half?" she quizzed.

"Let me speak... let me say something; I am very grateful for all you are doing for me, but I am well aware of the medical reasons for elevating swollen limbs, and everything else you've been doing." Alasdair grinned. "I also know I can't go on dosing myself with that amount of Laudanum, but I am the Doctor... half! That wouldn't touch a toothache... how about three quarters?" He tried to negotiate. "I don't know if I can stand the withdrawal on top of everything else."

"No! I am going to make another jug of the willow bark tea; drink it hot or cold, it makes no difference. The important thing is, Alasd – Doctor – fluid, before you start to tell me I know you know all about the need for rehydration. I bow to your superior medical knowledge, but I insist fluids are more important than you snoring in a drug-induced coma." Janet did not mean to sound sarcastic in front of Tam. She had tried to show respect for the Doctor and his superior medical knowledge and she had addressed Alasdair as Doctor because the less Tam knew about their personal arrangement the better.

"It's been a long day, you look worn out. Before I leave I'll put a notice on the surgery door cancelling all surgeries or house calls till further notice and tell the patients to go for Dr Henderson. At least until word gets around you're ill, that will have to do. I think that's it." Janet frowned. "Have I forgotten anything? Tam will bring me back about six o' clock to see how you are later, we might have to change the bandage but I don't think so. Tam will then collect Rena and bring her here before going to the The Pirates, right Tam? No point in him going back home, just to return two hours later to collect us." Janet wanted to sponge Alasdair down and make him comfortable before she left for the night... Rena would help chaperone, save any embarrassment.

"It's Friday, I always meet Jock Booman on a Friday for a wee dram." Tam pouted at first thinking she was going to prevent him going.

"I will give you money for a dram when we get back at six. Come back an hour or two later and take Rena and me home when we're finished?"

A wide grin split Tams old face from ear to ear; money from Janet for a wee dram wi' his pal... no bad eh?

"Who's Rena?" Alasdair asked suspiciously.

"Never mind, I'll explain when I return."

Janet finished adjusting the sling round the pole, turned to face the two men and announced, "I'll make up a bed for Tam on the floor in the room next to you Doctor; he will stay the night."

Alasdair raised his good arm to protest. "I can manage by myself, I don't need the man to stay. I am not a child and he's too old to sleep on the floor."

"Oh, don't worry, he's a tough old soul and he's slept in worse places. I assure you, this will be luxury for him. I had better bring Tam's own blankets and I have told him to sleep in his underwear. Don't get a fright in the middle of the night if he appears, it's not a ghost, just auld Tam. If you need to get up in the middle of the night, call Tam and he will come and help you." Janet ignored Alasdair's protests and finished her speech with a wave of her hand towards Tam.

Tam stood silent, gaping at the two... Alasdair in the bed, Janet at the side of it and in unison Janet and Tam turned and looked at Alasdair waiting for a reply. Tam, clueless as always, had no idea this was going to happen until this very moment. Tam turned to Alasdair and together they both turned to look at

Janet. Alasdair was right; it was getting more like a circus every minute. Janet was pleased, satisfied with her arrangements, but in case there were any arguments, placed both her hands on her hips, ready to do battle and stared at them.

"Well?" she prompted.

"The first av heard o' awe this. Dae ye play cribbage Doctur?" Might not be that bad a night after all, a dram at The Pirates and a game o' cribbage! Tam scratched his almost bald head, his bunnet still in his hand.

"What about my medicine?" Tired and debilitated, all Alasdair could think about was pain relief. He was past caring or arguing, whether Tam was staying or leaving.

Chapter 20

ALASDAIR slept on and off throughout the rest of the afternoon and early evening, tossing and turning, cringing in pain that at times disturbed his sleep. But when asleep he found himself in a strange land of drug-induced nightmares. Apparitions of unidentified missiles hurling straight at his head, veering off at the last minute, as he tried to duck, lashing out in fear, to deflect the non-existent objects from hitting him, only to find he had knocked a jar of cream off the bedside table. Strange voices came and went; he tried to call out, answer, only to find he was shouting at himself, for there was no one in the room.

'God help me, are these hallucinations my drugged patients told me of? When I think how I laughed at them and now I'm experiencing the same. What would they think if I told them, I saw a troupe of monkeys on my bed? Perched on the end, cranking it up! The bed rising, till I thought my feet were going to roll right over my head! Probably they would say, "I've been there too Doctor, now you know how stupid we felt telling you." I'll be more sympathetic in future, not just stand at the bottom of the bed and laugh at them. How could anyone actively want to become an addict...' The effect was horrible.

During the rest of the afternoon he slipped in and out of a troubled sleep. At times, startled, he abruptly woke up; found himself soaked in his own sweat; alternately throwing off the blankets to cool down and pulling the bed clothes back because he was shivering. The small dose of Laudanum Janet had allowed him to have had worn off. He was beginning to feel restless, the pain returning with a vengeance.

Where was Janet, had she abandoned him? She had no business leaving him in this state! Maybe he should have gone into hospital. 'Stop that, admit the truth, you've formed a dependency on her, a new experience for you, Alasdair! Something you have no control over' – feelings, emotions the problem was just that. He had no control over them, couldn't order to specification. The reason... not only because he needed her now, but another sensation he couldn't get out of his head, one previously unknown to him, was it love? That shocked him into reality; now awake, he had to face the implication of these new-found feelings. What would his mother say? He could not even begin to imagine! Introduce her to Janet?! Tell his mother he was in love and wanted to marry her?! Janet as far as he knew was little more than a gypsy. He had to face the unpleasant truth that his mother would be appalled.

'Think Alasdair, there is nothing to prevent you falling in love with Janet. The biggest challenge will be keeping it to myself. Irrespective of how she might feel about you, keep your distance. You're well aware of the social restrictions and you must abide by them for your own sake as well as Janet's.' But what good was unrequited love to a healthy young man? He wanted to shout out, tell the world about his new found love. He wanted to take her in his arms. Hold her close... feel her young firm body next to his, the swell of her breasts next to his bare chest; kiss her fully on her open lips. Tell her how he felt... would feel for the rest of his life.

He sensed as all young people falling in love do... his love was returned, he'd read it in her eyes, heard her call him dear. Returning to reality, there was only two ways to go, love her from afar or declare that love. Fly in the face of convention, marry the girl if she would have him and be cast out from his family and friends. No, the unhappy truth stared him in the face... he would stay single or succumb to his mother's demands and marry where he felt no love. Huh! He sneered... just like his parents' marriage, a front for society, he thought with contempt. 'Keep quiet, say nothing and whatever you do suppress any outward sign of affection. Apart from Janet using your first name for the present; nothing must change...

'If you let this take control of you, coming to Pittendreal will turn into a nightmare. This was supposed to be the promise of a bright new future so accept the things you can't change and change the things you can. Heavens above, we are now in China, I have just recited some old Mandarin proverb... I'm raving now! Maybe there's more to Janet's brew than meets the eye?' Unhappy, ill at ease, he dozed off again.

The next time Alasdair woke up, he could see the sun hanging low on the skyline. What time was it? He turned to pick up his watch with his good hand; thankfully Janet had left it within reach on the bedside cabinet. At last he heard the back door open, a soft click, and the person doing his or her best to keep quiet. Am I awake or am I dreaming? His eyes wide open, he was awake. Trying to sit up, he fell back forgetting to keep his left hand still. Ahh! The damn thing stung, throbbed like Hell. Falling back onto the pillow he stared in disbelief... what the hell! Slowly coming up the stairs, a soft silent light swaying from side to side. Moving up the wall and coming towards his bedroom.

'Should I shout?' Alasdair opened his mouth to yell as the light entered the room. He gave a sigh of relief; no, he was not hallucinating, it was Janet.

"Good grief, is it you? Mercy, you frightened me half to death, I nearly completed the job this stupid injury started. You nearly gave me a heart attack... but look at you with that shawl on your head! We are no longer in Pittendreal..." He chuckled. "It's – Florence Nightingale with her lamp, are we in the

Crimea?" 'God, just listen to yourself man, she will think you have been hitting the drugs again. Well I have, I'm not that brave.'

"I came back as quickly as I could; tried to avoid making a noise coming up the stair. I didn't want to disturb you, thought you might be asleep. What did you say… the Crimea? No, we are not in the Crimea… but my tea has that effect on people." Janet smiled.

"So do drugs?" Alasdair muttered to himself.

"Had things to do at the cottage and gave Tam his supper. If he is going to have a drink I like him to eat first." She removed her gypsy-style long-fringed shawl from around her head and as there was nowhere to put it in the room she went back out to the hall and hung it over the banister.

"Tam dropped me off on his way to The Pirates," Janet called over her shoulder. "He's gone to meet Jock Bowman. I have given him fair warning not to drink more than two measures of whisky."

"Dram, not measure," Alasdair interrupted rudely.

"Whatever. He does pay attention to me, well most of the time. He thinks I'm his mother! But I am very fond of the old man – I have no idea what would have happened to me – given the existence I had before…" Janet stopped mid-sentence. "No… I won't think about that."

Janet busied herself about the room, lighting the gas wall lamps over the bed and mantelpiece. Extinguishing the lamp, she fussed around the bed… straightening the bedclothes, distracting herself; avoided thinking she might be dead now, had Tam refused to take her in. She doubted she would have survived another winter on the road sleeping in hedgerows. Shuddering, she put those memories aside. Thankfully she was thinking less and less of the past now. Turning to Alasdair she felt sufficiently confident to look straight at him. In the brighter gas light, she was aghast at the sight in front of her…

"Oh! God, Alasdair, you look awful!" she blurted out without thinking, but restrained from crossing herself. Caught in an unsuspecting moment, a transient thought went through her mind. 'Why did I want to make the sign of the cross? Forget that, look at him!' His unshaven haggard face ravaged by days of pain and neglect, the man was a shadow of his former self. Normally Janet never gave an opinion on the look or state of the person she was treating, but with Alasdair it was different. Whether she liked it or not, a sensation previously unknown stirred her heart. 'Stop it Janet, you know why you're here. Or was it...fate? This would never have happened if Alasdair had not injured himself. Continue and these feelings will hurt you in the long run. Forget how you feel, focus on the job in hand: healing the sick.'

"I have put a little broth on the stove; I can't tell you how relieved I am to see you. I didn't know what I would find when I got back, or what state you would be in."

"Dead?"

"Alasdair, that's not funny. I've been worried sick… not to mention the responsibility you have inflicted on me by refusing to go into the hospital…" Janet tailed off not wanting to alarm the man any more than she may have already done. Better to leave the room.

"I will be back in a few moments with your soup and another jug of my special tea." With that Janet left, giving Alasdair no time to reply.

Alone Alasdair had time to think. 'I know I look and smell like Hell on earth. I know she's worried, I'm worried. I know only too well what can happen.' Alasdair stopped for a moment. Thinking about what she had just said, it occurred to him to take her remarks as a compliment, these being the first emotional words he'd heard coming out of her mouth.

The circumstance that brought them together meant they would never forget each other; they had a history now. Life would never be the same again. They were in love. He was in love, he could never admit it; never tell her, how could fate be so cruel? But from now on, he knew without doubt that no other woman would ever take her place in his heart. Maybe Janet's obvious devotion to the old man was a blessing; he doubted she would ever leave Tam, even if he was bold enough to fly in the face of convention and tell Janet he loved her... But if Alasdair had looked into a crystal ball, he would have been astonished, no, shocked, at what was about to happen in the next hour. The bond between them was about to be truly unbreakable.

Chapter 21

JANET returned to the bedroom. "Alasdair, I apologise for that stupid remark I made earlier. It was inexcusable, but the relief at seeing you... I can't tell you... I don't allow myself to become emotionally involved with anyone I am treating, but with you... it seems different... I don't understand." She shook her head, frowned.

"Janet, I know how serious my injury is and the possible prognosis. I know that better than anyone else on the planet. You have a right to be worried, but don't be – I have taken steps just in case." Alasdair looked a little sheepish. "This afternoon I unhooked my arm and believe me I almost gave up, you can't believe the pain when I lowered it. The throbbing returned with a vengeance. But with my arm above my head I managed downstairs to my desk. Got a pen, writing paper and an envelope." He raised his good hand to stop Janet protesting.

"I have written to Dr Henderson, you will find the letter locked in the top left-hand drawer of my desk in the surgery. The key is in the inside pocket of my tweed jacket, hanging in the wardrobe over there. Don't hesitate to use it; obviously it would mean the worst, but we have to be realistic. I had to make every provision... clear you of any involvement regarding my death." A short silence followed, Alasdair thinking the best way to proceed... how to explain.

"The letter is to my friend, Harry Henderson, you know him or at least you know of him. He knows me and my handwriting so he can certify that the letter was written by me. I have stated... this was my idea, what I wanted. I was never coerced or forced by you to stay at home. His surgery is in Leightham; if anything happens to me, go there immediately. My letter states you are to be completely exonerated, free from blame, regarding my demise. I asked you contrary to your advice to look after me. I did not want any other person to be involved and I certainly did not want to be admitted to hospital."

"But what would they do to me…?" Janet started to speak, but Alasdair cut her short.

"Janet, you are so innocent. Don't you realise the danger or legal consequences? If anything happened to me, you will be blamed. You could be held on a manslaughter charge, withholding medical attention for starters. They might even charge you with kidnapping me and holding me against my will. Killing me with drugs prescribed by a Doctor, but administered by an unqualified person… you! Considering what the police would find in that drawer." He pointed to the dresser where the laudanum was.

"I know you think I am being an alarmist, but believe me we have to be realistic. The Law can be a dangerous thing, dependant on interpretation. How could you prove otherwise with such evidence against you? Do you think they would ask old Tam? They would discount his testimony without even bothering to read it in a court of law. A judge would laugh at him! Now listen to me, before we go any further as I have not sealed the envelope. Correct me if I am wrong, but did I hear you say something about Rena McKay coming this evening?"

Janet nodded.

"We will get her to witness the statement I have made out. I am certain when she realises the gravity of the situation you could be in, she will be more than willing to sign. I thought of asking Tam, but I doubt he can read never mind write his name or understand what he was being asked to sign" – which sounded more than a little cruel on Alasdair's part, but unfortunately from a practical point of view it was true.

"Rena is not able to come till tomorrow. Tam went to collect her but she can't manage, her mother's not well."

"Then," Alasdair stuck his tongue out, made cockeyes at Janet, "let's hope I survive the night!"

"Thank you, I have to admit I had not given any thought to the legal implications. I only want to help in the best way I can, so you better survive the night! You don't want to think of me going to the gallows on your deathbed, do you?" Janet stuck her tongue out and crossed her eyes as Alasdair had done, glad to get that unpleasant business out of the way.

"Alasdair, I am grateful for your concern. But we have to come back to why I am here in the first place. Care of you and your hand. How is the dressing? Since you have been prancing around this afternoon, I hope it is still in place. You better not have dislodged the poultice on your travels, or you're in trouble young man." She examined his hand. "No, as far as I can see all's well, should be fine overnight. I will change the dressing tomorrow morning."

"So you are saying you will come back?"

"Alasdair, would I ever leave you? No... I mean, leave you in this state?" she added shyly.

Alasdair started to blush at the thoughts going through his mind, but worse was his physical reaction... his body... the way it was responding to her presence. He seemed powerless to control it. 'Drugs or willow bark tea... she's having some effect on you man.'

"I want you to try the soup I have brought while it is still hot. So let's get on with it. I don't have all night," she ordered, wishing she could stay. He was not the only one experiencing unnervingly strong desire.

"Sit forward till I fix your pillow, one is not enough. I found two others in the cupboard on the stair. I hope you don't think I was being nosey? That's better... comfortable?" Janet, holding him to her breast, placing the pillows under his head, made his

135

physical reactions worse. He had to do something to take his mind off it.

"Feed me Janet," he said cheekily.

"No."

Janet picked up a towel and wrapped it around his neck and shoulders, placed the tray on his lap, squinting sideways to observe his reactions.

"Eat!"

"Janet, I am not hungry actually; my stomach is rooted to the back of my throat, the very thought of food – I'm sorry."

"It's all right, but as long as you keep on drinking the tea. Is there anything else you would prefer? I will get it, but for now there's something else I have to do." She stopped, unsure; she watched Alasdair nod his head in agreement regarding his intake of fluid. But how would he respond to her next request? 'Janet, just tell him,' she scolded herself.

"Alasdair, we have to get you out of your underclothes. I am sorry, you have been sweating all day, your vest is soaking wet." She hastened to add: "It's sticking to you and that can't be comfortable." She continued: "I'd rather hoped Rena would be here to help me, but she can't come till tomorrow, and as far as I am concerned this can't wait." Without even looking at the man she continued talking, determined, giving him no opportunity to argue. "So I am going downstairs to get a basin of water to sponge you down. First we have to get you out of your vest and those Long John's. I know the last thing you want is to be disturbed, but trust me, the water will bring your temperature down and once we get you into your clean, fresh pyjamas, I assure you, you will have a much more restful night. Where are they kept?" Janet prompted. "In here?" She went over to the drawer at the bottom of the wardrobe.

A look of absolute horror was etched all over Alasdair's face. Turning back to face him and seeing that look, Janet almost burst out laughing.

"Don't worry, you have nothing I have not seen before. Who do you think puts Tam into the tin bath in front of the fire?" She was quite unconscious of the effect she was having on the defenceless man. Tied up to a hook on a clothes pole, he was at her mercy. All Alasdair could do was duck down the bed and pull the bedclothes up further under his chin with his good hand, till only his face was showing.

"Alasdair, these pyjamas need ironing. You can't go on working the long hours you do and have time to run this house. Which reminds me, I was going to talk to you later, but this is as good a time as any. Do you remember Rena McKay? I think you have met her? She was present at Agnes Gardner's delivery a few weeks ago," she prompted. "Might I suggest you give some thought to employing her? You need help in the house and I would recommend Rena. She is honest and trustworthy, but best of all in her favour – she never gossips or discusses anyone's business. She is a good soul and what happened to her is sad. Life can be so cruel to some people who deserve it the least."

Receiving no reply she prattled on: "Rena's a widow, her children are in school so she has time; work is hard to come by in the village other than following the fishing fleet to gut the fish. She can't do that and leave two children with her mother who is getting on in years. Her mother does what she can, but things are tight; I am sure for a few shillings a week she will do a very good job cleaning, washing and ironing. It would not surprise me if she would shop for food and even cook for you. I can assure you she will be very grateful; think it over and let me know tomorrow. In the meantime I have asked her to come help me until you recover… a chaperone to protect your modesty." Janet grinned at Alasdair, enjoying his discomfort.

"I am off down the stairs to the kitchen to put the kettle on, but I can tidy up while I wait for it to boil. What a state this room is in!" she said, changing the subject. Within seconds Janet was back with a collection of clean towels and fresh sheets she found in the hall cupboard, to change Alasdair's sweat-soaked bed.

"Tidy up… just look at where you have dumped your clothes, a heap on the floor, your trousers getting more creased by the minute, I had to hang my scarf on the banister in the hall when I arrived, there was just not one square inch of space on which to put it!" Janet said as she protested, hanging the offending trousers on an empty coat hanger she found in the wardrobe. Alasdair's crumpled shirt, other dirty clothes and towels he'd dumped in a corner she took downstairs for washing.

"This all needs to be washed; I'll put it in the laundry basket ready for Rena, if you decide to employ her. She can start with the washing," she called back, her head disappearing as she descended the stair.

Alasdair heard her as she meant him to: "You need Rena – you need looking after, Alasdair, give in –enough of this bachelor life!"

Alasdair started to think over what Janet had just said as she left – and what better recommendation than one from Janet? 'Rena McKay is known personally to her and I remember the woman… I think she was at Agnes Gardner's delivery.' Even in his desire to be independent, he needed to show his mother he could manage; but he had to acknowledge he needed help, he couldn't go on managing the housework by himself. The practise was picking up, more and more patients were signing on the 'Panel' leaving him less time for housework. He would make sure Rena came on weekdays and his mother at the weekend. He would tell Janet when she returned that she was right, he did need someone, and did she know how much to pay her? He thought about four shilling a week, for five mornings. When Janet heard of the princely sum, she blurted out: "For four shillings I would come and work for you myself!"

"I wish you would," he murmured under his breath when he heard her.

Chapter 22

STANDING at the kitchen sink, Janet looked out of the kitchen window at the river, waiting for the kettle to boil... but her mind was on anything but the view.

She was perplexed, confused over her feelings for Alasdair and could not understand why she felt different. She had never had to analyse her feelings for a patient before; her relationship with them was always strictly professional. She was there to relieve suffering, nothing else. What made this case different from all the others? Her body's longing, the throb of her heartbeat when she was with him – that's what was different. 'God, he's so handsome, his rugged good looks, hooded soft brown eyes and his hands so strong but gentle, he takes my breath away. I want to be caressed by him, I dream of having his arms around me and his body next to mine.' A warning voice in the back of her head cautioned... be careful, she might get hurt, but she would throw caution to the wind to have him all to herself... even for a short time. If ever the opportunity came to show him how she felt, even if it was only just once, she would gladly live on that memory for ever and be content.

The only affection Janet had ever been aware of in her life was the love she received from auld Tam and it was the purest form of asexual love, that of a man for his daughter. She had bathed male patients before, soaked their bodies in cold water to bring their temperatures down, just as she was about to bathe Alasdair, but never had she felt the slightest sexual urge or attraction toward them. She had delivered many babies but had given no thought to their conception. Janet had no idea if she had any sexual experiences before she came to Pittendreal. She did not know if she had experienced some horrific sexual assault in the past and had blotted it out of her conscious mind. As far as she was concerned she was still innocent and pure in body and mind, but without reservation she wanted Alasdair to change that.

She shook her head. Back down to earth, she reminded herself she was here to do a job and that it was unlikely she would ever find out what it was like to be loved or have a close physical relationship with the man she loved unreservedly. 'No point in dreaming, just do your work, keep your hands steady, your voice unemotional and most of all try not to betray how you feel with your eyes. Most of all be careful what you wish for, you might get hurt.'

Back upstairs, Janet sensed Alasdair becoming despondent and withdrawn. It began to worry her almost as much as the infection creeping up his arm. Seeing him lying there... staring out of the window. Janet moved towards the bed and placed the bowl ready to sponge him down on the bedside cabinet. They both knew what was going to happen and slipping her hand under his head drew him up closer to her breast so she could remove a pillow. Alasdair inhaled deeply, aware of the light floral fragrance that always surrounded her. She wondered if she was causing pain and gently laid his head back on the remaining pillow. Her close proximity almost made him forget the agony he was in and he was once again reminded of her close physical presence. It made him wish the pain would return... so he could concentrate on that, rather than resisting the sensations, the physical desires that threatened him. Her breasts, her shoulders so close, her perfume, it was Hell and Heaven at the same time.

At last he was ready for Janet to bathe him. Turning her attention to the bedding, she removed the layers one at a time. Folding them neatly she put them on an empty chair, which left

Alasdair with a sheet covering him and just in his underwear. Taking her time she moved up and down both sides of the bed; loosened the sides of the last remaining sheet still tucked into the mattress, leaving each edge curled up at the side of Alasdair's body. However careful, at times she inadvertently touched his arms and legs. She leant over the bottom of the brass bedstead to get on with the job at hand, but her good intentions to simply relieve the discomfort of her patient were beginning to dissolve.

"It's no use, I have to loosen the sheet that is trapped under the mattress beneath your feet at the bottom of the bed so I can get at your underwear. If I asked you to move back and forth to pull it out, that will cause discomfort. The less I have to move you and your arm the better." Janet shrugged her shoulders. "It's no good hauling at it between the spars of the foot of the bedstead; if I climb onto the mattress, kneel here at the bottom, then your Long Johns will slide easily down your legs." Janet slipped her shoes off and mounted the bed.

Alasdair's face resembled a rabbit caught in a trap; the thought of Janet on the bed with him... At least what you could see of his face. Janet climbed on the bed, slowly opened her legs to straddle his just below his feet.

"Alasdair, I will protect your modesty – I am not going to leave you altogether naked. I will leave the sheet on top of you but I must remove your underwear before I can begin."

Alasdair found himself with the worst dilemma of his adult life... should he hang onto the sheet... or underpants? Panicked, he made the wrong choice, chose his underpants.

"Let go," Janet pleaded with him. "Let go of the waistband, hold onto the sheet; can you undo the buttons, do you need help?"

He frantically shook his head. "No I can manage!"

Straddled over his ankles, it was easy for Janet to remove the now unbuttoned garment. Pulling her skirt up towards her waist freed Janet sufficiently to lean over his knees… slide her hands up under the sheet on either side of him. Alasdair turned his head to one side to avoid looking at the curve of Janet's breasts now protruding from the neckline of her blouse as she leant forward.

"Let go Alasdair," she repeated, using gentle pulling movements, easing the garment toward her, which enabled her to slide it under his bottom and down his legs.

Success, Long Johns in her hands and as promised the sheet still covering his body, clutched in his good right hand like a drowning man hanging onto a life belt. But he had enjoyed the sensation of his underpants sliding down his bare legs. The physical contact, the whole experience, certainly wasn't as bad as he thought it was going to be; in fact, it had been quite enjoyable. The vest however was going to be another story altogether, but even that painful thought couldn't quite take his mind off another predicament slowly forming in his mind or rather his body. Things were happening that he seemed to have no power over. 'What are you doing to me, Janet! Maybe you have cast a spell over me, maybe you are a witch after all… a beautiful seductive witch, more to your herbal tea than meets the eye?'

"Your vest has to come off." Janet brought him back to the present. "Listen to me, the bandage on your hand and wrist is bulky; I don't want to dislodge it by pulling your arm through the sleeve. To have to re-dress it at this stage, will cause you more pain. Destroying your vests, Alasdair, is the least of you problems."

His mind was on another matter. She could slash his sleeves to ribbons if she wanted, he couldn't care less.

"Oh, just get on with it, get your scissors, I've been through enough pain for one day, just cut it off… the vest, I mean!" he snapped in case she mistook what he meant.

Doing her best to keep his hand elevated, she hacked away at the tight cuff. At last, the Long Johns and the ruined vest lay together, a crumpled heap on the floor. The patient, stark naked but for the sheet and his arm once more secured above his head, Janet was ready to begin. Dipping a piece of soft muslin cloth into the cool water and wringing it out, she began to stroke his forehead.

"Ah, how wonderful that feels," he whispered. "They say you don't smell your own body…"

Janet put her forefinger over his mouth to silence him, to reassure him there was no need to talk at all. He fought the desire to kiss her finger. Systematically, she slowly worked her way down his chest, moving each freshly wrung out cloth in long sweeping movements to his waist and down his good arm. Returning to each part of his wet body, drying it with a soft towel, at last she reached his legs, using the same technique, lifting and replacing the sheet as necessary to save him embarrassment until she was satisfied every inch of the man in front of her was cool and clean. Never once looking directly at him, Janet encouraged Alasdair to lie back, close his eyes and let her do the work. She wanted him to enjoy the experience of having his needs cared for, for once, and he was rapidly becoming only too willing to accept that.

Relaxation was short lived… quickly it soon became the last thing on Alasdair's mind. A slow pulsating, throbbing sensation was rising in his groin. 'No… God, don't let this be happening to me! She doesn't know how inflammatory even her most innocent touch is, she doesn't realise the effect she's having on me.' Janet however was not unaware of the physical changes that were evolving. She saw the way he tried to guard the exposed parts of his body as she washed him. She did not blame the man, although she had not really ever stopped to think this light physical touching, a simple holistic and necessary bed bath, might have such consequences for her male patients.

Leaning over, she whispered, "Alasdair, take your time, I want you to roll onto your right side as I want to bathe your back." She lifted the sheet. Gratefully he managed to turn away from Janet, his cheeks reddening as she dropped the sheet back over him. He clutched frantically at it, did his best to ram it between his legs. Praying Janet had not noticed the ever increasing swelling between them. 'Get a grip man,' he thought almost hysterically, 'she might think it is another swollen limb and hang "it" on the hook on the clothes pole as well!' Acute embarrassment returning, he despaired at his mounting lack of control and the possible disgraceful outcome. 'Let the woman finish quickly and leave before something else happens,' he pleaded silently. His body yielded to the slightest touch of her expert hands and the hypnotic movements to and fro of the soft wash cloth. He clenched his teeth, but try as he might he just could not rid himself of the physical sexual need his body was screaming for. There was nothing he could do so long as she was present; she the unwitting cause. Of course, he knew she could not provide the physical solution. Unknown to him however, Janet had begun to feel her own desire gathering. Stroking his body and being close to him was affecting her more than she wanted to admit...

"I am nearly finished Alasdair," she whispered close to his ear. He drank in the comforting warmth emanating from her delicate skin, her soft voice, her perfume tantalising his senses. She took the cloth and dried his back with firm, long strokes going as far as she dared to the bottom of his spine. She then covered her fingers with a soft soothing ointment of oil and lavender that she had brought to complete her final task. With the fragrant ointment she massaged Alasdair from shoulders to the exposed cleavage at the base of his spine. Modestly missing out the area narrowly covered by the sheet, she continued down his muscular thighs in tightening and relaxing movements over and over, releasing tension and pressure… She heard him gasp involuntarily at each touch. He surrendered himself over to a sensual joy he had never experienced before.

"I am finished, you can move back, Alasdair."

'What the hell am I supposed to do now?' He knew the instant he rolled over, she would have the full view of what had happened and he would be powerless to conceal it. He closed his eyes as he rolled back to face Janet. A protruding mass beneath the sheet meant only one thing… He was now sexually aroused, the physical evidence undeniable and unavoidable, his body betraying his love and desire for her that his lips could not. No other woman had so moved him and yet he could not tell her. In his heart however he vowed to love no other but her no matter what happened from this moment on.

"It's all right, Alasdair," he heard her sweet voice at the side of his head… reassuring and strangely hypnotic. Was this an effect of the cocktail of laudanum and willow bark tea? "It is not unnatural you should feel this way, it is just nature trying to take your mind off your pain, don't fight it. Let your body tell you what you need to take your mind off your suffering. I will leave you – give you privacy." She pressed a piece of soft gauze into his hand and turning, she slipped quietly out of the room intending to go downstairs.

Something made her stand still on the landing. She listened... and heard the first sharp intake of Alasdair's breath. She had to fight a fervent impulse to return to him. 'Wait! Think, think what you were about to do!' Torturing herself, she closed her eyes and saw her love in the gentle glow of the bed lamp on the wall. How could it be so wrong to go to him now?

She wanted to take her clothes off right then and walk slowly, seductively, towards him. Lift the sheet and slip under it to lie naked next to him. Press her body close to his in the lavender scented room. Feel his strong body embrace her and make her feel safe and beloved. Because she hesitated it gave her more time to think of the consequences of such actions. What if he rejected her? Was offended, even disgusted with her? This shook her to her core. 'What if I have misread all the signs as he's never spoken out? For the rest of my life, could I endure the humiliation of knowing I had wantonly offered myself?' Bathing the injured man was one thing, but this was quite another... Weakly she willed herself to leave; go down the stairs. But instead she remained as in a trance, listening. Confused and longing, Janet stood still.

The sound of Alasdair's breathing became shorter, heavier. She could hear the rustle of the bed sheet. Closing her eyes, Janet allowed her mind to picture him there on the bed. Her body felt inflamed, so alive, so desperate for his touch. But she remained where she was, silently biting her lip, not moving a muscle, lest she betray the fact she was so close. Hypnotised, as if in a beautiful, sensual dream, she now leant back softly against the landing wall and slid slowly down to the floor. Bending her knees towards her chest she let her legs open. Without really thinking her hand was drawn to that most sensitive and intimate part of her body beneath her light summer skirt, now throbbing with need.

Gently, she began to circle her finger in unison with the sound coming from Alasdair in the bedroom. Gasping with the increasing intensity of her pleasure, she had to fight her lustful desire to stop and run back into the bedroom, throw caution to the wind along with her clothes. She saw herself lying with him, arching her back so that every part of her aching body was pressed next to his. Her other hand moved deliberately to her youthful, full breast under the cotton blouse and camisole. She could almost feel his strong male fingers teasing her taught nipple. Oh, how she wanted his hands bringing her body to such sweet ecstasy and not her own. Together yet apart, Janet and Alasdair achieved that intense pulsating explosive joy of total sexual climax.

Head gently leaning against the wall, still enjoying the fading eroticism of the last few moments, she smiled and wondered at the simplicity and beauty of two people joined as one. How peaceful it must feel to collapse breathless in your man's arms and simply lie together afterwards. Instead she had climaxed by herself... suddenly, she felt sad and alone.

She raised her head. All was silent but for the sound of Alasdair's breathing. Standing up, she straightened her dishevelled clothes, neatened her hair back into its hair net, hid the evidence. She stood at the top of the stairs, not sure what to do next. Had he heard her? Should she go back into his room? Pretend nothing had happened? 'Don't you dare... this is not the time or the place, leave the man alone.' She felt angry as she realised the exquisite dream had shattered and could now well turn into a nightmare. Go downstairs where you said you were going and should have gone in the first place. With that thought in mind, still shoeless, she went down to the kitchen. Perhaps Alasdair had not realised... she had to cling to that hope.

In the bedroom, Alasdair had felt that time had stood still. Yes, he had heard her and although they had not been together in the flesh, he felt sure they had been irrevocably joined together in spirit. He had no idea what the future might hold for them, but he knew in his heart he had met his soulmate for life.

Chapter 23

PANIC was the only word to describe Janet's state of mind, mortified, embarrassed, sitting in the kitchen chair, her arms clasped about her chest, rocking back and forth. What had possessed her? She had encouraged Alasdair's behaviour, but worst of all technically she had joined him and within his hearing. 'Oh my God!' Her mind was in turmoil. Did she encourage him when he was at his most vulnerable? But it was obvious that's what he wanted, she'd seen it with her own eyes. 'What am I saying – that I wanted it as much he did...? Maybe he didn't hear me; perhaps he thought I had gone downstairs. Who are you trying to kid? Of course he heard. Think, think; what are you going to do now? What on earth did you do that for Janet? To show him what it could be like for the both of us if only he would tell you that he loves you when it's so obvious he does. He has to speak first as he's the man... I can't speak first! Why doesn't he say something... anything! If he doesn't, then you get yourself out of this mess that you have made and let's hope he doesn't throw you out like a common tramp.' Janet rambled on in her mind:

'Janet, you have broken every vow you made when you arrived in the village. You have become emotionally involved, allowed your feelings in this case to rule. No emotion? What happened to your strict code of conduct? Now what are you going to do? Turn and run... to where? Who am I running away from? Myself or Alasdair? I have run before, I don't remember what I was running from, but this time at least I know.' Her brain was screaming at her to flee, but something was keeping her back...

Old Tam... until this moment she hadn't given him a thought. What would he do without her... what would she do without him? She owed it to him to stay. There was only one way out of this: however embarrassed or mortified she might feel, she would raise her head and with dignity, go back upstairs.

Having come to a decision, Janet, horrified, suddenly remembered she had left Alasdair stark naked, helpless, flat on his back with only a sheet covering him. 'Oh! My God, right Janet... regardless of the consequences, go finish the job. It's unlikely he will protest. He doesn't have much choice in the matter... the state you've left him in. Think positive; keep the atmosphere calm and normal, you're good at that ... but what's normal? Act as if nothing happened... How? There's only one way, Janet, you need a plan, make a noise, put the kettle on, set the tea tray, rattle the cups, saucers, teaspoons. First, take some of the lit coals from the kitchen fire on the shovel and go up. Say the nights are drawing in and the room will get chilly without a fire... Yes, that's it, busy yourself lighting the fire. Tell him you're making a cup of tea; light conversation, tell him Tam's on his way back.' Janet inhaled deeply then let out a slow breath. 'I hope this works, and if you have to apologize... do it, anyone can make a mistake, you're only human and would he forgive you?' These thoughts rattled around in her head as she began to blush, mortified at the memory of the last hour. 'If he does dismiss me, that's some consolation and maybe he will start to come to me in my dreams. Is there an alternative – go hide up the Coventry Road for the rest of my life?'

In trepidation, Janet steadied her trembling hands. One step at a time, with a shovel of burning coal from the kitchen fire, she climbed back upstairs still in her stockinged soles. Praying she wouldn't slip on the uncarpeted wood. 'Well done, Janet, congratulate yourself, you set Alasdair physically on fire... why not complete the job and set his house on fire as well!' The silence from the bedroom was ominous, no sounds of heavy breathing now, no movement from the bed.

Not daring to look at Alasdair, Janet walked over to the fireplace, tipped up the shovel, nearly all the cinders falling directly into the grate. A shower of sparks shot up the chimney but for a few pieces that fell into the fireplace. Deliberately playing for time, she reached for the tongs and lifting those bits placed them back into the grate. From a basket of logs at the side of the fender, she took one, put it on top of the cinders and a few more pieces of coal from the coal-scuttle. Still no sound from the bed... 'Maybe I have killed him, maybe he's dead. That would solve everything...' She raised her eyes heavenward. 'You're going to jail!' Slowly she stood up from the fireplace, turned and faced Alasdair, waiting for the axe to fall and seal her fate. Looking straight at him she could not believe the sight in front of her.

Alasdair had begun to think she was never going to turn round. He would never remember which part of that particular day would linger longest in his memory. It might have been the laudanum or Janet's herbal tea or perhaps a combination of both. 'The woman was only trying to help, let you finish what you so obviously wanted. You made no effort to conceal the effect she was having, nor make the slightest effort to control it. You didn't protest, ask her to leave, you were more than willing. Well, it certainly took your mind off the pain, I should be grateful. So don't you dare treat her with the slightest hint of contempt.

'Janet, what have I done to you?' Suddenly full of remorse, he thought, 'How could I have brought you to this? Just look at you, heaven only knows what's going on inside your head. A simple act of kindness, distraction, and now you're overwhelmed with guilt. Is it only the human race that's been made to feel guilty about sex? Is it the teachings of the bible, the fact that sex is never discussed openly, to be hidden as if it never happens? A sublime gift from God and nature to be used... only for procreation? Thou shall not indulge in any form of personal sexual pleasure however frustrated you feel... before marriage, that is. Who thought that one up? Sanctimonious hypocrisy... Sod it. What man and probably woman on the planet at some time has not indulged in personal sexual pleasure? Good for them, I say.'

Chapter 24

LYING FLAT, Alasdair had thought over the events of the last hour. After Janet had gone downstairs he'd fallen into a short primeval sleep. He woke, rested physically, depleted, but happy. Now faced with reality, what was he going to do, how to handle a potentially embarrassing situation and Janet? There is only one way out, reassure her how… play the fool. Talk a load of rubbish; sound as if you had hit the drugs again. 'If only I could get out of this bed, put my arms around her, say what I want to say, ask her forgiveness, reassure her it was not her fault. Tell her I willingly participated, she didn't force me, I enjoyed the experience.' Listening to Janet's own sexual response to his made it a unique experience… made it special. 'God, I wish this thumping headache would subside, let me think, maybe that's not a bad thing, don't think reassure, put her out of her misery. Let's hope my plan does not backfire… on me.'

"Ah, Janet, you have returned, welcome… come in, come in. What's that you have in your hands? Oh, a shovel of hot coal. I thought the room had heated up quite considerably in the last hour without the fire."

Janet stood still. Downstairs, it had taken every ounce of courage that she possessed not to flee. But here he was lying in front of her, a silly grin on his face, a cigarette hanging out of the side of his mouth, which wobbled up and down as he spoke. He looked like a clown, but Janet did not feel like laughing.

Refusing to respond to what Alasdair had just said, she managed to stutter.

"I thought... I would light the fire, the nights... cooler now.... make tea."

She did not complete the sentence before Alasdair interrupted her.

"Managed to get a cigarette out of the drawer... Could you light it for me? Couldn't find a match and I wouldn't be able to light it anyway... hand, you see." He took the cigarette out of his mouth with his good right hand and held it above his head. "Can't manage – only one hand."

"No, I certainly will not... Do you know what you have put me...?" Janet's anger was beginning to get the better of her, but she did not get the chance to finish her sentence before Alasdair interrupted again.

"Come here, Janet," he said, ignoring her reply as the cigarette had only been a prop to give him something to talk about. "Come, sit beside me, and get that basket chair from over there, beside the washstand... I have something to tell you." He looked furtively from side to side, as if to check they were alone.

Intrigued and more than a little curious to hear what he was going to say, Janet fetched the chair and sat down. 'Here it comes, he's going to dismiss me,' she thought. 'At least he has asked me to sit down... so you don't faint when he gives the reasons? Wait, I thought he would be angry with me, encouraging him to do what he did while he was so vulnerable.' She frowned at the expression on Alasdair's face, his odd behaviour. 'Something's not right; he's got a stupid grin on his face... hardly the look when you are going to fire someone. Are we on the same wavelength, are we on the same planet?' The planets certainly did figure in the equation, as Janet was about to find out.

"You have no idea what happened, I have to tell you… you will never believe it," he said, leaning a little further on his side. "Listen, listen." He crooked the fingers of his good hand indicating she should come closer.

Totally confused, Janet sat down. Her gaze neither wavered from his face, nor did she move closer. Maybe he was not going to fire her after all.

"I have had the most incredible, the most wonderful experience in my whole life. I would not trade what happened to me late this afternoon for all the tea in China. But Janet, I have a confession to make to you… I have been a bad boy."

Jesu-Maria what next, we seem to have descended into the realms of fantasy, she thought.

"I disobeyed you, I got up, went to the drawer… took more laudanum, drank all your herbal tea… wow, what a combination; but come closer, I want you to look at the wall… see over there, by the wardrobe near the floor, above the skirting board…. see it?"

"There's nothing to see, what am I looking for?" Janet asked, playing along. "I can't see anything."

"Ah, that's just it, it's not there now, but earlier there was a hole where I am pointing; you would never guess what came out of it… a whole troupe of monkeys!" He nodded to assure her. "At least four of them jumped up on the bed and danced round and round; one jumped up and sat on top of the clothes pole – what a sight, but the best is yet to come!"

'Which one of us is on the drugs,' Janet wondered. 'Perhaps *I* have taken laudanum. I think I am going mad. I think we both are. Here I am sitting, passive, listening, doing as I am told, with a man raving about monkeys dancing on his bed; next he will tell me he was up dancing with them.' Janet, uncertain what to do next, closed her eyes, hoping maybe when she opened them again this will all have been a dream, no, a nightmare.

"Oh Janet." Alasdair took a deep breath and slowly let it out as he spoke. "I heard voices, soft, so soft at first, but getting louder, telling me what to do." He pointed to the window. "Remember the seagull? It came back… told me to follow it. The next thing I knew I was soaring above the clouds… unreal."

"The whole thing is unreal, Alasdair," she whispered under her breath so he couldn't hear her.

"Yep, up through the clouds, flying higher, higher." He paused for a moment. "Then I saw her… La Luna… the moon, smiling, beckoning, beautiful, but best of all… oh Janet, Janet, you should have been with me to share the experience… I wanted you so much, but sensed you were close. I saw the planets in different colours near and far, I reached out, the stars got in the way… but the stars were the best of all. Starbursts, one explosion after another, each one bigger and better than the last, like fireworks exploding. I wanted them to last forever… then suddenly, here I was back in my bed."

'Well,' Alasdair thought, 'if this pile of gibberish doesn't reassure her nothing will. I have done my best, hope she realises I hold nothing against her, it was not her fault. A simple bed bath would never promote such a response under normal circumstances.' But Alasdair started to have doubts, began to regret he had fabricated such a story to save their faces. Maybe he should just have told her the truth; told her he held nothing against her and had loved every minute of their shared experience. 'Why did you not just tell her you coward?' Deep down he knew the answer, he just could not bring himself to. 'You are just using the same old excuse of your mother's prejudice to avoid the issue. Janet would understand and if she doesn't… well, goodbye Janet, and it's admission to hospital for you. Oh my God, where is she going?' Alasdair thought as Janet rose up.

Rising slowly out of the chair, she narrowed her eyes. "You have no idea what I have put myself through in the last hour, Alasdair Forman. I thought you would ask me to leave." Her words were deliberately calculated to have the maximum effect on Alasdair, so he missed nothing. She went over to the dressing table drawer, opened it, and picked up the bottle of laudanum. She retraced her steps to the fireplace, took great pleasure in opening the bottle and poured the whole lot on the fire, right on top of the burning coals.

"What the hell are you doing, woman!" he shouted at her. "How can I get through the night? It's agony – I needed that laudanum for tonight!" Starting to get out of the bed, he realised he was naked and had left the sheet behind. Pulling the sheet up to cover his nakedness, he tried to continue his protest. His hand, objecting to the sudden movement, started to throb with a vengeance.

"No more of this poison for you, young man. Do you think for one minute I am going to permit you to rant and rave... like a madman, make up stories drugged or otherwise? No more addictive poisons for you... keep drinking the tea. The tea won't have such a devastating effect on either of us. I was terrified to come back upstairs; I thought you would hate me..."

But that was some story he invented, she thought, making the excuse he was drugged. 'I don't think I've heard better... pure fiction; but that's not the point? He's given me the perfect excuse to get rid of the stuff; one excuse is as good as another.' With the air now cleared between them and no further need to dwell on recent events, Janet continued with the task of getting Alasdair's clean pyjamas on. There was little effort required to get the bottoms on now the main obstruction had reverted to its normal size. She'd only to ease them up his legs, over his hips and button them in place. Fortunately the pyjama sleeves were wider than his vest; his arm, once untied from the pole, slid

156

through quite easily without disturbing the dressing. With the bed made up with clean bedding, fresh pillows under his head, his arm back up in the sling, it was time for Janet to leave, her work finished.

Neither had spoken after Janet had thrown the laudanum into the fire. Alasdair, withdrawn, stared out of the window, no longer feeling remorse for the way he had treated her, anger and outrage having taken its place. His only other thought… how would he get through the rest of the night without pain relief?

The noise of the back door opening told Janet that Tam had returned.

"That's Tam, I will send him back after he takes me home as arranged." Janet turned round at the bedroom door. "I hope you will have a restful night's sleep, Alasdair. I will be back in the morning, but not alone. Rena will be with me…" She paused, then said in a lower voice: 'This must never happen again for both our sakes."

"What must never happen again? I rather enjoyed myself; I have no regrets… have you?"

Janet would never be able to describe the look on Alasdair's face as she left without answering his question. Weak and debilitated from days of illness, exhausted, he was tired and more than a little sorry for himself. A tear of self-pity slowly trickled down his cheek.

Janet, realising she had been more than a little harsh on the man, went back into the bedroom. Alasdair was a pitiful sight. On impulse she reached out and gently with her hand wiped the tear away. She had bent over Alasdair and lowered herself toward him so he could feel the heat from her body with her breasts almost on his chest; she was so close he could hear the throb of her heart. Her head nearly on his pillow, she kissed the cheek she had just wiped.

She drew even closer, slipped her hand under the bed clothes; let it slowly slide down till it reached his waist. Unknown to Alasdair it was for balance, but all he was aware of was her soft breath fanning his face. Her other hand moving at the side of the bed…. She stopped, was still. Her beautiful face resting so close… Janet whispered in his ear:

"Forgot my shoes."

Chapter 25

"AUNTY, I cannot express the feelings I have had while listening to you. Sadness... *disbelief...*" I emphasised the word disbelief. "What's wrong with the man, why couldn't he just tell her? Or at least give her an explanation as to why he couldn't allow their relationship to go any further. A deeply personal, sexual experience between them had just happened and all he did was turn the whole episode into a sick joke. Made a fool of himself to prevent betraying how he really felt; he thought he was protecting Janet, but who had he hurt the most, Janet or himself? No wonder Janet was angry." I stopped for a second. "Why, when she was so close to him as she collected her shoes to leave, did he not pull her closer and kiss her!? There was little danger of it going any further. But then this is fiction, isn't it Aunty? That bit, you know, between the couple, you made it up... no? Is this the first of Alasdair and Janet's sexual encounters...? I presume there is more to come?"

Aunty said nothing, only nodded.

"If this part of your story is fictitious, how can you describe such intimate sexual details without..." I hesitated. "...without some sexual experience yourself?" Was it my imagination, or had her head dropped like a young girl being caught out.

"Tell me... I know you are a maiden lady, but... how were you able to describe... where did you... you know?" I suddenly realised this old lady was no virgin.

"Of course I know, no one could make up what I have just told you!" she snapped, looking out the window. Regret

159

maybe, I wondered? Wanting to retract what she had just said? Then to my astonishment she added, "But don't tell the family…"

I managed to stifle the desire to burst out laughing, but hastened instead to reassure her of my promise when we started this journey, that all she ever told me would be in the strictest confidence.

"Your secret is safe, but good for you Aunty! I don't judge, I have no hang-ups about people's sex lives married or unmarried, including yours, it makes the story very human. Welcome to the swinging sixties Aunty… free love and all that and you never have to tell me any more about it, that's your business." I tried to reassure her. Can't say I was shocked by her confession, but it had been interesting and secretly I did wonder where and with whom? It was unlikely I would ever find out. I took a moment to reflect on what Aunty had said and it certainly was explicit! I don't think she realised how downright erotic her story telling was. I had to admit while I listened I found myself squirming in my chair, blushing slightly and clearing my throat to cover up my embarrassment, but I don't think she realised the effect she was having on me.

"I've written most of what you narrated today, but I think we need to quantify the event, it must be based on some truth to give it credibility. Even if it is fiction, what made you think there was more to what was going on, other than Janet nursing Alasdair? Janet was careful not to alert anyone in the village to the fact she was treating him. You said so several times."

"That's true," she had, "but Pittendreal is a small village and as I said before we began, everybody knew everybody else's business. Or they made it up. My grandmother told me of the rumours. No one knew for sure what was wrong with the Doctor, only the Minister Mr McDougall, Dr Henderson and Rena. And they never talked, but Carrick the butcher and

Lightmans the baker did and not all the fishermen left The Pirates drunk...

"Granny said there had been sightings of Janet coming from the direction of the Doctor's house late at night and early in the morning. So they put two and two together... and you are right, I did made their sexual encounter up, but it could have been true... as you will find out."

"You're something else, Aunty, I knew it... a maiden lady... you were unlikely to read the likes of *Lady Chatterley* and it's very sexually explicit... there had to be more... personal intimate experience?!"

"That's enough... we are now finished with that passage and no, I have not read that book. I felt sufficiently confident enough to be able to tell you everything, and nothing should embarrass you, you're a Doctor after all."

Ah, she's recovered... her proud old body once more sitting upright in her chair, any reticence regarding her past forgotten nipped in the bud.

"And enough of you implying I'm an old maid. Lucky for you I don't plan to die tonight. So do we continue, or are we going to sit here all day and discuss my sex life?"

"No, you are right, but I think I have heard enough for one day and I still haven't completed my notes. I want to do that while the facts are still fresh in my mind... thank you." I could scarcely hide a grin that was spreading across my face.

"What's so funny?"

"The part where Janet returned to the bedroom to... collect her shoes... made me want to laugh! Perhaps if it had not been so poignant it would be funny... heaven knows what Alasdair must have thought! Instead she was searching for her shoes!"

To my delight she laughed for the first time since I started to visit her and I felt more relaxed and happy in her company than I had ever been. So she's not the dried up crusty old maid I took her to be! I was delighted to find out she had a sense of humour after all. We had shared a joke, long may it last. I finished my notes and the details from today's visit before I forgot them. Not that I was likely to forget in a hurry. On the other hand I had a passing thought... Although this was very interesting, I began to despair of her ever reaching my request to know the answer to why Leightham House's roof had been removed. When was she going to tell me that and about her friend Alice who to date had not come into the equation? Anyway... I guess she will get to it in her own good time.

Sobering up, I asked, "Did they get married, Aunty? They are so obviously made for each other."

"Wait and see..."

"I have to go... see you in a few weeks." Here it comes... be careful driving on...

Chapter 26

A FEW WEEKS LATER, driving back to Aunty's house, I noticed a change in the seasons. The clocks had gone back and it would be dark much earlier. I had to get on with Aunt Jane's story before winter set in. Ice and snow in the coming months would make the road impassable, dangerous enough at the best of times. The winter as far as work was concerned, meant extra shifts because of flu epidemics. The staff at breaking point, trolleys lining the passages, patients waiting for beds to be found, in our own and other hospitals. An increase in R.T.A.'s because of the inclement weather... a nightmare. I knew I probably would have to put my visits on hold after this or definitely the next one. Put all that out of your mind for the present old girl, enjoy today... the story's getting more like *Lady Chatterley* every chapter. I couldn't wait to hear the aftermath, or the fallout from Alasdair and Janet's sexual encounter.

I hadn't risked bringing Kit-Kats... they didn't go down too well on my last visit. Aunty said nothing, her look said it all and she refused to eat one... insulted? On my way home that Sunday I'd smiled at her childish behaviour... better be a good girl today.

"Comfortable!" Aunty challenged me as I sat down in the sitting room. I heard the tea trolley being pushed through the hall.

"Hello miss, nice to see you again." Cathie was as cheerful as always. "Your Aunt wants the tea served now because the clocks changed. She knows you'll have to leave earlier." I

163

wondered why there was an expression of innocence on Cathie's face that said, 'I know nothing'.

"Thank-you Cathie, that will be all, I will serve the tea today, go." Cathie had been dismissed.

I showed no special interest in the tea… and smiled at Cathie who had winked at me from the sitting room door.

"Cake!" Aunt Jane announced triumphant, holding the plate out to me.

You old witch!

"Thank you Aunty, it looks delicious… Lightman's the bakers?" I asked innocently.

"Of course."

She had scored again – iced 'Ginger' cake instead of ginger biscuits.

"Ready to begin?"

"Ready!"

Chapter 27

JANET returned next morning and was waiting in the kitchen for Rena and Tam. No need for Tam to stay, so she'd left breakfast waiting for him at the cottage. Janet kept busy, lighting the stove and putting the kettle on to boil. For some reason, she was reluctant to go upstairs and face Alasdair by herself. She would wait for Rena, who shouldn't be much longer now. At that moment the back door burst open and a flustered Rena with a look of utter confusion on her face ran in.

"What's goin' on here Junet? Tam telt me last nicht to be ready in the mornin', you had a job for me. Ah didna ken it was at the Doctur's Hoose. Tam arrived at the back door, just efter the bairns left for school. He wouldn't tell me anythin'… said you would explain when a' got here. Junet, is there somethin' wrang with the Doctur?" Rena demanded, throwing her shawl from her shoulders on one of the chairs.

"Sit down Rena; you may need to sit down in the next few minutes anyway. First of all you must keep what passes between us strictly confidential, whatever you decide to do. Do you understand what I am saying?"

Rena furrowed her brow. Obviously she didn't understand, but she trusted Janet. "Tell me, for God's sake hurry up… you're worryin' me lassie."

"It's serious. I thought long and hard before I became involved. Therefore I must ask you to do the same. It's not all bad, first things first, let me explain. If you agree to stay and you have full knowledge of the situation, you could be implicated... if things go wrong with the law. So you must understand."

"Whit do ye mean the law! Like Mr Spence the Bobby?" she exclaimed aghast.

"Or worse." There was no point minimising the situation. "I take it you want me to continue... Yes?"

Rena nodded her ascent.

"I found Doctor Forman sitting on one of the dykes outside a patient's home in George Street. Right away I knew something was wrong. It appears he had injured his hand earlier in the week while attending to a patient. Subsequently the wound which is on the palm of his left hand had become infected... badly infected."

Rena sucked her breath in. "Oh, that would be sair!"

"My first instinct was to get Tam to help me get him into hospital, but it appears the Doctor had no more faith in hospitals than I do. He felt there was more infection in the hospital than out. He was also afraid that they might force him to accept certain treatments while not in a position to refuse. Do you understand Rena?"

Rena nodded; she knew only too well what Janet was meaning.

"That's why he is still here upstairs in his own bed. The Doctor and I decided to put it about the village he has the flu. No one is to come near the surgery or the house as they might become infected as well. I guess the news has not reached you yet?"

Rena shook her head.

"Naturally the Doctor and I have discussed this at length, so there you have it. He seems to be holding his own according to Tam, but I have not been upstairs. I have been busy... the fire had gone out... put the kettle on, you understand?" Janet turned away from Rena. She didn't want Rena guessing anything was amiss between Alasdair and herself.

"Yesterday I lanced the abscess on his left hand. I emphasise the *left* hand because the Doctor is right-handed. If things go wrong, hopefully he will still have the use of the right one. I'll come every day, dress the wound. Also assess the situation and decide the best course of action. That's why I asked Tam to fetch you; I need you here to help me."

While Janet had been explaining this to Rena it entered her head one more time, she must be crazy taking this on. Reflecting on the last twenty-four hours, Janet was angry at herself. But how do you deny chemistry between two people, how do you control feelings? She had no answer.

"Anyway, before we go any further there's another matter I have to discuss with you first; it has nothing to do with the current situation. Whether you decide to stay or not... the choice is yours either way. I have encouraged Doctor Forman to consider employing a housekeeper. He is proud, it is the first time he has lived on his own and wants to prove his independence.

"Anyway, I put it to him, or rather suggested to him; he cannot go on like this, his ever increasing volume of work and cope with the house. I hear new patients are at the door every day asking to join his Panel and it's only going to get worse with an increased workload. It could be the reason he injured himself... he's tired? If he does not look after himself how can he look after others...? He should be free to concentrate on his work and his patients and not clean a house at the end of a busy day."

"Aye you're right Janet, the young Doctur's well thocht of, he's gettin' quite a reputation for his skills at the Docturin'. Some folk swear by his treatment, the medicine he gives them, they dinna' ken what they would do withoot him. I kent there was somethin' wrang since I saw auld Tam flee'n' down the Comentry road wi' a clothes pole on his Kirt. That's a sight yae dinna' see every day, but I never would have guessed it was for this, or had anything to do wi' the Doctur."

Janet put her hand up to stop further discussion. "The Doctor agreed and I suggested three hours, five mornings a week. He needs someone to take care of the house, cleaning, washing, ironing and maybe a weekly shop and some cooking. I have recommended you. He will pay you for your services, but that you can discuss with him. Are you interested? Well?"

Rena was stunned… speechless.

"I take it that is a yes?"

"I canna believe it I'm hearing richt?… That's like gift from God, Junet," Rena uttered once she had recovered. "You canna believe how hard things have been for me and the bairns since Fred was droond."

"Rena, don't cry. I recommended you for several reasons; you are trustworthy and discreet. These are the most important qualities for a person working in a Doctor's surgery. You're perfect… am I right?"

"Aye your richt, am no gossip, ma mother taught me never to talk aboot others ahint their backs and they'll have nae reason to talk about you. I'll tak the job… dae ma best. When d'you want me to start? I can right away and still be back in time for the bairns gettin' out the school. But will three hours be enough?"

"I am sure that's more than enough for one man living on his own. Now I need you to make a decision on a more serious matter."

"What's that?"

"Doctor Forman with my best interests at heart has written a letter to Doctor Henderson in Leightham, regarding the situation here, which is unusual to say the least; he asks if you will sign the letter as a witness. You understand what I mean by a witness?"

Rena nodded.

"If anything happens to the Doctor you are to take the letter to Doctor Henderson without delay. I could be charged with a crime and you as an accomplice. The letter states Doctor Forman asked me to treat him, that he refused hospitalisation and in no way am I responsible for his death."

Rena, wide-eyed, nodded, as the enormity of the situation was becoming apparent to her.

"Now that you are going to work for him you can ask about the letter and its contents. You can also confirm that I in no way coerced the Doctor, pressured or forced him to stay at home. Sorry to keep on repeating myself, but it is vital you understand the implications for you and your children. But you are under no obligation to sign."

"Where do I sign... where's the letter, Junet?"

"In my defence Rena I did tell Doctor Forman... if at any time I became alarmed, regarding his illness, if he deteriorates, Tam and I will take him to hospital right away, no arguments whether he likes it or not."

"Aye your right Junet, this is no funny business, its serious richt enough."

"The letter is locked in the desk drawer in the surgery, the key upstairs in his jacket pocket, we can get it later. But first I need you to come with me. I've not been upstairs yet, so I don't know what state we will be greeted with. Tam said he was all right when he left, but the Doctor did have a disturbed night."

Rena appeared not to have heard Janet's request, to go upstairs.

"That's fine Junet, just give me a wee minute to look around, get ma bearing's, then I'll make a start. Mind you, if the state o' this kitchen's got anything to do with it... it's about time he got help. Ma feet are stickin' to the flair. Noo where's the scrubbing brushes and the dusters kept?"

Rena began to roll up her sleeves. "It's a guid job a' kept ma over-all's on, I was in that a hurry tae leave. I thought you must be in difficulties with another bairn on the way, but I couldna' work out why ye were at the Doctur's. So I just threw ma shawl about ma shoothers."

"Yes-yes, Rena, just a moment, then you can have a look around the house later – what you're looking for is stored in a cupboard on the stair. I believe the Doctor's mother arranged everything before he arrived and I can assure you the house is well equipped. There is everything here you will ever need to do the job. I want you to come with me to Doctor Forman's bedroom and meet the man, so we will waste no more time..."

"Whit! Go in tae the man's bedroom... with him still in the bed?" Rena was mortified.

"Rena, the man is ill; I doubt he would notice if you were wearing a pair of Garibaldi breeches in his present state. Who is going to know anyway? There is only the two of us and I certainly am not going to tell anyone. Are you?"

Rena, humiliated, informed Janet there was no way she would ever wear a pair of red flannel drawers, men's or women's... the very thought of it made her blush. On the other hand, this job wasn't to be sneezed at and no one was insisting how she dressed as far as she was concerned.

"Irrespective of how you feel about invading the man's privacy, it's important that you speak to your employer. Tell him whether you will accept the job or not and whether the hours suit you; if you are satisfied with the payment he is offering. It is better you ask him." Janet halted to see if Rena had any questions. None came.

"Half of the house is the Surgery as you know; I am sure that's where the Doctor files his confidential records. He probably will not want them touched. But the place also must be kept clean. Anyway it is not up to me to speak on your behalf. You will have to talk with him, get to know the Doctor.

Unfortunately things are upside down at the moment with his illness."

Once Rena made up her mind it was rare she ever changed it. With a determined look on her face, she took her overall off, undoing the ties at her back so she could loosen the garment from round her ample middle and bosom, and so she could get her arms out of the armholes. Throwing the garment on top of the shawl already on the chair, she got ready for the interview by smoothing loose tendrils of hair back into its net and fixing it in place with some Kirby grips. She tucked her blouse firmly back into her skirt and, satisfied with her appearance, declared:

"If I had known awe this was going to happen, I would have put my good Sunday claes on... the ones a' wear to the Kirk."

"Ready? Think Rena, if you had dressed in your Sunday best, you would not have been able to start work today or help me!"

"Aye that's true enough."

Having thus tidied herself, she indicated to Janet she was ready. Head up and shoulders down, a quick shake of her head, Rena followed Janet towards Alasdair's bedroom. At the bottom of the stair as Janet reached out to the bannister, Rena caught her hand.

"Junet, is everything a' richt, you look tired, pale – you'll need to tak better care o' yoursel' lassie. It's no just the Doctur that needs you, the village needs you as weel."

"I'm fine, nothing is wrong." Janet didn't look at Rena. "Didn't sleep last night... worried, tired."

"Ach I'm being an auld fusspot... I wouldn't like you to catch onythin'." Now Janet did meet Rena's gaze.

"I'm fine, just tired," she repeated. "Shall we go up?"

Pausing at the cupboards on the middle landing, Janet allowed Rena to look inside, hoping the noise would alert Alasdair to their arrival... Rena had never seen so much stuff in her life in one place; the cupboards looked like the storeroom of a General Merchants. What luxury, the Doctor's family must be wealthy to be able to afford all this.

As they entered Alasdair's bedroom, Janet was grateful to have Rena at her side. She knew her presence would help dispel any awkwardness. But not in the way it happened...

"Oh my God all michty!" Rena blasted forth. If Alasdair had been asleep he'd be well awake now. Janet nearly jumped out of her skin.

"Junet never warned me, just look at yersel' lawdie, that's an awfy state yer in. Does your Mother ken your that no weel?"

"No, she does not Mrs McKay, and on no account is she to be told."

In the cold light of day, Janet had to admit Alasdair didn't look much better than he had yesterday, but no worse. His cheeks flushed, cheekbones more prominent than ever, he had a pinched, gaunt look. Black circles under his sunken eyes told Janet they were far from out of the woods yet, but he had survived the night and the surgical trauma of yesterday, so he was in with a chance of beating this nightmare.

"I know I look like death, Mrs McKay, but believe me compared to how I have been feeling..." Alasdair closed his eyes for a moment as if to convince himself and Janet.

"Nature and Janet seem to work well together." He smiled to reassure Janet all was well. "Now Mrs McKay..."

"Just Rena, that'll dae fine Doctur."

"Well... Rena... Janet tells me I need a housekeeper and you come highly recommended. But that was not necessary. I remember you, how proficient you were at the baby's delivery in the Gardner household, a few week ago."

"Aye that's richt," Rena interrupted, "the Gairdner's hoose, how could a' forget it, or you Doctur!"

"Yes, just as you say. I propose to offer you four shillings a week for the five mornings. I am sure Janet will keep you right on the matter of what exactly needs to be done at the moment. I will tell you if there is anything else I want done once I am well. You are of course at liberty to make your own decisions regarding a routine that suits you for the present and Janet, she seems to be in charge. The surgery requires only dusting and the floors washed, I am sure you understand. Now how does that suit you, do you have any questions?"

"Four shillins... a week..." Rena almost choked, then recovering, "Doctur, like I told Junet, you'll never ken how thankful I am. I'll dae ma best to please you and I'll never let you down." Rena had made a serious attempt to modify her local dialect throughout the interview. "You just need to tell me what you're wantin' done an' don't hesitate to tell me if a' get it wrang. A canna believe it, it's like a wechts been lifted off my shooders... shoulders. The difference that money will make to me an' ma bairns..." Rena turned to one side to prevent Alasdair and Janet seeing her tears.

"I take it you have accepted the job... good! I need Janet to continue with my treatment, neither of you could have failed to notice the odour in the room. If that is everything... no, wait! I forgot I think, my memory is failing along with everything else. The letter for Dr Henderson... has Janet explained to you?"

"Aye she has, no problem, I would sign onythin' to help Junet. If there was any trouble I'd be right behind her. I'll tell you quickly Doctur; I can see yer gettin' tired. I used to get good marks at the school. Auld Mr Chambers the Headmaster used to say I had braw handwriting and good organisational skills. So you lie back and let Junet look after you, leave everythin' else to me, I'll deal with it."

"In that case, since I can leave everything up to you, my first request is... can you shave men, Rena?" Alasdair grinned.

Rena drew her eyebrows down, frowned at Alasdair's request. Initially believing he was serious, this request stopped her in her tracks, unsure how to respond. But Rena had a quiet sense of humour and a sharp wit to match his; she decided to play along with her new employer... tease him in return.

"Ah no, Doctur, you've got me there." Rena shook her head, pretended to be perplexed. "I dinna shave men, but since you've put me in charge, I'll send auld Tam up with his cut-throat when he gets back. He'll make a grand job o' it."

"Err, ah no thank-you... touché Rena..." Alasdair smiled a wan smile, warming to the woman, pleased she had a sense of fun.

"Dinna fash yersel' Doctur, a'll no be touche'n onythin... just the hoose. But among a' the other things that need sorting out, yer beard's the last thing for you to be worrying about. When you're better a' ken the very man, Danny Broon. He's just opened a wee Barber's shop on the High street, I'll get him to come to the hoose, gee yae a shave and a haircut, but ye'll need to wait till yer over yer 'flu'." Rena winked. "Oh and afore I forget a' hope you dinna think I'm gettin' above mysel, I couldna help but notice, the gairden needs a wee bit of attention... its fu o' weeds and the grass needs cutin'. Sam Taylor's no long retired and from what a' hear from his folks... he's bored." Rena paused for breath. "They're afraid he micht try to return to the fishing. You maybe remember the auld man he had a mild stroke, not that long ago, but he's recovered. Well it would give him somethin' to dae, you should see his own garden, the man's got green fingers... I'll get him; he'll dae it as a favour, nae need to pay him."

Alasdair lay silent in his bed. There was no answer to Rena's proposals, and they made right good sense. But he got the notion he was being controlled again and this time by more than one woman in his life. Being dependent, he let it go for the time being. To his relief Rena took herself downstairs, calling as she went:

"Am away to light the boiler in the wash-house. I saw a pile o' dirty washin' on the floor at the back door as I came in... Oh I hear the kettle, I'll put it aside, make us a cup o' tea once a' get back."

Rena's voice tailed off as she went down the stairs. The next thing they heard was the clank of the kettle as Rena moved it off the stove, the back door opening and closing.

"Janet," Alasdair asked wearily, "does she always prattle on like that? That's a weird mixture of the local dialect and English she's trying to impress me with... think I prefer the fisher folk's."

"No, I have to admit Rena is normally quite reserved, keeps herself to herself. However I think she's more than a little overwhelmed by her good fortune – that's why she is chattering so much; she might be trying to impress you? Rena's just realised how lucky she has been. You have no idea the misery inflicted on these young widows when they lose their husbands. They become totally dependent on their families and the Parrish Council, just to exist. A more decent, honest soul, you would be hard pressed to find in Pittendreal. Rena is one of the best."

"Time will tell, I hope so," Alasdair responded. "Let's get on with dressing my hand... I am certain you can smell the stench coming from it."

"Let's not dwell on that, it's temporary and a good sign." Janet spoke in her usual soft voice. "I have a fresh supply of seaweed lotion. So keep quiet, think nice thoughts. Mr McDade gave me a fresh supply of gauze cottonwool, bandages and something I have never heard of before... dommett. He says it helps stabilise the muscles, stops movement. I thought we would try it, so you won't need to worry about moving your arm and hand while you sleep."

"Now you're chattering, give it a rest, I know what dommett is," Alasdair snapped. "Get on with it..." He was anxious to get it over with. "Do you think I am looking forward to this? I know what's coming; the quicker it's over the better... I can try to get some sleep... more willow-bark tea? Please!" he added, not meaning to sound sarcastic.

Janet undid the sling from the hook, held onto his hand and slowly lowered it onto the bed. It was no use, the throbbing returned with a vengeance. Alasdair clenched his teeth, gasped in pain and threw his head back on the pillow, beginning to think his ordeal would never end... But it did.

One day becomes the next and the next... life goes on, relentless.

Chapter 28

IN NO TIME Rena was established as Doctor Forman's housekeeper. Some of the other widows in the village were angry. They were all in the same boat and had lost husbands in the harbour or at sea. They felt the job should have been advertised to give them all a chance at employment. When a disgruntled few heard Rena had landed herself a job housekeeping for the Doctor they called her a skivvy. But on the whole the news was well received; Rena was respected by the villagers as a good woman; reliable and always ready to help her neighbours. They were pleased to see her walk towards the High Road every morning, on her way to the Doctor's house, a clean apron under her arm and a paper bag of rolls from Lightman's for the doctor's breakfast. While he had been ill, Rena only saw Janet at his house in the morning. Whether Janet returned later in the day she'd no idea. That was Janet's business and had nothing to do with her. Rena would be hard pressed to remember if she ever saw Janet at the Doctor's house after he recovered.

Before long Rena, unknown to Alasdair, had all but adopted him as a sort of older son. Her life became devoted to the care of the man and his house as if he were family. Nothing was too much trouble; her personal crusade... to feed him as she was convinced he was starving. Alasdair discovered it was futile to argue with Rena on the subject of food. So to stop Rena spend her wages on him, he set up weekly accounts with the local shopkeepers. Rena made full use of those accounts. She didn't need to buy fish; Wullie Gairdner was only too pleased to give her all the fish and ice she wanted. Alasdair had not sent him a bill for his wife's delivery, and Wullie had not forgotten. The pantry and the icebox were always full. Alasdair insisted Rena took some of the food home for her family or anyone else who needed it, declaring:

"I hate waste, Rena."

"Thank you, I hate waste too Doctur, there's many mouths that will be glad o' something to eat in the village. I'll see to it."

When Alasdair had finished for the day, evening surgery over and no outstanding late calls, he looked forward to what Rena had left for his supper. A fine bowl of oxtail soup or a plate of potted beef, with cold potatoes left over from dinner. Alasdair liked cold potatoes as Rena found out, discovering him once with his hand in a saucepan helping himself to yesterday's leftovers. At times Alasdair smiled and shook his head. 'I am being manipulated here and Rena doesn't realise I know it.' Rena insisted he had his dinner at midday, like the rest of the village. Alasdair put up with it... but she had a point. When he'd fended for himself, had a late call-out, he never knew when he might be back, could be an all-nighter... Her way, he rarely felt hungry and the sandwich she'd left for him to eat when returned was welcome. But oh boy did he feel the need to have forty winks after one of Rena's midday meals! Thank goodness evening surgery didn't start till four. Once Rena offered to leave the children with her mother and return later, she never asked again, and Alasdair absolutely barred her returning. Until his illness he had relished his own company, peace and quiet to read his newspaper in the evening. He was aware of being alone in Pittendreal, but it didn't bother him. After a busy life in the City and a mother nagging at him, he could now do his own thing undisturbed. Loneliness? He'd never heard of it; loneliness would be a new experience for him in the weeks ahead.

A strange development took place in Alasdair's life after his illness. It seemed not only that he had acquired a housekeeper... but a family. Rena's children loved to accompany their mother to the Doctor's house in the school holidays and would sit patiently in the kitchen while their mother cleaned. It was inevitable Alasdair bumped into them when he nipped into the kitchen during morning surgery to pinch a biscuit. A friendship developed between the Doctor and Rena's son Brian. He was almost ten when his mother started to work for the Doctor, a quiet, serious wee chap with a head of tousled, brown curly hair which Alasdair frequently ruffled when he passed the boy… trying to get the lad to smile. Since the death of his dad, Brian found little to smile about.

Young as he was Brian vowed never to go to sea as a fisherman. It was not a fear of the sea or even drowning that bothered him. He'd overheard the villagers talk at his father's funeral… the general opinion being drowning was a quick, painless death. Dragged under in seconds by the weight of their seamen's boots and oilskins, they didn't stand a chance. None of that bothered Brian, because he'd experienced something worse, the non-existent financial help for his mum, after his dad's death. He was determined do better for himself and for his family.

Brian saw Alasdair as a sort of surrogate father, friend and mentor. It hadn't been long before Brian started to bring his homework in the evenings for Alasdair to check. By the time Brian was almost up to the Doctor's shoulder, his confidence had grown under Alasdair's tutelage to a point where Brian confided in Alasdair, telling him when he grew up he had decided to become a Doctor… just like Alasdair.

"Well Brian, if that's what you have decided to do with your life, we will just have to work on that together," Alasdair announced, secretly proud and pleased. He took it as a compliment from the young lad. As Rena had adopted Alasdair, so Alasdair adopted Brian.

Chapter 29

"OH, I DON'T MEAN to interrupt Aunty, but it seems to me that as the relationship between Alasdair and Brian developed, Alasdair saw the possibility of having a surrogate son. So far in your story it seems highly unlikely he'd ever have one of his own. Just wanted to say how I felt." Then I remembered something.

"Wait a minute, isn't there a Dr Alasdair McKay, in your G.P. Practice? I'm sure I've written discharge letters to him, but I don't know him personally."

"Excuse me missy, may I have your permission to continue? We have a lot to cover today and you are the one who's always yelping about time. No more interruptions – I don't plan to live forever and my local Surgery is of no interest or importance. Not relevant."

I put pen and pad in my bag…

"You're right. Here I am again yelping about the time, but you look healthy enough to me. The ginger cake was delicious, Aunty, but reluctant as I am to leave you, I have to go. I didn't tell you when I arrived I've been called in to do an extra night shift tonight… staff shortage."

"But how will you manage? You've not slept today. Can you stay awake?"

"Had a lie-in this morning, didn't get up till twelve, I'll be fine. Remember darling, we're the medical staff, not the nursing. When it quietens I nip off to the doctors' quarters and sleep. Sometimes, after three we're not called out at all, if it's quiet. The nurses are different. They have to stay awake… woe betide them if the night police… the night Sister, catches them."

"Maybe that's not so bad then."

"Worse still, it's unlikely I will get back till after the New Year. All the family and I will see you on Boxing Day as usual, but would it be possible to continue the story with them around?"

"I agree. You haven't discussed the reason for our meetings with any of them?" she asked, suspicious.

"Of course not. That was our bargain. I haven't forgotten; your secrets are safe with me, not that we have uncovered any yet."

"I don't have any secrets."

Really? I thought back about her sex life confession. "Don't worry, I can wait. I wouldn't miss what you have told me over the last few months for the world regardless of who it involved."

"What does your mother think of these visits? Isn't she curious?"

"Believe it or not… no She knows you are telling me about Leightham house, but seems otherwise disinterested. Let's face it, it's of no interest to her. I generally tell her we had a good time, enjoyed a cup of tea, had a blether… that suffices. I'm not sure how I would handle it if she asked a direct question…"

"You're right, better have some sort of reply ready. You know I like your dad, I always have, but I also know your Aunt Nan and he don't get along."

"That's putting it mildly, Aunty!" I smiled. "I'm off. See you boxing day with the gang, I'm working Christmas Eve and Christmas day, so will send your card as usual and bring your gift with me. I wonder what Cathie will have on the menu for us this year?"

"That's only a few weeks away, how time flies! See how the nights have drawn in… I look forward to your Christmas card arriving, and phone me!"

"See you over the festive season, take care, Aunt Jane."

Chapter 30

CHRISTMAS and the New Year passed in a haze of celebrations, parties, work, and the family's statutory visit to Aunty. I was more or less up to date with writing and had compiled much of the data, was now anxious to hear the next instalment of Aunty's story. She had promised to finish the first part by Spring. I had promised the old dear I would be back in January... fat chance! The flu had reached epidemic proportions and seemed like a plague on the young and elderly alike. I didn't dare visit Aunt Jane in case I took the infection to her.

When I arrived at Aunty's house I handed my coat to Cathie. "How is she? I just haven't had a minute to myself since we left after Boxing Day. Mum's been down with the flu – at one point her symptoms were getting pretty close to pneumonia."

"Are you two going to stand in the hall and talk all day?" a voice shouted from the sitting room.

"Oops Cathie, I'm being summoned to appear, Her Majesty calleth. I'd better jump to it!"

"Don't let your Aunt hear you; you're in enough trouble as it is."

"Why did I start this? I must have taken leave of my senses!"

"Not at all, lass, she's really missed your visits over the last couple of months. Your Aunty is always low in spirit in January... January, it's depressing. She kept asking if you had phoned and she knows all about your mother having the flu.

Your visits will cheer her up. Now away in ye go, face the lion in her den. I've left the tea ready on the trolley, just help yersels. Am awa tae ma sister Irene."

"Iced ginger cake, ginger biscuits, Kit-Kat?"

"No, Battenberg cake," Cathie announced with an expression of wide-eyed innocence. We collapsed onto each other's shoulders...,convulsing with helpless silent laughter.

"Better go face the music," I said when I recovered.

"Just take your time. Do you think I'm going to hang around here all day waiting for you and Cathie to finish 'gabbing'?" Aunt's agitated voice rang out.

"Where's she planning to go, Cathie? Hey, what about the local dialect, eh? She must hae been listening to you!"

Cathie smiled and shook her head at my attempted sarcastic humour; her coat now on, she made her way to the back door.

"That cake looks too good to miss... Hi Aunty... happy New Year!"

"Happy New year? A bit late are you not? H-mm, same to you, you're here at last," she nipped. "Get on and pour the tea, it's your turn, Missy." She was right, I had not been able to return as promised for it was now almost into early spring. I had a life of my own to lead and an interesting new development in it... boyfriend wise.

"You know fine well Aunty that I am an only child and when anything happens to the parents, the burden of responsibility falls on that child. With Mum ill I've nursed her, shopped, cooked... and worked at the same time," I defended myself, then smiled. "Forget it, I'm here now. What did you think of your Christmas present?" I asked, pouring the tea. "You know you're not the easiest of person to buy for." I glanced round the richly furnished room.

"Then don't waste your money... what was it you gave me? It seems a long time ago now. Yes – Estee Lauder Youth Dew... I ask you... do I look like I would use such a scent? I wore it at my New Year dinner party for Cathie and her family; it gave me such a headache, I had to take an aspirin."

Cantankerous! Did I come on a bad day? Straight to the point, don't think of hurting anyone's feelings will you?

"I thought, something different for a change. I bet you have drawers full of lace handkerchiefs. I thought you would like perfume. Maybe I should have stuck with English Lavender Water, respect for your age." I smiled, all innocent. Aunty narrowed her eyes at me. "Or what about Jean Patou?"

"Too expensive... No 5... Chanel no. 5, I've used it all my life. As far as I'm concerned it's the only perfume worth using. But here we go again... procrastinate... a prolonged discussion on the merits of perfume. Next you will be nagging – about the lack of time in your busy life, the purpose of your visit... you have to go... it's getting dark or your mother's waiting, dinner for you... It's you who are wasting time. So... fair warning, over the next few months we will complete the first half of our book. After the summer holidays we will continue with the other half. And as you have just reminded me about my age, we'd better get on with it. Drink your tea."

Memories of my childhood flooded back. I was breathing on her windows again! But I didn't wet myself or burst into tears this time! Pen and pad at the ready, Great Aunt Jane's personal secretary, her ghost- writer, was raring to go, though it did go through my mind this was going to take a lot longer than I had first thought

Chapter 31

RENA dropped in Sunday afternoon before Alasdair returned to work, to see if he needed anything; make sure he had eaten the fish pie she had left for his lunch. She brought the Saturday Courier for him to catch up with the local news. He thanked her for the paper and yes, he hastened to assure her, he'd eaten the pie, telling Rena he was looking forward to getting back to work next day. Although maybe a little weak in the legs from being in bed, Rena narrowed her eyes suspiciously, asking Alasdair if he was sure he was ready to return to work yet.

"Don't forget Rena, I have arranged for Dr Henderson to cover house calls and emergencies, another week should do it. Rena, your family will be waiting for you... go home, I'm fine and it's your day off."

"Aye, I'll dae that Doctur in a minute, it's Sunday... the bairns at the Sunday school in the Kirk hall and I hiv a wee bit o' time on my hands. I gled Doctur Henderson in gaun tae help yae oot, that's awfy grand."

"Thank you Rena." Oh for a bit of peace and quiet to read the newspaper and collect his thoughts on the next morning's surgery. He was not yet aware that in a few hours he would regret thinking these thoughts.

They both turned and looked towards the corridor at the sound of the front door opening and closing. Whoever it was, was letting themselves in unannounced. Doctor Harry Henderson had arrived.

"Talk of the Devil!" Alasdair muttered under his breath.

When Harry Henderson found out the real reason for Alasdair's illness, he had been horrified. The first time he visited Alasdair after the incident with the scalpel, duped into believing it was the flu, was bad enough. But the real reason a septic abscess and the action his young protégé had taken risking his life... deciding not to go into hospital! "An abscess on the hand!" he had shouted at Alasdair, "Sure it wasn't an abscess on the brain?" As for being treated by an unqualified person... had he lost his mind? Harry couldn't believe his ears. But if he was being honest, he wouldn't have placed a bet either way as to what the outcome would have been. Whether Alasdair stayed home or had been admitted to hospital, might have made no difference. Thank God he'd survived. That was all that mattered, but Harry was a reasonable man and under the circumstances he'd had to agree with Alasdair, there did seem to be some merit to the treatment. What had Alasdair said about salves and seaweed lotions? It seemed to him under the circumstances they had been every bit as good as the conventional products.

"See Doctur, it's just as weel a' came the day, you've got a visiter!" Rena smiled warmly when she saw who it was. "Doctur Henderson, come awa' in an' tak a seat. Keep the Doctur company, you ken he's not been his self recently."

"If I have not been myself Rena, who have I been?"

Rena ignored him; she understood what Alasdair had been through and it wasn't a surprise to her that he was sharp. She knew he didn't mean it.

"I'll awa' to the kitchen, put the kettle on, make the twa o' ye a cup o' tea afore a' leave. Then I'll need to go, the bairns will be back frae the Kirk."

"Yes, thank you, please put the kettle on. Dr Henderson and I would appreciate having a cup made for us." He changed his tone, answering Rena politely, slightly shame-faced about his previous uncalled for sarcastic remark to the woman.

Once Rena left the room, Harry decided to speak his mind – the purpose for the visit in the first place. Alasdair knew what was coming and tried to pre-empt the old guy… by speaking first.

"Good to see you Harry, owe you one… doubt I could repay you for all you have done... I am glad to be returning to…" was as far as he got.

"I'll give you GLAD! Getting back to work; it's a miracle you're not in your grave. Now it's my turn to speak, give you a piece of my mind and enjoy doing it." He puffed out, irate. "When I saw you lying in that bed last week… once I was allowed to visit, if you please! I nearly had a heart attack. The state you were in. Don't you ever… ever pull a stunt like that again, do you hear me?" Harry emphasised every word, pointing a finger at Alasdair.

Alasdair started to defend himself, but Harry held his hand up.

"Be quiet!" he snapped. "Don't you dare say one word in your defence, taking such a ridiculous, dangerous decision with your life. What were you thinking of?"

"I don't think I was in a position to think at all."

Harry ignored that remark. "As for me, addle brained old fool, duped into believing you were down with the flu… in the middle of the summer!" He banged a fist on his other hand. "I got you this job, I feel responsible. You're like my own son, I was one of your Godparents for heaven's sake." The older man's lips trembled slightly, anger and frustration getting the better of him. Recovering quickly, "If you'd only trusted me, I tell you laddie I would have got an ambulance, had you admitted to the cottage hospital in Leightham so fast it would have made your head spin, no argument!"

"Believe me, Harry, my head *was* spinning."

"That's not funny and don't interrupt. I would have supervised your treatment myself, never left your side." Then he remembered the secret Alasdair had sworn him to, making him swear never to break a confidence.

"As for keeping it a secret from your parents… that was a tall order. Your parents are old friends of mine. I've known them for years. What was I to say if the worst had happened, how would I have explained? 'Eh, oh sorry hem, yes. I knew all about it, but Alasdair, he's dead!' They would have never forgiven me. It goes without saying I would have never forgiven myself." He took a deep breath.

"When I saw you laying it that bed… forcing my way past that Rena woman standing guard. Your face flushed, shrunken, dark circles under your eyes, your cheek bones sticking out, emaciated, I thought it was too late. It was only when I saw you were still breathing I realised it wasn't a corpse I was looking at." He shook his head in disbelief.

Alasdair tried again to interrupt Harry's lecture… but he didn't get the chance. Harry was on a roll.

"The 'piece de la résistance'… your arm… hand, suspended over your head in mid-air, tied to a ridiculous clothes pole!" Harry stopped, realising how 'ridiculous' that sounded. Harry had run out of steam, he'd said what he had come to say, expressed his feelings… got it off his chest.

"Humph, thank goodness it's over."

Together they laughed. Remembering the 'pole' dispelled the tension in the room since Harry had begun his oratorio. Alasdair was relieved that Harry's speech had come to an end, because at times he'd bit his lip, to stop laughing at the sight of the portly old man strutting up and down the living room like some university professor delivering a lecture. There was a lot of truth in what the old man had said, but Alasdair did not want it rammed down his throat. He felt guilty enough, he knew the risk he had taken, but it was his choice, no one else's and he didn't need to be reminded.

Harry, all five foot-five of him, had taken advantage of what little height he had and had towered over Alasdair during his sermon. Alasdair had shuffled down in his chair, pretended penitence and guilt. He swore he would never do anything so stupid again. But Alasdair would never know of the sleepless nights, as Harry walked the floor struggling with his conscience; afraid, on the one hand, that the young man might die and whether to tell his parents on the other. What a dilemma; thank God it was over.

Harry's mood continued to improve when he heard the tea trolley from the kitchen. Rena appeared, trolley rattling, a pot of steaming hot tea, to be served in Audrey's Forman's second best fine bone-china. A plate of home-made scones, butter, whipped cream and strawberry jam on it. A veritable feast that brought a broad smile to his face, Harry loved his food. That was obvious from his ever increasing middle. The fact the buttons on his waistcoat were stretched to their limit, ready to burst open any minute, was proof of that. "Enjoy my food," he would announce to anyone who would listen, mainly his longsuffering wife. "and a wee dram as well of course."

"Will a' pour Doctur?"

"Eh, no thank you Rena, I will do it myself to prove to Dr Henderson that I am perfectly capable of using both of my hands. You have done enough, it's time you went home to your family."

He bade Rena goodbye, got up and ushered her out of the room by the elbow to make sure she left. Along the hall to the front door, he waved and tried to shut the inner glass door. Rena got the better of him, turning to put her foot in the door. "Just leave a' they dirty dishes, I'll attend to them in the mornin'." He nodded assent and went back to deal with Harry.

Chapter 32

"LET ME POUR Harry, demonstrate how well my hand has healed... see?" Alasdair announced once Rena had left. He didn't need to offer the plate of scones after he poured the tea... Harry had helped himself and was trying to lick a large dollop of cream from the end of his nose.

"It's a great pity that my 'physician' must remain anonymous – the treatment was worthy of a paper to the BMA. Believe me, I would never have survived but for such devotion. But something struck me, Harry. Something I had not thought of... how can I put it, the application shall we say... of psychiatry or rather the power of suggestion?"

Harry raised an eyebrow. Maybe Alasdair was still febrile, hallucinating. He started to mutter about psychiatry not being an exact science.

"No listen, I listened to you, you listen to me. I admit I don't think the person caring for me had any idea they were using the power of suggestion, almost like hypnosis. All I remember was being fed the will to live, not to give up. Even at my lowest, the pain excruciating, mind-numbing, I never wanted to relieve my suffering by dying... I knew I was being motivated to live. Well, physician heal thyself, so with a little help both physical and psychological I did." He waited for that to sink in, but Harry was pre-occupied with taking a bite of another scone, not apparently paying much attention.

Harry had been chewing the scone in his mouth. "What do you mean... hypnosis, a soothsayer, a gypsy... cross her palm with silver did you...? What kind of fool do you take me for? I don't believe in all that mumbo- jumbo." As he spoke he sprayed crumbs into the air.

"Maybe I did, maybe I didn't, but I am the living proof, whatever you think. I know I'll have a scar on my palm for the rest of my life. Maybe that's not a bad thing; it'll remind me to be more careful in future. But the proof's in the eating of the pudding! Look, I swear it will not be long before I have full movement of my hand and fingers." He demonstrated, wiggling his fingers in the air.

"I still can't believe it. What worried me the most, Harry, was not being able to use my hand. It would have been worse if I had gone into hospital as you wanted. I am certain that when the examining surgeon saw the infection creeping up my arm, he would not have hesitated to amputate and rightly so. A one-armed Doctor, no use to himself never mind anybody else. Ha! That's a fine joke!" Silent now, he thanked his lucky stars and Janet.

"Okay," Alasdair continued, "I agree it's not completely healed and I've been instructed to keep massaging a cream that was made for me into the wound. Also, to exercise my hand and fingers, like this," he demonstrated, "as if I was squeezing a ball and guess what? I was out this morning sitting in the sunshine, holding my palm upward to the sun. Apparently direct sunlight has... healing properties, what do you think of that, eh? Well?"

"What cream?"

Alasdair showed Harry the cream, but not too close to his nose. Alasdair did not want disparaging remarks on how it smelt like pig's fat. But Harry started to take an interest, dipped a finger in the jar, didn't remark on the smell and even rubbed some on the back of his hand to try it out.

"Who made the cream?"

"Ah, that must remain confidential." Alasdair made it clear he would say no more and changed the subject to distract Harry from further questioning.

"I am thinking of getting some of the creams and cleansing liquids analysed... I will get old Mc Dade to make them up for me. I am certainly going to use them on my own patients when the need occurs... Would you like me to get some for you Harry... for your own patients?" he asked, a benign look on his face.

"No...m-m-m... yes, I will think about it. Well-well, it's all over, forget creams, lotions, better to put it behind you, start afresh in the morning." Harry stroked his handle-bar moustache and beard. "By God you had a close shave lad, you don't know how close to death you probably came. I take my hat off to whoever it was took care of you." He thought: 'It looks unlikely Alasdair will ever confide in me, tell me who the man was, but he should be on his knees with gratitude to him.' The room had gone quiet. Alasdair knew what the wise older man was thinking... a miracle had taken place.

"Harry, do you think for one minute I don't realise how lucky I've been? I am a doctor for heaven's sake. But I keep telling you my recovery was not entirely down to luck, but the intensive care I received from someone who must remain anonymous. That had a great deal to do with it and I insist we do not discuss this any further."

Warmed by the fire, Harry sank back contentedly in the comfortable leather chair. Having demolished the scones, washed down with several cups of Ceylon tea, he now puffed on his pipe, at times sipping the whisky Alasdair had served up at the older man's request.

"Now it's you that is the lucky one," Alasdair smiled. "I always have a bottle in the sideboard for my dad when he comes to visit, I am not that fond of the stuff."

"Ach! You're too young to enjoy a wee dram; my father always said it was the elixir of life, kept him young in his old age. Some day you will saviour it as your dad and I do, a wee dram of himself never hurt anybody," he nodded.

"Yes but it loosens the tongue. Let me make myself quite clear, Harry, you will not disclose to my father any details on or off the golf course, or to my mother; this stays between us. I want no repercussions, no accusations, it was my choice and my choice alone to stay here and die in my own bed. Admitted to hospital… my mother weeping and wailing at my bedside, it doesn't bear thinking about. Think I might have wanted to die just to get away from her. I repeat, drunk or sober, you will not…"

"Tell Audrey?!" Harry sat bolt upright as if he had been electrocuted and almost choked on his whisky. Alasdair got up and gave him a few thumps on the back till he got his breath back, then sat down.

"It would be more than my life's worth to tell your mother… an abscess… infection creeping up your arm… you insisting you stay home, do you think I am crazy?" He felt aggrieved that Alasdair thought he could not trust him. He changed the subject.

"But what about the rest of the situation here… all this?" He swept his hand out over the room at the same time.

"What do you mean, the rest of all this?" Alasdair repeated.

"Oh come on, you know very well what I mean, something's changed since I first visited you. There's more to it than an abscess on the hand… more than lotions and potions. The house, its spotless… the grass has been cut, garden weeded and that's the second time I have seen that woman here, what's her name, Rena? Making scones, wanting to serve tea. Believe me, I'll be letting Audrey find out for herself, I'm certainly not going to tell her, but do me a favour, let me know when she's coming. I'll make damn certain I am away on holiday, better still… out of the country. So what happened?"

Harry leant forward, waiting.

Alasdair tried to think of something… shook his head as if sad. "It's the women in my life Harry, they have taken over… I have been womanized!"

"Womanized? What kind of word is that? Yer haver'n man… been hitting the dope again? Wait a minute, I know what's happened. You've met somebody…,you've got a girlfriend!" Harry grinned, leant towards Alasdair.

"No I don't!" Alasdair snapped.

That wiped the smile off Harry's face. Somewhat taken aback at the sharpness of Alasdair's reply, he must have hit a nerve.

"I didn't mean get married, right now. It's not like you to snap at me, Alasdair, you usually enjoy a joke."

"You didn't deserve that Harry, I apologise, and I know you have my best interests at heart. But, believe me the care I have received from the women in the community has been overwhelming. Go look in the pantry, more soup, more food than I can ever hope to eat. I don't need a wife." He hoped he was making sense distracting Harry from thinking there was someone special in his life.

"I thought I was coping… the practice… the house. I wanted to prove to my mother… to the world I could be independent, needed no one; I was invincible. But I was wrong and that probably contributed to my injuring my hand… that was carelessness. In my defence, I was probably tired and not paying attention, too tired to cook, do housework, cut grass… I didn't want to admit I was struggling, didn't want my mother to know. She was the one I fought to become independent." Had he convinced Harry?

"Fact is… the number of patients are increasing weekly. I listened to what was being said by those around me. I gave in, accepted their help, but very much on a business level. You know Harry, I am beginning to enjoy it. I don't have to think of what I'm going to eat for dinner or when I've time to do the washing. Shirts don't wash and iron themselves. Rena, that's the woman you met, she takes care of everything. I might even get time for a round of golf one of these days and there's one other thing I'd really like to do…"

"And what's that laddie?"

"I want to go out on one of the fishing boats, the summer line fishing will do. See how my patients earn their living." Alasdair had twisted round in his chair, looking out on the river, to avoid looking at Harry as he was about to make a statement, so Harry would understand in no uncertain terms…

Harry interrupted. "No point looking for trawlers today, it's the Sabbath, nothing moves on a Sabbath with the locals… might bring bad luck. I'm sure they will be glad to take you on shorter trips, line fishing in the summer. And you're tall dark and handsome, not a red-haired female!"

Alasdair decided to turn back round. "Listen to me, I don't want a woman girnin' in my ear. I've lived long enough with my mother to put me off marriage for… life… The last thing I need is a wife." But he *did* want a wife, he wanted Janet.

"Aye, I understand what you mean, but there's comfort in having someone to come home to on a winter's night. That aside, it looks like I've made a mistake giving you this practice; I should have moved here myself, let you take the one in Leightham. Seems your patients have taken you to their hearts, hold you in high esteem. I don't think patients would have done half as much for me." He raised his bushy eyebrows, nodded decisively.

"But you're not as young or as good looking as I am."

"Cheek!"

The two men sat staring into the fire, thinking over the afternoon. Alasdair frankly wished Harry would start making tracks... go home. Perhaps on account of the warmth of the fire, the whisky, or the conversation, Harry's eyes began to close, his chin dropping onto his chest and he nodded off. 'Oh Lord no,' Alasdair put up a silent prayer which was answered. The Lord works in mysterious ways.

The front door opened and closed and footsteps in the hallway could be heard coming towards the sitting room. Someone else had let themselves in, for the third time that day. Alasdair raised his eyes towards heaven. Harry heard the front door opening and was now wide awake.

Alasdair's friend, the right Rev Tom McDougall, the local Parish Church minister, entered the room. Tom wasn't your average man of the cloth, no tailcoats and gaiters for him... oh no; he had his own ideas about the Ministry. Many of his views and beliefs led to active debate with his contemporaries. He was not the university's usual divinity student; his views conflicted at times with his professors. He was of average height, good-looking rather than handsome, wore the cloak, cassock and scarf for Sunday services, weddings, christenings and funerals only. At times he felt a bit of a hypocrite when he toned down many of the church's accepted views in his sermons. He'd been welcomed by the villagers and many a day during the week Tom could be found in the town centre mingling with his parishioners, wearing an ordinary suit and dog collar. He hated the trappings of ministry; felt it led to a barrier between him and those he was there to help. The Parish Church was the Church for the people of the parish. Tom never discriminated between any man and his beliefs irrespective of Church Temple or Synagogue. Tom did not believe in Hell fire and damnation or bible thumping in people's faces. He'd only been a couple of years in his ministry, but was well-liked and respected. Listen and administer were Tom's ethics. But God rewarded Tom with the arrival of his friend Alasdair. The two professional men got on well with each other.

"Was passing... just thought I'd do a quick visit, Alasdair," he explained, "See how you are. How you feel about returning to work tomorrow? I can tell you the whole village is delighted... no disrespect, Dr Henderson."

"None taken," Harry growled.

"I warned them at church, urgent cases only. Once word got out you had the flu, I have been plagued with enquiries... when were you returning to work? It was grim at first when I had no answers to give. I think you're very popular, Alasdair, especially among the ladies." Tom smiled. "I am joking. Alasdair, their concerns were genuine, prayers have been said for your full recovery. Looks like they have been answered."

Hearing this, Harry snorted softly, reached for his handkerchief and pretended to blow his nose. 'Mind you, the minister seems a decent, honest sort of chap,' Harry thought, 'Quite genuine, in fact.'

"Well I am touched... I've only been here a few months." Alasdair shrugged his shoulders, pleased; it confirmed he'd made the right decision moving into general practice.

"Don't worry about me being overworked, I know Rena's got it all in hand; she will vet the patients as they arrive, sort out the genuine from the well-wishers. I hope she insists they take their well-meaning pots of soup home with them." The two young men smiled at the thought of Rena on guard duty.

Harry, wide awake, realised he was out-staying his welcome; it was time to go. If he stayed much longer it would be he who was suffering his wife 'girnin' in his ear. But that wasn't the only reason; Harry did not have much time for ministers. His local minister as far as he was concerned was a right canting, sanctimonious pain in the backside. He found it hard to keep his mouth shut when their visits to a dying patient clashed. Harry found it hard to believe any family could take comfort from being told the dying person had been such a good Christian they would go straight to heaven. Many were young children, had not done any harm to anyone in their young life, how could it be otherwise?

"Well that's me away," Harry announced. Tom helped to pull him out the chair, seeing the older man struggle to get to his feet. Harry nodded his thanks to the minister, straightened his tie, pulled his waistcoat down and buttoned his tweed jacket. Ready, he moved towards the corridor, stretching his legs that had stiffened while he'd been sitting. Alasdair almost heaved a sigh of relief at the old man's departure but Harry turned back one more time.

"Forgot to tell you, while you were off sick I was called in to see a patient of yours, a Mrs Agnes Gardner, or Gairdner, as the locals say. Her mother met me at the surgery door last week to ask advice. The woman was worried sick about her daughter. It seems she delivered about six weeks ago and according to her mother had not recovered. I believe it was a breech delivery and Agnes was in labour for several days. I did a house-call and gave Agnes a thorough examination but could find nothing physically wrong with her. The baby was fine... thriving. But it puzzled me, I felt something's was not right; it's difficult to diagnose in one visit. Maybe some kind of depression, a post-delivery psychosis, maybe? Anyway I decided to take a chance and suggested she might need admission to the asylum for a bit of shock therapy..." Harry shrugged his shoulders, unwilling to admit he had little experience of the condition. "I would keep an eye on her, Alasdair, as I have been unable to do a return visit. I must go; sorry talking shop, Mr Mc Dougall, but it's important to give a report when one Doctor is handing over to another."

Tom nodded, acknowledging the older man's apology.

"Thank you Harry, I remember that delivery, it was just before I went off sick. I'll get old Tam to drive me to any house-calls next week. My hand's tender and I don't want to handle the reins yet, but with Tam driving I will manage fine.

Yes, she will be one of the first I'll visit. I remember the family and will never forget Mrs Gardner's delivery, I was there." How could he forget, the first time he saw Janet! 'They say you never forget the first time you meet... love at first sight? How true.'

"No need to see me out, I know the way... without sounding sentimental, Alasdair, it's grand to have you back, laddie. I can't tell you how relieved I am you've recovered. I don't know who it was took care of you but if I were you I would be on my knees with gratitude to the person who saved your miserable carcass; I doubt I could have done any better myself. Cheerio!" Smiling, Harry left with a kindly nod and a wave of the hand.

Chapter 33

"ALASDAIR," Tom said, "I've prayed for your recovery, but the truth is… I don't know what I would have done or managed without you and your friendship. I don't know how I would have consoled myself, if anything had happened… maybe I was being selfish."

"Selfish?"

"Yes, selfish. What would I have done without my Friday night chess partner… no chance of revenge? I know… I know that's why you pulled through, just to teach me a lesson!" Tom felt confident he could tease Alasdair knowing the man had recovered and was now out of danger. "If I remember rightly, you won the last time, had me at check-mate in an hour!" Tom's joke had little effect.

"Don't worry; I can see you're becoming fit for nothing, but your bed… I won't get the chess board out tonight," Alasdair responded with a wan smile.

"I won't stay, but I have a confession to make."

"A confession… you're the priest!" he responded to Tom's light-hearted banter.

"I came under the false pretence of enquiring as to how you were… actually I came to escape the din in the Manse. It used to be a quiet peaceful place, but since the baby was born, the noise… it increases daily. What a pair of lungs that young lady has, she'll be an opera singer. I kid you not Alasdair, nothing prepares you for the birth of your first child… I can't believe the disruption; it goes on day and night. Help me out here, Alasdair… a question; you're a Doctor. Why do babies have to get up in the middle of the night? My friend, I will be renting that empty bedroom upstairs, to get peace to write my sermons and catch up on some sleep."

Tom paused to catch his breath.

"I love baby Helen dearly… that's her name after her great-great grandmother. Let me tell you her story. I believe you have an interest in Russia and Russian history. Well, it transpires that Isabel's family have a connection with Moscow and St Petersburg. Yes. it seems one of her ancestors was in Moscow during the Napoleonic wars. Did you know my wife's family are from the far north of Scotland? Apparently there have been strong ties between the two countries over the centuries. Anyway one of her ancestors was an adventurous young woman named Helen MacDonald who insisted on travelling alone to Moscow. Her family were horrified; she was there when Napoleon attacked the city. Seemingly she fled to St Petersburg with other well-to-do Muscovites. Loved it so much she refused to return home." Tom again stopped for a breath…

"Isobel's family seem to have a fascination with St Petersberg. I think Isobel's mother said at our wedding she has a cousin of her's still there. I'd love to visit someday but that will need to wait till we retire."

Tom could see this wasn't getting him anywhere. He decided to joke to see if that would work… all else had failed, why not?

"Well, like I was saying before I launched into that rather boring sermon about my wife's ancestors… Ah yes, that wee monkey Helen has me wrapped round her little finger and doesn't she know it! I am in agony, Alasdair!" Tom feigned a look of pain and started to rub his shoulder. "I have been infected with… 'Parrot Syndrome'… 'Long John Silver's Disease'. Seems it's an ailment all new fathers get! The symptoms are worse in the middle of the night… Oh, just remembered, that's what I came to ask you, so before I forget, Isabel and I want you to be Godfather."

Alasdair had paid little attention to Tom, too busy wallowing in his own self-pity since Harry left. Luckily he had heard the last part of the conversation…

"Tom, I am sorry, my thoughts… elsewhere, but what was that you were saying… parrot syndrome?" He frowned. "I've never heard of it… must have missed that lecture, what are the symptoms? I'll look it up – have a recent compilation of *Materia Medica*. Information for a G.P. in manual form; at last they acknowledge we can't remember everything. Perhaps it's mentioned in one of the articles, but if I can't help I know where I can probably… some cream… muscular…" Alasdair said tailing off.

"You really haven't been listening, have you? I am trying to lighten a one-sided conversation, Alasdair. I made it up, there is no such thing as Parrot Syndrome or Long John Silver's disease as far as I am aware… the only Long John's I know are men's underwear."

"Lord, Tom, I have been on another planet, but I remember old Tam saying something about your baby being born. Congratulations, I am pleased for you both. I would be honoured, delighted to be Helen's Godfather. Although I don't know much about being one… something about a silver Christening mug?... I'll get my mother to organise that." He frowned at the thought of having to contact her.

"Don't worry, Alasdair, all you do is turn up at the Church; I'll let you know in advance which Sunday. But it brings with it serious responsibilities… as Godfather. If anything happens to Isabel and me… you have to bring Helen up, adopt her…"

"Adopt!" Alasdair gasped. He'd heard that all right.

"Don't panic Alasdair, neither Isobel nor I plan to die anytime soon, at least not till we have had our tea. I am trying to cheer you up, you are making it very hard for me." Tom began to think maybe he should just say his farewells and go home. No, he would stay a while.

"So to continue what I was saying before the Godfather bit. Let me explain to you, because I wouldn't like you to miss-diagnose someone with the same symptoms I have. 'Parrot Syndrome' – I made it up in the middle of the night. It's when you throw one of those muslin square things on your shoulder and then you throw, I mean," he corrected himself, "place the baby over it... you know, like the parrot in Long John Silver, then walk up and down hoping it gets the baby to sleep." Tom gave a demonstration of the action, tapping his shoulder. 'I know there is something on his mind and it has nothing to do with his illness. He needs to talk about something or rather someone and I know who, but how to get him to open up?'

Tom realised it was no use, Alasdair was only half listening. 'This one-sided conversation is hard work and it's getting us nowhere,' he thought. 'Go for it man, be brave. The worst that could happen is that he'll throw you out!'

"There is a cloud hanging over your head, my friend... and it's not about your injured hand."

Alasdair looked up. Tom would never forget the expression on his face...of despair.

"You're in love with her... with Janet, aren't you, Alasdair?" Tom blurted out.

"How do you know...? You're guessing?"

"I'm not guessing, I knew the minute I saw you together. Unknown to you both I observed the two of you about two weeks ago. I'd come up the stair, I stood outside your bedroom door for a few seconds. Neither of you heard or saw me, but I saw both of you. There was no doubt, you love each other. The look on your faces in those few seconds said it all... I knew... you were in love. A few minutes ago when you thought there was something wrong with my shoulder... you were thinking of her. Such sadness; looks say more than words and they are unmistakeable. You can hide a facial expression but the eyes don't lie." Tom waited. "What are you going to do about it, Alasdair, what are you going to do about... Janet?"

"What do you think I am going to do, Tom, what the hell can I do?" Without thinking he spat out the next sentence: "Nothing... nothing to be done. Ha! Can you imagine my mother's face if I tried to introduce her to Janet? I can... Absolute horror! She would recoil as If I had tried to introduce her to a cobra, a street walker, a gypsy. Tell her I was engaged to a woman who doesn't even know her own name. God almighty, Tom, she would have a stroke. Forget it. My mother, her posh Morningside accent and friends..." He paused for breath.

"It would be like punishing Janet for something she hadn't done, had no control over; I can't do that to her. Tom listen, Janet has no idea who she is or how she came to Pittendreal, not any idea of how she got here. No papers, no documents, no evidence of who she might be, not even a surname. She tells me a sealed wooden box she had in her possession when she arrived, might hold a clue. I have tried... asked... begged her to let me open it. But she refuses, gets into a state, how can I describe it... sheer panic on the subject of that box. I will not force her and I don't have the courage to push her any further. I think she is afraid of its contents. But Tom, I love her so much, I owe her so much, I don't know what to do. I have heard that love can be painful, but this... this is excruciating and I have to learn to live with it!"

The two men sat together uncomfortable, but that didn't last long; it was interrupted by Alasdair hissing.

"The Lord giveth and the Lord taketh away, he gave me back my life and at the same time He has taken..."

"That's enough Alasdair! Stop feeling so damn sorry for yourself. Get a grip of yourself man!" Tom snapped.

Alasdair was shaken by Tom's reply, had hoped for a little more sympathy from the minister.

"By the way, Alasdair, damn is not a swear word, it's a blaspheme,' Tom said, trying to defuse the situation. "Look, you're still not a hundred per cent; give yourself time and be honest for both your sakes. Keep in mind the good people of the village, and they are good people, but if they got wind of an unmarried liaison between you and Janet..." Tom shook his head.

"It makes no difference to you, they might cluck their tongues in gossip, but they would get over it, they need you. But they would destroy Janet; she would be forced to leave the village. You know fine well what names they would hurl at her... they are not pleasant. Do you want to be responsible for her having to leave? Think man, she is a decent human being with an incredible gift. It puzzles me how she acquired the knowledge. Let's face it, her cures are simple herbal remedies... not the sanctimonious laying on of hands. Alas, to be honest, she doesn't strike me as being from the peasant class... quite the opposite, which might even bode well with your mother. Wait... gain her confidence and get that box opened, it's your only hope for a future with her." Alasdair knew he was right.

"You have made it quite clear you have no intentions of proposing marriage, am I right?" Alasdair nodded. "Then do the decent thing... let her go, don't risk soiling either of your reputations, she is worth better than that. A cheap affair? Forget it... from what little I know of Janet, it would never happen. I doubt she would allow herself to become involved in a cheap tawdry affair." Tom stopped for a moment to let his words sink in. "One way or another I am sorry for you both, sorry to sound so negative and sympathy is not going to help. You know me, I rarely preach about the sanctity of marriage, but for the grace of God there goes I... it could be any one of us in your position. All I can say to you if you want my advice... as things stand... get over her. If you can't, learn to live with it... maybe in time..." Tom dropped his voice.

Tom tilted his head, as if looking for some response from Alasdair. 'I hope he doesn't become too bitter,' he thought. There was nothing more to be said. With a heavy heart Tom took his leave muttering something about returning on Friday for their game of chess.

Turning back into the vestibule at the front door, Tom looked Alasdair full in the face... there was nothing much left to say. He placed a hand on his friend's shoulder. "Time does heal Alasdair. God works in mysterious ways. I know that's cold comfort but in my limited experience nothing stays the same for ever."

Tom left, glad to be going home to his wife and new baby. Never again would he complain about the noise of the baby's crying. Raising his eyes heavenwards, he put up a silent prayer of thanks to the Lord for his own life and asked another favour... remember his friend.

Alasdair turned back into the house and locked the outer front door for the night. The house now still, deadly quiet. After so much activity in the last few weeks, this was the first time he was truly alone. He hadn't seemed to notice how quiet it was before his illness. Now he found it strange, a new experience. Alasdair returned to the sitting room and sat down in the old leather chair. Thinking over Tom's visit, he felt grateful for his friend's compassion and understanding. In some ways he felt sorry for the man. Tom had tried, but could not offer a solution other than a religious one. He would have to work it out for himself. In a strange way Alasdair felt at peace. For the first time he had been able to admit openly his love for Janet. It had been painful, but wonderful to get it off his chest. He'd brought it out into the open with his trusted friend.

Tom had not preached about the sanctity of marriage, Hell fire and damnation for sinners of the flesh, for that he would be eternally grateful. Tom was one of the best.

Alasdair felt drained, exhausted after his visitors. Getting up, with one last effort he pushed the tea trolley back to the kitchen, happy not to have to wash the dishes. Back in the sitting room he put a few more logs on the fire and searched for the newspaper Rena had brought him to read. 'God knows what Tom will think of me,' he thought, 'I never offered the man a cup of tea.' He thought back to their conversation. Everything the good man said was true... physician heal thyself! He'd have to work on that one. Sitting back into his favourite chair, he opened the newspaper and started to read. Within minutes it fell to the floor at the side of the chair. He had fallen into a deep sleep.

Chapter 34

ALASDAIR woke up, startled... cold and disorientated. He became aware of the silence, the stillness in the room. He felt very alone. He must have slept for hours. Now fully awake, he noticed the fire had almost gone out. What time was it? Standing up he stretched, putting his arms behind his head.

"Ouch!" he yelped. He felt a painful stab from his still tender left hand which reminded him to take it easy.

The clock on the mantelpiece told him it was seven. Looking out of the sitting room window, he saw the sun dipping toward the horizon.

The sun setting earlier and with autumn approaching, he suddenly realised life had gone on regardless, without him being aware of it. 'You have been out of it old man, been out of touch with reality, never mind the season.'

The room was cold. Better put a few more logs on the fire before it goes out altogether.

"I'm hungry; it feels good to want to eat.' Alasdair bent down to the basket at the side of the fire and found a few logs and some kindling which he threw onto the dwindling embers. 'I've no intention of staying downstairs for much longer, so these will need to do for tonight. I'm damned if I'm going to get wood, I'll get Rena to fill the basket tomorrow... what am I saying, get Rena! The woman's psychic, she'll have the basket filled and the fire lit before I get down to breakfast." He stopped. "God almighty! I'm talking to myself! Well there's no one to hear so you can swear all you like Alasdair. Oh! Damn is a blaspheme, not a swear word according to Tom!"

Tired, he slumped back down in the chair… It was all over; a feeling previously unknown to him, a sense of loss assaulted him. He'd heard of some patients experience a lowering of the spirits when they survived some trauma in their lives, but he never thought it could happen to him.

"You have to face up to it, you're clinging to the past… you're afraid to let go… afraid of the future? By this time next week it will seem as if the last few weeks have never happened, a bad dream best forgotten. Stop thinking like a patient, you have to start thinking like the doctor. Do you want to go on feeling like this… miserable? No… then do something about it!"

This reasoning didn't help the idea of being alone in the house… quite the opposite. He began to miss the hubbub of daily life; missed the people and wanted to take comfort from his memories, just sit and reflect on those strange surreal days. He was afraid he might forget and for some unexplained reason didn't want to. But who in their right mind would want to remember? With facts staring him in the face, he had to acknowledge the enormous risk he'd taken with his life. In the cold light of day, was this what he was now feeling… a reaction to his stupidity? 'I could have lost my life,' he thought. 'I guess I wouldn't have known much about that. But the people I left behind, they would have had to suffer the consequences of my actions. But you survived, take comfort in that; draw a line under the past, it's over… live in the moment… tomorrow will take care of itself, go to sleep with a happy thought, think of something that made you smile… Isn't that what you would tell one of your patients? No, you would never have thought of that… that advice came from Janet, sane, sensible Janet.'

Looking back on the last month it wasn't all bad. One evening in particular he would never forget… the night he fell in love. After both the emotional and physical entwining of the body and mind, he had been willing to die… she had shown him heaven. He remembered other grim days when he thought he was on the ceiling looking down... as if he were out of his body, not just his mind. He sneered at himself... grateful to damn monkeys, he hadn't told Janet the truth... had lied to her to save her face, pretending he was hallucinating to save his own? Then he smiled at the memory of Janet and Rena rushing up the stairs, bursting into his bedroom and colliding in the doorway. Janet told him later they both thought they heard the death rattle coming from the room. 'I know I am not much of a singer but in my drugged state, the song wasn't coming from me, but from someone else. A Company... of Dragoons... came marchin'...doon! No wonder the girls panicked; thought they were hearing me Cheyne-Stoke breathing!' Alasdair smiled and shook his head. Sobering up, he remembered the old 'Dragon' who lived in Edinburgh. That wiped the smile off his face.

His thoughts turned to Janet. She was at his side day and night. Was it real? Each time he opened his eyes... was she there... was he dreaming? He'd survived a roller coast journey, ranting and raving, tossing and turning, sweat pouring down his face and through all that time Janet had sponged him, doing her best to keep his temperature down. Would he ever forget her kind hands...? With superhuman effort, she willed him to live... Janet never gave up. Now he was alone, facing a future without her. Was that why he was fixating on the times he had with her now? Was he ready for this...? Yes, he would miss the friendship. the closeness of those who had cared, but they were villagers, neighbours. In his darkest hours, throughout the fever the pain one constant presence... the one he could never repay... Janet.

"Stop it!" he shouted out loud. "You know fine well why you feel the way you do.... admit it!" He couldn't.

He got up, made his way to the kitchen to find out what Rena had left for supper.

'I'll have the sandwich,' he thought, 'I bet its cold boiled beef... yep, boiled beef, and it's like chewing string. What on earth do these people see in boiled beef; can't they roast a joint?'

Alasdair was in no mood to be magnanimous; normally he couldn't care less whether it was beef, ham or cheese as long as it was edible.

'I can't be bothered to heat up the soup.' He lifted the lid of the pan. 'Ugh! Just look at that layer of fat, it would make you sick!' He spoke out loud, not bothering to feel gratitude to his devoted housekeeper, who'd come in her day off to leave food for him.

Before Rena he would have had to fend for himself, probably had a bit of toast, but he had forgotten the past. Alasdair picked up the sandwich from the plate, bit into it and shuffled his way back to the sitting room, chewing on the way. Thankfully the logs had caught fire making the room seem a little brighter. Taking the poker in his free hand he prodded the logs and with some satisfaction stood watching the sparks fly up the chimney; then he sat down and took another bite. When he'd finished eating the sandwich, he turned to the side and put the empty plate on the side table. Looking at the glow from the fire he suddenly became aware of a sticky mess trickling from his hand to his shirt.

'Damn it, it's some sort of pickle or sauce she's put on the meat… thought it tasted better than usual.' He tried to lick the stuff off his shirt sleeve. 'Now I'll have to go back to the kitchen to wash it off!' For a second he felt ashamed of himself.

'When would the good fisher folk of Pittendreal ever be in a financial position to put roasts of beef on the table? You're selfish, think man… poor catches… money scarce. Every scrap of food eaten... no waste… you don't know how lucky you are. They don't have much choice in life, do they? You're a spoilt brat… you've eaten Rena's sandwich, show some gratitude. Be grateful to the woman, she's trying to do her best…" He shook his head, disgusted with himself. "Is this what your illness has done to you, unable to think of others? You've changed.

'Tom McDougal was right, you're feeling sorry for yourself,' he thought as he sponged his shirt at the kitchen sink. 'Then here's the perfect solution Alasdair, just run back to mummy; tell her you have not been well, you want to be petted, her little darling. Admit she was right, you were wrong.' He gave a sarcastic smile at the very thought… 'No problem, she would welcome me with open arms, but she would never let you forget she told you so…'

Returning from washing his hands, Alasdair wasn't sure what to do next.

'I need a cigarette.' He searched in his jacket pockets without success, 'I'll bet she's hidden them!' He remembered Janet's abhorrence at the smell of smoke in the house. 'Well it's not her house, it's mine… there you go again… get over her, she's gone… left you.' In the sideboard drawer at the back was the missing packet of Woodbine. Alasdair picked it up… took one out, stuck it in his mouth and returned to his chair.

'Blast her, where are the matches?' He couldn't be bothered to get up to look, so trying to light the cigarette from a smouldering log on the fire, nearly burnt his good hand in the attempt. In disgust he threw the cigarette onto the fire; it missed and it fell into the grate where it lay there, jeering at him. 'See, you can't even get a smoke in your own house without her permission!' He grinned. 'I always said she was a witch, maybe she put a curse on the cigarettes, or maybe she is trying to cheer me up!

'Well I didn't want a cigarette anyway.' He sat back pursing his lips, contemplating the immediate future… whether to sit staring into the fire or go to bed. Instead he reached over the side of the chair and fumbled for a few seconds to find the newspaper he'd dropped when he fell asleep earlier.

'I should be grateful for a bit of peace to read the paper and catch up with what's gone on in the world, then go to bed and try to get some sleep before I go back to work...' At least that was his plan, but fate ordained otherwise.

"I don't believe it!" he said out loud. "What now? Who the Devil's at the door, at this time of night?" Exasperated, he threw himself out of the chair at the second knock. "A patient? I'm not back at work till tomorrow; so maybe I should just ignore it. Well whoever's at the door they're persistent... I'll give them that."

Upright, irate, he threw the paper on the floor anticipating more visitors with their lectures... their useless advice! Still smarting from the tongue-lashing he took from Harry.... Tom McDougal telling him to get over his feelings, but not how... Let whoever's at the door wait, maybe if he ignored them they'd go away. He picked up the plate, went into the kitchen, bunged it in the sink with the other dirty dishes. In the hall he stopped, picked up the front door keys from the hall stand and deliberately taking his time, reached the stained glass inner door which he unlocked.

Walking over the tiled floor of the vestibule, he accidentally brushed against a castor oil plant in a large china planter, thinking that he must remember to get Rena to get rid of that eyesore. 'Some patient is going to knock it over and that china planter is going to smash... make a right mess. What's the use of decorative plants and ornaments in a doctor's surgery anyway? Alasdair, your gears are right out of sync! A plant! What does it matter, you're festering about nothing...

'God,' he realised, 'I'm beginning to sound like a right grumpy old bastard! Well, since you've decided to remain a bachelor... you had better get used to it.'

Slowly he maneuvered the heavy metal Victorian key into the keyhole. Turning it, scratching, grinding and complaining, till the lock finally gave way... 'Need to get old Tam to clean the rust out of it and oil it tomorrow,' Alasdair thought. He turned the handle, opened the door, intending to get rid of whoever was standing on the other side. He couldn't believe his eyes...

It was Janet, the love of his life!

Chapter 35

"I CAME TO... I wanted to see if... I don't know why I came!" Janet cursed her lame excuses for returning, but she just couldn't think of anything else to say why she was revisiting him.

Alasdair leant forward and took her hand.

"Come in, Janet, I'm delighted to see you, I felt like shooting myself... the silence was beginning to get to me."

"But I have no reason to take up your time now... I thought you might like Tam to return your clothes pole to George..."

"Rubbish, you came to discharge me from your care, like the caring professional that you are. Never mind the blooming clothes pole; I'm surprised Rena hasn't dealt with that already. Come in, don't stand on the doorstep like a stranger. I am about to have a cup of tea – will you join me?"

Janet gave a quick cursory glance to each side of the street before entering the house.

"Ah, don't worry, the neighbours are all in their beds by this time of night, no one is going to see you." His voice seemed to trail down the hall after him. Janet followed, closing the outer and vestibule doors behind her.

"Go into the sitting room, the fire's on; take your shawl off and make yourself comfortable. I will be only a few minutes – I'm going to put the kettle on.... oh no!" He put his hand out to prevent her following him into the kitchen. "My turn now to look after you; prove I am well, thanks to your care and show you what a good job you have done! I'm back to my old self."

'If only you knew the truth,' he thought. 'I'll never be my old self again.'

"Off you go." He ushered her towards the living room door.

Janet felt uncomfortable and started to doubt her motives for her visit. This was unfamiliar territory for her; she was no longer in charge as Alasdair was back on his feet, he didn't need her anymore. Why was she torturing herself like this? He would have sent for her if he needed her, but did he? No you fool he didn't, did he?

Janet removed her shawl, put it on the back of the couch, sat down and waited; at least he didn't keep her on the doorstep, she thought. She heard the rattle of cups and the saucers as Alasdair entered the room. Jumping up she went forward to help him; steadied his trembling left hand by placing her's gently over it. The impact of their hands touching made them look at each other as if they had received an electric shock. Falling back, Janet quickly removed her hand and looked away. Alastair cleared his throat… and returning to the kitchen he continued making the tea. Covering the pot with some ugly looking knitted tea cosy his mother probably got at a church sale, he returned to the sitting room to serve Janet.

"Sit down witchy, I remembered you don't take sugar in your tea!" He used the pet name he used when she nursed him and Janet smiled. He poured the tea for her, turning sideways to look at her. He grinned, adding the milk slowly to emphasise he had remembered she took milk and then he handed the cup to her. He poured one for himself then placed it on the side table beside his chair. But before he sat down, he turned back to face Janet who was still standing.

"Stop calling me witchy!" she laughed. "I don't have a black cat, so until I get one… no more names." The tension had disappeared.

"I know you don't have a cat, but look what animal thanks to you I have inside me… I am slowly morphing into a cobra; I have a snake creeping up my arm from one of your spells." He weaved his arm back and forth just like a snake in front of her.

"What!" she gasped.

He rolled up his shirt sleeve to expose his arm and hand. Right enough, it did look like a snake shedding its skin. His new healthy skin was discarding the old.

"Oh, don't worry." He saw her narrow her eyes, about to accuse him. "Don't panic, do you think for one minute I would dare forget to apply the cream. It's more than my life's worth not to. What else is in those spells and incantations…? Joking apart Janet, do you have any more, a new batch of cream? I can't return to work stinking of whale blubber. I think this lot's gone off." He held his hand out as if to let her smell it. "And before you ask, I was out this morning holding my hand up to the sunlight as instructed. What was that you were on about… the power of ultraviolet light?"

Janet nodded. "I'll send a new jar to you with Rena or Tam… never mind the light."

"Why don't you bring the cream?"

"No, I can't promise, I will be too busy… Rena will do it."

'Stop leading her on, that's not fair man; giving her false hope, this has to end tonight. You must make it quite clear you can only be friends. No, that's not possible… we can't stay friends either. What a lily-livered coward you are. God, what a mess…' He thrashed around in his mind for a solution to a nightmare.

"I come from Edinburgh, Janet… my mother," he began.

"Stop it! I know what you are going to say, spare me the details. You might say something you will regret. Please don't, I fully understand… *Doctor* Foreman." She emphasized his professional title… the old barriers rising between them. "I want to live in Pittendreal; I want to stay… never return to the past. Believe me, I feel safe, secure, accepted, I feel more confident, in my future than I have in a long time… No way would I jeopardise that. Old Tam is my saviour, my salvation. I would never leave him and even after what we have been through together... we can never be 'just' friends." She held her head up.

Alasdair was struck by what she had said and the manner in which she said it. Articulate, proud... 'You are a complete mystery Janet,' he thought, 'where the hell are you from? I'd bet my last pound you're no commoner.'

"All right, under the circumstances I agree, but if in future we are alone, I would consider it an honour if you would address me by my first name. There's little enough I can do to thank you... it's impossible to voice how I feel, there are no words to express... my gratitude." He shrugged his shoulders, dropped his head, ashamed how feeble these words sounded. "You saved my life," he added softly.

"I doubt that is going to happen, thank you for the honour, but from now on you're Dr Foreman in public or in private. I ask for no debts of gratitude, or thanks, I was just doing a job." Janet made a vow to herself to keep out of his way. "As far as the last few weeks are concerned, I am sure you have learnt your lesson and will be more careful in future. How many times would a community or your friends believe you had flu mid-summer, disappear for all of three weeks?" Janet's words were meant to convince Alasdair they were worlds apart and their relationship, whatever it had been, was at an end.

Alasdair sat silent, letting her speak, but could not bear to separate from her with this unhappy state of affair in his mind. He was loathe to part from her under the circumstances, as if they had quarrelled... fallen out with each other, when in truth they knew it was the opposite.

"Janet." She looked at Alasdair. "Have you ever wondered about your past, have you any idea where you might have come from?"

She sucked her breath in and visibly froze.

"That sealed box, have you never thought of opening it? It might hold a clue. It fascinates me Janet, you fascinate me, I am intrigued, puzzled."

He thought: 'Your features, I have seen them before, but I can't think where, maybe a painting... a portrait. Someday I'll remember.' He frowned trying to think where, and her teeth... the twisting canine, slight overshot jaw! 'Enough Alasdair, give up, do yourself a favour, this is going nowhere.'

Janet had no desire to discuss her past; she only wanted to sit a little longer by the fire; make a memory, take in every detail; remember his handsome face, deep-set hazel eyes and sharp, prominent cheekbones. His long hard muscular legs, firm buttocks, the physical response she had felt when she touched him, craved and longed for his hands on her body. She doubted this would ever happen.

She wanted the memory of every single moment engraved in her heart for ever. But his words had jerked her unwilling back to the present.

"No! I never will open that box. Alasdair, since I have been living in Pittendreal, my dreams, no, some would say nightmares, have lessened. I used to wake up soaked in sweat, trembling in fear, but had no memory of what I had dreamt or what I was afraid of, when I woke up. I don't want to remember my past. What would it accomplish?" Staring ahead and inviting no response, she continued. "I have no history... no family; I don't know where I was born or how I came to be in Scotland. Alasdair, I am terrified at the very thought of opening that box, it scares me to death. The only vague memory I have... is running away from something and someone pulling my hand." She closed her eyes for a second. "I know I must have been running, because in my dreams I am fighting for breath. It is very dark, flashes of bright light, loud noises. Someone had my hand... then no one... no one. Please, enough," she pleaded. "Stop!"

Alasdair had no idea his words would cause such a reaction. Moved by the pitiful sight in front of him he went over, sat on the couch beside her. Taking the teacup out of her hand which had been shaking with every word she uttered, he put it down and took her hand in his good one, casually encircling her trembling shoulders with the other.

"Sometimes when I see that box under my bed, I have a strong desire to take it... walk to the end of the pier and throw it in the river."

Still holding her hand, Alasdair hoped his voice would calm her.

"Then we will leave well alone, but I beg you not to dispose of the one possession that might hold the answer, prove who you are. Sometime in the future you might feel strong enough, confident enough to want it opened. Whether it does contain clues to your past or not, that remains to be seen. Put it well out of sight. Bring it here if you wish, I can store it in the loft. You have my word of honour it will never be opened without your permission and certainly never without you being present. I think we both know, unless things change dramatically, that will not be any time soon." He tried to reassure her.

"Look Janet, I have little knowledge of the workings of the human mind but, from what you have just described, if I attempt to give you an explanation from a medical point of view, it might help you understand. Might help you come to terms..."

"I am not going crazy?"

"Of course not, far from it, you are one of the sanest people I know," he reassured her.

"I am almost certain you are suffering from a condition known as selective amnesia. It sounds as if you have been subjected to some trauma; possibly you witnessed a situation your brain could not handle. I would guess it was probably when you were quite young. Your brain was unable to cope, so it obliterated the memory... Shut out that which you can't or don't want to remember. The experience affects your sub-conscious... in a subliminal form, presents itself... in your sleep. When we are asleep we have no control over our dreams. When we awake we have no recollection of the dream or the past, a sort of psychological protection... no memory of the event. God only knows what you have been subjected to." Alasdair shook his head... sad, he could not offer a better explanation.

"Stop it!" Janet implored. "Enough! Don't you hear me? I don't want to know, I don't want to remember, a trauma that caused me so much pain... my brain has obliterated it from my memory, except when I sleep. My brain has chosen to shut out this... this... catastrophe... I am grateful not to remember. My name is Janet; Tam gave it to me the night he found me on his doorstep. I want no other name... no other life." She pushed his hand away.

Alasdair watched as a visible shroud of closure, an impenetrable curtain descended over her face and eyes. Her cloak of anonymity had returned. Janet, the local howdie, was regressing, returning to that role, the healer, the village untrained midwife and her blue eyes were once again expressionless, unreadable. She stood up, picked up her shawl from the back of the couch, draped it over her arm and within a few seconds was at the front door, Alasdair hard on her heels. Standing in the vestibule, she turned to face him and put her hand out.

"Goodbye... Dr Forman."

He took the hand that was formally offered and feeling her warm soft flesh... did not want to let go. Then making the fatal error of trying to enclose her hand in both of his, in that impenetrable fraction of a second she sensed what he was about to do and jerked her hand away.

"No! No! This is getting us nowhere, it's over… over, do you hear me! We must return to our everyday lives, forget this ever happened, put it behind us… and you're right, I came to discharge you from my care. You once said I was a witch, maybe you are right… maybe I can read what's in people's minds. But what you give with your hand… say with your eyes… you take way with your mouth. It hurts, your dishonesty hurts."

To the onlooker Janet appeared unemotional, even cold, but inwardly Janet was suffering. How did she let herself become involved with this man? She raged at herself: 'Let him go, it's useless.' Her shawl round her shoulders, she made her way through Alasdair's front garden to the main road, paused for a moment but did not look back. Squaring her shoulders, she walked into the night… out of Alasdair's life. The only thing on her mind, to get home to the sanctuary of the little cottage… safety. Tam would be waiting. 'But you have to have hope Janet… nothing stays the same forever, maybe someday… maybe…'

Alasdair, smarting at her words, stood pensively and watched till Janet was out of sight. 'I should have told her the truth; she would have understood how things are. Instead, you wimp, you made pathetic excuses… my mother's to blame? What must she think of me?

Sad, he locked the outer front door, then the glass one. The key in the lock was silent now, reflecting his mood. Or perhaps he just chose not to hear. Deep in thought, he resolved to visit the library in Edinburgh, dig out modern history books, and see what he could find regarding wars and catastrophes in Eastern Europe. He knew there had been continuous conflict between Austria and Hungary, for many centuries. But none fitted the time for Janet's possible birth. He tapped his teeth with a forefinger, deep in thought.

'She cannot be more than twenty years old... less? What upheaval in Eastern Europe, or further afield perhaps, even Russia, would cause a well-to-do family, or even minor royalty, to flee their home with such disastrous result? She is too young to be affected by the Crimea... it had to be something else.'

Then it dawned on him, and he thumped his forehead with a clenched fist. "You fool," he said out loud, "you cretin, a medical man! Disease! An outbreak, cholera, typhoid, take your pick. If I remember rightly there was an epidemic in Russia around the time she might have been living there. Perhaps that's the explanation. Who knows, but that makes sense..."

Strangely comforted, Alasdair went back to the living room, walked to the window; stood a few moments looking out over the river. A calm still night, golden ripples on the water from the last of the sun's rays; clouds tinted pink, promised a good day tomorrow. He reached up to close the curtains.

'How do I go to bed with a happy thought now... tell me, Janet. Look what I have done... Betrayed the one decent person I know... for what? Kowtowing to society, condoning their values, their cold principles, you put your parents before honesty, betrayed your feelings and that of another's... hypocrite! Enjoy your self-imposed solitude, Alasdair, you deserve it.'

Alasdair reached up to close the curtains. 'How symbolic, closing the curtains, closing a chapter in my life. No turning back. Did I have another option? I think not. But until we live in a very different world from this one... can I, dare to hope?' He sighed. Another time, another place, perhaps. For the present he would have to endure the ear-splitting noise of... of self-imposed silence. Curtains closed, he went upstairs.

Many years would pass before Alasdair and Janet would come together again under different circumstances.

But morning comes and the curtains are opened once more... even after the darkest night.

BOOK ONE

Part Two

Introduction

LOOKING BACK on that last visit to my great aunt before my summer holiday, I remembered it had been a gruelling winter of day and night shifts. I had been ready for a holiday, to lie on a beach somewhere and soak up the sun. I assured my aunt before I left that I would be back as soon as I could. Unfortunately after I returned, I had to attend further training courses down south, so I knew it was unlikely I'd get back before August. Great Aunt Jane had assured me we would begin Alice's life story in earnest.

I remember lifting my handbag, fumbling as usual for my car keys and Aunt Jane following me down the hall to the front door, which was unusual for her. She stood watching me get into my car and head down her tree-lined drive. On impulse I stopped the car, got out, ran back and put my arms round her shoulders. She was standing stiff, proud as always, but I could not resist whispering in her ear: "I love you, Aunty." I swear that old body softened... not the cantankerous old besom any longer. Long may it last, I thought.

Returning to the car I continued my journey, vowing on my return I would demand to know more about my great aunt's own life.

Why did she not speak in the local dialect and where did all her magnificent possessions come from? I wondered if she would tell me or accuse me of prying... but I felt it was worth the risk and if she refused..., well, so what, I had the next instalments of her story to look forward to.

I had no idea what the next chapters would reveal, but I was then to understand what she meant by the people, the history and background of the picture she was painting in her story for me. I'd almost felt sorry to leave her.

That feeling did not last long as I found myself with old friends lying on the beach soaking up the Texan sunshine.

Chapter 1

FEELING more than a little emotionally wrung out, I had been glad to leave my aunt's house at the start of the summer holidays. Many of the subjects we had covered to date, although interesting from a medical point of view, had not even begun to tell me about Leightham House, or Alice. Prolonged breach deliveries, septicaemia, no antibiotics and patients with out-of-body experiences while under the influence of drugs were well documented, and hardly pertinent to the life story of Alice and Leightham House. I'd made the assumption Alice was the new-born baby but that as yet was to be confirmed. I had to admit I loved the story of Janet the howdie and Alasdair, however irrelevant to her tale it might be. It made me look at my great aunt through different eyes. However Aunty had thrown in some odd statements before I left, perhaps just to keep me interested in the couple, such as… why did Janet inadvertently cross herself, use sacred words? Was she Catholic or from one of the orthodox religions, and most intriguing, what was inside that box?

I wondered why she did not want to read what I had written. Perhaps she had good reason not to want to see her memories in black and white. I had also experienced a feeling of *déjà vu* as I wrote, sitting in the bay window of the sitting room. I had told her I felt as if I was actually in the picture and was not just the frame of it, but I could not explain why her story had affected me like this.

Her reply had been for me not to become emotionally involved with the characters, fact or fictitious. More confusing still, I was to reserve judgment until I heard all and was given to understand that I might wish I had not been so curious. She had also warned me, we would not always stay with the people of Pittendreal; nor would we always stay in the fishing villages as we follow Alice's story. Now I wanted to press on and get the answers – no more procrastinating.

However, I would have to tell her that there were a couple of changes in my own life and put it to her there was good and bad news. The bad: I had changed my job and was going to work in Community Health back in the city and had decided to commute thanks to the new road bridge. The good news: I was free every weekend, so I would be able to spend all day Sunday with her if she was agreeable, and perhaps we could accomplish a lot more in a shorter time. I was keen to hear what she thought of this new arrangement.

In the proverbial twinkling of an eye I was glad to be home and driving along the coast road. Familiar landmarks greeted me and the dry stone walls on either side of the road reminded me to drive on the left-hand side, after weeks driving on the right. Fields of ripening corn, waving in the late summer breeze seemed to say… your great aunt's waiting for you. Reaching the bend in the road past the source of my curiosity for so many years, there it was on the hill, Leightham House – the sun streaming through vacant windows, trees growing inside the ruin as if to say 'welcome home'. The derelict façade seemed to ask, why are you fascinated by my history? Then I wondered, why have I never thought of going to look inside the ruin? There is no reason not to; no 'Keep Out' signs anywhere… but the very thought made the hair on the back of my neck stand up.

Turning into the stone pillared entrance of Aunt Jane's broad tree-lined drive, in spite of the number of times I've driven up it, I never forgot the feeling, the anticipation; the thrill of arriving, wondering where Aunt Jane's story would take me. There's no an answer to that question, except wait and see. Parking the car at the front entrance, I grabbed my tote-bag off the back seat and slung it over my shoulder and slammed the car door shut. No need to lock the car, never anyone around to steal it. I ran up the wide pillared entrance steps and rang the doorbell. Remember, I lectured myself, you are expected to sit down, be quiet and speak when spoken to. Like the good little girl Aunt Jane thought I still was? 'I have news for you Aunt Jane, I've grown up a lot in the last year and I think I know you well enough to start asking questions.'

"Hi Cathie, I'm back!"

Cathie reached out and hugged me and pulled me into the outer circular vestibule and then into the main hall.

"Come in, come in, it's grand you're back, lassie, and in one piece! That America's an awfy dangerous place." Her welcome was heart-warming.

"I hope I'm back in one piece." I patted myself down pretending all of me had arrived. We both laughed at my antics. "Yes, I'm all here Cathie. Believe me I got fed up living out of a suitcase. I wasn't just on holiday, I had to attend several medical seminars down south, on my return. It's great to be home. I feel as if I have been away for ages."

"Your Aunt Jane is waiting for you in the conservatory, been counting the days till you returned. She's harassed the poor Postie half tae death, demanding to ken if there were letters or postcards frae the States!" Cathie shook her head and clucked her tongue. "Between you an' me I think she's missed ye, but we'll no let on that I'v telt ye that," Cathie whispered.

"Really, Cathie, she's missed me, honestly? At times I felt she couldn't get rid of me fast enough. To tell the truth I've missed her. I never thought I'd hear myself say this, because I was terrified of her as a child, but I've grown to love the old dear and that will be our little secret."

"Ach, it's just her wey, her barks worse than her bite, pay nae attention tae the auld besom and what I'v just cried her... that'll be oor little secret as well. Your visits have become important tae your aunty, they've given her a new lease of life. I think she's gonna live forever!"

"Well I hope she lives long enough to finish the story she has been telling me."

"I'm telling you, since you left there's no been a minute's peace. I think you call it 'swatting'. She's been knee deep in auld newspapers, diaries, documents, photographs, the mess a' ower the dining room table and flair, you wouldna' credit it." Cathie raised her eyes to the heavens. "I'm gled I didna' have tae clear it awe up, but she wouldn't let me near... banned me from entering the room, did it a' hersel'."

"Never mind Cathie, it's in a good cause, but you probably already know half of the story she's been telling me."

"A' dinna ken onythin' aboot what goes on between the twa o' ye. She never discusses your visits wi' me and I'm not so sure I'd want tae ken. Sounds like it awe took place a long time ago, ask her to show ye the photograph she showed me a couple of weeks ago... a woman frae the last century... fair gave me the heebie-jeebies."

"The what!"

"Ach never mind, a fricht, couldna' sleep a' nicht for thinkin' on it, but you're changed, I hardly recognised ye."

"The changes are only skin deep," I assured her. "This will cheer you up, take your mind off ghosts and ghoulies. I brought you a wee minding from the States."

"That's awfy kind o' yae lassie, thinking about me, yae shouldna' hae bothered."

Exactly the self-effacing response I was expecting. Cathie ducked her head in genuine pleasure.

"Okay, here we go." Slinging my tote-bag off my shoulder and dumping it on the central hall table, undoing the drawstrings, I dug in and brought out a book. "An American Cookery Book, Cathie. *Better Homes and Gardens.* Since you and Aunty have a sweet tooth, I chose recipes for cakes and desserts."

A broad smile spread over Cathie's face.

"Also a set of cups," I said as I dug deeper into the bag and brought out a set of measuring cups. Cathie's facial expression was a picture of confusion.

"Cups, you mean for a cup o' tea like?" True enough I could see why she would think a tea-set an odd sort of gift.

"No Cathie, I'm dragging you into the twentieth century – measuring cups! Luckily I remembered to buy them at the last minute before I left the States; otherwise the cookery book would be useless. No one in the States uses scales to weigh ingredients for baking now; everyone uses cups to measure flour, margarine, that sort of thing," I explained, handing over the various sized baking utensils. Cathie stuck the cookery book under her arm and took the cups from me and looked at them suspiciously. I think she was wondering how to get margarine into a cup! I have to admit I was thinking the same thing.

"Wait till I tell you. I ran into 'Big Mike's Home Store' on the way to the Airport. Cathie! The minute I opened my mouth he kept asking me if I was Scotch! I tried to explain you drink Scotch and I was Scottish. It was hilarious! I don't think he'd ever met a native Scot before... then he turned and shouted to the back of the store: 'Kam'eer Billy-Bab... we got a Scotch gal in the store!' Then after big Mike and an even bigger Billy-Bab served me, they both shouted as I left, 'Ya'all cum back now ya hear?'

"What do you think of my Texan accent Cathie? Ach, never mind that... let me explain." The bemused look on Cathie's face regarding my Texan accent and the cups said it all; I might as well have spoken in Chinese and handed her a wok.

"It's easier using these measuring cups, Cathie, less mess and everything over the pond is geared to simplicity. Guess what my favourite American dessert is? Something I've never tasted before... never even heard of... cheesecake. The recipe is in the book, you can make it for my next visit."

"Cheesecake?" Cathie's facial expression was priceless. "Cheesecake... made with what, Gorgonzola or Cheddar?"

"No Cathie!" I couldn't stop laughing. "Neither, you need cream cheese."

"Cream cheese, whit on awe the earth is cream cheese?"

"Yes, cream cheese." I tried to reassure her it does exist. "The best place to try, is the Co-Op in Leightham, or one of the new Deli's that's recently opened; they're more likely to stock it. But you will have to use digestive biscuits for the crust; we don't get Graham Crackers in the U.K."

"Digestive biscuits?"

"Oh-o! Sour cream; spoke too fast, I doubt you'll get sour cream in the whole of Scotland!"

"Sour cream... cream that's gan aff?"

"No Cathie, I don't know how to explain it to you. It's... it's like a sort of double cream that's had a culture added to it. It doesn't taste... sour." I struggled to explain and I gave up trying. I realised if I continued we would be there all day; maybe the cookery book wasn't such a good idea after all. "Try adding fresh lemon juice to cream and see what happens," I suggested.

"Fresh cream with lemon juice... to curdle it?"

"Cathie, stop repeating everything I say, go read the book; you're a brilliant cook, make something up." Cathie wasn't convinced. Digging back into my tote-bag to find the tin of Tuna fish I'd brought, I handed it to her.

"Drain it, then mix the tuna with mayonnaise and black pepper, make sandwiches for lunch," I suggested. "I love tuna mayonnaise... in America they add it to baked potatoes as well. Have you any cucumber in the kitchen, it goes well with tuna?"

Cathie's raised her head, stuck out her chin and straitened her shoulders, implying she knew precisely what to do with tinned fish. Also inferred I should know lunch was already organised, thank-you very much. 'Oops, I've upset her.' The poor woman turned and marched towards the kitchen muttering loudly:

"Tuna, tuna, what kind o' fish is that?"

"Cathie," I callout after her. "On my next visit we will make Hamburgers. I'll phone you before I come – we'll need Lightman's rolls. Oh! A jar of Dill pickles..."

No response from Cathie as she disappeared down the back corridor to the kitchen... She probably thought Hamburgers were made from ham. God only knows what she thought Dill pickles were. Better not tell her about the chilli I had in Texas... she'd be away to find me a jumper, thinking I'm feeling the cold.

Chapter 2

I **SHOOK MY HEAD**; I'd teased Cathie but she's a good-natured soul and wouldn't hold it against me. Digging into my tote, I searched for a small package, buried among the junk… one of these days I might get round to clearing the rubbish out. I'd added a fresh supply of jotters and pencils to the old ones. I hadn't looked at my notes since I'd left Aunt Jane's at the beginning of the summer. I thought to myself: 'Let's hope I can remember where we are or I'll be in trouble. Don't worry old girl, there's someone in the conservatory only too willing to remind you. Ah! Here it is… the Chanel No.5 I'd bought in the Duty Free shop in transit from New York to London.' I knew it was a stupid thing to do; Aunt Jane's favourite perfume probably cost more as a French import in the States than it cost in Fordyce's Emporium. But it was worth the expense, no more American perfume for Great Aunt Jane… I didn't want to get my nose bitten off again. I also wanted her to know I had not forgotten her favourite perfume and I had thought about her on holiday; which was true – I had missed the old girl.

As I was ramming the junk I'd spread about the table back into my tote, I looked up at the surroundings. I'd never given much thought to Aunt Jane's home before. Perhaps I had been too preoccupied, obsessed even with the history of Leightham House. As a child and teenager I guess such things were of no real interest; it was just Aunt Jane's house, so what? I was used to it. I was puzzled because for the first time I realised there were no framed photographs. Cathie said Aunt Jane had shown her a photograph of a woman, so why none on display, no family, friends, views, past or present... odd.

Apart from a pearl necklace and earrings, Aunty never wore any other jewellery that I'd ever seen. No rings on either hand that might give a clue to her status. Maybe she had been the mistress of a rich businessman... He might have set her up in salubrious surroundings before he died. 'Don't be ridiculous,' I reprimanded myself, 'you're letting your imagination get the better of you... behave!' But I knew that on a previous visit Aunt Jane had admitted to being no virgin lady, so she must have had a partner at some point in her life. But I couldn't stop thinking, how did one old unmarried woman, who as far as my family were aware, had never worked or married, accumulate so much wealth? My family wasn't poor... but compared to this, we were paupers!

Suddenly questions flooded my brain as I become aware of the opulent décor around me. Panels of light, *eau de nil*, coloured walls, set between half convoluted marble pillars reaching up to overhanging swaged coving. A deep snow-white freeze connected elaborate plasterwork cornicing, from the upper wall and well onto the ceiling. Above my head, like icing on a wedding cake, was a central rose that resembles a lace doily. A huge crystal chandelier suspended from its centre, cascading in all directions – how on earth did they get it up there? Explosions of intricate white plasterwork cascaded down the walls either side of the marble pillars flowers, bunches of grapes, ivy leafed trellises in abundance. Gold framed oil paintings of various sizes were mounted between the plasterwork. An elaborate cabinet stood against the main wall beneath one of the paintings. Thick with inlay work of different coloured woods, embellished with gold metal scroll edges and drawer handles. I think they are called... Boules? A large gold ormolu clock centrally placed on it, had an unusually deep, oblong base. It supported various rearing animal and between gold fluted pillars a tiny clock, but the face was so small – how could you read the time?

The pale colouring of the walls was complimented by the warmth of a central crimson carpet runner on each white marble stair reaching to the upper floor. A black ebony handrail sat atop a fine filigree frame of wrought iron railings as if crocheted, with flowers and leaves on their stems; were they stapled with gold leaf? It seemed too bright, too fresh for ordinary gold paint. The first three rails of the staircase were set into the first circular edged step at floor level; supporting a carved circular block of dark wood on which stood an antlered bronze stag – he looked as if on guard duty. Looking up I saw the stair leading upward to an overhanging semi-balcony on the upper floor, large enough to accommodate the most enthusiastic Romeo and his Juliet; and this was just the hall… what was concealed behind the doors on the upper floor?

Coming down to earth I realised the house had been well named 'Mount View' inside and out. Standing back from the cliff face and surrounded by gardens that reflected the imposing grandeur of the house. Views of the harbour, the beach and the river to the front and sides were unimpeded. I looked out of the hall's vast windows and wondered if Dr Forman ever got a dog to walk on the beach with. Casually slinging my tote-bag onto my shoulder, I stopped. Lord, what was I thinking? I could have scratched the hall's mahogany, circular pedestalled table with my carelessness or knocked over the large floral display in the middle.

From Boxing-day visits, I knew the door on the right led to the dining room; the left one the study. Aunty's gift in hand, I walked towards the dining room door… and stopped as if I had been winded. A life-sized oil painting in front of me – how could I have missed it in previous visits? It was partially hidden by the stair, but was I blind? It was huge! Framed in heavy ornate gold, the portrait of an arrogant black stallion; so captured by the artist, so real I could imagine the horse rearing its head, see the tail swish back and forth. The horse stood in front of a late seventeenth-century Renaissance Palace. A young lady sat side-saddle on its back. Proud, upright, her dark blue velvet riding habit draped the horse almost to the ground. Gloved hands held the reigns, her eyes staring down at me from an aristocratic unsmiling face. Her large wide brimmed hat, trimmed with chiffon drapes round her head and neck, partially concealed her long dark ringlets cascading to her waist. A large plume encircled the brim of the hat swinging gaily up into the air. The hat spoke of another time, the riding dress another century?

I continued to stare at the girls' face… Did the beautiful young lady on the horse have something to do with Aunty's story? Where did this all come from? I was annoyed at my own lack of observation and blind acceptance. Wake up, I admonished myself, stop accepting all she tells you, you need answers; you need to know the truth!

Chapter 3

DEMANDING ANSWERS from Aunt Jane was one thing, but how to go about it another. Cathie said Aunty was in the conservatory. I'd never been in it, but I knew where it was. The conservatory extended the entire south-facing wall of the house guaranteeing full sunlight on sunny days. A Victorian reminder of a bygone age, frilled curling iron spikes outlined the glass sections of its roof and framed the glass windows till they reached the low brick walls. Inside huge ugly metal chains attached to cogged wheels at knee level to open and close the windows. Heavy linen blinds above and on the windows to shelter plants and we humans from strong sunlight. Large circular metal pipes for central heating, skirted the lower brick wall, obviously to keep the place warm in the winter. It seemed money was no object – the heating bill must be astronomical, I thought!

The conservatory resembled a giant tropical forest. From floor to ceiling greenery formed a semi-circle enclosing half of the far end windows and the house wall. Palm trees with branches that sprayed in great arks, others resembling Egyptian fans, gave height and width. Wide spreading ferns at a lower level seemed to grow like weeds. Ivy crept up the house brick wall and formed a canopy over the roof of the conservatory at the far end. A collection of orchids and other rare tropical flowers bloomed in abundance, planted in decorated ceramic and brass pots. Now I realised the need for winter heating. The Botanical Gardens would be green with envy if they saw this; I doubted they would have half of such rare plant species.

A basket weave Chaise lounge covered with a tartan throw and soft multi-coloured cushions were placed under the palms, but Aunty was not sitting or lying on it. She was sitting upright on one of the basket chairs at either side of a matching coffee table, with cross-stitch embroidery in her hands.

"Well, you've decided to come back!" she barked. "I hardly recognise you, what have you done to yourself?"

Aunty's opening remarks brought me down to earth; all desire to ask questions evaporated.

"Hi ya'all!" I give the cheerful Texas greeting and sat down opposite her.

The face frowned; I realised the Texas drawl was a bad idea.

"What did you say I am... a sea-gull?"

"No Aunt Jane, I'm just being silly. How are you, did you miss me? I missed you, brought you a little something." I put the box with the perfume on the coffee table.

"Humph! What are you wearing, did you forget to get dressed again... you're half naked. What happened to the mini-skirt? Come closer." I complied, getting out of the chair and drawing close.

"What happened to your beautiful long hair?" followed by, "And how much weight have you lost?"

"Oh, don't worry Aunty; as I explained to Cathie, the changes are only skin deep."

"Skin deep – that's your opinion."

"Perhaps I have become Americanised. My friends in Texas tell me there's no such thing as ugly or fat girls, just lazy ones. Losing a bit of weight won't hurt me – it was about time I lost my puppy-fat anyway." But I had to admit that Mum had walked past me at the airport, not recognising me. Digging into my tote I brought out a tin of Metrical to show her.

"Metrical – I take it to work with me," I smiled. "Readymade, calorie counted, makes life easy. I put it in the freezer before I begin my shift and it's ready by lunchtime. It's sort of like drinking a frozen milkshake." I couldn't think of another description. "It's okay once you get used to the taste. There's different flavours – I like vanilla best. I brought it with me from the States, but I'll have to find something else now I'm home. I don't think it's available in Scotland yet."

"Well, you will get no Metrical here. You might think it makes you look beautiful, but just look at your hands, they look like claws... what does your mother think?"

"The same as you, but when I arrived in Texas I felt so provincial and out of fashion. I went straight into Neiman Marcus, it's a huge store on the outskirts of town, bought these hot-pants and a pair of knee-high leather boots to wear with them. What do you think?" Not giving her time to answer, I pressed on.

"Then I went to a hairdresser, a brilliant wee guy called Carlos, a refugee from Cuba – he's a scissor-wielding genius. Honestly, Aunty, it's so simple, no more plastering my hair with Amami, rollers or sitting for hours under a hairdryer burning my scalp. I remember the nights I could hardly sleep, rollers the size of beer cans jabbing into my skull. No... no more, I'm done with all that. I have a hand-held hair dryer now; you use a brush and blow-dry your hair, its dry in minutes, fantastic!"

"Hump... and what do you call that style anyway? It's uneven at the edges. Perhaps Carlos needed glasses?"

"Five points, it's all the fashion – three points down the back of the neck and two long ones at the front, below the chin, designed by Vidal Sassoon. I love it, easy to keep and it's meant to be like this." I shake my head from side to side to demonstrate the movement of my hair. I can see she's not impressed and I find myself agreeing momentarily with her, as I tuck the right side of my hair behind my ear one more time so I can see out.

"Danny Brown, the hairdresser's grandson, has opened a ladies salon down the front on the Mid-Shore," Aunty said. "Phone him for an appointment and get him to straighten the edges."

"No I won't Aunty," I bravely argued. "I love the style. Anyway Brown the hairdressers have been there for ever; I'd probably get a short back and sides. Nothing changes here – you're still living in the dark ages. Whoever is running the salon will not be up to date with the latest styles, probably has never heard of Vidal Sassoon."

"Clever, that's where you are wrong missy, the dark ages, eh? Yes, you are right, Alec Brown inherited the Barbour's shop from his father and he still runs the men's hairdressers; but young Danny recently returned from London. He's opened the new Ladies salon and has a partner Sally Barkley, Brown and Barkley's now. From what I hear he has clients from all over the County... so there!" Aunty was triumphant.

I gave her a benign smile; suppressed the desire to burst out laughing. Out-manoeuvred by a crafty eighty-year-old... Suitably admonished, put in my place, I dug into my bag and brought out the fresh jotter and pencils. But in an effort to get my own back I turned the tables on her...

"But just look at you, I hardly recognised you either, a Tweeny-Twink perm and a crimplene pinafore dress! Very modern, it suits you!"

Aunty shuffled in her chair. "Well, Cathie's getting older and finding it difficult to cope running up and down to the dry cleaners. I read about crimplene in a magazine – it can be washed in the washing machine. It saves her a lot of trouble, doesn't need ironing either, you just hang it on the pulley to dry." Thus Aunty stuttered out a disjointed explanation to justify her arrival into the twentieth century.

She noticed my writing gear and the conversation returned to the practical.

"Cathie will serve morning coffee in about an hour. I ordered a fresh supply of Kenya Blue Mountain from Thompson's last week. I am told they import it from the Paxton Tea and Coffee Estates in East Africa. I know they drink coffee in the States, but I think it's Columbian from South America. I prefer Kenyan, its Arabic. We will have lunch in the dining room."

I had learnt to appreciate real coffee in the States, black, no sugar. This was good news.

"Real coffee, Aunty. I hate the powdered instant I've had to endure since my return." Since Aunty doesn't do fake, I guess it won't be tinned fish sandwiches for lunch either.

I began to realise I couldn't write with my elbows on a level with my shoulders; the armrests of the Lloyd Loom basket chair were high; the writing pad would end up under my nose if I had to raise my knees to support it.

"Now we will move to the sitting room – I can see it's difficult for you to write sitting in the Lloyd-loom."

"Thank-you Aunty, it will be just like old times! But can I ask you a question before we begin?"

"A question?" she looked suspiciously at me.

"Cathie said you let her see a photograph of a woman while I was away. She suggested I ask you to let me see it."

"Don't bring Cathie into it... just ask what you want and, as for the photograph, the answer's no!"

That was clear enough; but I refused to be side-lined.

"All right, I guess you have your reasons, but I was curious because you have no framed photographs around the house. So I want to ask you..." Aunty narrowed her eyes as if daring me. "The painting in the hall, the girl on the horse... do you know who she is, where it came from and who painted it? You have so many beautiful things, and last, where did you live before you returned to the village? Mum says you didn't always live here."

"You are being nosey, too many questions miss; it's none of your business where I lived, but since you ask… Canada."

"Canada!" I gasped. That blew all my theories, and it would have been the last place on the planet I would have guessed. Wow! How did she end up in Canada? That explains why she speaks with virtually no trace of the local dialect, except when she is telling me her story and her French is excellent. I took in a breath, ready to press my case… but before I could utter a word, she interrupted.

"Shall we continue or sit here all day wasting time? Now where was I before you left for the States … the birth of the baby?"

"No, Alasdair Forman's love life."

"Don't be facetious."

Suitably admonished, I followed Aunty to the sitting room, like a sheepdog, tail between my legs. Back in my old chair, the one I usually sat in, pad and pencil at the ready, I waited for her to begin the next chapter of her story… the reason why Leightham House is roofless.

Chapter 4

TODAY BECAME TOMORROW and tomorrow became the next. Relentless, time seemed to stand still. Aunty began.

What a perfect summer's day, Maggie thought, staring out of the kitchen window as she washed the dishes in the sink. Gannets, flying high above the harbour on hot air currents, ducking and diving into the sea to catch the surfacing fish. Fishing boats moored in the harbour, silent from the still water, not a ripple on the surface. Today was perfect for the celebration Maggie had planned. She smiled with pleasure at the thought of the fine fish pie she had made, now cooking in the stove's oven next to the fire. A clouttie dumpling bubbling away in the big saucepan of boiling water over the fire was giving off a grand spicy smell, making Maggie's mouth water. The family would be back soon from the Shows in Leightham.

"Better get on and sweep up the rest o' the flour that I'v spilt under the table," Maggie muttered.

Then finishing the dishes and drying her hands on her apron, Maggie grabbed the broom from the wall at the side of the fireplace and swept thoroughly under the table.

"Now I can get on settin' the table; they'll be hungry, that's if they haven't spilt their appetites wi toffee apples and candy floss."

While Maggie burled about the kitchen cooking and cleaning, Jock sat and watched, not moving a muscle to help. He wouldn't have dared. The house was Maggie's domain and no one could satisfy her cleaning standards. She was no fanatic, but as far as housework was concerned she was convinced no one could clean as well as she did. Scrubbing the floor on her hands and knees from back bedroom to the pavement... then chalking the doorstep till it was snow white.

Jock sat contented in his rocking chair beside the fireplace. Sucking noises emanating from his favourite Dutch pipe announced the lack of tobacco in it. Leaning forward, he tapped the pipe on the edge of the chimney to make sure it was empty. Standing up, the old chair creaked as it rocked back into its original position. Jock picked up a packet of Virginia tobacco from the mantelpiece and taking a finger and thumb of loose shag, stuffed it into the bowl of the empty pipe. Bending down, he took a tapper from a jar by the fireside, lit it on the coals, then laid it over the bowl of the pipe. He huffed, puffed and 'sooked' repeatedly till the shag was finally lit. His tobacco-stained fingers were made of asbestos and felt no pain as he poked the burning shag further into the pipe. Heaving a contented sigh, he slumped back down into the old rocker and proceeded to blast mouthful after mouthful of smoke into the kitchen to make sure the tobacco was well and truly lit... much to Maggie's annoyance. With a benign smile on Jock's unshaven face, he reflected on the past.

"Aye, I remember it weel, the day she was born. I canna believe five years have passed already."

Maggie had been counting her blessings that this day had arrived, the bairn healthy and about to go to school. Maggie was more than ready to celebrate, but not look back on a time that caused her so much pain.

Jock and Maggie had been together from early childhood – holding hands in the playground, swimming, playing on the sand in the summer and sitting together in the Kirk on Sundays. A 'till death do us part' couple right from the start. Jock never failed to admire Maggie's fair hair. Blonde, it was almost white. He took delight in teasing her, saying she was a throwback to the Vikings who'd come a-raping and a-pillaging down the Scottish coasts in past centuries. Fair hair, soft white skin and cornflower blue eyes, Jock fell in love from the first time he saw her. When the fishing fleet returned from the winter fishing, Maggie, shawl wrapped about her head, was seen at the end of the pier, scanning the boats from bow to stern as they docked; worried... had Jock survived another fishing trip in the treacherous North Sea? She would never forget the overwhelming sense of relief she felt when she saw him waving to her from the wheel house.

It came as no surprise to the fisher folk that on a certain September day the pair were seen at the Manse, waiting to be married by old Mr Thompson the Parish Minister. It had been a hastily arranged wedding, between the sixteen-year-old Maggie and the seventeen-year-old Jock. Maggie wearing a new hat and her mother's shawl draped loosely from shoulder to knee; Jock in his father's shirt and tie, both hastily spoke their wedding vows. Even Mr Thompson who's eyesight wasn't great, could see the reason for the urgency. Equally it was no surprise to him the young couple returned to the Manse for the christening of their first-born barely two months later. Aggie, when she grew up, frequently asked her parents why they had waited so long to get married. Jock tried explained... no, insisted he had gone to fight in the Crimea. He had enlisted, lying about his age. It was just possible the story Jock told Davie Muir regarding his army coat had some truth in it and why he had disappeared for six months... without knowing Maggie was pregnant.

That was the start of a long happy marriage, but nothing stays the same for ever. As Jock got older he began to enjoy a dram or two, or three. At the fishing he stayed as sober as a judge; but after he retired and had no son of his own to hand his fishing boat over to, he decided to give it to his son-in-law – and after that there was nothing to restrict his drinking habits.

Nothing gave him more pleasure than a night at The Pirates... in the company of the older men and in particular Auld Tam. They were a fine pair; a couple of drams of 'Himself' and a game of cribbage or dominoes kept them occupied for hours.

If Jock stuck to that routine, Maggie had no quarrel with him and it left her free to enjoy a night out with her daughter, at the Women's Guild in the village hall. Jock however did not always stick to this arrangement; occasionally he was so drunk when he left The Pirates that he slept in a coal cellar or the first washhouse he could find with the door open. Next morning would see him tiptoeing into the kitchen, a sheepish look on his face. With his head throbbing, he'd sink into the rocking chair hoping Maggie hadn't seen him arrive. Maggie never said a word on those occasions; she had her own way of getting her own back. For the next two days Maggie neither cooked for Jock, nor did his washing, ironing, nor lay out his guid Sunday clothes for the Kirk. Repentant or hungry, Jock learnt his lesson... till the next time. They had married for better or for worse, but when Jock had been binge drinking, it was definitely for the worse for him.

"An whit part o' that day would you be remembering. Jock Booman? Noo let me think... would it be efter Auld Tam joined yae in The Pirates and Davie Muir let the pair o' you wet the bairns heid till yae were that drunk, yae couldna bite yer finger?" Jock slowly began to sink down in the chair, his neck gradually disappearing inside his collarless shirt, a flush appearing on his weather-beaten cheeks.

"Or would it be when you took a tummel doon the Kirk Wynd? Trippen' ower the hem o' that auld coat o' yours, with yer great muckle tacketty boots? Or was it when Auld Tam and you singing at the tap o' yer lungs... wait noo, whit was it you were singing?" Maggie pretended to think, tapping her forehead with her hand. "It could be heard awe ower the village... 'You tak the high road, I'll tak the low road... aye, I wish yae had taken the high road, oot o' ma sicht. A've never been sae affronted in awe ma born days Jock Booman!" Jock's head had all but disappeared inside his shirt. But Maggie wasn't finished.

"When a' opened the front door and saw Mr Spence the Bobbie there, wi the pair o yae. It's a miracle he didna' arrest you and Auld Tam, charged yae wi breach o' the peace… and you wi blood pourin' doon yer face. A' thocht drunks were no supposed to hurt themselves? Dae you remember me hauling' ye tae the kitchen, eh? Aye that'll be richt. Thank goodness young Dr Forman was in the hoose attendin' Aggie. I'll never forget him pitten' stitches in yer heid. Maybe you didna feel the stitches gaun in, but boy did ye suffer when ye sobered up… twa black een, a thumpen' heid… deserved yae richt!" Maggie took a breath. "Twa an six I had tae pay the guid Doctor… twa shillings an six pence and another twa shillings tae Dr Henderson tae get the stitches oot… by God, felt that richt enough, in yer heid and yer pocket!" Maggie's voice reached a crescendo.

"Wheesht noo, they'll her yea in the street Maggie and a' did disgrace myself," Jock agreed for the sake of peace and quiet; and he hadn't forgotten Dr Henderson removing the stitches.

He frowned, thinking back. Life in the village seemed strange, odd things happened without explanation. He'd never forget seeing Auld Tam belting up the Comentry Road with a clothes pole sticking out the back of his Kirt. Mr McDougall the minister coming to the house telling Maggie they would need to go to Leightham and get Dr Henderson to take the stitches out, Dr Forman had the flu… summer flu? Weird. Jock shook his head and when Janet arrived to help Aggie after the bairn was born, she had a strange look on her face… preoccupied, seemed to run in and out of the house, never staying any length of time. Yes, it had all been very confusing… drunk or sober.

"Ah weel it's in the past, best forgotten."

"Forgotten! I'll never forget as if a' didna hae enough to cope wi… Aggie in a state, the new bairn and you four sheets tae the wind… was the last thing I needed!" Maggie droned on.

Jock thought it better to leave while the going was good, got up from his chair and sidled round the kitchen table to the door. "A think I can hear the bairn shouting Dey, I'm gaun oot tae meet ma bairn. What time did you say they'd be back?"

"A' didna'!"

"Come on Maggie, let's make up, dinna spile the day because o' the past."

"Aye that'll be richt!"

Maggie took a step back as Jock came towards her.

"Gimme a kiss then."

"A kiss! Whitever's gaun on in that mind o' yours Jock Booman... forget IT!"

"Forget IT Maggie... I canna mind what 'IT' was. A' hiv 'na had 'IT' for twenty years. A've forgotten what 'IT' feels like." Jock loudly emphasised the 'IT' word.

"Wheesht, now it's you they'll hear in the street, and am mair likely tae give ye a dunt aside the heid wi ma broom, Jock Booman. You'll no forget what 'IT' feels like in a hurry. Noo get oot o' ma road, let me get on and don't you dare go near The Pirates." Maggie made a few threatening gestures with her broom.

Jock made for the kitchen door. Maggie finished sweeping under the table and bent down to pick up a piece of paper. He seemed to appear from nowhere; he had tiptoed back into the kitchen. Maggie stood up... Jock with surprising strength grabbed her round her middle, turned her to face him and managed to plant a kiss on her cheek. A right smackaroo with his course unshaven face and at the same time he nipped her ample buttocks. Before she had time to protest or carry out her threat with the broom, Jock beat a hasty retreat. Maggie, pretending to be insulted, clucked her tongue, but smiled, pleased at his show of affection.

"Enough of that yae daft auld gouk!" she shouted at Jock as he left...

Chapter 5

MAGGIE, secretly pleased at the attention Jock had paid her, wasn't sure what part of her anatomy to rub first. Her cheek smarted from what probably would develop into a rash from his unshaven face. Still, the man had a point; those days after Aggie's delivery were strange, the events unreal. Returning to the sink Maggie looked back out of the window, thinking they had been the worse six week of her life. She knew she couldn't go through that again and thankfully she'd never had to. She felt sad as she thought back on the three days Aggie was in labour, but grateful Aggie was now past childbearing. Even although it had meant there would be no male heir to the family fishing boats.

Life in the village after Aggie's delivery and Dr Forman's illness, went on as usual, that's if it ever had changed in the first place. But life was far from normal in the Gardner household at that time. Maggie had moved in with her daughter and she had all but given up hope Aggie would ever recover. After six weeks tiptoeing around, walking on eggshells, never knowing from one minute to the next what mood Aggie would be in, had begun to take a toll. Even the simplest suggestions were met with a disdainful shake of the head or ignored. Maggie was at her wits' end. Aggie's constant plea to be left alone was the worst of all... life was anything but normal since the birth of the baby.

Enough was enough – something had to be done, but what? The nets from the winter fishing needed mending. Great piles of them stacked in heaps up the laft needed two or three women to do the work. Rena McKay normally would have been glad of the work, but she was working as housekeeper to Dr Forman and no longer available. After one hellish day of not being able to do anything right without getting a mouthful from Aggie… "Don't put that here, pick that up, not these clothes, this Barrie-coat is damp!"…Maggie felt exasperated. Damned if she did a thing and damned if she didn't, so she felt she might as well be damned. Funnily enough, it was Jock who offered a solution on one of his infrequent visits to his daughter's house. Jock and Wullie had been avoiding contact with the women because of the reception they got from both daughter and wives. Poor man, he couldn't do anything right either.

"How about the twa o' yea treat yersels? I'v got a wee bit o' money put aside. The fishing's no been that great this winter and we didna' hiv bawbee's tae waste, but if this gets yae back on yer feet Aggie, it'll be money well spent. Have yer tea in Lightman's new tearoom, buy wool, whatever it is yae dae when yer in the toon. I'll keep the bairn; you'll no be that long."

"Jock Booman, I widn'a' leave a dug tae be looked efter by you, never mind the bairn!"

Jock, head hanging, beat a haste retreat.

But Maggie had thought about what Jock said and there was a lot of sense in his suggestion. A change of scene was a good idea, but how to go about it? 'Well,' the exhausted woman thought, 'you've nothing to lose Maggie Booman, you've tried everything else. I have to do something.'

She decided, because nothing including Janet's elixir had worked, she would take matters into her own hands. If Aggie never spoke to her again she didn't care. So Maggie wrapped her shawl around her shoulders, plonked her hat on her head and left without a word to her daughter, determined to demand answers from Dr Forman, whether he was ill or not, what was wrong with her daughter. She marched up the High Road towards Dr Forman's surgery, only to be met at the door by Dr Henderson. Harry Henderson had been the Gardner's Doctor long before young Forman had arrived and he knew the family well.

"Hello Mistress Bowman, you've caught me just in time. I am off to do house calls. I haven't seen you since I removed the stitches from Jock's forehead, just as Dr Forman became ill. Normally I would ask how you are, but I've known you long enough to tell something's not right. You're as whites as a sheet! Well, you are always white as a sheet, but those black circles under your eyes tell me a different story. Not getting enough sleep… new baby keeping you awake at night?" Harry asked kindly, remembering neither the Bowmans nor the Gardners troubled the Doctor without a good cause.

"No… well… yes, Doctur," Maggie managed to stutter, feeling embarrassed about troubling Dr Henderson again, "but it's not the bairn, she's fine, coming on a treat, disnae' give us ony bother… oh dear maybe I shouldn't have come!" Maggie, having doubts, started to turn away.

"Now, now Maggie, that's enough, you're not the type to bother the medical profession without good reason," Harry encouraged the woman. "Tell me what's on your mind, maybe we can work on a solution together."

"It's Aggie, Doctur, I'm at my wits' end, she's no recoverin' like she should… Lies in her bed a' day and its wae past the lying-in. She feeds the bairn, but apart from that takes no interest in the wee soul. Never smiles or talks tae the bairn, it's not like her."

"M-m." Harry stroked his beard. "Not really my field, childbirth; that's women's business… I never interfere." But the man stopped for a moment to think. "In my opinion, for what it's worth, it sounds like a sort of child-bed fever, but not of the body... of the mind. I've heard about it. Aggie's not rejecting the baby, is she?"

"Oh no, Doctur, that's just it," Maggie hastened to assure him. "She feeds and dresses the bairn, but has no interest... it's as if she is afraid to love the wee soul."

"Now listen... I need you on my side with what I am proposing."

"Proposing?" Harry could see she didn't know what he meant, but he pressed on.

"Go back to Aggie's house and wait for me. I have a call to do in George Street. Then I'll arrive unannounced as if I have just called in... a courtesy call. Now Maggie, it is imperative, I mean act surprised when you see me and agree with everything I say. Do you understand?"

"Aye Doctur."

"We will give my plan a try first. Go home, I will call in about an hour. Do not tell Aggie, I do not want her either alarmed or prepared for my visit."

"Whatever yae say, Doctur, I'm awa back hame... see what's happening. Oh afore a' forget, how is Dr Forman?"

"Much better thank you, he's taking morning surgeries, but he will be glad to get back to full time and believe me I will be glad to see him back to work; I'm getting too old for this double workload."

Back at Aggie's with a brown paper bag containing a selection of tea bread bought in Lightman's the bakers, she saw Aggie feeding the baby. Maggie busied herself putting the kettle on thinking when was the last time she had to buy scones and pancakes! 'I can't remember, it seems so long ago, I hardly get time to sit down these days never mind bake.' Fetching plates, cups and saucers from the press, Maggie set the table adding the scones, butter and a jar of bramble jam. Deliberately keeping quiet, she busied herself tidying the house for the Doctor's visit.

Aggie finished feeding the infant without looking at it; staring into space, she rubbed the baby's back to break her wind. Putting the infant across her knee, Aggie changed the nappy and dumped it in the pail ready for her mother to wash. Then she swaddled the wee thing in the shawl and put her back in the cradle to sleep. She got back into bed, pulled up the bedclothes and lay staring at the ceiling. Maggie kept silent, although she had been tempted to comment that if Aggie didn't stop rubbing the baby's back she'd rub a hole in it.

Hearing the front door, Aggie muttered, "Who's that at the door now, another nosy parker spierin' aboot ma business… is there never gaun tae be ony peace!" Maggie ignored her daughter's comments, comments she had heard a hundred times over the last few weeks, sighed and went down the hall to let Dr Henderson in.

"Oh, it's you, Doctur Henderson!" Maggie, acting her part, greeted the man. "Come awa ben the hoose Doctur, what a surprise. I was beginning tae think you had deserted us since Dr Forman took ower. We missed ye, but the young man is doing jist fine at the Docturin'."

"Yes he is... I was in the next street and thought I'd look in say hello. I hear Aggies had a new baby." Harry winked at Maggie and pushing past her marched down the hall in his usual brisk manner without looking back at the woman, now scurrying behind him to keep up.

"Watch yer heid on that stag Doctur." Maggie called out an unnecessary warning to the short man regarding the animal head hanging on the wall.

Once in the kitchen old Harry, who never put up with any nonsense from patients, walked over to Aggie's bed.

"Now what's all this then, you still in your bed in the middle of the afternoon?" he accused the hapless woman. "It's a beautiful day and that infant could do with a breath of fresh air before the winter sets in."

"I can't, Dr Henderson; I'm no weel, always tired. The bairn's too heavy for me to lift. A need my sleep."

"Are you in pain... do you have a fever?" Harry asked as he threw back the bedcovers, then feeling her forehead. Finding there was no rise in her temperature that he could detect, he announced: "I want to examine your stomach." Which he did in his usual no nonsense manner. "Any pain?" he asked as he poked Aggie's stomach with a firm hand. "No...? No pain?"

"No."

"Well, I'm off then, nothing physically wrong with you, Aggie."

Harry turned to her mother so Aggie couldn't see and winked again. Maggie had stood silent while this was going on. She now followed Harry as he strode out of the kitchen toward the front door. In a loud voice Harry informed Maggie:

"Well, Mrs Bowman, I can't find anything wrong with Aggie, that is physically, of course, so it must be psychological – a condition we are beginning to recognise as 'childbirth psychosis'! Generally only the symptoms appear after the woman's had her baby. If Aggie doesn't improve, then I will have to admit her to the Asylum." Harry had reached the front door and before leaving turned to Maggie and in a soft, but more serious voice, informed her:

"There's no medical name for the condition yet, Mrs Bowman. I've seen it a few times in my career; normally it rarely lasts more than a few days to a few weeks at most. I prefer to refer to the condition as a lowering of the spirits due to exhaustion and the realisation life has changed forever, but for it to last six weeks is not right. Some further thought is being given to hormonal disturbance and it can lead to unusual behaviour, so we need to keep an eye on Aggie. Honestly, there's nothing else for it, if there's no improvement... in your daughter's mental condition when I call back in a couple of days. I'm sorry there is no alternative; we will have to admit Aggie to hospital. I cannot take the responsibility and do nothing. Keep a close watch, of her own behaviour and with the baby. I hope you understand what I am saying, but I doubt it will come to admitting her."

Maggie gasped, astonished, as she realised what Dr Henderson had said.

"Are ye shure we're no takin' an awfy big risk, Dr Henderson, supposin' she does hurt hersel or the bairn?"

"I am prepared to take the responsibility. I have known your daughter since she was a child and I am certain my plan will work, or believe me I wouldn't take the risk. After forty years you get an instinct for these things, for instance the hairs not standing up on my arms to tell me to do otherwise." Harry tapped his nose. Then returning to his normal happy-go-lucky demeanour, he raised his voice.

"Unfortunately I will have to admit your daughter and it will mean finding another woman in the village to nurse... err, look after the child... nothing else for it." Harry's smile reassured Maggie and thankfully Maggie caught his drift.

"I can hardly believe what you're telling me, Doctur! Of course we must tak your advice, but the lunatic asylum..." Maggie spoke in an equally loud voice, knowing fine well Aggie would hear her.

Wylie old fox, Harry knew there wasn't that much wrong with Aggie; aye, she was low in spirits and tired. Her delivery would have knocked the feet from under the strongest. But worst of all she was using her mother shamelessly; it was time to put a stop to it. 'I hope you know what you're doing Harry,' he thought, 'or it will be you they admit in the asylum if this goes wrong.'

"Cheerio Doctur, thank you for dropping in. If nothing's changed by Friday I'll have her case packed ready and I'll find one o' the village women tae feed the bairn!" Maggie called out after Henderson.

Aggie had heard the conversation and had shot out of bed and was standing in the middle of the kitchen floor when Maggie returned.

"What did he say, Mum…? He's going to come back in a couple o' days and if a'm no better he's gaun tae put me in the lunatic asylum? Did a hear him richt? The bairn tae be looked efter by another woman?"

Maggie looked at her daughter's anxious face with sympathy. But sympathy wasn't going to help.

"Aye, that's what Dr Henderson said. If you're no better when he comes back in a couple o' days then he has nae alternative but tae admit yae tae the asylum in Leightham."

Aggie gasped in horror. Maggie hastened to reassure her daughter.

"That's if yer no getting ower the bairn's birth. It's more than six weeks noo Aggie, I'v been that worried… am at ma wits' end."

"You dinna understand Mum!" Aggie sank into the rocking chair and taking hold of her nightdress dabbed at her eyes and tried to dry the tears pouring down her face.

"Try and tell me, am yer mother. How can a' if yae dinna tell me?"

"It's the grey rain, the grey rain Mum, a' wake up, the sun is shining, but inside my heid it's raining grey rain – I canna' explain ony better than that. Now you'll think am aff ma heid and call Dr Henderson back and admit me tae the asylum!"

"No, a will no let Dr Henderson dae ony such thing, admit you tae hospital, never, and a dae understand how ye feel Aggie, as much as ony woman that's gone through childbirth. The feeling life will never be the same again, exhausted, numb. Worse if the woman has lost a bairn afore, suffered the pain of a wee one dying afore its ony age and you've lost twa. Nae wonder ye feel the way ye dae." Maggie slumped down on her knees beside her daughter and put her arms around her and held her tight... and let Aggie sob her heart out.

"Aye, it's no much comfort tae yae, ma lass, but nearly every woman and family in this village has lost a bairn at some time." Maggie's voice faltered... remembering her own wee boys buried in the cemetery. It seemed like a long time ago since Jock and the men took the tiny white coffins out of the house for burial.

"But a canna love her, Mum; a dinna want to love her. A don't trust her or mysel, what if she doesn't survive? If a' ever have tae put one o' ma puir wee lassies in their cauld grave afore their third birthday... a' swore the last time a'll throw mysel' in as well."

The last words Aggie spoke shook her mother to the core.

"Now you jist listen tae me, Aggie Gairdner, you're made o' stronger stuff than that. There are nae guarantees in this life. Why should you be different from onybody else? In life there is death. Ma granny gave me good advice a long time ago; got me through some heartbreken times a' can tell yae. Now a'm gonna give her advice tae you... Granny said furget about yesterday, dinna' look back yesterday's ower... nothing tae be done aboot it. For a wee while live only in the now... be grateful for whatever the guid Lord sends ye. Tomorrow's no here yet and it'll tak care o' its sel. She used to say... life is short at its longest."

If Doctor Henderson had had himself admitted to the asylum if things didn't work out in the Gardner household, Maggie would be right at his back pleading to be admitted as well...

Chapter 6

SATURDAY dawned bright and sunny; Maggie decided to take Jock's advice... a change of scene for her and her daughter. Aggie had made an effort to put the past few weeks behind her and was pleased at Maggie's suggestion to catch the bus into Leightham and do a little shopping. Then a real treat, afternoon tea in Lightman's new tea rooms, paid for by Jock. It had taken Aggie a few days to get the strength back into her legs, weakened from prolonged lying in bed, but now she was back on her feet and looking forward to the trip. Unfortunately the Link's Market was going full tilt in St Creils and most of the women who might have babysat were there. Wullie, backed by Jock both unanimously, volunteered to babysit. The two men would have looked after the devil himself, they were that thankful Agnes was showing some sign of recovery. Both men assured their wives they should be finished delivering the nets to the boat by lunchtime and would be home in time to let them away to catch the bus.

"Mum, I'v a mind tae buy cloth, lace trimmings and the like. Wilkinson's in the High Street will have what a want. A'm gaun' tae make the bairn a new Christening robe..."

"No you'll no! You will dae nothing o' the sort. A ken fine weel what's gaun on in that heid o yours, Aggie Gairdner. You think the christening robe that's been in our family fur generations has brocht bad luck. Get that richt oot o' yer heid. Ma great grandfather brought it from India when he sailed in the tea clippers. Fine cotton... Indian cotton, embroidered in Ayrshire and sent back oot tae India fur the British soldier's tae christen' their bairns." Maggie held her hand up to stop Aggie arguing with her.

"His sons and daughters were all christened in it right through the generations to you and there's nae reason why the bairn shouldn't be christened in it. So that's an end tae that, but a' can understand why ye feel that wi." Maggie thinking, worked out a plan.

"A'll tell ye what a'll dae, the robe is oor long, must be all o' five feet in length. The last time I held a bairn wearing it, a' near fell aw ma length on the hem. No jist that, but it trails in the dirt and its some job tae clean it. Shortened, it shouldna' mak much difference tae the style as mist o' the heavy embroidery is nearer the bottom. It's a bonnie robe Aggie embroidered wi tropical flowers, thick wi birds o' paradise, your great grandfather telt me that's what they were called. Chrysanthemums, leaves and the like."

Maggie nodded as if agreeing with her own plan. "A'll cut out the plainer upper third of it and join what's left o' the skirt tae the bodice. That'll make aw the difference, what dae ye think Aggie? Get a few yards o' white lawn and deep lace in Wilkinson's, a'll mak a new petticoat, trim it with lace to gan under the robe; that I'll mak a big difference, give it a new look. Oh! And before I forget, I'll mak a new bunnet fur the bairn, how do you feel aboot that?"

But before Aggie could answer her mother forged ahead with the shopping list, in case she forgot something while in town.

"And dinna let me furget we need to gan tae Cormack's the wool shop, I need six unce o' sock wool, am sick o' darnin' the holes in yer faither's socks, there's mair darn than sock. Ma granny used to say you should always have a sock on the needles... oh! And white Shetland wool, a' was thinking the bairn could dae wi a new shawl. That auld one's gey yellow and weel dugged in, it's been washed that often. Your dad can help me wind the wool, haud the hanks on his hands, no doubt girnin' and whinin aboot his airm's gettin' tired… ach, he's no such bad soul efter awe. One o' these days I'll get one o they wooden wool winders. I saw an advert in the *Dundee Press*, once you stretch the hank on its circular arms it spins so you can wind the wool by yourself."

The ladies laughed at the thought of husband and father complaining about doing women's work, both agreeing a wool winder would be a good idea.

"Its grand tae hear ye laugh again ma lass!"

Aggie smiled. "Of course you're richt Mum, the christening robe is bonnie and a family heirloom – shortening it's a guid idea. A' was bein' over sensitive… superstitious, it's hard no to look back." Aggie put her hand up to stop her mother interrupting. "A'm making progress and trying to do as you said… live in the moment. What would a' do without you? A love you Mum." Aggie, still weak from her delivery, had tears in her eyes.

"Ach haud yer wheesht lassie." Maggie smiled shyly at the rare show of affection from her daughter. "Let's get on; you've fed that bairn till she's nearly burstin, but she'll no last forever withoot wantin' fed again'."

"Mum, a think she smiled to me when I spoke tae her jist the noo!"

"Rubbish, its wind, yer haiverin."

"No, a' hiv been talking tae her and I think she recognises my voice."

"Weel its aboot time, but let's face it she's heard yer voice for the last nine months, so its nae surprise she recognises it." The front door opened and footsteps were heard coming down the hall.

"Now who's that… oh, it's your faither and sober! It's either the Sabbath or The Pirates is shut. What dae yea want,

Jock? Let me guess, you're leaving Wullie on his own tae keep the bairn?"

"That's enough o' your bliddy cheek, Maggie Booman! Dae ye think a' canna hear yae? Trust you tae think the worst o' me, am sobers a judge. Am tellin' ye efter the tongue lashin' ye gave Davie Muir fur letting Auld Tam and masel get drunk efter the bairn was born. He only lets us hae twa drams at a time noo," Jock blurted out. Up till now he had not informed his wife about Davie's new rule, because it meant Maggie had won. Privately the two pals were furious, but Davie Muir was adamant except for the New Year when he'd bend the rule.

"No, a' came tae offer the twa o' yae a lift in tae Leightham. Auld Tam and mysel are gaun tae the railway station tae collect the new nets Wullie ordered from Edinburgh last week. Mr Spence telt Auld Tam they'd arrived and they're waitin' tae be collected the day. His brother Malcolm Spence, the station master, wants them aff the platform afore Monday. Tam telt me last nicht aboot it, it'ill no tak long once we've dropped you and Aggie. Wullie will keep the bairn till a' get back."

"A lift on Auld Tam's Kirt?"

"Aye, there's plenty room on the way there, but no back – you'd hiv tae get the bus."

"Jock Booman… if you think fur one minute, Aggie and I would be seen deid or even consider getting' on that filthy, stinking' Kirt, you kin think again. Of awe the daft ideas, are ye shure yer no drunk?"

"A' wish a were drunk, a' widn'a need tae listen tae your voice drummin' in my ear Maggie and a jist telt ye, if ye'd stopped the racket long enough and bother tae listen, nae mair than twa drams at a time… and The Pirates' no opened yet… mair's the pity"

"You better be back in guid time tae help Wullie, or you'll no hear the end o' it frae me."

Jock escaped out the back kitchen door and went off to find Auld Tam, leaving Wullie behind to babysit. After they pair of them got back to Pittendreal they would go straight to the Mid-Shore and unload the new nets on the pier beside the boat. Auld Tam would then drop Jock off at his son-in-law's house to help with the baby sitting… At least that was the plan.

Maggie ignored Jock and turned to the matter of getting Aggie ready for their trip.

"Aggie, Junet left a wee jar o' lavender oil last week. She said tae pit a couple o' drops in a bath o' warm water and soak a wee while in it, it'll relax ye. What dae yae think?"

"Aye Mum, that's a guid idea; can yae manage the tin bath frae the wash hoose? I'll put a couple o' pans o' water on tae bile, take the chill off the cauld water. It's a grand warm day, a good soak is just what I need."

Maggie left the kitchen to get the bath. She arrived back with it in her arms, puffing and panting.

"Here, let me help ye mum."

"Aggie there's something I hiv been meaning tae ask yae aboot?"

"Well?"

"It canna wait much longer, the Minister and Councillor Bird the registrar in Leightham council want tae ken… they want tae ken when the bairn's gaun tae be registered. A tried tae explain we hidna agreed on a name yet, but it's urgent Aggie. The bairn should be registered afore she's six weeks tae get her birth certificate."

"Alice," Aggie interrupted her mother. "And before you start aboot tradition a' will never use my granny's name again. A'm no saying it brought bad luck, but a' dinna believe in third time lucky. Ma bairns, ma twa wee lassies…" Aggie's voice caught in the back of her throat. "Never again will I risk it."

"Alice...Alice?" Maggie repeated. "Whaur on awe the earth did yae cum up wae a name like that? A doubt there's onybody in Pittendreal wae a name like Alice."

"A' read it in the *Courier*. It's a book: *Alice in Wonderland*. The wee lassie in the story disappears down a rabbit warren, but reappears. The story's fiction, but it helps me believe if my Alice disappears like the one in the story, a' ken she'll find her wae back to me!" Now Maggie's jaw was hanging open. "You, Wullie and dad can all gan tae the Registrars... add whatever names to her birth certificate ye like, but she will be kent as Alice Gairdner... By the look on your face, you think a've gone daft so get Doctur Henderson... hae me admitted tae the Asylum!"

Chapter 7

A COUPLE OF HOURS later found Aggie and her mother standing at the bus stop on the High Road. They had reluctantly left Wullie alone for the first time with his baby daughter. It was no real surprise to the three of them Jock had not appeared as promised and was nowhere to be found. Wullie assured Aggie and his mother-in-law he would be fine. So the women made the decision to go, Jock or no Jock.

They didn't have long to wait for the bus, so Maggie took the time to bring Aggie up to date with the village gossip.

"Did a' tell ye Rena McKay got a job as housekeeper tae Dr Forman and afore a' forget tae tell ye, Mr McDougall's the minister's wife had a bairn the day efter you had Alice... Aye Alice, I like the name it kind o' slides aff the tongue. I'll get a Christening Mug ordered from Bird's the Jewellers wi her name on it, now that we ken whit the bairn's name's gaun tae be." Maggie's thoughts had wandered to her little grand-daughter, then returned to the subject, relating the latest gossip. "Noo where was a?"

"Mother! You were telling me aboot the McDougall's bairn and I already knew aboot Rena. I'm plaised for the woman, she's a decent soul and the money will mak aw the difference tae her and her bairns."

"Aye so it will... but what was I saying? Oh aye, the minister's wife... she had a wee lassie the day efter you had Alice, but she went tae the hospital tae have her and they had a nurse biding wae them for a while efter she was discharged. I wonder what they'll call the bairn. Goodness me, talk o' the devil, there's the Minister wi his horse and buggy!"

Both the ladies looked towards Tom as he approached, preparing to nod and smile at the man when he passed them. But instead of Tom driving on, he drew in the reins forcing the horse to stop.

"Good afternoon ladies." Tom smiled and took off his hat. "Where are you going?"

"Into town, Minister," Maggie acknowledged the man's greeting and answered his question.

"So am I, can I offer you a lift? I believe you have been ill, Mrs Gardner; it would be my pleasure to drive you both into Leightham. I can drop you wherever you want to go and that would save you a walk from the bus station." Tom got down and came round to the pavement to help Maggie and her daughter get up onto the buggy.

"That's awfy kind o' ye Minister, ye can drap us at the High Street if ye dinna' mind."

"Watch your hats ladies, there's a bit of a breeze; are you comfortable Mrs Bowman?" Maggie nodded, pulling her skirt in tight so Aggie could have more space. "Be careful your skirt doesn't catch in the wheel when we move off, Mrs Gardner," he warned Aggie as he flicked the reins. "How are you feeling today? My wife is still a little shaky on her legs, and I believe you both had your babies a day or so apart."

"Aye Mr McDougall, I was telling my dochter aboot yer bairn. What name are you gaun tae cry yer wee lassie?"

"Ah, my wife Isabel and I have decided she will be named Helen. There are no other Helens in our family. Isabel and I like the name, but believe me it has caused quite a furore among the relatives. We are not following family tradition you see, naming her after her grandmother… the family is outraged!" The young man laughed. "I guess you will follow that tradition, Mrs Gardner, name her after your…"

"No!" Aggie snapped. Tom was taken aback.

"No, she is to be cried Alice," Maggie interceded to halt any further discussion on the subject of the name.

"Oh how lovely, what a beautiful name! Alice Gardner – it has a ring to it." Tom diplomatically parried any further discussion regarding naming traditions. "With a name like that she must be meant for great things. And I have it on the best authority she is a beautiful young lady."

Aggie and her mother looked at each other and then turned sideways to look at Tom.

"Don't worry, ladies, I'm a bit of a poet," Tom laughed, put a hand up to excuse his poetic declaration regarding the baby's name and beauty.

"Now what about a date for the christening, have you decided yet? Could I suggest next Sunday? I realise it's not a local traditional to baptise babies in the Kirk, but Isabel and I want to change some aspects of village life, so we can get to know everyone a little better. And what better, happier way than a christening and perhaps a cup of tea for the congregation in the church hall after the service. What do you think, ladies?" Tom waited for an answer from the now speechless women who had assumed that the Minister would have come to the house to christen the bairn.

"Isobel and I would be delighted to entertain your family, along with the parishioners. I know the ladies in the women's guild will be more than pleased to organise the tea and I'm sure will bring a surfeit of home baked scones to eat. Our little one has not been christened... she's a right little madam and has taken a lot out of her mother over the last few weeks. Isabel didn't feel up to it... but now it's time. What do you think – I baptise them both together on the same day? Have you chosen Alice's godparents yet? Dr Forman has been persuaded to be one of Helen's now he's recovered."

Tom smiled. "Then after the ceremony I will write their names and date of their christenings on their birth certificates and sign them myself with a special message before I record their births on the church register. Now I must tell you my news, I am sure this will help promote the idea of church christening in future." Tom had his fingers crossed.

"You will never guess what I found, stored in the basement of the church, a beautiful carved early Victorian christening Font! Old Mr Thompson my predecessor must have removed it for cleaning and forgot to have it returned to its rightful place in front of the alter; he was getting a bit absentminded before he retired, but if christenings took place at home, well you can't blame him. It looks like it hasn't been used in years, so I'll get the verger to give the stone a right good scrub and polish the copper water bowl till it shines. Then it will be returned to its rightful place in the church where it belongs on the right side of the Alter. I think there is a mark on the floor where it once stood, near the congregation so everyone has a good view of the baby. I hope your whole family can attend and our girls will be the first to be baptised in the newly resurrected Font." Tom stopped, thinking he was talking too much... sermonising? But he pressed on while the going was good.

"Which reminds me, talking about the copper bowl – we need water... I'll send to the Synod of the Church of Scotland for a supply of Holy Water from the river Jordon. It should arrive in good time for the christenings. I hope as the girls grow up they become good friends, attend school together and so on. So Sunday, what do you think?"

Maggie had been listening to the minister, and then complimented him on his daughter's name, echoing his sentiment regarding the girl's future friendship and waiting for Aggie to respond to the proposal of a church christening. Aggie still sat silent. Maggie felt one of them had to speak.

"That's awfy kind o' yae minister… did you say eleven o'clock at the church?" Tom nodded. "We'll be there, as yae can see Aggie's feeling an awfy lot better." Maggie decided against giving Aggie a say in the matter. "Withoot being for'et Mr McDougall, could I ask a favour?"

"Of course, what can I do for you?"

"Am awfy fond o' the hymn 'All things bright and beautiful'…"

"Mrs Bowman, you took the words right out of my mouth! It's a favourite of Isabel's. I will instruct Miss Simpson the organist to play it on Sunday and the congregation will sing the hymn while I christen the babies."

Aggie however had sat silent staring at the road ahead, till she seemed to summon the courage to speak.

"Mr McDougall, forgive me, a'm overwhelmed at yer generosity, wantin' the bairns' tae be christened the gather, it's a privilege… but in the church…" She hesitated, making up her mind whether to continue.

"Go ahead, Mrs Gardner; there is nothing you can tell me that I probably have not heard before. Nothing shocks… or upsets me." Tom had sensed something was troubling the woman who had sat silent during the journey. "I believe in talking about what troubles us. We dour Scots are known for being unable to express our feelings and holding them inside. So Aggie, may I call you that?" Aggie nodded her consent. "Tell me what troubles you, and if you don't mind your mother listening… go ahead; or I can arrange to meet you at a time that suits you… at home?"

"No, ma mother is my closest friend, there's nothin' I would keep secret from her; its jist… I hiv tae be honest Mr McDougall… my faith's been sair tested in the last few years. Am no sure if a believe in God any mair. How can a God dae what he did tae ma bairns? They suffered so before they died…" Aggie managed to choke the words out, fighting her tears at the same time.

"Aggie!"

"It is all right, Mrs Bowman, let your daughter speak."

Maggie gasped, horrified at her daughter's revelations in front of the minister.

"It's all right, Aggie, I understand. I don't believe in sanctimony or sanctimonious platitudes… Hell fire and damnation, just because of what you said. It takes a great deal of courage to admit how you feel about your faith. All I can say is with the loss of life you have had to endure over the years, who can blame you? Your faith's been sore tested. What I have come to believe… call it God if you wish, but I have found, He makes no promises, does not negotiate, but offers faith, trust and belief. You more than most are acutely aware of the fact there are no guarantees in this life and you have had to learn that lesson the hard way. It is hard to be philosophical when little ones are taken from us." Tom stopped for a few minutes to let the ladies digest his words as the horse trotted into town. As they were about to reach the town centre Tom added:

"May I make a suggestion, Aggie, without sounding parsimonious? My advice would be… take one day at a time. Trust in the good shepherd, attend the christenings on Sunday of our two wee girls and pray… for their health and happiness. What more can we do, what more can I say? Except let's rejoice in their safe births and marvel at the joy they bring. How about that for a bargain, and maybe your faith will return, Aggie?"

The horse and buggy drew up at the kerb in Leightham High Street. "Ah, here we are ladies, stay where you are till I come round to help you down."

Now standing on the pavement, Tom shook hands.

"Thank you, Mr McDougall, for the lift. That was awfy kind of ye. A believe we would have still been standing at the bus stop if ye'd no come by and gien us a lift. Aggie and I are grateful." Maggie fumbled in her purse. "Afore ye leave... tak this and press it intae yer wee lassie's hand. It's a silver sixpence... to ward off the devil... mind noo there's nae herm in oor auld traditions or superstitions."

Tom smiled. "I will, Mrs Bowman, thank you... see you Sunday. Enjoy your shopping trip." Tom put his hat on, got back into the buggy and with a flick of his wrist set it in motion. He looked back at the two women to wave and was heartened to see Agnes with a happier look on her face.

Chapter 8

"THAT'S A FINE LOOKIN'** hat in Wilkinson's
window, Aggie – come on, let's gan awa in and you
try it on."

Maggie and her daughter had alighted from Tom's buggy at
the far end of the High Street. Arm in arm the two women
made their way down the High Street looking in their favourite
shop windows. Maggie spied the hat – just the thing for a
christening, she thought.

"What dae ye think Aggie? It's plain enough tae be worn
on a' occasion and it'll gan weel wi thon blue Paisley shawl o'
yours that you've hardly worn."

"Mum, look at the price, dinna be daft! I'm no wasting
dad's hard earned siller on such gee-gaws and the fishin's no
been that great last winter."

"Dae ye think a've only have a pound wi me? A've got a
bit put aside as well, that yer dad kens nothing aboot," Maggie
grinned. "For his funeral," she added.

"Mum! You're terrible!"

"Am only kidding, now let's gan in… it canna hurt tae try
it on."

"You shouldna joke about these things, it'll bring bad luck
and no look at the price, twelve shillins and six pence!" the
ever frugal Aggie protested.

"Well, I'll touch wood for luck." Maggie touched her head.
"Yes, you will try that hat on." Aggie knew not to argue with
Maggie when her mind was made up.

"A hiv twa pounds tae spend and wi the christening next Sunday you're gaun tae have a new hat tae wear. Twelve and six, we can manage that. If a' remember richt, the fabric we want is aboot a shillin' a yaird, the lace no muckle mair. Ma sock wool's six pence a hank and the bairn's Shetland shawl wool a shillin, an' only need six o' wan and fower o' the ither. Noo If I'v calculated that richt? That leaves us plenty for oor tea in Lightman's and the bus fare hame wi change in oor pockets. So yer getting' the hat, nae argument!"

"Oh, Mum, what wid a dae withoot ye?"

"Niver mind that ma lass, let's get on wae it, a' dinna want yae gettin' oor tired or leaven' the men in charge o' the bairn oor long. A'll get yer faither tae haud the hanks o' wool the nicht when a' get back. A'll wind the wool and get on wi ma knitting... ach, he has his uses!"

The hat now safe in a large brown paper bag, Aggie looking like she was guarding the crown jewels, clutching the bag with both hands in case someone bumped into it. Maggie had charge of two flat paper parcels tied up with string tight under her armpit: soft white cotton for the new petticoat in one and the other with yards of crisp lace for the trimming, both the new petticoat and bonnet. Shopping now complete in Wilkinson's, mother and daughter set off in the direction of Cormack's wool shop. Maggie with the determination of a knitting junkie examined every hank of four and two ply wool, in every colour in the shop; every skein of silk embroidery thread and every reel of thread, thoroughly examined with the skill of the professional needle woman, till she found exactly what she wanted.

"Cup o' tea next a think Mum!" Aggie's strength was beginning to flag, never mind her spirits with the length of time Maggie was taking to choose the wool.

"Aye, your richt lassie, a' dinna want ye getting oor tired, it's your first trip out. It's time we made our way doon the

High Street tae Lightman's the baker's; his new Tearoom's upstairs above the shop overlooking the prom. Ye get a grand view up the High Street and the river in front."

Contented with their purchases, the happy pair made their way to the tea room, Maggie arguing more with herself than her daughter regarding the quality of the wool and whether or not she should have bought more of the sock wool because it was such a bargain. Aggie gave her support regarding the purchase of wool, but announced the hat was a sheer extravagance…

"Weel, lets tak it back then Aggie," her mother had threatened. "I'll return it on the way tae the bus stop."

"No you'll no!" Aggie retorted instead of joining in Maggie's empty threat of returning the hat. She decided not to protest against the expensive handmade lace her mother had insisted on purchasing for the baby's outfit.

"You never know, Aggie, my great grandchildren micht be christened in the robe with the petticoat and bonnet someday. That makes me content, fur I'll no see it, but it'll be handing down generation efter generation." Aggie felt a lump rise in her throat as she echoed Maggie's sentiments, assured her mother if she was spared, she would make sure all her grandchildren would know the story of the christening gown.

"I'm sure they will all be christened wearing it Mum, and a'll tell them about our shopping trip and how it came to be… a day we celebrated. Here we are at Lightman's Tearoom. Now there's a bit o' luck, a' forgot the Market's on in St Creils – the place will be half empty for a Saturday. We'll hae nae bother getting' a seat."

Sam Lightman's wife Elsie had decided with the fast approaching new century the town needed a Tearoom for the local ladies to sit down and be served afternoon tea. She had seen a rather grand Tearoom in Edinburgh, a Miss Margaret's, and decided to copy the concept, but not the décor, feeling it was a bit extreme for the locals. Elsie's Lightman's Tearoom was a simpler version and had gained an excellent reputation among the locals. Young Martha Lightman, Elsie's daughter, was in charge and greeted Maggie and her daughter warmly.

"Ladies, grand tae see yae. Now I'v a fine table in the bay window; as ye can see we're half empty the day… everybody's at the market."

Comfortably seated the two women enjoyed their tea served in fine china from a silver teapot. Both women agreed homemade Lightman's scones with butter and homemade bramble jelly were the best in the world.

"My, that was grand, Aggie; see if there's ony mair tea left in the pot."

Aggie managed to squeeze another half a cup out for each of them, declaring it was now tepid but they'd need to get a move on. Alice would need to be fed soon, so they decided against ordering another pot.

"Aye you're richt, but what a fine day oot we've had. A hiv tae be honest lassie, a began tae think this day would never come and while I'm being honest… a dinna ken how tae put it…"

"Jist say what's on yer mind mother… what's bothering ye?"

"Aggie, it's non o' ma business… but…" Maggie lowered her voice, not that there were many others around them to hear what she was about to say, the place being half empty. Which as it turned out was just as well.

"Well?"

Maggie blurted out: "Aggie, God forgive me, but a hope ye hiv nae mair bairns… there I'v spoken my mind!"

"Yer in guid company mother, a' feel exactly the same. But what's tae be done aboot it? Wullie's already started grousing… he says its cauld sleepin' in the back bedroom… In the middle o' the summer, who's he trying to kid? I'll hae a talk wi Junet, maybe she can suggest something."

"Make shair ye do."

Aggie leant over the table to get closer to her mother. "What did you dae, Mum?"

Maggie looked about her making sure no one was listening. "Aggie, it's personal but yer a grown woman and we women hiv tae stick the gither..." Maggie lowered her voice even further, drew in closer to her daughter and whispered in Aggie's ear: "The Haymarket."

"What are ye talkin' aboot? Wullie's no gaun tae Edinburgh is he? First a heard o' it and dae ye no mean Waverley?"

Maggie quietly repeated: "No, the Haymarket."

Aggie frowned. "I don't understand, Wullie's..."

Exasperated, Maggie shouted out: "No Waverley! Tell Wullie tae get aff at The Haymarket..."

A silence fell over the room. Some customers turned to see where the source of the information had come from. Others started to giggle and young Martha stuffed a napkin into her mouth to stop bursting out laughing. Realising what her mother had just said, Aggie felt her cheeks redden, but with great dignity, calmly lifted the cup to her mouth and finished her tea. She placed the cup back in the saucer and after wiping her mouth with the napkin, she put it on the plate. With the resilience gleaned from generations of fisher women facing adversity, Aggie straightened her hat, rearranged her shawl round her shoulders, picked up her handbag and parcel from the floor and stood up.

"Collect your parcels mother, we dinna want to miss the bus," Aggie announced solemnly with head held high, betraying nothing of how she was feeling inside. Continuing for the benefit of the assembled company, she stated in a much louder voice as she walked between the rows of tables:

"Mother, you are richt, a' believe Wullie is going to Edinburgh next week on 'BUSINESS...' A'll remind him to buy a ticket for Haymarket and not continue on to Waverly."

Maggie scrabbled about the floor to retrieve her handbag and parcels, which seemed to have taken it into their heads to move out of her reach. With her hat slightly askew, her shawl trailing from one shoulder onto the floor, Maggie walked alone, scarlet in the face towards Martha at the desk to pay the bill. She had never felt so embarrassed. She was sure all the customers were looking at her. Head down, she whispered to Martha...

"How much dae I owe yae?"

Young Martha was grinning from ear to ear, thinking she had never enjoyed such an entertaining afternoon in the tearoom before.

"That'll be three shillings Mrs Bowman."

That brought Maggie down to earth, humiliation forgotten as she gasped out loud.

"Whit! Three shillin' fur a cup' tea and a scone! There'll be nae tip fur you Martha Lightman! What's Sam Lightman planning tae be... a millionaire wi they prices?"

Chapter 9

"**WILL I RING** for Cathie to serve us coffee?" Aunty asked me. "Are you still writing? Do you want more time? The coffee's late, I wonder where the woman's got to!" Aunty looked at me still scribbling in my notebook.

"No, I am nearly finished, I wanted to add some of my own thoughts and opinions on the topics you covered this morning. You said I could make changes as I saw fit when we started, remember?"

"Of course I remember, but which opinions of yours are you adding?"

"Well, for instance, post-natal depression and family planning. Post-natal depression has not been recognised as a separate psychological condition until quite recently, and in my opinion the old doctor took a bit of a risk with Aggie. I guess prior to clinical recognition, women were told to pull themselves together, or they were just looking for attention and to get over it. To be honest I'm not sure if they will ever find out what causes it in an otherwise healthy woman, with no previous history of psychological problems other than childbirth. There's a degree to which the condition affects individual women. Some women sail through the post-natal phase with no adverse effects, but for others post-natal depression begins a few days after they deliver. Thankfully for most it passes relatively quickly, even before their six week check-up. But for others it's a different story altogether." I stopped to recollect my thoughts, before continuing.

"I remember one young woman, Aunty – first pregnancy, normal delivery, a healthy baby, the couple and the family were delighted. I'll never forget her distraught pleading: 'Take him away... I don't want him!' a day later. There was no option; a psychiatric referral had to be made. Both mother and baby were admitted to the psychiatric ward for observation right away. The obstetricians and psychiatrists couldn't risk discharging her in case she harmed herself or the infant. It's also important mother and baby are kept together to bond. She was the woman who came to mind because she gave a description of what post-natal depression felt like. However irrational, she said it was as if 'rain... grey rain was raining inside her head'. So I included it in your story as it made me think of Aggie."

I didn't think I would ever be able to forget that girl, the lost expression on her face. She just could not understand why she felt the way she did; she thought she was going crazy.

"But there is something else that bugged me while I was listening to you... Maggie's family planning advice! Not much has changed for the single woman either."

"How much more of this do I have to listen to?" Aunt Jane snapped. "It's your interpretation; write what you want, that was our agreement, but I don't think adding a chapter on family planning is pertinent. I assure you there will be no more on that subject."

"I am not adding it to the narrative. I thought you might be interested in how little has changed for single women. We have a new pharmacological miracle called 'The Pill', and its only being prescribed for married women. I ask you Aunty, have women no rights, no needs, no feelings? Are we not allowed to satisfy our own sexual desires? Men don't think about it, not a single thought, but it's the women who have to bear the consequences. Who makes that vital decision for us? Doctors, politicians, priests, and they are nearly all men. So what is available to unmarried girls? Nothing! Can you imagine the look on Brown's face, if any of the local girls went into his 'Barbour's' shop to buy condoms? What about the withdrawal method Maggie described to her daughter, relying on the man – and you know how reliable men are!"

"Where is this getting us?" Aunty attempted to dismiss the conversation. "I wish Cathie would hurry up with the coffee."

I pressed on regardless about the subject, interesting to me both as a young unmarried woman and doctor, to fill in time before the coffee arrived.

"As you know Aunty, there's nothing a woman can do on the spur of the moment to prevent pregnancy, when love or lust take over; do we supress our feelings? What, are we only fit for breeding purposes and denied sexual pleasure? And if a woman becomes pregnant and the man refuses to marry her… double punishment, for her, not the man. Admission to the 'Home for Unmarried Mothers', the birth certificate with only the mother's name on it, broadcasting the child's illegitimacy; advised to have the baby adopted, the baby taken from its mother at birth, inhuman, cruel, personally I cannot imagine the pain. The memories the woman has to live with for the rest of her life and never be able to confess her sin. It's as if they have committed a crime. Things have to change, Aunty."

"That's enough of that; we will not discuss this subject any further. You will say no more."

What was bugging her? I couldn't believe it, Aunty the prude, after her confessions of unmarried sex. She must have got lucky and the man she had sex with must have been reliable in the coitus interruptus department, or sterile. For a fleeting moment however, Aunty looked pensive, sad even as I spoke; maybe she wished she had had family.

At the sound of the tea trolley Aunty's demeanour radically changed. "Ah, here's Cathie! I can hear the trolley coming down the hall. But what's that smell? Has Christmas come early?" Aunty, sarcastic as always, asked, wrinkling her nose, but there was no doubt; a strong spicy smell was emanating from that direction towards our nostrils and became even stronger as Cathie entered the room.

"Sorry Cathie, I didn't mean to tease you this morning," I apologised.

"What are you talking about?" Aunty demanded to know.

"It's nothing, Miss Jane, a' ken the lassie weel enough no tae tak offence. Oniewey it's my turn tae get revenge," Cathie chirped.

"I am more confused than ever! Will someone tell me what's going on between you two?"

Cathie served the coffee, ignoring Aunty. "Here's yer coffee the wi ye like it… black, nae sugar, richt?" I nodded. She didn't need to ask Aunty what she took in her coffee, knew obviously and served the old lady's white, heavily laced with brown sugar.

Aunty's eyes narrowed as she tried to see past Cathie, as Cathie had turned back to the trolley and bent down to the lower half, obstructing Aunt Jane's view.

Cathie stood up, turned round with a plate covered with a tea towel from the bottom shelf in her hand. With great aplomb, like a magician whisking a cloth off a dove, Cathie uncovered the plate with pride.

"Just for you miss… date, walnut and cinnamon cookies! A' jist happened tae hiv the ingredients in ma pantry and yer richt, the measuring cups are grand, they dinna mak sae much mess wi the flooer."

"Cookies!" Aunty exploded. "Cookies are they… iced buns in disguise? These are *biscuits*, Cathie, *biscuits*, and why so many flavours in them? What a waste!"

"A' decided to tak a recipe from the new American cookery book I was given this morning," Cathie looked at me. "This is the American equivalent of our biscuits, but they seem tae be softer. I didna like tae leave them in the oven ony longer in case they burnt."

"They still look like biscuits to me," was Aunty's tart reply.

"Thank you Cathie, they are delicious and go well with the coffee" – which I had been savouring, while Cathie and Aunty continued to argue the toss whether they were biscuits or cookies. I took a deep breath deciding whether I should leave well alone and just let the pair of them argue it out, or join in. I could see neither was going to give way, Aunty being in a quarrelsome mood and Cathie digging her heels.

"Aunty, in America biscuits are… well, how can I describe them? Let me think… yes, I have it, in the States biscuits are more like Yorkshire puddings, except they are savoury and called pop-overs."

"Pop-overs! Well, now I have heard it all… get on with your coffee or we will never get finished. Cathie, you can clear the dishes while we are at lunch."

Summarily dismissed, Cathie smiled triumphant and left us on our own. Aunty leant toward me and glancing at the door to make sure Cathie couldn't hear, whispered, "These cookies are delicious."

Refreshed, Aunty continued with her narrative.

Chapter 10

BACK AT THE GARDNER household in Pittendreal, Wullie Gardner was a troubled man. To start with, Jock had not appeared and now he was alone with his baby daughter. All had gone well for the first hour after his wife and mother-in-law left, leaving Wullie with a hundred and one instructions ringing in his ears. The baby slept soundly as Wullie sat in the rocking chair puffing away at his pipe, rocking the cradle with his foot and reading the *Courier*. But for the last half hour, the infant had been yelling holy murder. Wullie frantically rocked the cradle till the infant was almost banging her head on its wooden sides.

"Am telling yae, yae dinna' need tae torture prisoners. Just mak them listen tae the racket you're makin' for an hour or two and they'll confess tae onythin tae get peace and quiet. You'll need tae hid yer wheesht – stop greetin', yer gien me a headache!" Wullie scratched his balding head trying to remember… what was it Aggie told him to do if the bairn cried? Pick her up, you stupid man, walk her up and down the kitchen, rub her back, she might have wind, she'd settle down and go back to sleep once she broke it. Wullie emptied his pipe in the grate, threw the *Courier* on the floor and did just that, tried everything he'd been told, but the baby screamed on… By now the infant had managed to break free from the tight swaddled shawl, her little fingers becoming snarled in its cobwebby pattern. Scarlet in the face, it looked like she was doing a frantic form of semaphore with the shawl, the only problem… Wullie couldn't read semaphore.

Picking the baby up, Wullie announced to the empty room: "That's it, a've had enough! I'll need tae find another wuman tae help me, a' dae ken whit's wrang." Wullie left the house and walked into a deserted Rodger Street. Good grief, not a soul in sight, where is everybody? 'I forgot the market's on in St Creils, no wonder the street's empty,' Wullie remembered, 'but you must like being walked, you've stopped bawling.' The movement did seem to quieten the screaming infant, but as soon as Wullie stopped the bellowing started; the more he walked the less she bawled. Proceeding along Rodger Street, Wullie followed a well-worn track that found the pair of them at the bottom of the Kirk Wynd.

Straight ahead *The Royal Diadem*, his own fishing boat, was waiting for the new nets. Subconsciously, Wullie was making toward The Pirates. In the back of his mind, he was sure he would find Jock and Auld Tam there, but The Pirates was shut.

"Whar's that daft auld bugger got tae, a'll kick his backside when he gets here!" Wullie was getting angrier by the minute. Standing on the quay he became aware of the rasp of a brake handle grinding on wooden wheels becoming louder. 'A Kirt coming down the Lang Brae? Tam's Kirt with Jock and Auld Tam sitting on it!'

As they reached the quayside, Auld Tam pulled up alongside Wullie and the infant. Jock put his hand up to pre-empt a predictable tongue lashing from his son-in-law.

"Ah dinna you start, Wullie Gairdner, you dae ken the half o' it, ye have nae idea what we've been through. We were on oor wae back frae Leightham mair than an oor ago, when we hit a pothole on the main road and a wheel fell aff. Luckily Mr McDougall the minister was cumin' along the High Road frae the direction o' Leightham. He saw what had happened and stopped tae help us. If it hidna' been for him we wud still have been there."

"Aye Wullie, thank God for the Minister. Nellie got the fricht o' her life, but we managed tae get her oot o' the harness and stuck her in a field," said Auld Tam, echoing Jock's words.

"Got the fricht o' her life? She was the only one who didna get a fricht when that daft auld bugger Stanley Whitehill frae ain o' the Estate farms, cam flee'n' doon the hill and shoot's aff his blunderbuss. I thocht a' was back in the Crimea at the Charge o' the Licht Brigade. Wud yae believe it Stanley wanted tae charge us for the neeps Nellie was helpin' hersel tae in the field. A telt him tae get lost and if he didna stop fire'n that gun he'd lose mair than the money frae his neeps, the coo's in the next field wud stop milkin'."

"Are yae shure yae were at the Crimea?" Wullie interrupted.

"Niver mind that, I'm trying tae tell yea it took up time staundin' arguin' wae Stanley, but we a' managed tae get the nets aff the Kirt. Stanley, then offered tae help as, so between the three o' us hauden the bliddy contraption up, Tam managed tae get the wheel back on. But noo Auld Tam' I'll have tae gaun back up the Comentry Road tae get George Watson tae sort it and it looks like the axel's got a crack as weel. Ma back's killin' me. Awa ye go hame Tam, we'll get help on Monday from some o' the lads, tae get the nets aff the Kirt and on tae the boat, it's no urgent."

"Ma backs sair as weel Jock Booman frae liftin' that wheel and they nets back on the Kirt... is that yer new grandochter Jock? Eh what a bonnie bairn, thank goodness she has no got her faither's nose!"

"Aye big nose Gairdner!" Jock echoed delighted.

"Well let's hope she gets longer legs than yours, Jock Booman," Wullie said, exchanging insult for insult with his father-in-law. "Yer the tallest in the Kirk as long as yer sutten doon man, but the minute ye staund up yer the shortest!"

285

"A think we should wet the bairn's heid afore a go Jock," Tam interrupted, seeing a quarrel brewing between in-laws. When Jock's chin began to stick out, Tam sensed a war was about to erupt, and thought it would be better if Jock moved out of the line of fire.

"A'll gie ye wet her heid the pair o' ye... ye'v wet her heid that much ye'v fair droond the bairn. Have yea no noticed The Pirates' shut?" Wullie had had enough for one day.

"Aye, so I see, but yea didna need te worry Wullie. As a telt Maggie earlier, Davie Muir only lets Auld Tam and me hae twa drams at a time."

"Aye, but the secret is, Wullie," Auld Tam butted in, "Tae gan in twice when Davie's busy. Then he forgets we've already had oor twa drams so we get served again..."

"Haud yer wheesht man, Wullie disnae need tae ken aboot that," Jock interrupted, changed the subject, hastened on to distract his son-in-law.

"Mr McDougall telt us there's to be a Christenin' on Sunday at the Kirk, fur Alice and the minister's bairn. A canna mind the last time a bairn was christened in the Kirk. Oniewey we're a' tae gan and there's a cup o' tea in the Kirk hall fur everybody efter. Are ye cumin' Tam?" Jock announced winking at him, thinking he'd remember to fill his hip flask. Drink tea at a christening? You've got to be joking.

"Aye a' wid nae miss it, thanks for the invitation Jock, but a canna guarantee Junet will be there, she's been awfie busy lately."

"First a' heard o' it, a christening in the Kirk! And tell me since yae seem ta ken everthin' aboot Alice, whaurs that name come from?" It seemed to Wullie he'd had no say in the matter; it had all been arranged without telling him, including his daughter's name. Tam beat a hasty retreat, did a U-turn with the creaking Kirt, and made his way back up the Lang Brae.

Alice, who throughout the discourse had continued to sob and hiccup, now exhausted, was quietly going blue in the lips.

"Ma back's no that sair that a canna tak the bairn. Here, gie her tae me, whit hiv ye been daen' tae her? Cum on ma wee cooshie-doo, cum tae yer auld Dey. A ken what it is ye need, a wee shoogle on the boat."

A large ball of wind had erupted from Alice's mouth, along with a fountain of spew landing on Wullie's shoulder and down his back from the movement of Jock taking the baby from him.

Pulling an old grey hanky from his trouser pocket, Wullie busied himself wiping the sick off his jumper and paying no attention to Jock, now with the baby. When Wullie looked up, to his horror he saw his father-in-law preparing to board the fishing vessel with Alice. Wullie shouted at the man:

"Don't you dare!"

Throwing superstition to the wind and ignoring Wullie's protests, Jock negotiated the pier and boarded the *Diadem* with Alice tucked under his armpit.

"No Dad! Dad!" Wullie shouted. "Bad luck tae tak a red haired woman on board. Weel a' jist hope we dinna' awe droon this winter! On the other haud oniethin's better than listenin' tae that racket," Wullie conceded.

Alice, her trapped wind now relieved, was sleeping contentedly in her grandfather's arms and being rocked gently to and fro with the movement of the boat. Jock grinned from ear to ear triumphant, he'd proved Alice's point – she liked movement, but not a stomach full of wind.

But far from being unlucky, quite the opposite occurred. The following winters saw catch after catch of herring and cod landed by the crate-load and sold at record prices. Alice the red-haired young lady had brought the family good luck, not bad. In no time the story of Jock and his granddaughter got round the village. At first the superstitious fishermen were initially as horrified as Wullie had been. Their usual crew were loath to sail with Wullie that winter, but soon changed their minds as their share of the profit from the catches grew. By the time Alice was three years old, the family had accumulated sufficient resources to buy a new fishing boat, grandly named *The Alice'n Maggie*.

Turning back to the stove Maggie shook herself out of her reverie, returned to the day and the bairn's fifth birthday. Bending over the bubbling pot, she carefully lifted the scalding cloth by the string tied round its neck. Balancing the slippery bundle on a plate, she carefully tipped it sideways to drain off the excess liquid. At the kitchen table Maggie untied the string, folded back the cloth and slid the dumpling onto a fresh dry plate, then placed it in front of the fire to dry and form a skin on the surface. Maggie allowed herself a pat on the back, and announced to anyone who might have been listening: "A dumpling fit fur auld Queen Victoria herself!"

Maggie rarely agreed with Jock, but on this occasion in one of her rare sentimental moments she agreed with him. "A canna believe five years hiv passed. A'll awa oot and meet Alice… wish her a happy birthday."

Chapter 11

THE COFFEE BREAK rapidly followed by lunch had come and gone. Now I was at saturation point, I'd had enough, felt I couldn't write another word. Some aspects of Aunty's story seemed more vivid than others... but which were the true events and which were the ones she made up? I felt as if I was being sucked in and we would never reach the end... but when we reach the end, will it just be the beginning? I hear my great aunt telling the tale, but I no longer hear her voice; I hear the voices of the characters she describes in my ears.

Suddenly I wasn't sure if I wanted to continue. I felt as if I was becoming too emotionally involved. Something was nagging at me, casting doubts, but I couldn't work out what. Did I really want to know the answer to my question? It's no use trying to do a post mortem when there's no corpse. Was I wasting time on a pointless exercise? It was beginning to get on my nerves; I realised I had to pin my aunt down and ask her how much longer this was going to take, and whether all this background information was necessary. I had to get out of the house for a breath of fresh air.

Cathie had left for her usual Sunday visit to her sister Irene's. Aunty and I were left alone in the house. I'd suggested she take a siesta, to which she offered no resistance, but she asked what I was going to do with myself while she took a nap. I began to wonder if a whole day was too tiring for her. We had covered a lot of ground and made considerable progress and at last we had reached the fifth birthday of her friend Alice. Alice-in-Wonderland, but did Alice really exist, and where was the proof? And what did she have to do with the roof being removed from Leightham House?

"I am going down to the beach for a walk," I told her. "I want to clear my head. You warned me before we started our journey I need to separate fact from fiction, but I have to admit I am finding it hard."

I drove down the Lang Brae to the harbour, parked my car on the Mid-Shore and started to walk along the quayside to the beach. A row of, red tiled, irregular sized old houses were on my right. I guess there was no need for planning permission when they were built. The Pirates Inn must have long since disappeared and now a new café was in the place where it must have stood. Café Allan looked interesting and modern; if I ever came back on a Saturday I must go there for a coffee, I thought. On the Harbour side I stopped suddenly, realising I was probably standing at the very spot Wullie, Jock and Auld Tam had stood with the baby. I paused for a moment and took in the view of the harbour. The fishing boats moored alongside the quay, still bobbing up and down as they had for over a hundred years, still protected from port to starboard by their huge jute-filled fenders. In front of me were heaps of fishing nets with rope and cork trimmed edges, fishing creels lying on their sides, wooden boxes with Pittendreal stamped on them stacked in rows and old ships' tackle. Seagulls fighting with each other for fish scraps left behind from the fish-market scuttled out of my way, crying their discontent, the same today as it was yesterday; some things never change.

The strong nagging doubts I had experienced when I left the house seemed to vaporise with the breeze. I felt light hearted and I sensed the closeness, the spirits of the people aunty had described all round me. I could see their thick hand-knitted seaman's gairnseys, their flat tweed caps, tacketty boots and I could hear their strong local dialect in my ears. They held me spellbound for a few seconds, but I felt no fear or threat from these spirits; these were my ancestors, they were my kindred folk and I was one of them. Aunt Jane had said I was involved somehow and I did not believe her then, was even shocked at the thought. I'd asked for proof, now I have the proof standing here on the Mid-Shore. This is the inheritance from my great aunt, but where do I come into it, who am I?

'Wake up, you stupid woman, you're deluded! The sentimental fog lifted from my brain. They are not your people, they are not even Aunt Jane's relatives or ancestors, they're Alice's!' I almost shouted out loud. Doubts crept back once more, but they didn't last long, for in the next ten minutes I had a very strange encounter with someone. Something happened that reawakened my thirst, my desire to know exactly what did take place between Alice and the Leightham Estate.

Walking along the deserted Mid-Shore I reached the end of the quay and went down the sloping stone jetty at the far end. I sat down, took my boots off, left them behind me and walked onto the sand. The bulrushes on the right of the beach headed up towards a grassy incline, in the direction of the High Road. It was the end of August and the holiday-makers had long since left – that's why the place was deserted. The regular July west coast holidaymakers had all gone home and would be back at work, in the shipbuilding yards on the Clyde after the Fair holidays. I knew from early childhood, the visitors booked the same accommodation with the local landladies for the same two weeks every year before leaving. I wondered how they got here now, by bus I supposed, since Beeching closed the railway line along the coast.

The sand scrunched beneath my feet and I breathed in the fresh salty air savouring every moment. This was the cure, be by myself on an empty beach, clear my head. I had earlier begun to question my motives for the time-consuming commitment I had made for myself. Was I becoming bored, regretting even starting, what did it matter what happened to some stupid old house? 'Oh, stop analysing it old girl, you're giving yourself a headache... you started it. Stop right there lady, this is getting you nowhere... take Maggie's advice and live in the now.' So I decided to calm down and live in the present at least for an hour or so and do no more than watch the waves. Listen to the cry of the seagulls and feel the breeze on my face and in my hair.

I hadn't brought a towel with me, but I couldn't resist playing a childhood game of chase with the waves to see if I could avoid getting my feet wet. Which of course I couldn't – they were faster, trickier than me and now my feet were soaked and covered in sand, but it felt good. I gave in and just stood still in the freezing water and looking out toward the North Sea. If I had a boat and sailed out of the estuary, turned north and kept going I could sail right up the Neva River and berth in Leningrad, but doubted they would let me in, with this wretched cold war. A sudden noise attracted my attention, woke me out of my daydreaming and I turned round to see what it was.

I thought I'd heard a dog bark, which was odd because I had not been aware of another presence on the beach when I arrived, probably because I was both lost in thought and concentrating on my game with the waves. A short distance from me was the figure of a man, playing with a dog. I guessed it was his dog because there was no one else around. I couldn't understand how I had missed him. I waved and smiled to the man as the Alsatian bounded towards me, but it swerved past and ran into the sea to retrieve a ball, then returned to the man who ignored me. I had a fleeting memory of my dad telling me when I was quite young that this breed of dog was originally named German Shepherds, but because of the two world wars had been re-named Alsatians because of the association with Germany. Man's inhumanity to man extended to the re-naming of a breed of dog... as if the two wars were the dog's fault.

The dog bounded back to his master, the man bent forward and I saw him put a lead on the animal. They began to walk towards me, still neither acknowledging my existence. I shrugged my shoulders – well, not everyone's friendly. As the man came closer I noticed how tall, rugged and handsome he was. Not young, not old, distinguished only by slightly greying hair at his temples. I couldn't see the rest of his hair as it was covered by some kind of Panama hat. The man was wearing a thick tweed jacket, waistcoat and cravat; I thought that's strange for a warm August afternoon. As they passed I saw the man tip his hat to me… or did I imagine it?

Oh well… turning back to the waves and my game, I decided to ask Aunty about the man and his dog. There couldn't be too many locals with that breed, which suddenly reminded me it was time I got back, I looked at my watch and turned to leave in the same direction as the man, who should have been a few yards in front of me… He had disappeared, dog and all. It was an open beach, he could not possibly have made it to the quay so quickly or the bulrushes, he'd vanished. I shook my head and shut my eyes tight, thinking you need to get your eyes tested. But no, when I opened them I was alone on the beach – nothing wrong with my eyes.

A fog lifted from my brain… In a moment of clarity I realised, Aunt Jane was telling the truth and there was precious little fiction in her tale. Engulfed by today's experiences I realised there was no escape from the Svengali-like hold my aunt had on me, or the spirits of the people on the Mid-Shore. It was as if she had sent them and the man on the beach to find me. Having almost lost interest and loathe to write any more, I now felt like a drug addict in need of a fix. Hypnotised by two strange encounters, I was more than ready for the next instalment. With all reservation and doubts gone, I made my way back to Aunty's house.

I found Aunty back in the lounge waiting for me.

"That walk has done you the world of good my dear, your eyes have a sparkle in them and your cheeks are glowing. Let's begin. There is not much more to cover today, then you can be on your way home."

"You're right Aunty, I was at saturation point before I went down to the beach. I don't think I could have taken in another word." I hesitated for a moment... Feeling spirits around me was one thing I would keep quiet about, but to say I actually say saw something or rather someone who disappeared in front of me was quite another. I'd no idea how my aunt might respond; she'd probably think I'd lost my reason and tell me to go home. But I wasn't prepared for her response.

"Aunty..." I hesitated, chewing on my lip for a second wondering, should I ask her or not, but decided I would, as it would bother me all night if I didn't. "Aunty, I saw a man on the beach with an Alsatian dog... When I looked in his direction a second time he seemed to have disappeared as quickly as he appeared. Do you know who he was?"

"Ah...you've seen him too." Turning away, she looked out of the lounge window assuming the usual impersonal distant pose she always assumed when narrating her story. Then she launched into the last chapter, without further ado.

Chapter 12

"I HAVE A PROPOSITION for you, Janet."

'God almighty, what a stupid thing to say! You fool, you've ruined it, frightened her before you have even begun. Heaven only knows what she thought you meant. Get on with it; hurry up before she realises, takes offense and leaves.'

Janet stared up at Alasdair in disbelief. She knew exactly what that statement meant.

"I... I put that badly, please don't be offended," Alasdair managed to stutter, aware of his reddening cheeks. Janet made to walk away and he hastened to prevent her by reaching out and taking a hold of her arm. Her eyes looked down momentarily at his hand before she slowly looked up at him.

"I am sorry," he repeated. "We have a history Janet, a connection."

'What connection?' Janet thought. She was rarely sarcastic, but felt justified in thinking just that, considering the statement Alasdair had just made.

"Wait Janet, do you think I would jeopardise that, by proposing something indecent? I would do whatever it takes to preserve the memories that I have of you... us... you caring for me when I was desperately ill and I thought I was going to die. You gave me the will to live, even in the strangest of ways. I have never forgotten. Let me make it up to you."

They both stood silent, each with their thoughts regarding those few fateful emotional weeks. Alasdair thought, 'I have never shown much gratitude or told you how you changed my life. I fell in love... have loved you ever since, but can't admit to it.' Alasdair rarely allowed himself the luxury of looking back because it hurt. 'Well, get on with what you wanted to do... already you've nearly blown it. She's not your patient and you're not her doctor.' Looking down at Janet's calm expression, he might have been surprised to know what was going through her mind at that precise moment.

She was not in the least bit offended, a little surprised maybe, but in fact was wishing he would propose something indecent. At least it would make a pleasant change from the usual silent treatment she received whenever they met. Somewhere along the line she had realised he had deliberately avoided and ignored her over the years.

"I can only repeat, don't be offended."

'Plod on Alasdair with your big flat feet, but she has the oddest effect on me. When we are close, she reduces me to a drivelling idiot. Maybe that's why I avoid her.'

The two had met at the top of Rodger Street, by intent on Alasdair's part. He knew she had been attending one of the local girls that had recently given birth and he was on a routine return visit to old Martin Anderson next door. Alasdair hung about the pavement outside the Anderson's house, keeping one eye open for her and pretended to write up his notes. When he saw her coming out of number twenty, he walked towards her.

Janet prepared to dip her head slightly to acknowledge his presence and to pass by as she usually did, expecting him to give the usual perfunctory nod. They were now standing side by side, but facing in opposite directions. Every time Janet moved with the intention of moving on, Alasdair tightened his grip. He became pleasantly aware of the throb of her pulse and the warmth of her body through the sleeve of her blouse and it stirred old memories.

Janet stood still, made no attempt to walk away. He moved round to face her so he could look down into those steady blue eyes. She met his gaze, unwavering. Even being a little surprised at his unusual behaviour, her eyes still betrayed nothing, looking up steadily at him with that same impenetrable veil he knew so well. Where had that unemotional shield she had imposed on herself come from, and would he ever know? He recognised that look when he first became aware of Janet the girl, but now she was a beautiful young woman. Tall, slender, her fine white skin, the throb of her heartbeat at her throat that he knew so well; he silently cursed her, but secretly was pleased she had not married. He hoped the reason was him and felt disgusted at the pleasure he took in the fact she was still single; but then he was still a bachelor and his mother took no pleasure in that.

"Doctor Forman?" Janet queried.

'How the hell is it that after all these years you can still be · dominated by your mother, fearful she will think Janet is not good enough for you, when the truth is I am not good enough for her. Is there a point to these thoughts, Alasdair? Janet would probably turn and run if she knew what you were thinking; you love her? Ha, that's a joke, when you have avoided her at every possible encounter, terrified in case you betray your feelings. God, how cruel can life be? My feelings have never changed over the years and shame on me I have passed you in the street, as if it was beneath my dignity to acknowledge your very existence. Driving away, not stopping to offer a lift, even in the rain, any other decent man would have offered you a lift. Shameful! And you justified your behaviour by pretending it's your mother's fault and you are shy? So stop wasting her time and tell her what it is you want to discuss.'

But looking down on Janet's beautiful face, his heart quickened and he almost forgot the purpose of stopping her in the first place.

"Doctor Forman?" Janet repeated.

"Ah, yes, as I was saying." He cleared his throat. "Would you be willing to, if you could, come to the surgery tonight? There is a matter I would like to discuss with you. Please don't concern yourself; I am certain you will find the information I have is to your advantage," he bumbled on, realising he was making a complete ass of himself. "Would six thirty suit you? I have asked Rena to stay a little longer tonight, as I thought we could all share a cup of tea and please bring my friend Old Tam with you – I have not seen him about the village recently." He thought: 'Give me some sort of answer Janet, don't make me beg.'

"Tam has had a cold recently and I have made him stay at home, probably that's why you have not seen him about and he is not as young as he used to be. Soon he will deserve the title *Auld*," Janet replied, defusing the situation. She knew exactly what had been going on in Alasdair's mind. She could read him like a book.

"You are not giving me much time to think about it, Dr Forman,"

Initially Janet had wondered what the man was on about, 'a proposition'. That was a quaint way of putting it. Talking about Tam had helped stall for time so she could think about the invitation to the Doctor's house, and also to make Alasdair wait for an answer.

"Well, think about it," Alasdair urged, but it was very important Janet came.

She watched the Doctor walk back to the buggy and take hold of the horse's reins, but he then dropped them, turned back and walked towards her.

"Until tonight?" he asked, not letting her off the hook and raising an eyebrow. 'Witchy, you're not the only one who can read minds. You'll come.' He was sure of it.

298

She stood still and thought back on that fatal night that changed their lives. That very special night they shared – it seemed so long ago now and she would never forget it.

Alasdair went back to the buggy, climbed up, took up the reins and flicked them at the horse. As the animal pulled away from the pavement he looked over his shoulder and called out to her:

"Bring that old box, the one you said was the only possession you had in the world that belonged to you. It might have some important information in it that could be useful. Have you opened it yet…?"

Chapter 13

"OH, HELLO JUNET, Tam, we're expecting yae, come awa ben the hoose." Rena welcomed the odd looking pair with a bright smile. "The kettle's coming tae the bile."

"Tam, remember, take your bonnet off before we enter the house and make sure you give your feet a good wipe on the scraper at the front door," Janet had ordered Tam before they left the cottage for Dr Forman's house. So Tam stood at the doorstep, having just about scraped the soles off his boots as instructed, and followed Janet down the hall to Alasdair's sitting room.

Janet glanced back to make sure Tam was still behind her and not bolting back to the horse to make his escape.

"Tam, your bonnet!" Janet hissed.

"Oh aye, my bunnet." Tam grabbed the offending item of clothing from his head and began to wring it between his gnarled old hands to conceal how nervous he was, then followed Janet down the hall like a lapdog with its tail between its legs.

"Just hiv' a seat the pair o' you, the Doctor will not be long, he's finishing wi the last patient. I'm awa tae mak' the tea, make yersel comfortable on the settee, I'll be back in a minute." With that warm welcome ringing in their ears, Rena turned and left for the kitchen.

"Whit is this awe aboot, Junet? Yae ken I'm no that happy tae be here, a' telt yea a' didna want tae come."

"To be honest, Tam, I don't know any more than you. I met the Doctor in Rodger Street this morning and he asked if we could both join him tonight. It seemed to me there was no reason to refuse. I guess it affects us both as he asked specifically for you to be here, so just behave yourself and sit still. I am sure we have nothing to worry about."

The pair, now seated very uncomfortably on the edge of the couch, waited side by side in silence. Tam had taken his jacket off and Janet her shawl when they arrived and hung them on the hall stand. Thankfully over the years Janet had finally managed to get the smell of manure out of Tam's clothes by soaking and boiling them in turn, so sitting beside him now was quite bearable. Simultaneously they turned at the sound of a trolley being wheeled from the kitchen into the sitting room.

The trolley entered carrying fine china cups, plates and a matching sugar bowl, milk jug and a silver tea service on the upper shelf. The smell of fresh baked scones wafted towards them, accompanied by the necessary butter and jam in crystal dishes, and a plate of iced buns on the lower. All the reassuring sounds and smells put Janet and Tam at their ease as they simultaneously sat back on the couch. Rena, smiling from ear to ear, proceeded to serve the tea. She had been in control of the Doctor's household and all his domestic needs from the day she arrived. Having catered for the Doctor's mother and another woman who she took to be his Aunt, she felt she could please the pair if not the Queen herself!

"Ah dinna think I'v thanked you enough Junet for getting me this hoosekeepin' job. A dinna ken what I would have done or what would have happened tae me and ma bairns, efter ma man was drooned. It's been such a blessing. Did a tell yae ma lawdie, Brian want's tae gaun tae the University in Edinburgh? Aye I was tellin' Doctur Forman how weel he's been doing at the school and how he had admired the Doctur that much, he wants tae be a Doctur like him!" Rena continued, her chest puffed with pride: "Am that prood Junet and between you and me the Doctur is gaun tae help oot wi' the fees and gawn to get his mother to find accommodation for Brian in the big city, keep an eye on him ye ken? But that will be a couple of years yet, he's still ower young."

Rena stopped, a smile crossing her face. "Ah, here's the Doctur, I kin hear him locking the surgery door. I've been telling Junet aboot Brian," she announced looking towards the door as Alasdair entered, still drying his hands on a towel. He wanted to look like a confident, professional man, cool and collected.

"Now Rena, that was to be strictly confidential between you and me, but I know Janet and I know she will keep it a secret." He turned his handsome face towards Janet, smiling broadly. Turning back to Rena, he asked, "What about that cup of tea Rena? Two scones please, butter and some of your bramble jelly, I am famished! I'll get my supper later, after we have finished our meeting."

Rena duly placed the cup of tea with milk and two sugars on the side table next to the big armchair, which was obviously the doctor's chair. The two scones as requested came next. 'Where to begin?' Alasdair wondered as he mulled over the options as he chewed the scone. 'The beginning, you idiot,' he snapped at himself, 'try the beginning, but at least let everybody finish eating and you better not speak with your mouth full and spray everyone with crumbs like old Harry.' With a few more pleasantries and enquiries to everyone's wellbeing between mouthfuls, he was ready. He had to smile at Janet kicking Tam on the side of his ankle after he'd asked about their health, as Tam had started to tell the Doctor about his 'awfy sair back'. That delightful relationship between the young woman and the old man had never changed.

"Let me begin." Alasdair was not smiling now.

Turning his full attention on Janet, he remembered how serious the subject of the meeting was. His facial expression had changed as he placed his cup and saucer back on the side table. He was not joking now or exchanging pleasantries. Rena, sensing the meeting was about to begin, rose to clear the dishes away.

"No! Leave it. You can do the clearing up when we have finished; I need you here, Rena, as you already know." A little startled at the Doctor's sharp words, Rena resumed her seat. '

'Let me get this over with, as quickly as possible,' Alasdair thought. 'I am about to offer Janet something on one hand and threaten to take it away with the other.'

"I have asked you here on a serious matter, Janet."

A temporary frown crossed Janet's face as she failed to comprehend what Alasdair was talking about, but the facial guard returned, unreadable.

"The law has changed Janet, it will be mandatory for anyone working in any aspect of nursing to be registered with the newly formed Nursing Councils.

"From now on, Hospitals will be obliged to train their nursing staff both in practical and written work to a standard that will satisfy examiners of their competence to practice, and that means studying and sitting exams. In Scotland, successful candidates will be placed on a register. They will then be 'State Registered Nurses' with written documentary proof. In future when applying for a nursing post, these documents will need to be submitted." Alasdair drank the last of his tea. Turning to Rena to break the tension, he asked, this time a little more politely:

"Could I have a little more tea please, Rena?"

"I'll make a fresh pot Doctur, this one is cauld."

"Good." Alasdair turned back to Janet. "This will give you time, Janet, to think over the information I have just given you. It's a lot to take in."

Rena returned from the kitchen with the fresh pot of tea and sat down. The room was silent. All were deep in thought, except perhaps Tam. This was beyond him – all he could think of was Jock waiting for him in The Pirates.

"So," Alasdair continued, "what has this got to do with you? Just this, my advice: apply to a training hospital and train for the required three years, sit the exams and be awarded your certificates." Janet opened her mouth to speak but Alasdair held his hand up to silence her.

"Let me finish." Calmly he continued: "With the recent change in the law, they are going to come down heavily on anyone working in this field unregistered; in other words, not qualified to practise caring for the sick. Those found guilty of practicing without certification by the courts, maybe fined or sent to jail." He looked straight at Janet to observe her reactions. Finding none, he continued:

"I propose to support your application to one of the Nursing Schools in Edinburgh. I know you will do well. I have the utmost respect for your intelligence, integrity, ability to keep a confidence and your healing instincts are phenomenal. God only knows I am the living proof of that. As for your academic abilities, had you held the high-school certificates necessary to study medicine, I would have had no hesitation applying for admission to the University's medical school for you. However as things stand that is impossible. Please accept my apologies; I have no wish to offend you. Instead I will do what I can to help." He paused.

"Before I ask for your thoughts, I must also inform you that with these changes in the law, if I at any time I observed you to be involved in medical-nursing practises, I would be legally bound to report it to the authorities. That is a decision I don't ever want to have to make. Do you understand me, Janet?" He leaned towards the woman. "You would be practicing illegally and I would or could be suspended for condoning it. I would be as guilty as you for not informing the authorities. I would have no option, even if it goes against the grain because of my respect for you. If one of my patients ever came to the surgery and complained about you, my hands would be tied." He held both his hands up in the air to express the seriousness of the situation, although silently he had to acknowledge none of his patients had ever complained to him about Janet.

"For the sake of the patients and the law I have to be ruthless. This is a good thing; it is progress and about time too. I already have an old witch in my sights to report, the widow Dickson. I believe she lives at the back of St Creils and no one sees what she gets up to for a few miserable pennies. I have not only heard stories, but seen evidence of her butchery and I know the patients are too embarrassed or afraid to report it." Alasdair narrowed his eyes in contempt for the woman. How many painful deaths had she caused with her dirty crochet hooks and knitting needles?

"She is the first on my list to be reported and the quicker the better before another young life is lost."

Rena stood up and duly poured out the fresh tea, adding milk and sugar to all who wanted it. It was her way of breaking an uncomfortable tension that had spread throughout the room.

Janet had listened carefully to all Alasdair had said and had absorbed every word with her calm calculating mind. A few minutes passed as they drank their tea. Janet put her cup down on the side table, straightened up and leant forward to speak directly to Alasdair. He closed his eyes for a second, tried to fix this moment in his mind, thinking if Janet chose to leave, it might be a considerable time before he saw her again. 'Ditch conventions, man, go and sit beside her, reassure the woman, push Tam out of the road, hold Janet's hand, and help her decide what to do for the best.' And most of all, he thought, spare himself the horror of having to report her to the police if she decided not to take his advice—some choice! Was he being selfish, thinking of himself and not Janet? Maybe he should just turn a blind eye?

"Thank you, Doctor Forman, for giving me this information and your advice on the matter, offering me a way out because of the forthcoming changes in the law. However, although you have not given me much time to think things over, my principal objection would be this..."

"Tell me what concerns you. I can understand you are worried, but the power to change what is troubling you lie in our own hands Janet, and nothing is set in tablets of stone."

"First and foremost, it's Tam." She turned slightly, leaning towards the old man. "I cannot leave him. Who is going to look after him?" She turned back to face Alasdair and Rena. "He did not abandon me in my hour of need so many years ago, just as I did not abandon you, Dr Forman. I will not leave him to move to the City for weeks on end and as you very well know, he cannot come with me. I love this old man just as if he was my real father; he is the only father I have ever known, so in a way you are asking the impossible..." She hesitated before announcing: "I-I think I would rather go to jail than leave him."

Alasdair and Rena burst out laughing; even Janet gave a wry smile. She had just confirmed the very situation Alasdair was trying to avoid, by suggesting the same difference, the jail or the training school.

Out of the back of the settee a deep guttural voice spoke. Tam had sat silent but now, pulling an old handkerchief out of his pocket, he dabbed at his eyes, moved at Janet's speech. Putting the hankie back, he spoke in an emotional voice:

"A hiv been listening tae awe you've been saying. Now a ken I'm no that bright but I understand some o' it." Looking straight at Janet with his soft wrinkled old eyes, he went on, "Dinna fash yersel about me lassie, I'll be fine. Whit dae ye think ah did afore ye cam tae live wi me?" The old man stuck his chin up with pride. "A' kin look efter masel, I'll no stand in yer way. The Doctur's makin richt guid sense..."

"Wait Tam," Alasdair interrupted the old man. "We haven't finished yet and thank you for your support on the matter, but Rena and I have given it some considerable thought and I am sure we have come up with a solution we hope will be acceptable to you both."

"An' whit's that?"

"Aye Tam," said Rena, glad of the chance to speak at last and add her contribution. It was also Rena's chance at last to repay Janet for what she had done for her all these years ago.

"The Doctur and I have given a lot of thocht tae it and if you are willin' we are gaun tae' look after yae. Whit dae yae think o' that noo, Tam?"

"It is Doct-or... Rena... Doctor." Alasdair patiently one more time tried to correct Rena's pronunciation; in fact there had been times when he was at home, when he had described himself as the 'Doctur', just to annoy his mother, but Marjory laughed at his colloquial antics and advised him not to torment the poor woman.

"Aye whatever yae say, Doct-hoor."

Alasdair raised an eyebrow. 'Give in laddie, you will never change the way she speaks, and do you really want to?' No, he supposed not. "Now tell them our plan, Rena," Alasdair magnanimously handed the floor to his housekeeper again.

"Tam, we're baith prepared tae care fur yae while Janet's awa' at the training. All you need tae dae is bring yer dirty washin doon here on a Monday an' I'll hae it ready for yae tae collect on Wednesday dependin' on the weather. Pass by every day at teatime, I'll mak a wee bit extra food so your supper will be ready every nicht, you will jist have tae warm it up when you get hame. Noo how does that sound Tam... Junet?" She looked at each of them in turn for an answer.

Tam was the first to respond to the 'plan'. Turning to Janet, he said it sounded grand to him and he was pleased the Doctor and Rena had thought so much of them both.

"Sounds grand tae me, Janet, I'll no stand in the wi o' yea bettering yer sel and I'm dammed if I'll stand by and see yea sent tae the jile – sorry aboot the language Doctur." A thought had also passed through Tam's mind: no more nagging from Janet regarding his drinking habits with Jock, or about the dirt he was bringing in the cottage with his dirty feet. He'd get a wee bit of peace and quiet. Then it struck him, he'd be alone, but this time not for ever.

"Thank you Tam, that's very good of you, and don't worry, I am sure every holiday Janet gets she will be back," Alasdair nodded. 'And I will have a reason to see more of her and enquire how she's getting on.'

"Now down to business, what is your full name Janet... middle name or names, if you have more than one, and your surname?"

"My name Doctor Forman ... my name..." Janet gasped. "You don't understand, I don't have a name, first, middle or last! Janet is the one Tam gave me the night I arrived in Pittendreal. I felt sure you already knew that."

Alasdair noticed Janet becoming tense as she sat forward as if preparing to rise up. This was the last thing he wanted her to do. Leave before they had settled things.

"Yes, I remember now. How about we open that black wooden box? There could be documents relating to your birth in it. The box, the one you told me about a few...'

"No!"

Taken aback, Alasdair had forgotten how badly she reacted the last time he talked about the damn box. He decided to ask Rena and Tam to leave. He thanked Rena for staying and providing such a fine cup of tea and her delicious scones as always, but now if she did not mind, clear away the dishes and go home. Or better still she could wash up in the morning when she came back. Rena readily agreed to go, realising the Doctor wished to be alone with Janet and her family would be waiting for her. Obviously there was some serious business to discuss and the Doctor wished to do it in private with Janet. Tam stood and nodded as usual with that stupid look of innocence on his face when in actual fact it was the look that said 'time tae get tae The Pirates'.

"Tam you have been a great help, perhaps you could give Rena a lift into the village, do you have your cart with you? Yes, well, coats on and I will escort you to the front door." He raised his hand to stop Tam protesting about leaving Janet behind.

"She will be safe with me Tam, no need to worry, I will take good care of her, and when we have completed the business in hand I will walk with her to the cottage."

At the same time Alasdair, unseen, slipped a shilling coin into Tam's hand and whispered to him, out of Rena's earshot, as they walked down the hall:

"Enjoy a wee dram on me, Tam, and thank you for getting Janet here. I knew if you protested the visit she would insist on coming." He winked at the old man and in a louder voice, "Come and visit me when Janet's away, I enjoyed our last game of cribbage, not that I can remember much about it, the state I was in. Perhaps we could try dominoes next time?"

"Hurry up Tam, ma bairns are waitin'," Rena called out.

Tam, grinning from ear to ear, whispered "Thanks Doctur" as he went forward to help Rena up onto the cart.

Chapter 14

ALASDAIR returned to the living room, unsure what Janet's reactions would be now they were alone. Janet was still seated on the couch. She had looked around the room during Alasdair's absence and had realised nothing had changed; curtains and chairs were the same from the time she had nursed him. He had insisted the room stay exactly the same as it had been during his illness to preserve his memories of Janet and those few precious weeks he'd shared with her. It always seemed to him whatever he encountered in life he took comfort in that room; now with Janet in it, it seemed as if she belonged there, but suddenly Alasdair felt nervous, unsure of himself and he began to make inane comments.

"The evenings are drawing in Janet, soon it will be winter and this room gets cooler at night, so I am going to light the fire. What we have to discuss won't take long, but it will be warmer and more pleasant for us with the fire lit." With that he took a match from a jar on the mantelpiece and lit the fire. As the flames appeared, he turned and gave Janet one of his endearing smiles to reassure the both of them. The firewood was tinder dry after a long hot summer and caught alight quickly, giving the room a soft flickering glow.

Janet stared into the dancing flames reminding her not to get too comfortable as she would have to leave soon. Deliberately, Alasdair picked up his pipe from the small table at the side of his chair, took his tobacco pouch from a small drawer in the same table, shook out the shag and filled the pipe.

Pressing it down tightly with his fingers, he lit it with a taper from the fire and sucked in the smoke, trying not to cough.

"Does my smoking bother you? I can put it out," he hastened to assure Janet as he saw her nose wrinkle at the smell. "The truth is I am not that fond of smoking; I just do it to show my mother I am a big boy now."

'Are you trying to reassure me you are all grown up, Alasdair?' Janet refraining from shaking her head and thinking here we go again... his mother. Alasdair and Janet looked at each other across the fireplace, neither willing to look away. Alasdair did, resisting the temptation to go and sit next to her and hold her in his arms, tell her how much he missed her and had longed for her company. Instead he turned back to the fireplace and tapped the tobacco out of his pipe. They both watched the sparks of light from the tobacco disappear up the chimney and relished the unspoken communication between them. He finally summoned the courage; he got up and went over to the couch to sit beside Janet. To his relief, Janet did not object.

"Janet, I am reluctant to break the silence and I am loathe to interrupt the peace after a long day at work, but we must make a start resolving the problems I have made for you."

'So now it's your work that's the problem between us, work... just get on with it Alasdair, the quicker we get this charade over with the better. Nothing has changed; what you say with your eyes you never confirm with your mouth.'

"Janet, I will do whatever you are comfortable with. I did give some consideration to this and thought long and hard before I made the proposal in the first place. In the hope you accept Nurses training, we have obstacles to overcome and the first most important as I said earlier, is a surname. To the best of my knowledge I have never heard anyone use a surname when they speak of you, Janet, is that correct?"

"Yes," she answered simply.

"I am guessing now so please forgive me if I get my facts wrong, but before we can go any further it is essential to have a birth certificate to forward with your application to the Royal Hospital's school of nursing. They will not accept you for training without one. Getting references to go with your application is the least of our worries, but a birth certificate is mandatory." Alasdair opened his hands towards Janet, raising his shoulders slightly in a sort of questioning manner, waiting for her to answer.

"I have already explained about my name and you know full well that I don't have a birth certificate."

Sensing her distress Alasdair seized the opportunity to move closer to Janet on the couch and put one arm round her shoulder, holding her hand with the other. Now close to Janet on the couch he could feel the heat from her leg next to his. Breathing in, he inhaled that intimate scent of lavender that always came from her. Here, sitting next to him, reminding him of that once close personal relationship that he couldn't seem get out of his head. 'Enjoy it, Alasdair, it's not going to last long.' Oh, if only things were different, but nothing had changed, nor his mother's attitude and she never stopped harping on about him not being married.

Janet's head was inclined a little towards her lap. What to do next? She wasn't sure. She turned to Alasdair and her deep blue eyes met his; suddenly she reached out and with both hands, lifted his left hand and turned the palm upwards. The wound, long since healed, had left an ugly scar right down the centre of it. Gently she stroked the long white indurated mark, put his hand to her mouth and kissed it, then very quietly spoke as if she was talking to herself.

"It seems so long ago, Alasdair." She realised at once what she had said and done. Overcome with embarrassment, she quickly dropped his hand and apologised for her familiarity. "I am so sorry, I don't know what overcame me Doctor Forman, I forgot myself."

"Janet! Look at me, Janet," he said sweetly. "You saved my career; you saved me. As far as I am concerned, without you I would be nothing... maybe not even alive. " He smiled. "I want you to call me Alasdair. Before we blink you will be back in the village, a professional woman, a qualified nurse; though the public may not see us as equals, we both know we are." He frowned a little before he continued:

"You have always puzzled me, Janet. I look at your face and I cannot place your features. The serenity, the high cheek bones, those dark blue eyes; their hidden depths give nothing away. You have another feature that makes me think... but that is for another day. Let me say from the moment we met there have been times I have felt an air of majesty from you and maybe it should be me kissing your hand." He thought: 'Shut up Alasdair, she'll think you've been hitting the laudanum again.' "But I am no further forward in trying to trace your origins now than I was all those years ago. I'll be honest, I did a considerable amount of research when I went home to Edinburgh. I researched the middle and eastern European crisis and came up with nothing. I hit a brick wall simply because I had nothing to go on; just a hunch and your facial features, but that box you spoke of might give a clue. Don't panic, it's not necessary to open it; we will leave well alone, leave the past behind for the present and create a new Janet. How does that sound to you?"

"I do not want to know what the contents of that box are." Janet, now unemotional, emphasised every word, so Alasdair would make no mistake about it. "Perhaps sometime in the future when I feel more confident about being allowed to stay permanently in Scotland, to be able legally to tell the world I am a true Scotswoman. Till then I trust you to proceed as you see fit."

"Well, I have made some enquiries; it seems you are not the only person who has emigrated without papers. It seems we have an ever-increasing population of Polish, Italians and people from other countries arriving in Scotland. Some have documents, but the registrar can't read the writing or the language they are written in. Also the immigrants may not speak English so can't help immigration decipher it. Or the surname is impossible to pronounce even if they do speak English. So the immigration officer asks the family what surname they want to be registered with. That's why we have surnames like Barbour, Baker or Butcher. The family looked in the street around them and opted for the name above a shop front. Very intelligent. in my opinion." Alasdair thought for a second before he returned to the question in hand.

"But back to the present, I spoke in confidence about this with Tom McDougall and he asked if you would be willing to go to the Manse and be christened, privately mind you, not in church. Tom, he's a very decent guy, he will record the baptism in the Pittendreal Parish church records and issue you with a baptismal certificate to take to the Registrar in Edinburgh and possibly the registrar will issue you with an official birth certificate. It is possible together with the hospital's application form and references from Tom and me you will be accepted. I know it all sounds very improbable but it is our best hope. Tom says they issue birth certificates to all the abandoned babies in the orphanages without any parental information, so there should be no problem for you to get yours."

"Please don't hold it against me Doctor, I mean Alasdair, but with my history I have found it very hard to believe in a God who abandoned me."

"It may come as a surprise to you Janet, but you are echoing much the same sentiments I also hold regarding religion, but let's see it as a means to an end and Tom would understand, so you don't have to feel like a hypocrite. Let's face it Janet, desperate times call for desperate measures. I am sure if there is a God he will forgive us. Just think, if we were Catholics we could go to confession, confess our sins to the priest, ask for forgiveness and do penance!"

"Please Alasdair, don't joke."

"Jail, Witchy, jail, that's the alternative!" he continued to tease Janet.

In the present situation Alasdair had thrust Janet into, she was far from thinking it was a joking matter – and she wished he would stop calling her Witchy.

"But," she said, "what about a name – a surname?"

"Well, I wonder if you would do me the honour..."

Janet's eyes, normally the size of saucers, enlarged to the size of plates. What was he going to ask? And what would she say if he did?

He quickly realised he had made another ridiculous statement and hurried on. "Do me the honour of accepting my surname. Miss Janet Forman? You probably would prefer Tam's surname, but I doubt he remembers what it is and I am certain he will not have a birth certificate we can show to the Registrar as proof of his existence, but I have mine here. We can take it with us when we go to Edinburgh."

'Mrs Alasdair Forman would suit me better Alasdair, but that's not going to happen,' she thought sadly.

"Well, what do you think, Miss Janet Foreman? It has a ring to it." If only it was a ring he was offering her. Alasdair was genuinely sad.

"I do." Janet used the words of the marriage ceremony, hoping they would not be lost on Alasdair. "I do accept your proposals; I will gladly be christened by Mr McDougall and I will go with you to Edinburgh, but I am sorry Alasdair... I cannot accept your family's surname, no."

"As you wish, but you still need to come up with an alternative…"

"I know, Mr and Mrs McDougall – as you just said, they are kind compassionate people. I will ask them if they would do me the honour of allowing me to use their surname."

"That's settled then, for the future and a professional career for you, Nurse Janet McDougall. However, I must warn you it won't be easy. I don't want to put you off before you begin, but those ward sisters rule with rods of iron. They bullied us as students, registrars and even the consultants at times. Can you believe they sleep in a sort of bedsit just off the main ward so they see and hear everything that goes on day or night? Privately I think they are a load of bad tempered dried up old maids. Remember Janet, once you start… good, bad or indifferent, there can be no turning back. You cannot continue as things stand, but any time you want to let off steam during your training, come back on your days off and holidays and visit me." At last, a good excuse to see Janet on a harmless regular basis.

With all the clinical details discussed and hopefully resolved, the two sat on, comfortable in each other's company. Each loathed breaking the spell. Alasdair still held Janet's hand; both looked at the flickering of the flames and listened to the crackling of the logs. Reluctantly Alasdair laid Janet's hand back on the couch and stood up.

'Ah Janet, if only things were different, a different time, a different place and goodness only knows when we will be together again like this,' Alasdair thought.

"Time to move, it's been pleasant having you here to myself, but I have to get you home. I promised Tam and I bet your cat's waiting for you, Witchy."

'I do wish he would stop smiling that lop-sided handsome smile at me,' Janet thought.

316

"You know very well I don't have a cat," she smiled, "and after I have completed my nurses training... don't you dare call me Witchy!"

"It's a bargain! Tomorrow's Friday and it's always a busy surgery. Rena tells me the patients turn up because they know I will see them before the week-end, as I don't have the heart to turn them away."

"Why don't you think of starting an appointment system, Alasdair?"

"Brilliant idea Janet, for Harley Street, but far too modern for this neck of the woods. I would have a mutiny on my hands. The patients think it is their right to see their 'Doct-ur' whenever they feel like it. Come on, Miss McDougall, let's get you home. I think you left your shawl on the stand by the front door."

Chapter 15

EMBOLDENED by his earlier success with Janet at the house, Alasdair slipped his arm round her shoulder and as she offered no resistance he drew her in close. Together they walked up the Comentry road. Both silent, Alasdair felt in complete harmony with her, but Janet was not talking because she was deep in thought regarding the last twenty-four hours. This strange turn of events, so deep in thought, she was unaware Alasdair had dislodged her hair band when he put his arm round her shoulders. Her luxurious thick brown hair tumbled down her back, curly wisps framing her face. Alasdair looked down at the enchanting vision walking beside him and his heart skipped a beat. A profound sense of longing for her, which had been stifled for so many years, invaded his soul.

Now and again Janet had felt Alasdair's arm tighten, pulling her close and she could feel the heat from his body. Now back in the present she wondered why he didn't just speak and say something. Should she risk speaking first, simply tell him how much she loved him? She always would and nothing he did or say would ever change that love. No other person would take his place in her heart and as far as she was concerned their past history made him hers. There were times she had to admit it had been painful to experience the contempt which he seemed to have treated her with since his illness, but it was her own fault, she had laid down the law on that last evening when they parted. She had no one else to blame but herself. At times she felt hurt he had not protested against her wishes, had not tried to stop her, had fought for her!

But she sensed his eyes following her when she passed on the opposite side of the street from him and was aware of his fleeting glances when they met at a patient's house.

Today his gestures, his facial expressions as he looked at her and the tone in his voice, made it obvious how he felt. But for Janet the biggest confirmation of his love for her was that he was still a bachelor. Why had he not married, a man approaching his thirties? It was very unusual. Still neither spoke. The cottage was coming into sight and it was almost time to say goodbye. It seemed as if they were the only two people in the world. The light breeze, the sun slowly beginning to dip behind the trees and the stars appearing in the darkening sky, there could not have been a more romantic setting and they both knew it. The peace and quiet amounted to a surreal silent stage as if set by an unseen hand, just right for a young couple to express their love for each other.

Arriving at the cottage, Alasdair, caution thrown to the wind, suddenly stood in front of her preventing her from going any further. She raised her hand to shake his, thinking this was what he wanted, otherwise why was he standing in front of her? Abandoning all of his engrained principles, he wanted her right now, wanted to glorify in her young firm body and know the joy of possessing her. Her shawl fell slightly with the movement of her arm and he stared, mesmerised, at the exposed smooth flesh of her shoulder. Any rational thinking was now futile; he felt consumed with his long denied craving for her and could wait no longer. Neither of them would remember the exact moment of recognition in each other's eyes, that fraction of a second. Like two well-trained ballet dancers in a Pas-De-Deux who sensed every movement the other would make, Alasdair lifted Janet up in the air with his muscular arms, her head now above his. She looked down at the love and adoration etched on his face and then gently cradled his head with her arms, arching her spine to press herself blissfully closer to him, and looked up contentedly into the star filled sky. She felt she could lose herself in that unrestrained moment forever.

Alasdair's strong hands still enclosed her waist, breathing deeply as he buried his face deep between her breasts, drinking in her scent, and she gasped with joy. As she slid slowly down Alasdair's body he hurriedly undid the ties of her blouse, skirt and underclothes which rapidly fell to her feet as he lifted her onto the edge of the dry stone wall at the side of the cottage. Except for her camisole which reached down to her hips, Janet was otherwise naked but she felt no shame, only joy. She had waited all her life for this moment to be with the man she loved. She wanted to share the most intimate human experience of her life with Alasdair. All her supressed longings forgotten, whatever happened, tonight he would be hers.

Alasdair's right hand found her breast and holding the naked flesh in his hand and with gentle circular movements he caressed her nipple till it hardened under his touch, her body responding with a throbbing wet sensation between her legs that continued deep inside. All Alasdair's pent-up sexual frustration, too long denied, surfaced. He began to explore the skin on her breast with his lips and tongue, working his way up till he found the base of her throat. She felt she could not stand such sweet torture any longer, and then he found her waiting, parted mouth. Groaning, she opened her thighs wide to encircle Alasdair's, instinctively pulling him towards her. She slowly moved her legs down his till they were wrapped tightly round his knees. His merciless kiss deepened, his tongue seeking hers, and he revelled in her ardent response. With his free left hand he slowly stroked the inner naked flesh of her thigh, reaching the most sensitive moist part of her body with his fingers. She pulled her head away from Alasdair's kiss and gasped out loud with sheer ecstasy, desperate for more.

Slipping her hands between Alasdair's and her own body, she searched downwards, eager to feel him, to know for sure that he wanted her as much as she wanted him. With both hands she opened the buttons of his trousers and gently reached inside, coaxing his swollen erect penis out. She was now fully aroused, burning for him, and more than ready to share this most intimate primeval sexual experience, her first time; arching her back and closing her eyes in anticipation of what would unite them forever in body and soul; transport them to that paradise of erotica the poets wrote about. Alasdair felt her complete submission and quickly put his hand behind her hips, pulling her closer to him, instinctively rocking them gently back and forth together, positioning her, ready for him to enter her.

But that first thrust from Alasdair, so long desired, never happened. Janet opened her eyes, questioning to look at Alasdair... what was wrong?

"I can't do this," a strange voice whispered in her ear that almost deafened her. Stunned into silence, she couldn't believe what she heard. Within a heartbeat the dream had turned into a nightmare.

Alasdair reached up to Janet's hands still round his neck, freed himself from her hold and gently placed her back onto the rough ground. Moving back a little he frantically started to rearrange his clothes, pushing the evidence of his desire for her back inside his trousers.

She opened her eyes wide, mortified; she could not believe what had just happened. The throbbing between her thighs had not subsided any quicker than his wilting erection.

Shamefaced, he could not look at her. She sensed his growing regret, the turmoil going on in his mind and her love for him, rising to the surface, was about to forgive him, when his next statement caught her off guard, changed everything.

"I should not have done that, led you on. You see my friends, my mother… wouldn't understand."

"Stop, just stop it!" Janet's strangled voice was distraught. Alasdair said nothing as Janet realised she had been rejected yet again.

Again, the same old story, the same excuses. Humiliated, Janet had wanted to give herself willingly to Alasdair and she had not initiated, or encouraged him or suggested they made love. She truly had believed they would have ended their walk with a handshake and part. For the first time in her life she felt shame. She dropped to her knees, frantically searching the ground about her for her clothes whilst at the same time clutching her camisole over her exposed breasts. Alasdair knelt clumsily down beside her and tried to help her get dressed, but she knocked his hand out of the way in contempt.

"No!" she cried, humiliation etched all over her face. He saw that look and that beautiful pitiful face that he knew would haunt him for a long time to come.

Horrified at his behaviour, his betrayal of her, Janet allowed her anger to rise to the surface and she let Alasdair know it. Loud and clear without caring or thinking about what she was saying, standing a few inches from his face, she whispered fiercely:

"How dare you!"

The serenity that Alasdair had admired so much in the past had suddenly disappeared, as she gave vent to her feelings.

"Just look at you, standing there all self-righteous, justifying your rejection of me with your usual excuses and platitudes! Do you think I am a gypsy, do you think I would grovel like a serf or a prostitute? Are you going to offer me money, pay me now? No? Did I not come up to scratch, or did you discover with your amateur fumbling, you are just as inexperienced as I am? Do you think I have no pride? What have I ever asked for… nothing!" She now shouted: "I want nothing from you, nothing but your love and respect, and you have betrayed both. What you give with your eyes and your body, Alasdair Forman, you take away with your mouth!" Janet hardly knew what she was saying. Her anger came from bitter rejection and disappointment.

"Why are you still here? Go home…just go home, forget about me," she said in a quieter voice, embarrassment at the tirade of verbal demeaning abuse she had hurled at him.

Proudly raising her aristocratic head, now modestly dressed again, she stood up to look straight at him.

"Alasdair Forman, you are tall, handsome, intelligent and strong, like a magnificent, solid granite stone mansion, with its doors wide open, offering warmth and security, a welcome within its walls, its arms outstretched, shielding those inside from the storms of life, with its embrace…" Janet, unrestrained, made every word count. "But your foundations are weak, unsupported and your house leaks. It lets in the cold, and rain and wind saturates any hope of happiness. Alasdair Forman, your house has no roof. I know what I am, but do you know who you are?" She paused for a moment, seeing his dejected face, and tried a different tact.

"For God's sake, Alasdair, grow up. Damn your mother…,to hell with your mother… she's not even here! Why do you care so much what she thinks?!"

Alasdair stood mute, had nothing to say, silently agreeing with every word she said.

At first feeling defeated, Janet turned to leave, but anger gained the upper hand. All the discipline that normally governed her life left her and, totally out of character, she saw red, swung back and with all the strength she could muster belted Alasdair hard across the face. He felt the unexpected, astounding blow to his face, the crack from which sounded like a bullet ricocheting through the trees.

Aghast at her outburst, Janet collapsed once more to her knees. Her slender shoulders heaved in distress and she covered her face with both hands in shame. What had she done; this was the end, it was all over now. Worn out from trying to control her feelings, she sobbed quietly, and wished Alasdair would just go and leave her alone.

He had been totally unprepared and was stunned by Janet's behaviour. He hadn't seen the blow coming. His cheek was throbbing in pain and it felt as if his eye had exploded. He was astonished at her physical strength. It went through his mind, 'Hell hath no wrath...' He bent down and picked up the shawl, leant forward and helped her to her feet. She rose up with as much dignity as she could muster. With one majestic movement she tossed the hair that had partially covered her face and breasts, a simple gesture that tore at his heart as he put her shawl round her shoulders.

"Look at me," he said, "I deserved that, I more than deserved it and I don't blame you." What indeed had he done to her, he asked himself. What a brute he was. "What have I done to you?" he tried to console her.

"I don't want your pity."

Taking her soft cool hand in his, he gently placed it against his throbbing face, tilted his head to the side till he could kiss the palm. She stood absolutely still, offered no resistance, passive... a pitiful shadow of her earlier self.

"I am so sorry. Look at me, Janet," he repeated.

She looked up and saw a bright red weal developing round his cheek and eye where she had walloped him, but tonight he could take care of himself; she had nothing to offer.

"You are right," he said, "I have made a complete ass of myself, betrayed you, the person I hold in such high esteem. You have every right to despise me, but I will not promise what I cannot deliver. I am a shameful coward, but listen to me, even if you disagree, it would be you who would suffer in the long run from our relationship. And it must be a true and meaningful relationship! If not that, I could never just use you and toss you aside when I was finished with you, and believe me I know how to prevent you becoming pregnant, but I cannot do that to you… I will not. I use the vagaries of the culture I was brought up in and my mother… I know, I know it's a pathetic excuse…" He held his hand up, shook his head, hating himself. "But it would be reprehensible for me to allow my family to cold-shoulder or treat you with contempt."

"But I asked for nothing… never have!"

Coming a little closer to Janet and dropping her hand, he spoke in the softest and loving tones. "In my defence, Janet… I was trying to save you the humiliation and embarrassment you would suffer if I allowed things to go further between us and not just from my family. I care too much for you to let that happen, but I cannot offer you anything else however much I want to at this moment, except the future we planned for you an hour ago." Janet stood silent. "I would not hold it against you if you never wanted to see me again."

Desperate to give her, and him, hope in this desolate moment, Alasdair said in earnest, "Remember, nothing stays the same forever." And with a heavy heart he turned to go, wondering which of them was in the most pain, physical or emotional.

'Don't leave it there, you stupid man! Say something to defuse the situation, make her smile again, and look at her face!'

"I'd better get some ice on this eye of mine before it turns into a right black eye… you pack quite a punch Janet… I'll let you know when I have arranged the trip to Edinburgh." There was no more to be said, he'd done what he could, prayed his behaviour this evening would not affect the future for her here in the village.

She walked into the cottage. The embers in the stove were still burning. Filling the kettle, she put it on to boil. The cottage, her haven, her refuge from the storms of life... its walls were strong and its roof did not leak and the one consistency in her life lived there, Auld Tam. But Alasdair was right, nothing stays the same forever... He had thrown her a lifeline, he had given her hope, given her the possibility of a better future. Emotionally exhausted, she sat down in the old rocking chair to wait for Tam's return.

'Serf? Where did that come from?' Alasdair thought as he walked into the darkening night.

Chapter 16

"**P**ARDON MY FRENCH, Aunty, but it was about bloody time... Good for her! I'm surprised she only hit him, the rotter. If he had done that to me... he'd have swallowed them and he wouldn't have known how they got up the back of his throat! Sorry to be so graphic. At last she's asserted herself, but she still loves him... Women are so vulnerable when they are in love."

When I thought about Aunt Jane's first erotic descriptions of Alasdair and Janet's last sexual encounter, this time it was almost verging on the pornographic. Our relationship had certainly reached a whole new level. I had just stated I would knee a man in his testicles and neither of us batted an eyelid. On the other hand I would have to weigh up the pros and cons as to how much of that last chapter I would write for posterity.

"Any idea how Alasdair explained his black eye to Rena?"

"He told Rena he tripped, fell down the stair and hit his face on the banister and she repeated the story if asked. But the men in the village loved the explanation and kidded with the Doctor that if he had been drunk he wouldn't have hurt himself. All you need to know is that Janet left the village shortly after the event to do her general training in Edinburgh."

"I am pleased to hear that. It's been a long day and I wondered if it was too much for you."

"No, I am fine and we have covered a great deal, although the nap in the afternoon was welcome. Don't you worry about me. A few more visits and you will know the truth about

Leightham House. Are you sure you still want to?" Her look challenged me.

"You are so sensitive it's scary, Aunty; intuitive, as if you know what I'm thinking. I didn't tell you, but walking down the front earlier I did have some reservations regarding future visits." I paused momentarily, then continued. "But I had a strange experience on the Mid-Shore. Standing on the Pier and walking on the beach, I think it is fair to say I shivered, but not from the cold. I got goosebumps and the hair stood up on the back of my neck. It was spooky. I sensed the spirits of the people you have been telling me about around me and I saw something which I realise now must have been a ghost. Strange, but I felt no fear. Don't laugh at me, but it's almost an obsession to get to the end of your story now. I feel as if someone from the past wants me to know everything and not just what you have already told me..." I shook my head in disbelief, as if someone else's voice was coming out of my mouth.

"Why would I laugh?" she said soberly. "You are not the only person to sense the spirits of those who have gone before you in the places they inhabited."

"But I had begun to doubt my reasons for being here, to tell you I quit... Till I realised those spirits were the people you were telling me about. Their message was so strong, at one point I was sure I was related to them and that's impossible... they were Alice's relatives, not even yours."

"Anyone who has a connection to this village, is related, and remember your witches' thumbs – perhaps you sense more than most of us, have the second sight!"

"Got me there, Aunty! Well, I'd better get on my way. You don't need to let me out, but I have to tell you something." I turned back at the lounge door. "I am going back to America in October for ten days' holiday, and after that back to hospital duties in November."

"America again, so soon! Let me guess, that look in your eyes when you returned after the summer… tells me you have met someone."

"Maybe, but before I go let me ask a question, a quick one?"

"Well?"

"The two fishing boats, the *Alice n' Maggie* and the *Royal Diadem*, I guess they no longer exist? Ended up in the scrapyards years ago?"

"You are right, they no longer exist, but they were not broken up. They were appropriated, requisitioned by the Government at the start of the First World War as mine sweepers. Both boats were blown to smithereens in the North Sea with the loss of all hands."

Aunty never showed much emotion, but I could see it on her face, sadness at the loss of life, and I wondered if she knew or was related to some of those men. I felt it was more than time I asked her about her own life, but there never seemed to be enough time or encouragement from her.

"Am I ready to go home? You bet I am, Cathie," I answered Cathie's question when she met me in the hall as I left. We had continued our meeting far longer than intended.

"A thocht a would come back early, tae see if the pair o yae wanted a cup a tea!"

"That was kind of you, but no, I have to get back. Mum will have dinner ready… you know, get ready to start my new job tomorrow and I'm already late. By the way, did your grandmother ever tell you about Janet leaving to do her nurses training?"

"Aye, ma granny spoke a lot about it. The village missed her, but she came back for… a while."

Chapter 17

"MERCY ON US lassie, are yae gaun tae a waddin?" Cathie exclaimed, just the reaction I was expecting from her.

"You too, Cathie? I have just had the same reaction from my mother this morning before I left home, except she demanded to know if I was going to the Kirk with Aunt Jane."

"Well, yer lookin awfie weel dressed the day, a hardly recognised yae!"

"Sh-h-h...I want to surprise Aunty." I put my finger to my lips. "I don't think she was too impressed with my hot-pants or hairdo on my last visit."

"One things fur shair, she'll notice the day!"

"That will make a change. Here Cathie, hang on to my duffle bag. I've put a pair of jeans, a T-shirt and sandshoes in it to change. I can't sit looking like this all day."

"Ah, a mind noo, where a've seen a frock like that afore! Jackie Kennedy, noo you've put the hat on. Pair lassie... and to shoot the President... what a death tae get!"

"I know, one of my Texan friends told me Dallas is a city still in mourning, smarting from the pain of his assassination in their city and how it happened; they feel they will suffer the shame for many years to come. They say everyone remembers where they were when the news of the shooting broke."

"Dae you remember where yea were?"

"Vividly, I was in London visiting some old school friends, who married and moved there. We had tickets for Pickwick. When Janice, John and their friends Mick, Jan and I came out of the theatre and got into the car; John who was driving couldn't understand why the traffic was almost at a standstill. I have never seen anything like it... we thought the Third World War had been declared. People were screaming, newspaper vendors were running like lunatics, John and Mick hung out of the car window trying to get a paper; we couldn't believe it when we read the headlines. I'll never forget as long as I live. Well, I better go find Her Majesty."

"Jist a minute, a hear yer gaun back tae America?"

"Yes, in October, but only for ten days. I don't have any more annual leave left."

"Am no shair a like the sound o' that."

Cathie trundled down the hall, muttering loud enough for me to hear.

"A hope yea dinna plan tae move there... that's an awfy dangerous place, they're awash wae guns."

'Cathie, you have been watching too many episodes of Rawhide,' I thought. Yet it wasn't far from the truth regarding the guns.

"Hi Aunty, how are you?" I made my entry, pillbox hat on my head, clutch-bag in my hand and stiletto heels on my feet.

"That's more like it, at last you're decently dressed," she announced as I made an entrance fit for the catwalk and did a quick twirl.

"Balenciaga, I recognise that designer's work! The slight bubble skirt at the hips and the straight front panel give it away. You know I am not much given to giving compliments, but that particular shade of blue certainly suits your colouring and the hairstyle is beginning to grow on me."

Praise indeed. I often wonder who I got my colouring from; no one else in the family has my dark auburn hair. Dad is so swarthy his ancestors could be French, and Mum... well, pure Scandinavian, so blonde and those cornflower blue eyes. She must have been a real beauty when she was younger. I always remembered Dad teasing her, telling her if Hitler had won the war they would have taken her into the breeding camps to produce the next generation of Aryan Germans. I doubt they would have kept her for long – I was the only child she ever had. Not good breeding stock!

"She was very blonde, and very beautiful. Sit down, then we will begin," Aunty ordered.

"Sorry Aunty, but I can't possibly sit for the next hour with a hat on my head and my feet are killing me in these shoes. I'm going to find Cathie. She has my ordinary clothes in a bag. I need to change and get my writing gear."

"Hurry up but first tell me, where did you buy the dress? It must have cost you a fortune. And in future leave those shoes at the front door; I don't want my floors pockmarked with those heels. The gardener says these heels are only fit for planting leeks."

That sharp remark suddenly propelled me back to my childhood… got it wrong again, worse, I was marking her floors with my shoes – not breathing on her windows this time.

"The dress didn't cost me anything. My Texan friend Mary gave it to me – since I lost weight we are almost the same size. Her father's a wealthy rancher up the Texas Panhandle, he's so rich he changes her car every year for her, can you believe it? It's a whole different ballgame living in the States. The endearing thing about Mary is she takes this as normal, new cars and designer clothes."

Having changed and come back into the lounge Aunty asked me, "Do you like America?"

"Everything is bigger and better in America, that's what they say. It's different, Aunt Jane, I don't know how to describe life there. Very friendly and family orientated, but at times I think a little superficial; you live in the now. There's little social back up; if you're injured, unemployed, have a sick child or illness in the family, it can be financially catastrophic.

No National Health Service, nor is there ever likely to be one. America's not ready for social medical care, we don't realise how lucky we are.

"Americans are immigrants from all parts of the world and are expected to fend for themselves. The only true Americans are as you know native Red Indians, wrongly named because the early explorers thought they had reached India. It's every man for himself in the States; if you can't make it in the land of the free, that's your problem. As for the first amendment, I think it's a hangover from previous centuries of lawless gung-ho cowboys, for self-protection. The constitution permits the carrying of firearms and they make full use of it, but it's hard to feel sorry for them when a child innocently shoots its mother or a friend, finding a gun in her handbag thinking it's a toy. That's bad enough, and several other situations made me feel uncomfortable; I hope we never change here in Scotland."

"That's terrible, we rarely hear news of shooting's on the BBC, but what do you mean, situations that made you feel uncomfortable? I don't know what you mean."

"Aunty, the first time I flew to New York, I took a *T.W.A* flight from London. It had come in from Germany and was partially full of U.S. servicemen going home on leave from the American base there. Innocent, looking for a seat, I saw an empty aisle one. I had put my hand luggage in the overhanging compartment, fastened my seat belt, and reached for the flight information leaflet in the seat pocket in front of me. A stewardess appeared from nowhere and insisted I move. Protesting and assuring the woman I was fine, she would have none of it – I had to move. She reached down and released the buckle on my seat belt, took my stuff from the overhanging luggage compartment and almost hauled me up the aisle by the sleeve!" I shook my head at the memory.

"Pardon my dreadful American accent, Aunty, but she announced loud and clear for all to hear. 'Cum on honey, you can't sit there,' she drawled. 'A've found you a real nice seat for you next to the window. Cum on now!'

"So I found myself sitting next to two white gentlemen, businessmen as I found out later in conversation with them. They told me they had been asked to move their seats to the middle and aisle ones, to let me have theirs. It took me a while to realise… I had unwittingly sat next to a black American couple. The stewardess had been horrified; she must have thought I was colour blind. Wish I'd had the chance to tell her as far as I am concerned the pigmentation of people's skin is of no importance to me, and in that case I am colour blind. Strange, though, it took me a while, but looking back I remembered, the black guy next to me turned his back away as I sat down, he didn't want me sitting next to him. What do you think of that? My first brush with racial prejudice!"

"We live in a backwater here, so I am not surprised. I'm sure you witnessed worse while you were in America," Aunty said.

"You are right Aunty, I did. Before I left, my friends held a farewell dinner for me. I overheard Mary phoning to book a table at my favourite restaurant, but no, she was asking if the restaurant allowed coloured people to dine there. I leant over her and cut the phone off. 'It's all right, I agree with your principles,' she assured me, 'but this is America and I don't want Stella to be turned away at the door because of her colour and that's why I am checking if they allow blacks.' I told her if Stella wasn't allowed in then I'm not going. Aunt Jane, Stella is Latino; she comes from South America, one of the most decent human beings you could ever meet, a devout Catholic. Worse still, another member of staff, Ruth, tried to justify the restaurant's colour ban; she said it goes both ways. The white mothers teach their children not to sit next to the coloured children in the school bus and vice versa; she was using this as an excuse to condone such prejudice." I shook my head, paused for a moment not sure if I should continue, but Aunty seemed to be taking an interest.

"That's not all. The Universities have fraternity houses, a form of student accommodation, and a good idea really. It's a family tradition to belong to the fraternity your father or grandfather belonged to, and each house has a Latin name, identification rings and the like. I had no idea when I arrived that there was a separate fraternity house for the black students. They were intelligent kids studying for the same medical degree. I asked why they were not allowed to join a fraternity house of their choice. Can you imagine my horror when one smart ass medical students sneered and with an attitude that can only be described as superior took pleasure in telling me, it had been medically proven the African skull bones were thicker in diameter than European ones? In other words they could not join because of the diameters of the skull! I was stunned! It's not true Aunty, he was just a bigoted racist. I don't know if I could live in such a society, but I got homesick as well, although I did have a good time and made many friends." This was true.

"Martin Luther King's got a hard job on his hands… a long row to hoe," I added as an afterthought.

"That does not surprise me," Aunty said, "but we can't sit talking and not get on with the purpose in hand, dear, I'm not going to live forever. Go change your clothes and tell Cathie to bring the coffee early; two more full days should just about do it and your burning question should be answered. All will be revealed… remember, not all I have to tell you has a happy ending."

"Are you trying to tell me Janet won't be back?"

"I didn't say that… Wait and see."

I left to get changed and returned, sitting in my usual seat, pen and paper to hand, wearing my jeans and ignoring the look of disapproval on Aunt Jane's face. She began to speak and I began to write.

Chapter 18

"GET THAT FILTHY BEAST oot o' here!" Aggie demanded. Alice had arrived back from school with Helen in tow and was standing at the kitchen door with the biggest black and grey striped cat clutched to her chest that Aggie had ever seen.

"But Mum, that's no fair, it's Christmas and you said…"

"No buts… get rid o' it. I'm no having that flea infested animal in ma hoose!"

"But you and Dad promised, I could have whatever I wanted and I want the cat. It's been waiting for me in the playground every day this week and he's followed me hame every afternoon, isn't that right Helen?"

"Yes, that's right Mrs Gardner," Helen said, siding with her best friend.

"I have tried tae get rid of him mum, but…"

"Well yae didna try hard enough. Pit it doon, your nearly chokin' the beast, it's a wonder it can still breathe."

Alice obliged her mother and dropped the cat. Aggie turned her attention to the problem of a cat in her kitchen. Lifting a dishtowel off the chair, Aggie went towards the cat and flapped the towel at it to shoo it out, but to her amazement the cat remained completely unfazed by her actions. Instead of running towards the door to escape, it shot between her and the kitchen table legs, jumped up on the rocking chair by the fire and proceeded to groom its fur. It then tucked its front paws underneath its chest, and sat blinking at Helen, Alice and Aggie.

"Weel… wid yae credit that, the cheek… he thinks he's biding, weel see about that!"

It was true; Wullie and Aggie had promise Alice she could choose whatever she wanted for Christmas. But, as far as Aggie was concerned, it did not include a live animal.

"Please mum, he's not got fleas, Bodger's clean. Awe just listen, he's purrin'… I think he's smilin' as weel."

"Bodger, whaur on awe the earth did yae cum up wae a name like that? And how dae you ken it's a male?" Why was she even having this conversation? Aggie shook her head. This was not going well.

"Oliver Twist," Alice smiled brightly.

"That's right Mrs Gardner. Oliver Twist," Helen echoed brightly.

"Miss Laird at the library, she's been reading the book tae Helen and me on Saturdays. It's a story aboot the Artful Dodger and a wee boy called Oliver. Bodger's been dodging in and out o' the dykes like the Dodger on ma way home from the scuil, following us. I just made the name up, and it suits him. Mum, Bodger's lovely, he never bites or scratches." Alice put on her best wheedling voice, the one that usually worked with her parents, not realising that tactic was about to backfire.

Aggie shook her head. 'She's getting' that auld fashioned, what a lassie. She thinks she can get round me. We'll see about that.'

"Ah dinna' care how lovely he is or whit his name is, oot he goes, dae ye hear me? In any case, if he's as tame as you say he must belong tae somebody, they'll be missing him. We better ask aboot the neighbourhood. How dae ye ken it's a boy oniewey? And if he is, he'll smell the hoose out."

'Stop discussing the cat Aggie, you're going to lose, change the subject.'

"It's aboot time yae went hame Helen, your mother will be wondering whaur yae are."

"You're right Mrs Gardner, see you at school tomorrow, Alice."

But Alice was not giving in; after Helen left she sensed her mother beginning to weaken. "I talked wi' Auld Tam on the wae hame frae scuil... no, on the way home from school; Miss Phimister says we have to speak clearly in English. And Tam told me it was a boy."

"Eh, what's the world cumin' tae... English!"

"I asked Tam if he'd seen Bodger afore. Tam kens everything and everybody in the village. He said no, he'd never seen him before. He picked Bodger up an' looked at him. Tam says he's clean, he's no got fleas and if ye pit a rub o' Lye soap on the back o' his neck every week it will keep them awa'... away." Alice hardly paused for breath and forgetting her English accent, hurried on. "And Auld Tam says there's a man coming from St Aundrey's next Monday, to neutralise the pigs on the Leightham farm. I've to tak Bodger tae Tam and he'll tak Bodger tae be neutralised... what's neutralised Mum?" Alice frowned.

"Ah dinna' ken onythin' aboot neutralizing pigs or cats!" Aggie knew she was slowly losing the fight. "Wait till I see Auld Tam, I'll gie him a mouthful, encouraging you like that! He micht hae asked me first."

Alice moved round the table to the rocking chair and knelt down beside the animal, scratched his head and ears. The animal, purring loudly, pushed his head against her hand, enjoying the human contact and working his feline magic.

"Can yae no gie Bodger a saucer o' milk mum?"

"Indeed I will not, dae yea think am' gonna encourage Bodg... eh, the beast? Just you wait till your faither gets here. Mind you I hiv' tae say that animal's tame, it wouldna' surprise me if he's no been done already."

"Done mum?" Had Bodger been completed, finished... done, what did her mother mean?

338

Wullie and Jock arrived back together with a newspaper wrapped round a fine Cod. Wullie put the parcel down on the dale table and smiled at his wife and then the cat.

"A see the cat's made himsel at hame," and turning to look at his daughter, he winked.

"You'll need tae talk tae her Wullie, or is it too late? It seems tae me it's a' been decided. You're a' in it thegither, the three o' yae. A' micht as weel haud ma tongue. Was this your idea Dad? You twa canna' refuse that bairn onythin', you've got her spilt. Well it looks like av' been out voted, so a' richt, the cat can bide... In the washhoose... He's no living here, stinkin the place oot!" Aggie sniffed to emphasise her point of view on the subject. Jock moved round the table to the fire, lifted the cat onto his lap and stroked the purring animal for a few minutes. Bodger stuck his nose in the air... whiskers twitching... he smelt fish? He promptly jumped off Jock's lap as he sensed the source of the smell was coming from the kitchen table.

"Ach dinna' fash yersel Aggie aboot whaur the animal's gaun tae sleep the noo. Just look at the braw fish I caught us fur oor tea. I ken it's the bairn's favourite, fish an' chips, eh Alice?

"Aye Dey, I love fish and so do cats," Alice assured her grandfather, getting up on his lap now that it had been vacated by the animal and put an arm around the old man's neck. The pair rocked back and forward on the rocker.

"A'll look efter Bodger mum, you'll not need to do onythin', give me that auld blanket that's in the Kist in ma bedroom; a'll put it in the claes basket in the washhoose, that it'll keep him warm." Having tried to emotionally blackmail her mother about Bodger's sleeping quarters, and getting no response, Alice decided on another tack.

"Auld Tam says cats catch mice better than traps. A' bet if you let him sleep in the hoose mum, he'll watch fur them cumin' oot the press and catch them for ye."

"The lot of you hiv ganged up on me, a micht as weel hiv been talkin' tae the wall!"

While Aggie had been making her position clear on what Bodger could and couldn't do, she had moved from the stove back to the kitchen table, turned her attention to the fish, unwrapped the newspaper and started to gut the cod for their supper.

"Mercy me..." Aggie nearly jumped out of her skin, startled by what felt like a fur coat rubbing against her legs.

"*Miow-miow!*" Bodger cried pitifully.

"Awe he's starving Mum!"

"Awe richt, awe richt, I'll no have the animal gaun hungry, he can bide in the hoose till he eats his supper. I'll bile the cod's heid for you Bodger then oot yae go. Why am I talking tae a stupid animal as if it were human? That cat, it's got me bewitched as weel!" Aggie declared.

The four conspirators stood close together, cat and humans, grinning from ear to ear. They had won a great victory. Maggie returned from her weekly visit to the Seaman's Mission and joined in the feast of fresh fried cod and chips, followed by Aggie's roly-poly.

Chapter 19

"A' COULDN'A HAE cooked better masel Aggie, that was awfy grand!" Maggie sat back in her chair, content.

Alice smiled with happiness, clapped her hands. "I must be the happiest girl in Pittendreal. Oh, a' forgot tae tell yae, I'v had my name on the blackboard, top o' the class for a week now. Miss Phimister says I've tae keep up the good work. She gave me a pandrop and said I'd be taken' her job when I grew up."

"Oh no, you'll no..." Wullie interrupted his daughter.

"That's enough Wullie," Aggie intervened. "She's just a bairn, plenty o' time to discuss what she's gaun tae dae in the future." Aggie refused to talk about the future as far as her daughter was concerned. She had learnt the hard way with the loss of her other two babies, not to tempt fate; she had taken her mother's advice and was content to live in the present, a day at a time.

Jock interrupted. "I jist happened to have another wee surprise for ye, ma bairn."

"Oh Dey, what is it?"

Jock handed Alice a small paper parcel. She took it from her grandfather, knelt down by the fire and began untying the string, then the paper. Inside she revealed a small hard blue jeweller's box.

Wide eyed with pleasure, slowly, Alice clicked open the catch. Inside the lid of the box was written:

341

Alec Bird Jeweller
High Street,
Leightham.

Nestled in soft cream coloured silk was a brooch, a solid silver broach for a child, in the shape of a caramel sweetie. The 'wrapper' twisted at each end gave the impression of a frilled paper edge. The child gasped in surprise… across the centre of the brooch was her name *ALICE*, written in gold italic writing.

"It's beautiful, Dey! I love it with my name on it, and I'll keep it safe forever. I'll wear it only on Sundays at the Kirk!" And with that, Alice snapped the box shut, put it up on the mantelpiece, turned and threw her arms round the old man's neck and kissed him on the cheek.

"Ouch! Your face is prickly, you need a shave Dey!" Alice smiled and laughed with the old man.

"You're richt there Alice, God only knows when he last shaved." Maggie, agreeing with her granddaughter, joined in the general laughter.

"That's a handsome gift Dad, where did you get it?" Aggie wanted to know.

"A took the bus intae Leightham and had a word wae Alec Bird – the jeweller, and ye ken the local councillor as well. Telt him whit a' wanted, he said tae leave it wae him, said he knew exactly whit it was a was efter and tae come back in a week. He knew it was for a special wee lassie. It's fully stamped on the back wi the Scottish assay marks. Ye see a' met Miss Phimister in the street and she telt me how well the bairn was duin at the scuil so I decided she should have a wee minding."

"Yae ken Dad, apart from my wedding ring, ma granny's jet mourning beads and a pair o' earing's made o' pinchbeck, that's awe the jewellery a' hiv. You're a lucky lassie, that's a fine start tae onybodie's collection."

Bodger, grinning like a Cheshire cat from ear to ear, a gut full of fish and milk, contented, was stretched out in front of the fire.

"A' ken how lucky I am. Look at the cat Mum, he's thinking how lucky he is as well and happy he belongs tae me!" Alice sat on the rug in front of the fire with the cat, stroking him and enjoying the sound of his contented purring. He did a few rolls onto his back to show off his spotted belly and entertain his new found friend.

"Yer an awfy lassie Alice, how dae yae ken what a cat's thinking? But let me tell you whit I'm thinkin'. If that beast starts tae claw that rug... oot he goes, nae arguments. And he better start earning his keep and catching mice to pay for his board and lodgings'!"

The happy family scene was too much for Aggie. To Alice's surprise, Aggie got out of her chair and gave her daughter a rare cuddle. Aggie never had much faith in the future as far as Alice was concerned, and found it hard to show any form of affection, verbal or physical. Suddenly she felt obliged to break up this happy family gathering – things were going too well and it was tempting fate. A recent family bereavement came into Aggie's mind: five-year-old wee Betty Gardner, Alice's cousin who lived in St Creils; the two families had visited each other frequently.

Aggie would never forget the heart-stopping day when Janet arrived at the door and told her to scrub the entire house with Lye soap and bleach. "Boil all the family's clothes that had been in touch with Martha Gardner's five-year-old daughter, Betty." Janet had been called to Martha's house in St Creils just two days after the families had been together on the Sunday. She immediately ordered Martha to take the child to the Sanatorium outside Leightham. Janet realised there was nothing she could do; the little girl had contracted whooping cough and diphtheria at the same time. One infection required the patient to be nursed sitting up; the other, lying flat with a tube in their throat. Five heart-rending days later, wee Betty died.

Aggie would never forget the little girl lying in a white coffin dressed in a long white nightgown and lace bonnet as if she were asleep. A doll, her Christmas present, was placed in the little girl's arms before they closed the lid. The men were in tears as they left the house with her little white coffin on their shoulders to walk to the Cemetery up the Comentry Road behind Mr McDougall for burial.

"Richt, that's enough. Bedtime, young lady. Mum, Dad, time you were awa hame."

With that Aggie unceremoniously ushered her parents out of the house.

"It's no that late Aggie, sometimes I think you're ower hard on the bairn and yer mum and dad," Wullie complained later in the evening when Alice was in her bed with the cat curled up at her feet.

"I'll decide what's late and how a' deal wi mum and dad is none of your bliddy business!" Aggie snapped at Wullie.

Wullie shook out his newspaper and ducked his head behind it. Better not to argue when Aggie was in one of her moods.

Chapter 20

"**M**UM, I can't go to school!" twelve-year-old Alice lamented to her mother one Monday morning.

"Whit dae ye mean ye canny gan tae the scuil?" Aggie demanded, looking at Alice with suspicion. "Whit's wrang wi ye, are you no weel? Or are you and your pal Helen up to some tricks again? Yer gaun to the school and nae nonsense; ye dinna look ill to me." Aggie peered closer.

"Oh Mum, it's not the first time it's happened, I thought I'd scratched myself on that paper, it's so hard."

"What paper?" Aggie asked flabbergasted.

"The toilet paper," Alice answered hiding her face.

"Toilet paper!" Aggie gasped. "Dae you ken how lucky ye are tae hiv that new toilet paper I buy, it's bloomin dear!" Aggie almost exploded, offended that an expensive modern commodity such as toilet paper could provoke complaints from her family. "Maist o' the folk here are still cutin' up newspaper!" she sniffed. "What are you goin on aboot for Heaven's sake! Get your school bag. Helen will be here any minute and you no ready yet, you'll mak the two of you late. I have put a roll in for your lunch." Aggie relaxed, became her old practical self again but not for long as she realised Alice hadn't moved an inch.

"But Mum, please." Alice shuffled her feet and would only look at the ground, twisting her school apron into a crumpled mess, her face becoming redder by the minute. Aggie peered closely at her daughter.

"Mercy on us, gie me peace! What is the matter, you have to tell me, I canny guess, can I?" Aggie asked, getting more than a little exasperated with her daughter.

"I am bleeding mum," Alice managed to blurt out, scarlet in the face, tears forming in her eyes. "Am I going to die? This is the second time it's happened; the first was a few weeks ago, that's how I know it canny be the toilet paper this time."

Alice could not understand why Aggie was speechless. Why was her mum saying nothing? Maybe she was angry with her for making a mess of her underwear.

"I scrubbed my knickers clean myself so you wouldn't see the stains but, now it's happened again and this time my stomach is sore and I can't get the stains out." By now Alice was in tears, not only for the present situation she found herself in, but dreading the possibility of having to suffer Aggie's standard treatment for all ailments – a dose of Syrup of Figs. Yuck. "I'm not constipated, mum," Alice hastily reassured Aggie.

Aggie wasn't speechless; she was just trying to work out the best way to deal with the situation. How to overcome the desire to laugh which would only make matters worse for Alice or more realistically, how to overcome her own embarrassment. Recovering her usual brisk, no-nonsense approach to life, Aggie felt a stab of sympathy for her girl.

"Now, now," she said, putting her arm around her daughter's sagging shoulders. "It's nothin' ma' lass, you are not ill and you are definitely not going to die," she reassured her daughter, but was not too sure how to continue. "I haven't been very forthcoming about what's happened. There's nothing wrang wi ye, it's normal; you are just becoming a woman. I should hiv had a talk with you aboot this, told you what to look for and no tae be afraid long afore the day but, I wasn'a sure how tae tell ye. My mum never said anything to me, I just had to figure it oot masel wi some help from my chums and the older lassies in school when I was your age. However a mysterious pile o' these towelling rags jist appeared in my drawer that my mum had put there. She must have guessed what had happened. That was my introduction to womanhood." Aggie cringed from the memory of stains through to her petticoat.

"Noo that it's happened tae you, hiv ye noticed onythin' else?" she asked. Turning to the old dresser in the kitchen and opening the bottom drawer, Aggie took out a pile of what to Alice looked like the same white towelling rags that her mum had just described. 'It must happen to all the girls then, I'm not the only one, that's a relief!' Pink colouring returning to Alice's face, she shyly indicated her chest to Aggie.

"Well, my dresses seem to be a bit tighter under the armpits," she volunteered.

"Weel that's part o' it, you are developing a chest."

'I thought I had a chest already,' Alice said to herself. Aggie responded by dumping the rags on the kitchen table with two huge nappy pins. "You'll need these aboot every fower weeks so mak shair ye gie them back to me for washin'. Pay attention! Don't forget we don't need the world tae ken awe aboot this, are ye listenin? I'll get them ready in yer drawer for the next time, that will be unless..." Aggie hesitated, thinking. "No wait a minute, no need for you to ken any more about these things jist noo." That can wait, one thing at a time.

'So that's what mum was hanging on the pulley in the kitchen to dry now and again.' When Alice asked her mother what they were, Aggie said they were dusters.

Every four weeks? Did her mother say *every four* weeks!? Alice's jaw dropped. She couldn't believe her ears, and she thought this would be only once. And for how long, for a month, a year?

"Dinna look at me like that Alice Gairdner, I was nae prepared for this tae happen jist yet either." Aggie shook her head. Time passes so quickly. It seemed like only yesterday Alice had been born. "I never thocht ma wee lassie would turn intae sic a beautiful young woman so soon, it always seemed as if it would be sometime in the future," Aggie said, giving a rare compliment and trying to soften the reality of womanhood.

Aggie tried to cover up the fact that she had not given much thought to the inevitability of her child growing up. She should have been more observant; her daughter's dresses were getting tight under the armpits, and she hadn't noticed. She was so skinny, yet tall for her age, but that's no excuse. Aggie mulled these thoughts over in her mind realising the steps she would have to take because of the physical changes in her daughter and how to fit in the time to do what she had to do. "You'll jist hiv tae put up with your claes as they are till the weekend, but I'll get the Singer oot and mak these pads a wee bit smaller today. You can tak the mornin aff the scuil and a'll send word tae Miss Phimister wi Helen when she gets here, if she ever gets here. She's late, she'll be dawdling again! Sometimes I wonder about that Helen…" Aggie tailed off.

Alice sat down at the kitchen table agonising over how she was going to attach these chunks of towelling to her knickers with the two nappy pins and keep the whole thing a secret. Alice thought things couldn't get much worse. Oh yes, they could, as Aggie delivered the next blow.

"This is you becoming a young lady like I said, so I will let all the hems o' your dresses an' skirts doon this weekend. I'll not have you showing your underwear or your legs in public, that's no' ladylike, so keep your skirts down. A' dinna want you to give ony reason for the auld village gossips to talk about your behaviour." Aggie, staring straight into Alice's now astonished face, added in a commanding voice: "And don't go near boys!"

Don't go near boys? Alice, thoroughly confused, had the feeling that all her male childhood friends and playmates had suddenly developed terrible infectious diseases that she could catch if she went near them. "Are the boys' ill mum?" Alice asked innocently as she thought about what her mum had just said. Aggie clucked her tongue, turning to the sink in the window to hide her embarrassment at her inability to enlighten her daughter any further about the facts of life. Only the married woman of the village huddled together in the street or in the corner of the village hall at some function, discussed such matters. Normally in very hushed voices, whispering so no one could over hear. The stories they exchanged with each other about conception, pregnancy and childbirth were hair-raising. The gorier the details the better these worthy matrons of the Parish enjoyed their conversations.

Suitably attired and in a much better frame of mind, Alice waited by the door for Helen, who had promised to return at lunchtime to accompany Alice to school for the rest of the afternoon. 'How am I going to tell Andy Patterson I can't play tig anymore? I know there's no problem keeping away from the boys at the school, they have their own playground. Helen and I always walk together home.' Alice paused for a moment to think about it. 'But if that Andy Coule pulls my pigtails or touches my clothes, he will get a mouthful from me he won't forget!' The morning passed and Alice sat patiently waiting for her friend, thinking over recent events.

"Oh, there's Helen Mum, see you after school!"

Aggie went out into the street to watch her daughter and her best friend walking away together. That's odd, Aggie thought, she'd never noticed before, Helen's skirts were longer too. 'Well, well, how quickly time passes. The pair of them young women, but still bairns! Seems like only yesterday they were being christened... Look at them, their heads together like a pair of fishwives. I wonder what they are talking about.'

Chapter 21

HAD AGGIE OVERHEARD their conversation, not only would she have been surprised, but would have split her sides laughing.

At the top of George Street Alice said to Helen, "You never told me why your mum let your skirt hem down." Alice felt aggrieved Helen had not taken her into her confidence.

"My mum said it was a secret and not to tell anyone." Helen hung her head in embarrassment.

"My mum says she is going to let my skirts down this weekend, and you'll never guess what else she said."

"What?"

"Don't go near boys!"

"Ha, you got off lightly. I almost died when my mum said 'Don't let them touch you… you know where'!"

"No, I don't know, do you?" Alice, wide eyed, looked at Helen in astonishment.

Both girls fell silent, each with their own private thoughts.

"Well, it looks like from what your mum said Helen, whether we like it or not, from now on there will be no more playing tig with Andy and Eric. I think that's what she must have meant." Alice frowned and sighed, thinking growing up wasn't all it was cracked up to be.

"Never mind that, we will just have to get over it. Listen, I know something. I overheard my granny asking my mother if Mrs Lesley was better yet. You remember our old teacher when we first started school, the one who left to get married last year?"

Alice nodded.

Helen drew in closer to Alice. "My mum said to granny, yes, she was better, and she had a wee baby boy yesterday."

"I didn't know Mrs Lesley was ill."

"No, neither did I, but I saw her in Mr McDade's the chemist about a month ago, when I was in there with my mum. She didn't look ill to me either, only a bit stouter as if she had put on weight. My mum told her how well she looked and marriage suited her." Helen twisted her lips in thought. "Mr McDade then gave Mrs Lesley a bottle of pink medicine and told her that would do the trick... she had to take a big spoonful three times a day. Imagine medicine three times a day... Ugh!"

The girls walked on. Helen suddenly stopped in her tracks and put her hand out to prevent Alice walking any further.

"That's it Alice, I've just worked it out!" Helen smiled. "First you get married, then you get a bottle of pink medicine from McDade's, take three spoonful's a day... that's it... that's how you get a baby!" she announced, triumphant. "But you better be careful what colour medicine your mother gives you in future," Helen warned, her imagination running wild.

"So if that's the case and it's the medicine that's making the babies... Do you remember in Sunday School last week, Miss Laird our Sunday School teacher telling us about the African missionaries? She showed us books with pictures of the African children and mothers with their babies, remember?" Helen prompted.

Alice nodded her head slowly, not quite understanding the point her friend was making.

"Well, if what you say is true, they must have a big supply of Mr McDade's brown coloured medicine in Africa... that's how they get brown babies. Now I get it!" Helen snapped her fingers, proud of her thesis.

"But Dey's married to ma granny and he's been taking bottles of McDade's brown mixture for ages." Alice stopped for a second, remembering. "I think it's called Cascara and he's not had a baby yet, brown or white."

"Well he can't be taking enough of it... tell him tae try more!"

"I'v smelt it, Helen, and it stinks! I'll bet the pink medicine isn't much better... I don't think I'll bother having a bairn." Alice shuddered, grue'd at the very thought of it.

Imaginations running wild, the girls ran the last few yards to the school gates, the school bell ringing in their ears.

Chapter 22

A UNTY INTERRUPTED my concentration… not like her at all. I looked up, thinking, had she forgotten where she was in her story? Could she be getting absent minded?

"What is it?"

"I am surprised you have not noticed, but I came to a decision before you arrived today not to include my name in the history of Alice's life."

"But you must have been there, I sensed it, even if you didn't mention your name. You give such a personal account and it's so sweet, it's beautiful, the innocence of youth. Without doubt there's no fiction in this part of your story – it's all you, wee girls on the threshold of adulthood. I can see the three of you in the painting you talked of when we started."

"Yes I know, they were innocent times and for me nice to remember and look back on, but I am superfluous to the need. I am telling the story, it's ridiculous to have me in it, and far more important we concentrate on the life of my friend Alice, not me. Youth is fleeting and there won't be much more on this part of her life anyway."

"Well okay. I suppose it cuts down on writing, but are you sure?"

"Would I have made such an important decision without due consideration?" she snapped.

All right, no need to raise your blood pressure… keep you hair on.

"Here's Cathie with the coffee, I hope she's not baked any more of these biscuits from that book you brought back from the States. I can hardly get into my corsets, I've put so much weight on," Aunty announced without a trace of humour. I bit my lip to prevent myself from bursting out laughing at the thought of her hooking up her stays.

"Ach yer lookin' a lot mair comfortable in thae trousers, and no, Miss Jane, no more biscuits, I baked butterscotch brownies!"

Aunty rolled her eyes heavenwards. "I thought we agreed, no more recipes from that American book! I warned you I am going to confiscate it… and what are brownies anyway?"

If Alasdair thought Janet and Tam bringing a clothes pole into his bedroom was like a circus, this definitely was turning into one. I wished I hadn't brought the stupid cookery book.

"Drink your coffee and let's get on with it," Aunty stated. "By the time you leave for home I think you will be pleased to know I will be on the brink of answering your question. You will be standing at the gates of Leightham House!"

Chapter 23

AGGIE shook her head and smiled as she turned back into the house. There was no doubt Helen and Alice were inseparable. From early childhood the girls did everything together. An improbable relationship, the fisherman's bairn and the Parish Minister's, the two had formed an unbreakable bond. Helen's father Tom McDougall, a very down-to-earth man, did not believe he was any better than his parishioners, nor did he want his children to give themselves airs and graces. So the minister's children went to the local school same as every other child in the parish – no private schooling for them. The two girls now well on their way to school were deep in conversation. Aggie noticed for the first time Helen's clothes had also been let down. Looks like the pair of them were now young woman. 'Mercy on us, overnight the world has changed; time passes too quickly, childhood gone in the blink of an eye.' Aggie shook her head, mystified.

The girls were complete opposites. Helen, full of life, bubbly and a bit of a chatterbox, a bright young lass, with a leaning towards the Arts, English, and had considerable artistic talent for design. Whenever it was time for the summer fete or the Christmas play at the church hall, Miss Laird always called on Helen to help design the costumes and the scenery. Alice, on the other hand, was the academic, a real bookworm, Aggie frequently had to shout at her to get her head out of a book as her tea was ready. Alice got it right away, no need for any of the teachers to have to explain her maths problems twice. A joy to teach, said her report card, and most of the term it was

Alice's name that was on the school notice board, top of the class for English and Mathematics. "I am top of the class again, Mum," she would announce on her arrival home from school.

Alice and Helen could be found most Saturday afternoons in The Phimister Library with Miss Emily Laird, their English teacher, who doubled as the Librarian; all three of them poring over some book or other and not just fiction or children's literature. The girls loved books on the arts, history, travel books and journeys of the explorers. What a blessing the Phimister sisters had come back from India after their parents' deaths and had invested in the village. A fine Academy purpose built for all the children of the Parish to attend till the age of 17. A library, and they had renovated the church hall so that the whole community could get together for local functions.

"These folks are rich," Wullie had announced to Aggie one evening while they sat at the fire. "My Father remembered the Phimister sisters. Mother, married twice, caused a scandal at the time. Harry Paxton hardly cold in his grave and his Mrs marries Phimister, that's why the ladies have a different surname to their older half-brother Fred. No, it was Phimister who made his daughters wealthy. Phimister had shipping and tea estates in India, but he made the most of Paxton's fortune that Mildred and Fred had inherited on Harry's death. That's what caused a sensation in the villages, which was talked about for months. I wonder what happened to Fred Paxton, he must be in his fifties by now. My father told me the Phimister family rarely came back, but they kept the big house on the main road with just a housekeeper. Old man Phimister came back when he had business in Edinburgh, but only for weekends. It was quite a surprise when the lassies returned, announcing they were home for good."

Coming out of her revelry Aggie decided she better get on. 'I better go see if the water's ready in the wash house boiler or needs more wood; if I don't get going it might rain. There's a good chance of getting the washing dry or Wullie's long Johns will be dangling in our faces up on the pulley while we are eating our dinner. Now where's that scrubbing board? I'll need to get some more yellow soap and some soda crystals with the messages this week and a new scrubbing brush as well; mercy, the list never ends. Thank goodness Wullie and the crew had some fine catches this winter, the money will tide us over till the fishing starts again in the winter. Wullie was just saying only the other night that the crab and lobster creels were doing well and he'd had some enquiries from the big Hotels in Edinburgh for the shellfish. Seems they want to buy shellfish for their restaurants; it appears the rich and famous like shellfish and willing to pay for it. How he's going to get them there I don't know!' Aggie shook her head breaking out of her revelries. 'Get on!' she ordered herself. 'Aye, a woman's work is never done.'

As Aggie started the chores she thought maybe it's not that bad a thing the lassies are learning about the outside world. Maybe Alice was right, the only drawback were the times when Wullie and Aggie had no idea what their daughter was talking about and didn't know how to answer her questions and they had a fleeting sensation Alice was drawing away from them both socially and academically. Alice was beginning to wake up to a whole new world and she wanted to travel and to learn of other lands, the people who inhabited them, their culture and habits.

Sitting by the fire when Alice was in her bed at night, the couple occasionally acknowledge to each other the changes in their only child. She was growing up and becoming aware of her surroundings and had begun to realise there was a whole new life outside the village that had once been the centre of her universe. Aggie had some sympathy for her daughter and would have liked to see more of the world beyond the fishing community. She secretly hoped her daughter would not end up with the backache and raw hands of the fisher lassies. If Aggie had any say at all or could influence Wullie about Alice's future she would. Wullie however had none of these aspirations for his daughter, she would just do as she was told and that was that.

Aggie's experience of the world was her journeys up and down the East coast following the fishing fleet. Sometimes Aggie would look at her small collection on the dresser of tea cups and saucers with 'A gift from Peterhead' written on them in gold. They reminded her of her youth, the only evidence of her own limited travels. Sighing to herself, she thought there was no point looking back – nothing would have changed. It was inevitable for these young girls, that was their lot in life and none questioned or expected it to be different.

'Oh Lord,' she sighed, 'all those torn nets up the laft waiting to be mended before Wullie gets back. It won't be long now before Alice is old enough to give a hand. Maggie is teaching her to help in the house and she does make a grand pot of soup, even a decent cup of tea but the wee soul doesn't have the strength yet to do the mending. It's heart-warming though to see her knitting and sewing on the old treadle, what a patience granny Booman has. What a pair they are, right kindred spirits, every afternoon after school, that's Alice's first port of call, her granny's. Help! What a future for her to look forward to, mending the nets!' Aggie burst out laughing at the memory of Alice's first attempt to make scones without her or her grandmother present. There was more flour on the floor and on her than on the scones: she looked like a snowman, but at least she got them out the oven before she set the house on fire! Aggie smiled. 'Bless her, she'd wanted to surprise them and make the tea. What would my life be like without her? I don't even want to think about that – don't tempt fate, Aggie! M-m-m well, I better get on.'

The girls were well out of sight, probably nearing the school by now.

'Get a move on, Aggie.'

Chapter 24

THE NEW YEAR blew in like a scene from Dante's Inferno weather-wise. The January winter weather caused much anxiety among the fishing communities. Snow up to the knees, roads impassable, snowdrifts blocking the roads, gales of wind. Freezing temperatures that normally would have kept the population indoors, huddling at the fire to keep warm, but this particular January all was not well in Pittendreal.

Doddie Spence the Bobbie was sick to his back teeth chasing the womenfolk off the outer seawall. Silent, anxious, shawl draped women huddled together, staring out to sea in desperation. Fear made them unaware of the soaking they were taking or of the danger of being pulled into the sea by the next massive wave. There had been no sightings of the fishing fleet and they were long overdue. The fisher folks began to think the worst. The North Eastern gales were treacherous; many a boat had been sunk in one of its gales. They began to fear the worst the whole fleet had been sunk. Although the families did not celebrate Christmas to any great extent, generally only the children received small gifts. Fruit, when available, a sugar pig in their stocking, along with some practical clothing that had been knitted for them by their mothers or grandmothers, and maybe a new pair of baffies. The fishermen however never wanted to miss celebrating the New Year. At last there was a lull in the weather and the fleet was sighted! Everyone breathed a sigh of relief and laughed a little when the men told them they had taken shelter, hidden from the storm on the south side of Mary Island.

Cake day came on the second day of the New Year and thrilled, excited children plagued Lightman the baker for their cakes, with their name iced on each individual small bun. It soon became apparent that one loved member of the community was missing... Jock Booman. He and Auld Tam had well and truly brought in the New Year with a vengeance. Davie relaxed his usual ban on no more than two drinks for each of them, so they had been more or less legless when they left The Pirates. Davie wasn't particularly worried about the two old codgers; the pair like homing pigeons always turned up sleeping on a doorstep, in some wash house or garden hut. By the third day they knew Auld Tam had made it home safely – but not Jock. The community was now seriously worried and began a fruitless search.

Again Doddie couldn't believe his eyes, coming out of the police station which was little more than a Mizzen hut on the Mid-Shore, in which thankfully the local council had installed the telephone. In front of him were two children, their thick Kelly-gravat wool scarf round their necks big enough to cross over their chests and secured at the back with large safety pins to keep them warm. Warm they might be but not for much longer, the tide coming in with a vengeance and the waves once again threatening to scale the seawall. The spray had already started to soak the inside walk of the wall where the fishing boats were berthed and the girls would be soaked. 'Aye, two lassies,' Doddie Spence shook his head in disbelief. No point putting his bicycle clips on and cycling along the Mid-Shore to warn the girls: the wind would have him blown off his bike in no time. So the frightened man ran all his might, yelling at the top of his lungs for the pair of them to get back. The girls looked up as they heard Mr Spence the Bobbie and turning back walked towards him.

"What on awe the earth dae yea think yer up tae? I'll gie yea skelpit backside. Oh my God, it's the Minister's bairn and

Wullie Gairdner's lassie!" he said out loud when he got close to the girls and recognised them. "A'll tell yer faithers on the pair o' yea. What are yea thinking about walking even on the inner sea wall in such weather! Yea could hae been drooned. Your mother will be looking for you Helen McDougall, and yours as weel Alice Gairdner!"

Helen, always the first to speak, announced, "We were trying to help find Alice's Dey, he's missing and we are all worried."

Doddie could never quite get over the lack of east coast dialect when most of the children who went to the Academy spoke. That would be because of the posh Miss Phimisters, he thought.

"Fine a ken your Dey's missing, but dinna worry lass, he'll turn up, nae doubt wi a sair heid, but you pair will gie them a bigger sair heid if yer dragged intae that herbour and drooned!"

"I know Mr Spence, but it's nearly a week now," Helen argued. Alice stood silently, unhappy.

"Wherever he's hiding you'll no find him doon here onywey, Auld Tam said yer Dye turned back because he'd left his great coat in The Pirates, so he'll no catch the cauld Alice," he tried to offer some comforting words to the obviously distressed child.

Spence suddenly felt as if someone had walked over his grave. Maybe the girl's instincts weren't far from wrong and it was possible the sea had claimed the old man.

"Well get awa hame… am watching the pair o' yea till yer at the top o' the Kirk Wynd and don't you dare let me catch you back here again in weather like this."

Several days' later word went round the village that an army great coat had been found at low tide in St Creil's harbour and two days after that a body.

Now all the local men had gathered at The Pirates awaiting the cortege to arrive, to pay their last respects and attend the funeral.

"It looks like your prophesy came true Davie… his auld army coat was the death of him. From what I hear his coat was found first, his body washed up on the beach further along the coast. That was some distance he travelled! A' bet he planned it just tae keep us a' guessin'. Bet he's lookin' down on us richt noo… havin' a rich guid laugh." Aund Dunsire smiled as he shook his head at the thought.

"A' wonder what party tricks he's got up his sleeve to entertain us at his funeral?" Iain Moir quipped in.

"Well, let's get on wi it, the quicker we get it a ower the better, a' dinna like the look o' that weather and it'll be dark by fower o' clock the nicht and it's depressing tae look at thae blue mourning bands round the fishing boat masts," Davie Muir said, "And I'll never understaun why he's decided tae get buried in the cemetery up the Comentry Road?"

"Well they blue bands are a mark o' respect for dead fishermen, it's obvious you've never been tae sea Davie Muir. I'll bet he picked the Comentry road, just tae mak us walk the twa miles ahent the hearse in the freezing cauld… better hae another dram. Davie, double's awe round, am payin'. Jing's that's aboot six I'v hid," Aund Dunsire announced.

"You'll need it tae keep yea warm, here's Davie wi the drinks… slangivah! Here's tae Jock!"

Davie Muir looked about the men gathered at The Pirates for the funeral procession and asked, "Whaur's Auld Tam? I thocht he micht hiv gien a lift tae some o' the older lads on his Kirt."

"He's no cumin' tae the funeral, he says he disnae believe Jock's deid… droned," Iain Moir added as an afterthought.

"Ach Auld Tams losin' his marbles," Aund chipped in, "but it's not like him tae miss awe the free booze!"

"To be honest gentlemen, I find it hard to believe he's awa masel and I have tae live wae the guilt... It was me that flung them oot that nicht. The weather was closin' in somethin' terrible... one o' the worst gales o' wind a've ever experienced... Oh dear, if only..." Davie sighed.

"Dinna fash yersel man, it's no your fault or the first time the pair o' them got drunk and yae flung them out... yea canna go on blamin' yersel," Iain added. "Drunk men dinna hurt themselves, he'd no suffer, yea hiv tae believe that."

It had been a harrowing week for the little community. Several of the houses had their red Dutch tiled roofs blown off and the men thankfully had brought a new consignment from Holland on one of their last trips and had taken a lull in the weather to repair the damage.

Jock left the house as he normally did on Old Year's night when Auld Tam hammered on the kitchen door for him to hurry up. Maggie knew what was coming, thoroughly disapproved of the drinking and refused point blank to join in what she believed was a Pagan festival. She didn't mind a glass of ginger wine, a bit of homemade shortbread and black bun to celebrate the New Year, but she never touched alcohol. A strange turn of events took place that winter's night. Instead of slinking out the back door like a thief in the night avoiding a tongue lashing from Maggie on the ruination of drink, Jock stopped halfway out and halfway in, as if trying to make up his mind about something. For a fraction of a second Maggie thought he had changed his mind about going out... no such luck. Turning back he headed straight for Maggie and to her astonishment and before she could protest, Jock took hold of her, held her by the shoulders with both his hands and placed a long lingering soft kiss on her cheek.

"What's this awe aboot Jock Booman, dinna think your gaun tae get aroond me," she uttered rubbing her face where

Jock's course unshaven beard had scratched her skin; but Jock had seen that sweet loving smile he knew so well.

"A' just felt like it... it must be aboot sixty years we've been the gither Maggie."

"Aye ye're richt Jock, but a think yer gaun soft in your auld age... ye daft auld fool. Remember am no bid'in up for yea... when ye and Auld Tam get the gither ye furget the time and it's an awfy like nicht... Hell mend the pair o' ye."

"A'll no be long Maggie, it's an awfy like nicht and Tam, I'll need tae get up the Comentry road afore Junet throws a hairy fit, his chests been botherin' him again."

That was the last time Maggie saw Jock alive. Within a few days the whole village was out, led by P.C. Spence to search for him. Every out-house, wash house and coal cellar was inspected without success... Jock had disappeared without a trace. High seas, gales of wind and a further foot of snow prevented searching further afield.

When questioned by Spence, Davie Muir quite openly admitted to throwing Tam and Jock out of The Pirates before midnight, around nine o' clock in fact. They were the only customers left in the pub and as far as Davie was concerned they had drunk enough. He decided to close early because of the weather and it was unlikely there would be any more customers venturing out on a night like that. Watching the pair of them leave weaving their way towards Nellie and the Long Brae, he saw Tam get on his Kirt and leave and Jock getting off the Kirt to turn back for his coat before Davie locked up. In retrospect Davie thought what a pity he had forgotten the coat, because Tam was well away before Jock got it on or could run after him for a lift. He'd never forget the last he saw of his old friend staggering along the Mid-shore clutching his old army coat about his chest and head.

More bad news came when Eric Stevenson the Bobbie from St Creils was seen peddling along the High Street with a suspicious parcel tied to the back of his bike and making his way to the Mid-Shore. Arriving at the Police Station Doddie let him in. About half an hour later Stevenson left minus the parcel.

Giving bad news was part of the policeman's lot in life and Doddie was not looking forward to this. He put his trouser clips round his trousers at the ankles, tied the same parcel on the back of his bike, slung his leg over the bar and cycled towards Rodger Street and the Bowman household dreading every minute of it. The great coat had been found floating in St Creils harbour; it wasn't concrete evidence, but it was highly suspicious. With a certain sense of foreboding, Doddie reached the house and was relieved to see Wullie was there with his mother-in-law.

Wullie answered the door. "Come in Mr Spence, we're expectin' ye."

Once in the kitchen Doddie placed the parcel on the table and began to undo the string. Maggie stood up and looked at the coat.

"Well now, Mistress Booman, I ken it doesn't look good and it certainly isn't conclusive, but I have to be honest. Can you identi…"

"A ken Mr Spence, its Jock's!" Maggie interrupted; it was obvious it was his – no one else had an army great-coat in the village, only auld Sodger.

"A'm very sorry Mrs Booman, but until a body's found we have to keep the case open and of course we'll a' keep on searching for Jock."

Lowering his voice as he left the house, Doddie turned to Wullie.

"We canna say for sure he's droned, Wullie, but that gale o' wind the nicht he was last seen leaving The Pirates… the sea was hammering ower the sea wall; it's just possible a wave could have cawed him off his feet and dragged him intae the herbour. Unfortunately a have to prepare ye for the worst." Spence shook his head.

The discovery of the coat now made it imperative for another search, to focus on the beaches. Sadly before this search could be organised P.C. Stevenson arrived back out of breath from his six-mile cycle from St Creils along the coast road. Fortunately he met the men about to leave from The Pirates with Davie Muir in front leading the search.

"Stop!" Stevenson yelled at them. "Stop... a body's been found on the shore of the Link's golf club between St Creils and Leightham. The body was found by a couple of golfers out looking at the greens this morning, which was lucky because they could hardly play golf in this weather... A'm awfy sorry, Wullie, but a hiv tae ask yae tae come wi me tae identify the body, we hiv it in the mortuary at Leightham police station."

"Aye Mr Stevenson, one o' the lads will lend me their bike. Yer not tellin' me anything I dinna already ken and I'd better no gaun hame until Jock's been identified." Wullie was obviously shaken.

Chapter 25

IN THE LIVING ROOM now draped in black, the women sat with Maggie and her daughter in equal sombre attire. Patrick Wright and his sons lifted the coffin from the bedroom to the hearse – a magnificent black and gold vehicle with wide glass windows offering an all-round unobstructed view of the coffin. The hearse, pulled by four black horses, each horse supporting three black feather plumes sprouting from the top of their harnesses. A wreath of artificial wax flowers supplied at extra cost by Wright's on top of the coffin. The cortege was ready to set off but not to the cemetery – no, Jock had stipulated in the past he was to be met by the men outside The Pirates. The fishermen would then walk in procession from The Pirates, through the village and on to the Comentry Road for his burial. Only Mr McDougall and Wullie set out to follow the hearse as it moved down Rodger Street towards the Long Brae. Every window in the village had its blinds and curtains drawn, every shop in the High Street had closed out of respect for the dead man. Although occasionally a curtain flicked to the side to let the occupants see the passing hearse.

Once Jock's body had been identified and brought home, Maggie had insisted on dressing him ready for burial herself. From the bottom of the Kist Maggie brought out a white sheet saved from their wedding night to be used as a shroud. Wullie, Wright the funeral director and Doddie Spence protested, explaining Jock was not a pretty sight. Maggie was adamant and lying in front of her on the bed they had shared for so many years, she saw only the handsome young man she had married.

Mr Mc Dougall arrived at seven o' clock the evening before the funeral and gave a fine ceremony to the family relatives and friends, as many as could cram into the house. Jock was a popular man and the house was full to bursting – it was standing room only and many of the mourners shed a genuine tear.

Next day the men were ready to fulfil Jock's wishes and waited sheltering in the pub door stamping their feet and blowing on their hands to keep warm while waiting for Jock to arrive.

"A hear auld Wright's hearse coming doon the Lang Brae noo! It's aboot time, am freezing tae death," Iain Moir complained. "And whit a bliddy racket, they damn wheels are needin' oiled, it's aboot time he handed oor tae his sons. Is he trying tae alert the Heavens that auld Jock's on his wi? That noise would wake the deid!"

Iain wasn't far wrong. The screeching and grinding from the axels and the brakes made a racket that could be heard for miles around. The clatter of the horses' hooves on the cobble stone roads could hardly be heard either.

Hip flasks full of warming whisky in their pockets, heads down and silent, the procession slowly headed up the Lang Brae, along the deserted High Street towards the Comentry Road. At the head of the mourners walked Mr Wright with Mr Mc Dougal behind him and Wright's sons riding on the Hearse. Behind walked the chief mourners, Wullie Gardner, his cousins, Iain and Aund and Davie Muir. Behind them in rows were the rest of the male mourners, all in sombre black suits and hats. No one spoke until they were halfway to the Cemetery and past Auld Tam's cottage.

Willie in the front row, twisted his lips sideways and whispered to Davie who was next to him, without looking up.

"A canna believe Auld Tam's no here. A thought he micht hae turned up frae his cottage. So he obviously hid nae intention o' comin' tae Jock's funeral. Am surprised thou they've been pals from school."

"Aye, yer richt Wullie," Davie whispered back, "and drinkin' pals ever since, but a' think you should complain tae auld man Wright, that's some bliddy racket they wheels are makin' – downricht disrespectful if yea ask me, it's a aboot time they were oiled."

"It's a guid job the Minister's oot in front or he'd hear yea swearin'."

The procession made its way slowly for the next ten minutes or so. Looking back, no one could really remember the exact moment it started and it wasn't that bad at first, but gradually it became almost impossible for the front row of mourners to breathe, never mind the row at the back it was so strong. The vile smell becoming stronger by the second was choking the men, till finally Wullie reaching for his handkerchief to cover his nose broke the silence.

"My God auld Jock's turned awfy quick!"

"No, it must be auld Wright that's losin' his marbles and no screwed doon the coffin lid ticht enough… Gawd almichty, the stench!"

Breaking with convention, the front row of mourners suddenly halted. Wullie, Davie Muir, Iain Moire and Aund Dunsire halted in their tracks without warning. The rest of the men, row on row, still with their heads looking at the ground, collapsed into the row in front until they were in a heap on the ground.

Everyone looked up… they had missed the turn for the cemetery and had walked straight on at the crossroads. So instead of following Wright's creaking hearse, they had been following Auld Tam's creaking Kirt with a fresh load of hot, steaming, stinking manure on it.

"A kent it, that auld bugger and Tam had one last trick up their sleeves! A'll bet auld Sodger peyed Tam and Wright tae separate at the crossroads, tak a different route tae the cemetery and Tam waitin' fur us tae follow him instead!" Davie burst out laughing, joined by the others, all the men now upright and brushing the snow off their clothes.

"Weel lads, we better get on, aboot turn... the licht's fading fast. If we tak the short cut oor the field we'll be there afore Jock – micht turn the tables on him if he's watchin' us from above. We'll pit the auld boy to his rest, and then we can hae a richt guid laugh in The Pirates at his wake later the nicht!"

"Wait till Maggie and the rest of the village hear about this, it'll be the talk of the toon for weeks," Wullie announced.

"A wonder if Maggie had auld sodger buried in his great coat?" Davie asked of anyone who was listening.

Chapter 26

"**Y**OU MADE THAT UP! Do you really want me to believe such a story?" I burst out laughing at the thought of the men tramping up the road, deep in respectful thought, following a cartload of dung!

"No I did not!" was the sharp retort. "Believe what you want, that's up to you. Now let's go to the conservatory for lunch. I have asked Cathie to keep it simple, more like a buffet. I know how attached to that Minnie-mouse figure you are."

Sarcasm, aunty? I ignored her.

"Salad to be served first, separately American style, salmon and a baked potato, but no sour cream that you keep talking about. Cathie hasn't been able to find it yet in the shops. So you will have to put up with good Scottish fresh butter, then strawberries and cream. Oh, and I've ordered a fine Chablis to go with it."

'Oh Lord, here we go again, she already knows I don't smoke. How am I going to tell her I don't drink alcohol ether? She's going to think I am a right puritanical, sanctimonious bitch! She'd be in good company – my friends think the same. Here goes.'

"Sounds wonderful and I was beginning to feel peckish, but if you don't mind, and you brought it up, my Minnie-Mouse figure... I will pass on the wine, it's full of sugar and I'm driving. I want to go back down the Mid-Shore this afternoon while you have a siesta." I put my hand up to avoid any arguments. "I insist you take a rest, it's good for you. Don't argue, I'm the Doctor, I know what's best." The old eyes narrow as she realised her mistake teasing me about my figure.

"I wasn't going to argue, I'll take a rest, but when I decide its time. What you find to do down at the harbour on a Sunday... I don't know!"

She just couldn't resist getting the last word!

Back in the lounge, having eaten a rather delicious lunch and now with a cup of Aunt Jane's special non-fake Kenyan coffee on the coffee table, we continued with her story.

Chapter 27

AGGIE AND WULLIE began to realise Maggie wasn't eating and it seemed to them she was losing interest in life. They insisted she came to stay with them for a while and close up the house, arguing there were too many memories for her to stay alone.

Maggie had begun to think back on that awful day of the funeral. She felt it would never end. The last she saw of Jock was his coffin leaving the end of Rodger Street. She had begged to go with the cortege, but Wullie point-blank refused, saying it wasn't seemly for women to be at the graveside. She couldn't get the sequence of events out of her head. Jock going missing, his body being found on the beach and then his funeral. If she hadn't seen his body she would never have accepted he was dead. The house crowded with mourners, well-wishing neighbours, Maggie had to stifle the desire to shout at them: 'Go away, leave me in peace!'

Why had Jock turned back on that fatal night and totally out of character had hugged and kissed her? Did he have a premonition something was going to happen to him? She would never know.

In the privacy of her bedroom, Maggie gave way to her emotions. Falling onto her knees, she rocked back and forth with grief. How could she, how would she recover without her soulmate? What would she do without him?

Maggie gave up the desire to live, turned her face to the wall in the little bedroom off Aggie's kitchen and prayed for death to come and take her. Sometime in the middle of that long dark winter night, the wind howling down the chimney, rain battering against the window, a pair of small hands threw back the quilt and blanket and a small body slid down between the sheets next to her. Two little arms reached out and held the grief-stricken old lady around the shoulders. A soft childish voice said in Maggie's ear:

"Do you still love me Granny?"

Those words shocked Maggie out of her depression, and she realised she had no option but to live. This little girl, her only grandchild, needed her, brought her to her senses and she needed the comfort and warmth of the child's love. Also, death was not so accommodating as to take her at her will. She recognised, too, that for Alice to lose her adored grandfather was one thing, but to lose them both was another; it would break the child's heart and she would not be responsible for that. The best outcome was to get a life back and she would visit Jock in the Cemetery whenever she got the chance. At least she knew he was there waiting for her and not down the Mid-Shore in The Pirates with Auld Tam.

As one day became the next, so did one year become another and time passed quickly, waiting for no man to catch up, giving Maggie no option but to go on living for her family's sake and her granddaughter in particular.

Chapter 28

"**WHERE'S MY MOTHER?**" sixteen-year-old Alice asked, bounding into the kitchen and dumping her schoolbag on the deal table.

"Awa wi a sodger," Wullie responded. "Alice, if you ever come into the kitchen and say hello Dad, a'll faint wi my leg up in the air!"

"Dad, this is important, stop joking," Alice interrupted, knowing the last thing her mother would do was run off with a soldier. As Alice had thrown her heavy schoolbag onto the table it had burst open scattering books, pencils and jotters all over the floor. "Now look what I have done, I've lost it!" she said searching for something in the bag and on the floor.

Wullie stopped rocking in his rocking chair, smile beginning to fade. "Look at the mess you've made!" he yelped, taking the pipe from his mouth. "Here a' am enjoying a few minutes reading the *Courier* withoot your mother yapping in my ear. Can a man no get ony peace? Yae better hurry up and get that mess cleaned up afore your mother arrives back."

"It's the last day of term and I have my final school report home with me. Miss Phimister wants me to discuss the results of my final exams with you and Mum. Here it is, a note from her." Alice waved a piece of paper in the air. "She wants me to stay on for another year and study more advanced work. She says I should be given the chance to become…"

Alice realised it was probably useless going on about it with her dad. He had that look in his eye that meant, 'Don't start on that again.' The family had had this discussion already. Once Wullie's mind was made up, that was that.

Seeing the beginning of another negative response to her pleas, Alice jumped into Wullie's lap and with her arms round her dad's neck, planted a kiss on his stubble covered cheek. 'Pins on my lips!' she thought. Her head now rested on Wullie's chest, she felt his hand stroking the luxurious tumble of her natural curls and ringlets.

Wullie would normally have called his daughter a redhead, but he'd heard the Rev McDougal call it Titian. That description appealed to Wullie even though he had no idea who Titian was and normally was not that interested in anyone's looks. Alice, aware of her dad stroking her hair, cuddled into him. 'How can I distract him?' she thought, 'Let him think he's won!'

In a wheedling voice, hoping to convince Wullie she had lost interest in the school report, Alice said: "Dad, Mum's got blonde hair, it's so fair it's almost white and I have red hair. You once said we got our family's colouring from the Vikings who came raping and pillaging down this coast centuries ago." She frowned. "What's pillaging, Dad?" she asked mischievously with an air of innocence that would have done credit to an angel.

Wullie ducted his chin into the polo neck of his fisherman's gairnsey and swallowed hard, practically knocking Alice onto the floor. Was it astonishment or embarrassment? He knew he had been caught out by his daughter. Stuttering and stumbling, he managed to blurt out:

"Eh? Well, it's the man who came doon frae the north and opened the local sweetie shop. Aye that's it, he's been pillaging our pockets ever since to pay for the sweets." Wullie hoped this would suffice and quickly changed the subject, just in case the next question was about the 'R' word. The only thing he could think of as a diversion was the school report.

"You'll no get round me that wi, you ken my opinion on further schooling for young lassies, a waste o' time."

'Good, back on track,' Alice said to herself, 'progress.'

Wullie never ceased to be proud of his girl and her incredible school reports. She damn near sat top of the class from the day she started school. Who did she get her brains from? Aggie, Wullie conceded, was the smarter of the two of them.

"Dad, I have my school report here, but Miss Phimister says to discuss it with you and Mum – if there's any possibility of staying on for another year. She says I have every chance of going to the University. It's in the note I have here." She offered Miss Phimister's letter to Wullie.

Before she could finish speaking, Wullie held up his hand to silence the girl, refusing to accept the letter. But Alice pressed on.

"Miss Phimister said she would apply for a scholarship for me if my academic progress continues. So it would not cost you and Mum anything and I'd just have to sit the entrance exam, which she says I'll pass."

"Are you arguing with me?" Wullie rapped out sternly. "Am yer faither, yer no listening, you'll dae as yer telt. How often dae a' have to repeat mysel?"

"Dad," Alice pleaded, "I can apply to St Andrews if you don't want me to go to Edinburgh; I know you might be anxious if I have to travel too far…"

Alice tailed off. Wullie was now looking directly at his daughter with his brows down, never a good sign. She knew when to quit. There was no point arguing once he had made his mind up. 'Why didn't I wait till mum to get back? Two against one is better odds.'

"Where's Mum anyway, Dad?"

Wullie went back to rocking in the chair, retrieved his pipe from the fireplace and started to puff away at it, making loud sucking noises; realising the tobacco had finished, he put the pipe in his pocket, lifted up the newspaper from the floor and with a sigh of satisfaction convinced himself he'd won.

"Ach, your mother is probably up the cemetery with her knitting, a've nae doubt clashing with the neighbours. What puzzles me is they sit on blooming tombstones, and you'd think it would be cauld on their dowp's. A' asked her did it no bother them tae sit in the graveyard among the deid; you'll niver guess what she answered! 'We're no bothered aboot the deid, efter a' we're among our ain folk, what harm wid they dae us? It's the living you have to watch.' A' think your mother's a wise wee woman," Wullie chuckled.

"Your mother being here will no mak ony difference," he went on. "A've made my mind up, so dinna think getting her on your side will change matters. Martin Wilkinson telt me he needs another assistant at his Draper's shop to stock the shelves and serve the customers. Lightman's the Bakers are looking for staff to help serve the customers and dae the accounts. A telt them you're grand at the sums and hiv your school report to prove it. Both these businesses are expanding and they are looking for staff." Wullie stopped, proud of his achievements in getting offers of employment for his daughter.

"A' was talkin' wi Mona Simpson coming oot o' the Kirk last Sunday; she does the accounts for Wilkinson and Lightman's. A telt her what Miss Phimister said and Miss Simpson says with your ability with the arithmetic she guarantees you a job in Lightman's office. Yae ken what that means?" Wullie smiled slyly. "When yer banking on Friday wi Miss Simpson, you'll bump into young Andy Coull the cashier at the Bank." Wullie could scarce contain himself.

"A'v seen him lookin' at yae in the Kirk on Sundays. A widn'a mind him as a son-in-law!" Wullie was now thinking out loud more to himself. "Mak your choice and be thankful that am no sending yae to gut the fish. That's a hard wae o' life for ony woman, a' widn'a want that fur my lassie."

"Dad, stop!" Alice put her hand up, beginning to blush at the thought of young Andy. Mercifully it sounded like she would not have to go to the fishing with the other women. Following the boats from Peterhead to Yarmouth to gut the fish in the freezing cold, standing at the gutting tables, the salt stinging any open wound on their hands. The speed they had to work at left ugly callouses and scars behind. Worse still, carrying heavy baskets of fish on their backs till they ached from lifting such weights. 'I should be grateful that my dad wants to spare me from such a life. So keep quiet, let him speak.'

"Weel," Wullie now demanded an explanation, "what's the guid o' French and in the name of a' that's Holy, what's Diction? You're never gaun tae use these subjects; it's they Miss Phimisters putting they notions in yer heid. A pair of Lady Mucks, they've nae experience of real life and how hard it is for us to earn a living. Earnin' a living frae the sea's no joke, at the mercy of the tides, the weather and whither we land a good catch, tae put food on the table. I ken it's a hard life but it is oor life and a'll no have it changed." Wullie looked back on what he'd just said, ignoring the look of disappointment on his only child's face.

"There's nae need for ony mair education and you've hid an extra year at the school already. No! Tak your pick o' the jobs offered, I'll even let you keep some of your pay," Wullie offered magnanimously, trying to get back in Alice's good books. "You can start collecting stuff for your 'hope Kist', I've nae objections tae that, you're oor only child and we can afford to feed you." Wullie smiled. "Although it wid nae surprise me if your mother has already started to collect stuff fur yae."

"Dad," Alice interrupted her dad, "I have no intentions of marrying soon, believe me, and don't be angry but I sometimes wonder what is worse for the girls in my village; following the fishing fleet doing work you tell me you don't really agree with, or back-breaking housework. Scrubbing floors on hands and knees, getting the messages, cooking, cleaning, washing the dirty clothes, at the same time mending nets and having babies or going out to work? Some choice! But no more talk of me getting married. I will get a job and I will work until I decide what I want to do. Change is coming Dad, women are beginning to assert themselves!"

Wullie was silent for a moment or two, frankly stunned with the speech Alice had just made.

"Whaur did you get such a notion?" he gasped.

"I read the papers, there is discontent all over the country from men and women. We are being taught in school to think for ourselves. Dad, I don't want to quarrel with you or Mum, but young people should have confidence to disagree!" Alice tried to make her dad see how she felt. Wullie also had read the papers and the news from home and abroad was disconcerting, especially from Russia; thankfully that country was a long way away. It was all very unsettling.

"We'll have nae mair o' that revolutionary talk!" Wullie had had his eyes opened at his young daughter "A'll gie yae change!" Indignant, he was unable to cope with her desire for independence. "How many o' your pals are oot earning money, paying their wages to their families, paying for their keep? You are a lucky, lassie, what more do you want?"

"Helen's staying on at school; she wants to go to Art School."

"Eh! The Minister's lassie, what a surprise! That's their business, none o' ours."

Wullie was up to high doh! He had indulged his only daughter most of her young life, taking pleasure in spoiling her, but this was different. She was frankly disagreeing with him and arguing for the first time in her life. "My lassie's grown up and she is thinking for herself – we'll see about that!" Willie didn't like this turn of events.

"Listen tae me!" Wullie demanded, in a stern voice. "A'm still your father and a'll decide what is going to happen, no you. No, a'll no let you gamble on an uncertain future. A dae care how clever you and your teachers think you are. You have been offered a grand opportunity, so you'll just tak the job and show some gratitude. There's no place in this village for lassies with further book learning. College, University… a've niver heard o sic a like thing, nothing but a waste of time and wi your looks you'll no stay single long. Furget it Alice," Wullie ordered his daughter. "You are leaving the school; I mean it, no arguments and that's that!"

Alice resisted the temptation to disagree – 'Quit while you are ahead, but you've given him something to think about.' Wullie's eyes were beginning to narrow; his chin protruding, he challenged Alice to dare to disagree. Alice, from experience, knew this was not a good sign and it was better to keep quiet. She knew he loved her dearly and the last thing she wanted was her father changing his mind about the job offers he had found for her and sending her to gut the fish instead. 'Well, the jobs were not so bad,' she consoled herself, 'and you never know what might happen. Life is a funny thing, you think you are on one path and suddenly without warning you find yourself on another. Anyway, Mum will be back any minute now and she has not had her say. Let us wait and see.' Alice quietly went to put the kettle on, but Wullie was not convinced at her submission.

'She is up to somethin',' he thought. 'Women! A'll never understand the workings o' their minds!'

Chapter 29

MAGGIE met with her friend Jeannie Tarvet at the monthly meeting of the Seaman's Mission in Leightham. During the tea interval, Maggie happened to mention that Alice had now left school and hadn't made up her mind what she wanted to do... much to the disgust of her father.

"Mercy on us, is she leaving the school already?" Jeannie had gasped. "A remember the days when she used to come to the Mission with you, a wee lassie afore she went to the school. Time passes oor quick!"

"Aye, I remember thay days weel," Maggie had agreed. "It's a pity they hiv tae grow up. You ken why she came, don't you? Only came to feed that old dug o yours at the tea break, what was its name, Bruce? Once she gave it the biscuit, she'd had enough and wanted tae gaun hame. Every time I vowed I would niver bring her back, but she always wheedled me intae it."

"Happy days, Maggie! A remember the time yae gave her yer crystal beads tae amuse her and the thing burst, scattered all oor the flair, sparking and twinkling in the sunlight from the mission windaes!" The ladies laughed at the memory.

Suddenly Jeannie sat bolt upright.

"Maggie, did a hear yae richt... Alice doesn'a hae a job yet?" Maggie had nodded.

"Weel, that's divine intervention... a jist minded... am gettin' that donnert in my auld age. A was talking with ma sister Lizzie last week, the one that's no married; she has a

grand job up at the big hoose as housekeeper. She was tellin'
me she's lookin' for an under housekeeper to train, as she's
getting' on a bit now."

"But Alice is only sixteen," Maggie interrupted.

"True, a' ken that, but she could write tae ma sister for an
interview. She says good staff is gettin' harder tae find and a'
hear Alice is a bright lassie and she'll need tae be. Leightham
House is no the biggest of the Leightham estates, but the work
managing the accounts is just the same as in their bigger
mansions. She micht get Lizzie's job when she retires."

Alice wrote to Miss Tarvet, had her interview and got the
job as junior housekeeper to Miss Tarvet.

The following Saturday dawned bright and sunny. Maggie
and the village womenfolk made their usual Saturday
pilgrimage up the Comentry Road to the cemetery.

Chapter 30

APART FROM a light breeze and the sound of the birds, the peace and tranquillity of the graveyard was broken only by the clicking of the ladies' knitting needles and the clacking of their tongues. "The devil mak work fur idol hauns. Always keep a sock on the needles, somethin' tae dae," was Maggie's mantra.

Aggie and her mother had made the usual journey and enjoyed the walk to the cemetery, meeting Rena McKay on her way to visiting her husband's grave and Martha Gardner visiting wee Betty's grave. They all walked together up the Comentry Road, with Alice and Helen ahead deep in conversation, the girls' arms around each other's waists.

"Jist look at the twa o' them Mother... a think they're joined at the hip. Heaven only kens what there gaun tae dae without each other when Alice leaves tae gan intae the big hoose," Aggie commented.

"Aye, the pair o' them and yer dad when he was alive, they got up tae some mischief, but Alice's no gaun tae the moon! They can get the gither on her days aff."

Comfortably seated on Jock's grave, a plaid thrown down to sit on top of it, the four women were happily exchanging the latest gossip. Aggie felt her mother had come to terms with the traumatic death of Jock and looking up was pleased to see a smile on Maggie's old face.

"You've gaun awfy quiet, Mum – what are you thinking about? Are yea thinkin' o' Dad?"

"Aye." Maggie let out a long sigh as she answered her daughter. "A miss the auld scoundrel, but he's at peace and a ken whaur he is." She paused for a moment. "A' was thinkin' aboot some o' the antics he got up tae!"

"Tell us mum. It's grand tae celebrate his life and no longer tae feel the need tae mourn."

"Dae yae remember the summer days when the three o' them, Jock, Alice and Helen McDougall, spent on the beach wi their pails collectin' wulks from the rocks? In the kitchen waitin' for pan tae bile on the stove so they could eat them… pickin' the wulk oot o' its shell wi a safety pin. Dae ye ken Mrs McDougall's hid a bairn nearly every other year since she had Helen? Somebody forgot tae tell the Minister tae get aff at The Haymarket!"

"Wheesht Mother! Helen's nearly here wi Alice."

"There's enough stories aboot Jock tae fill a book," Rena announced, looking up from the sock she had on four knitting needles. Rena kept Dr Forman and her son well supplied with home-knitted socks, after Alasdair had expressed his pleasure in wearing the homemade garments. "Nothing like them," he had said and Rena could turn the heel and graft the toe like a professional. While Maggie had been talking about Jock, Rena had been basking in her own thoughts about her son Brian. A qualified Doctor now, he was gaining experience in the city hospital and Alasdair had offered him a job in his practice once he had sufficient practical experience. A new surgery was to be built on the High Street for them to work in.

Rena had been shocked when her daughter Susan announced she would also study medicine. Brian and Rena had been against the idea. "No you'll no!" Rena had protested, aghast at the very idea of 'A woman Doctor' – but support came from Alasdair who backed the girl. He stood by Susan declaring "they needed more women in the medical profession". Rena wondered where her children got their brains from – 'Certainly wasn't their dad or me,' she thought, 'must have been all that fish I ate when I was carrying them!' She smiled, shaking her head.

"Tell us some mair, Maggie," Rena re-joined the conversation.

"Aye, his antics would fill a book and that's the sober ones. A was thinkin' o the time Kitty Macintosh, a posh distant cousin of ma father's and her man frae London, were invited fur their tea," Maggie obliged.

"Aye, who could forget that day Mum, bakin' and cookin' for a week! I remember what a spread we laid out wi the best china, table cover and awe. Sandwiches o' pressed tongue, potted beef, scones, you name it, we'd made it!"

"But a' canna mind who's bright idea it was to show Kitty the new dry lavatory in garden," Maggie laughed.

"Mum, do you remember what we fund when we came back in?" Aggie prompted her mother.

"Would I ever forget… you wouldna believe it Rena… Martha, Jock, Helen and Alice were in the kitchen efter been banned frae it, while the visitors were there fur their tea."

By this time the girls had joined the ladies and were sitting on the ground with their hands over their mouths, trying to stop themselves laughing.

"Aye, the pair o' yae a' wi a sandwich in each hand and Jock pretendin' tae eat the potted beef. A was that affronted, what would the wuman think! The lot o' yae had been warned tae keep weel awa frae the hoose till the wuman left."

Aggie shook her head as she remembered the three criminals trying to explain. They declared they had been hungry, but a certain young man in a fur coat lay innocently by the fire grooming himself, grinning from ear to ear, settled down to sleep on a full stomach.

"Dey saved the day, Rena; when we went into the kitchen to collect the pipe we nearly died – there was Bodger up on the table helping himself to the potted beef and he'd nudged the sandwiches open and eaten the pressed tongue! Dey said to pretend we were hungry, he was the one who prevented Bodger from getting flung out!" Alice finished the story.

"I always loved the antics of your grandfather, Alice, especially at the New Year," Helen joined in. "When he was aping the 'band o' hope' he always made me laugh prancing about the floor singing 'Yes we'll gather at the river', shaking his hand up in the air with his pretend tambourine!"

"Helen McDougall, you better no let your faither hear you makin' fun o' another religious sect," Aggie cautioned.

"Let the bairn alaine, Aggie, she's no dain' ony herm. I think my favourite memory o' your dad was the New Year's Day. He brocht the Russian sailor hame wi him frae The Pirates!"

"Aye, that's the best one yet, Mum. We were a' in the kitchen waiting for the auld devil tae arrive, the steak pie dryin' up in the oven. Well…"

"Am tellin' the story Aggie!" Maggie interrupted her daughter. "Like a was sayin' Jock arrives back wi a man we'd niver seen afore. We didna ken a Russian fishing boat had taken shelter in the herbour. The man just smiled, niver said a word."

"He couldna get a word in edgeways, Mother, yae niver stopped naggin' Dad!"

"Kin yae blame me, the dinner awe spilt and yer faither no botherin' his shirt… Jock sat the man doon at the kitchen table – a' couldna believe ma eyes! He slung a kitchen cloot around the man's neck and proceeded to cut his hair!"

By this time the whole ascended company were splitting their sides laughing.

"A canna believe it, Maggie, Jock cut the man's hair?" Martha gasped.

"That's not the half o' it, tell them Mum," Aggie butted in again.

"Weel yea see a' hid created such a racket... the man jumped oot o' the chair, threw the cloot tae the flair and ran oot the door wi only one side o' his hair cut. We niver heard o' him again. Sometimes a wonder what he telt the crew when he got back tae his ship wae only half a haircut. Mind you, he was lucky yer dad was drunk... he micht hae cut the man's ear aff as weel!"

By now the assembled company were pleading with Maggie to stop and were wiping the tears from their eyes.

"Aye Mum, that's a grand story to stop on, finish the afternoon with, but it's time we went hame. Come on Alice, get up, brush the gress aff yer skirt. You too, Helen."

"Aye he's entertained us the day, he doesn'a want us tae gan hame feelin' sad. He was an awfy man. I wonder what he would think aboot his beloved granddaughter going intae service at the end o' the month. Am no that sure masel', a' hope your Wullie's made the richt decision. Maybe the bairn should bide at the school. A' think her Dey would have supported that." Those few words of Maggie's brought the present company down to earth.

"No point thinking about that now Granny," Alice interrupted her grandmother. "No turning back, I am glad to get work." Turning back round to face Aggie, Alice announced: "I forgot to tell you Mum, Miss Phimister told Helen that on my days off she and Helen will join me to continue with my studies." Alice, determined, was not going to give in that easily. Proudly straightening her shoulders and raising her head gave Aggie a twinge of conscience.

Having been bitterly hurt by her parents' lack of support, Alice wondered why they had allowed her that extra year in school, just to pull the academic carpet from her feet at the end of the day. Disappointed, she would never look at or trust them again. When she next needed their support, could she rely on them? Could she trust them? Alice now saw her parents in a different light, backward, insular. Presented with the options her father had given her, stacking the shop shelves or gutting the fish, she had chosen to go into service to spite him. Now she wasn't so sure she had made the right decision. Walking back to the village, Alice remembered that long, silent walk up the drive of Leightham House for her interview. Holding back her tears, she felt she was walking away from her family, friends, Helen and the security she had known all her young life. Helen, sensing her distress, squeezed Alice's hand to reassure her.

Standing on the precipice of life, on the brink of the unknown, a strange turn of painful events in her young life would have catastrophic results for her sometime in the future. She would find herself in a cruel world of reality.

Innocent, she went forward to face the future as a servant in Leightham House.

Chapter 31

I'D LEFT AUNTY resting in the conservatory. It had seemed like it was a good place to stop her narrative before I left for the States. On my way out I bumped into Cathie. Since I had begun to stay the whole day, Cathie had had the extra job of preparing a coffee break as well as lunch. There had been little time for us to enjoy our usual banter, but I collared Cathie at the front door.

"Cathie, do you know why that derelict old house on the coast road is a ruin?" I chanced my luck at a quick answer. Cathie frowned.

"You mean the one wi nae roof?" I nodded. "A dae ken, it's always been like that, has it no'?"

I left the house no further forward and made my way down to the Mid-Shore.

"A penny for them!" a cheerful voice sounded in my ear. A pleasant young man placed a cup of steaming hot black coffee on the table I was sitting at with one hand and pushed the other out to shake mine.

"Alan Addison, proprietor of Café Allan, at you service!" His friendliness made me smile up at him.

"What are you writing?" He indicated the collection of notes in front of me on the table. "And why are you frowning... might never happen. Are you studying for an exam or something?"

"You are right, I was deep in thought." I shook his hand and exchanged the usual pleasantries. "Thank goodness you're open and on the Sabbath, you're risking it with the locals are you not? And no, since you asked, I am past studying for the present. You're not from here with that accent?"

"Aye, that's right hen, I'm frae Glesca, the city where we phone for the Polis, no the Bobbie!" he answered, exaggerating the distinctive sing-song dialect of the west coast. "Home of The Barrowlands dance hall, home of the male patter merchant, have ye heard of 'Are ye dancing... are ye askin'?" Before she had time to reply Alan translated in his poshest English accent: "'Would you like to dance? Are you asking me to dance?' Glesca, the dancers are the best in the world; you should see them do the Twist. It's the city of the Teddy Boy lacquered cowlick hairdo, sideburns, skinny ties and bovver boots. Rangers and Celtic football teams, famous for opposing fans fighting after a football match. The Gorbals, the midden men, the Broons, maw, paw and the wee-yins in the *Sunday Post!*" Alan laughed at the speech he'd just given.

"Aye, I'm a Glaswegian, but when I saw this place up for sale... well, I just had to have it. Ma auld Maw said 'follow your heirt son' and as they say, the rest is history. I believe it used to be a Pub in its hay-day, was closed for years. What a state the place was in, almost a ruin, I had to strip the plaster back to the bricks... put a new roof on and new windows in and whether the locals like it or not, I'm opening on a Sunday, so they will just have to get used to it!"

"I'm sure they will, just give them time. I believe this was The Pirates Inn?"

"That's right, how do you know that? You don't have much of a local accent either."

"I have come to know quite a lot about Pittendreal, its history and its people over the last year," I said, ignoring his question regarding my accent. I had warmed to this friendly young man and wanted to talk to him. Tell him about my visits to Aunty. The first time I had opened up to another human being about them.

"You could say I am trying to get my head round these notes. I've been trying to get answers to a question that has plagued me from childhood. It seems my great aunt is the only person who knows the answer, but getting it out of her is like drawing blood, no pun intended, and believe me I am good at that!" I found myself smiling as Alan had not picked up or questioned me regarding my ability to take blood.

"Aunty insists on answering my questions, by mixing fact with fiction. When we began she explained she had wanted to write the book herself, but never did and she regrets it. Believe it or not, not a word is to be discussed with anyone or printed before she dies." I shook my head again. "Some bargain, eh? I get my answer and she gets the history recorded for posterity. Sometimes I don't understand any more now than I did when we started." I smiled. "And you're brilliant at your job – I have just broken her confidence!"

"Is that the old lady who lives in the big house on the outskirts of Pittendreal, Mount View?" I nodded. "Wow! Well, don't worry, I don't know her personally and am like the priest in the confessional!"

Encouraged, I continued, "Some things are downright weird, Alan. Some tie-in but others are a mystery. For instance, I stopped to look in the church graveyard on my way here and I couldn't find one headstone with a name or date on it regarding the people she has been telling me about. There was one massive headstone in a corner, but I didn't have time to look closer." I stopped there thinking the poor bloke must be bored to death by now. "Oh, by the way, just out of interest, do you know anything about the old ruin between Leightham and Pittendreal?"

"Naw it's always been like that has it no? At least that's what I was telt."

"That's what Cathie said."

"Who's Cathie?"

"Never mind, it's not important. What are your plans for the café?" I changed the subject.

"I want to introduce a new menu. At the moment I get my cakes and deserts from Lightman's the bakers and I've decided not to do fish and chips or ice cream that might put Marcello's nose out of joint. I was thinking more of 'Chicken in a Basket' – battered chicken in an open basket with chips and the customers can eat it in the cafe or take away. What do you think?"

"Good idea, I've recently been in the States and enjoyed their Colonel Saunder's Kentucky Fried Chicken... it should go down well."

"You've been in the States? My wife and I were there last year visiting her sister and boy, do they Americans know how to eat! I brought recipes back with me; just have to source the ingredients. What did you think of Strawberry Shortcake, and what about Cheesecake?"

Oh no! Any more discussions about the merits of American desserts and I would end up with nightmares – being chased along Fifth Avenue by a giant New York cheesecake?! Time to go, I decided.

"Sorry, I have just realised the time. I must get back to the old dear; she will be waiting for me. Good luck Alan Addison. I hope I haven't bored you to death."

"Naw it goes with the territory, listening to the customers."

Looking for my purse to pay for the coffee, Alan put his hand out to stop me. "Naw, have it on me hen." What is it with these Glasgow folk? They'd give you their last penny, the shirt off their backs, they're so kind.

Back sitting in the car I took a few minutes to look out over the river, make a memory, to take with me to the States. I knew Johnny was going to propose and I had fallen in love with him... but was I ready to leave... emigrate? I argued the pros and cons, but how could this small Kingdom have such a hold on me? The answer was simple, just like Alan; my countrymen are friendly and our culture indisputably recognisable in other parts of the world, so why would I want to leave?

My wedding was on my mind and American friends had asked in the past, 'Is it true Scotsmen don't wear underpants under their Kilts?' If they are true Scotsmen it's true, the men like the freedom! They take pride swinging their hips; exposing their legs, enough to set any girl's heart aflutter and with Scottish country dancing you never know what you might get a glimpse of! I remembered the eightsome reels I'd danced at weddings, although I never saw anything except knobbly knees and hairy legs.

I tell my friends abroad that there is nothing as exhilarating as a Ceilidh at a Scottish wedding and nothing so moving and emotional as the lilt of the bagpipes playing to announce the beautiful bride's arrival at the church. I had often been automatically served Scotland's national famous drink, whisky, on a night out in Texas, but I assured my friends that at weddings and other events "a wee dram" was mainly served to the men.

I shivered with excitement, realising I could have two weddings, one in Scotland and one in America! Kilted men, bagpipes at the church and traditional fruit cake with marzipan and Royal icing, for the Scottish one; and two American wedding cakes, one vanilla sponge cake for the bride and one chocolate for the groom at the American one. They don't like fruitcake in the States. I thought, I bet Mary will try and make a fruit one just for me. It also meant I'd get to wear my wedding dress twice. I wondered if Johnny would wear the kilt just for me. He might. I think I heard him say he had Scottish ancestors once.

Having come to a decision and being in love, how can I not remind myself of another of Scotland's most prized possession and export, Rabbie Burns? His memory was immortalised all over the world in January, on his birthday, with traditional Burns suppers. 'My love is like a red red rose' – his poetry moves me almost to tears. Scotland, you own half of my heart, but a certain handsome American airline pilot owns the other half. Smiling, I knew what my answer would be. I started the car engine and waved cheerio to the view. I made my way, refreshed and happy, back to Mount View and great aunt Jane, to do the same.

Epilogue

HUMMING **WITH PLEASURE** in anticipation of my probable engagement and a wedding or weddings to plan, I parked my car and walked to the front door. But hard as I tried I could not dispel a nagging doubt creeping back into my thoughts. I felt the nearer I got to the answer regarding Leightham House, the further away I got from the end of great aunt Jane's story. Alice, her best friend, named after a fictitious character from a children's book… was I the sequel? She told me to separate fact from fiction, but I was no closer to deciding which was which? I had begun to think it was either all fiction – no local gravestones? – or was it all truth? Only one way to find out – to keep visiting the old darling. 'Enough,' I thought, 'you will be back in a few weeks and with good news to give Aunty so keep visiting.' Although I had other things to think about now I was still consumed with the same passion I had had all my life – to get to the bottom of the mystery that only one old lady had the answer to: The House with No Roof!

Happy, I almost skipped up the few stairs to the front door. The door was open and Cathie was nowhere to be found. The house felt cold, eerily silent. I ran to the conservatory where I'd left Aunt Jane, but it was empty. I began to feel anxious about her, wondering if she was all right. I called her name, but there was no reply.

Eventually I found her in the lounge sitting upright in her high backed leather chair. For one heart-stopping moment I thought she wasn't breathing. Slowly, she turned to look at me, cold, unemotional. I slid into the chair opposite. I don't know how long we sat in silence, a minute, an hour? I felt hypnotised by her Svengali-like hold over me. Lowering her eyes and pointing toward the coffee table, she indicated an old sepia photograph.

I hesitated, then leaning forward, I picked up the photograph.

"Ah-h-h!" an involuntary gasp escaped from my lungs. I clutched at my throat. I am not easily shocked, but looking at the photo I gasped in horror. A woman on a chair dressed in a long gown. Wearing a high-necked collar with long sleeves. The eyes black, sightless, staring. The hands abnormally discoloured, folded in a high position on her lap. The head and torso tilted as if unsupported to the side of the chair.

Fearful, I looked up at my great aunt.

"Yes," she said, "the woman is dead... she was my mother."

The End of Book One

Glossary

Aye	Yes
Sma	small
Awfy	awful
Skelpit	smacked
A	I
Yersel	yourself
Awa	away
Sair	pain
Bairn	child
Beilen	septic wound
Bobby	East coast for the Police
Bonspiel	a curling match
Braw	beautiful
Craiter	creature beast or devil
Cannae	cannot
Cauld	cold
Dinna'	do not
Dae	do
Dye	East coast for Grandfather
Fou	full

Gaun	go
Haar	mist from the sea
Hapit	cover
Haun	hand
Himsel'	the boss
Haud yer wheesht	be quiet!
Masel	myself
Naw	West coast for no
Ken	know
Lowp	throb
Maun	you must
Mauna	must not
Neeps	turnips
Ower	over
Oor	hour
Poke	a paper bag

To
Sheila

With very Best Wishes

Jessie Ritchie

August 2019